Y0-BYZ-851

CHRISTMAS LOVE

There's no time of year more special or enchanting than Christmas and there's no better way to travel back to Christmas yesterday than with Zebra's newest holiday collection, *A Christmas Embrace*. Setting their stories against a backdrop of Christmas balls, blizzards, and battles, Colleen Faulkner, Carol Finch, René J. Garrod, Doreen Owens Malek, Dana Ransom, and Bobbi Smith introduce us to six dashing heroes and six independent heroines who are about to discover the true meaning of Christmas magic when they fall in love for the first time.

So as the snow begins to fall and the wind starts to blow, put an extra log on the fireplace, turn on the Christmas lights and curl up in your favorite chair with *A Christmas Embrace*.

TODAY'S HOTTEST READS
ARE TOMORROW'S SUPERSTARS

VICTORY'S WOMAN   (4484, $4.50)
by Gretchen Genet
Andrew—the carefree soldier who sought glory on the battlefield, and returned a shattered man . . . Niall—the legandary frontiersman and a former Shawnee captive, tormented by his past . . . Roger—the troubled youth, who would rise up to claim a shocking legacy . . . and Clarice—the passionate beauty bound by one man, and hopelessly in love with another. Set against the backdrop of the American revolution, three men fight for their heritage—and one woman is destined to change all their lives forever!

FORBIDDEN   (4488, $4.99)
by Jo Beverley
While fleeing from her brotners, who are attempting to sell her into a loveless marriage, Serena Riverton accepts a carriage ride from a stranger—who is the handsomest man she has ever seen. Lord Middlethorpe, himself, is actually contemplating marriage to a dull daughter of the aristocracy, when he encounters the breathtaking Serena. She arouses him as no woman ever has. And after a night of thrilling intimacy—a forbidden liaison—Serena must choose between a lady's place and a woman's passion!

WINDS OF DESTINY   (4489, $4.99)
by Victoria Thompson
Becky Tate is a half-breed outcast—branded by her Comanche heritage. Then she meets a rugged stranger who awakens her heart to the magic and mystery of passion. Hiding a desperate past, Texas Ranger Clint Masterson has ridden into cattle country o bring peace to a divided land. But a greater battle rages inside him when he dares to desire the beautiful Becky!

WILDEST HEART   (4456, $4.99)
by Virginia Brown
Maggie Malone had come to cattle country to forge her future as a healer. Now she was faced by Devon Conrad, an outlaw wounded body and soul by his shadowy past . . . whose eyes blazed with fury even as his burning caress sent her spiraling with desire. They came together in a Texas town about to explode in sin and scandal. Danger was their destiny—and there was nothing they wouldn't dare for love!

Available wherever paperbacks are sold, or order direct from the Publisher. Send cover price plus 50¢ per copy for mailing and handling to Penguin USA, P.O. Box 999, c/o Dept. 17109, Bergenfield, NJ 07621. Residents of New York and Tennessee must include sales tax. DO NOT SEND CASH.

A Christmas Embrace

COLLEEN FAULKNER
DOREEN OWENS MALEK
CAROL FINCH   DANA RANSOM
RENÉ J. GARROD   BOBBI SMITH

ZEBRA BOOKS
KENSINGTON PUBLISHING CORP.

ZEBRA BOOKS are published by

Kensington Publishing Corp.
850 Third Avenue
New York, NY 10022

First Printing: November, 1994

Printed in the United States of America

TABLE OF CONTENTS

The Other Christmas Story

by
Colleen Faulkner

Prologue

Christmas Eve, 1711
Maryland Colony

"Time for all good children to be abed." Lissa stood beside the cradle at the hearth. She tucked the goosedown quilt around her sleeping infant son. "Now, boys!"

"Good children? You couldn't mean us then," Matthew, Lissa's eldest, answered. He stood at the kitchen table patting gingerbread dough into a black spider pan. The pungent aroma of gingerspice filled the cabin. "You said yourself that we were all too bad this year for gifts."

Lissa crossed the cozy room to tug on a lock of her son's black hair. "Give me mouth, boy, and you'll find yourself out cutting wood with your father." She brushed a bit of flour off the ten-year-old's nose. "Now put the gingerbread near the coals and see to your brothers."

"Mama!" Little Luke, almost three, wrapped his arms around his mother's striped petticoats and hugged her knees. When she tried to walk, she dragged him with her.

"Luke. I said it was bedtime. Be a sweet and get your nightshirt on. Mama's busy."

Luke giggled. "Don't want to go good night. Want a pony ride."

"Mama!" Mark, aged seven, called from the kitchen area.

"You said I could help with the gingerbread and now Matt's done it all. You said I could help."

Matthew threw a handful of flour at his brother. "Did not!"

"Did so!"

"Did not!"

Lissa stood in the center of the cabin room and let her hands fall to her sides with a sigh. Dealing with four children and the harsh winters of the Maryland wilderness was a difficult life. She smiled. But what a blessed life it was. She tousled Luke's hair as he hung on to her knees. She wouldn't give up this world of bickering children, sleepless nights with a colicky baby, and long days of cooking and cleaning. Not for all the kingdom of heaven.

The white lantern light glimmered off a precious glass window and she caught a glimpse of a man outside. His back was to her as he swung his axe rhythmically. His long black hair rippled in the wind as he cut away at the log. Just the sight of him brought a lump to her throat and tears to her eyes.

John, John her lover, John her beloved, John her savior . . .

"Mama! Make him stop!" Mark shouted, racing around the table with Matt in hot pursuit. "He said I was getting cinders for Christmas. He lies! Tell him to stop. Liar!"

"Boys!" Lissa snapped back to reality with a sharp snap of her fingers. "Enough. Now get dressed for bed."

Luke plopped down on her foot, still clinging to her knee. "Will you tell me and the brudders a story if we get ready for bed quick, Mama?"

"It's late."

"Please?"

"Please? Please, Mama?" The two older boys stopped chasing each other around in circles.

"We'll be good. We'll get ready for bed," Matt promised.

"Please?" Mark begged. "Just a quick story? You tell the best stories, Mama."

"Pwease, Mama?"

Lissa looked down at Luke. He was staring up at her with the roundest, darkest eyes. How could she resist such an angelic face? "All right," she gave in with exasperation. "But if you're not quick about getting into your nightclothes—"

"We'll hurry!" Matt shouted.

"We'll hurry," Mark repeated, forever his older brother's echo.

Matt came running across the cabin floor and swept Luke off the floor, disengaging him from his mother's legs. Luke giggled as he wrapped his arms around his big brother's neck.

"We'll be right back, Mama! Race you!" Matt dared Mark as they both bolted for the ladder staircase leading to the upper loft.

"I beat! I beat!" Lissa heard Mark call as she went to the fireplace to check the Christmas baking. By the time she had turned the gingerbread and put on a pot of water to boil John's tea, the three boys were coming down the loft ladder two rungs at a time. All three were dressed in long muslin nightgowns and wool stockings.

"We're ready!" Matt hollered, balancing Luke on his shoulders.

"I beat," Mark called, flopping down on the wool rug in front of the great-room fireplace. "I beat you all."

Leaving her apron on a hook near the door, Lissa went to her children, taking a seat on a low footstool. The boys tumbled on the floor like puppies. "Enough, gentlemen, enough." She clapped her hands to get their attention. "Now what story shall it be?"

"The Christmas story!" Matt piped up.

"The Christmas story," Mark chimed.

"The Cwist-mas story!" followed Luke.

"The Christmas story it is, then. Mark, fetch me the family Bible."

Mark covered his face with his hand. "Not that Christmas

story," he groaned, acting as if she didn't have a streak of good sense.

"Not that Christmas story?" Her eyes widened with a sparkle. "Well, what other Christmas story is there?"

Little Luke giggled. "You know . . ."

Matt rolled his eyes. "You know which story we want to hear, Mama. Stop teasing us."

Mark punched his older brother playfully. "Yeah, we want to hear the other Christmas story, about you and Papa."

"Oh." Lissa drew up her knees beneath her striped petticoat hugging them to her body. "You want *that* Christmas story. Why didn't you say so?" She took a deep breath, her gaze moving from one son to the next. They were all eyes, their attention completely hers. "Once upon a time," she began softly, "there was a woman called Lissa . . ."

One

Lissa was so cold that she was beyond shivering. She had lost all feeling in her feet hours before; her bare fingers were stiff and numb. And still the snow fell, and the temperature dropped.

Lissa let her eyes drift shut for a moment. It would be so easy to just go to sleep. She rested her head against the rough lodge pole she was tied to. It would be so easy to give in to the Mohawks, to give up the battle of wills. It would be so easy to die right now, so peaceful.

Lissa forced her eyes open to the stinging snow. There were two things keeping her from dying here in this miserable, frozen place. She looked down at her swollen abdomen. The first was her unborn child, a child of rape, but a child nonetheless. Her second reason, and perhaps the better reason, was Honeek.

Honeek, a Delaware Indian, had been captured and brought to the Mohawk camp last spring shortly after her own capture. Lissa and the twelve-year-old boy had immediately found a kinship. Just being able to speak English to someone was a comfort to Lissa. The two had clung together in the wicked Mohawk camp and she was convinced that it was Honeek who had given her the will to live, to keep fighting.

"Honeek!" Lissa called through the darkness. "Honeek, can you hear me?"

"Lissa?" she heard his gentle voice. "Lissa, I'm cold."

Lissa's eyes would have clouded with tears, only it was too cold for tears. It was her fault they had been tied up as punishment again. She had let Honeek sneak out of the village. She had tried to escape with him. They had only gotten as far as the frozen stream bed when Crooked Knee and his men had caught them. Then had come the curses, the beating, and finally this—being tied out in the cold. But it had almost been worth it. The taste of freedom, the smell of it had been worth the beating.

Only Honeek couldn't take much more. The child was stubborn and was punished often by the heavy-handed warrior Crooked Knee who owned them both.

It was Crooked Knee who had burned her family's cabin. It was Crooked Knee who had dragged her to the Mohawk Camp somewhere in the foothills of the Catskill Mountains. It was Crooked Knee who had grown drunk on English whiskey and raped her that first night in the village.

Lissa knew it was wrong to hate, but she hated Crooked Knee. She hated him enough to kill him. She hated all Mohawks. She hated their taunting, their abuse, their lack of respect for her and Honeek as human beings. They were the Mohawks' prisoners, their slaves, and they were of less worth than the shaggy ponies tied up in the lean-to barn at the far side of the camp.

Lissa tried to wiggle her hands tied behind her back. "Honeek!" She couldn't tell if she was touching him or not; her fingers were too numb. "Honeek, answer me!"

"I'm tired, Lissa. Tired and cold."

She could feel his body slumped against hers.

"Honeek, listen to me! You mustn't sleep! You'll die if you go to sleep. Talk to me. Tell me about your brother. Tell me about how he will come for you."

"He won't come for me," he answered dully. "It's been too long. He's given up. He won't come for me."

The tone of the boy's voice frightened Lissa. He was giving

up. After all these months, he was giving up. And if he did give up, he would die. "He will come for you," she called into the bitter wind. "Tell me about him, Honeek. I want to hear about John." Her voice trembled. "Please, Honeek, for me?"

She heard him sigh. Then after a long moment of silence, he spoke. "My . . . my brother John, he . . . he's coming for me, Lissa."

"Yes, he is, isn't he? Soon."

"His, his name is John. He's my big brother. We have different mothers, but the same father. His mother died a long time ago and our father remarried."

"Does he live in the village with you?"

"No." Honeek's voice was growing stronger. "John lives in a cabin. He . . . he grows tobacco and he sells it. He has a cow and . . . and a table and chairs."

"Tell me about the table and chairs, Honeek. I love that part."

"My brother John, he can make anything with his hands, but . . . but he wanted this table to be special. Me and him—"

"He and I," she corrected gently.

"He and I, we went to the big village of Philadelphia, Lissa! And . . . and there were brick lodges that stretched high into the sky. And horses, and glass windows, and shops with sweet meats."

"And you bought the table and chairs?"

"Fine cherry wood. Made in Philadelphia by a master woodcarver. Not from England. My brother John, he didn't want no English table."

"And it's a beautiful table and chairs, isn't it, Honeek?"

"Oh, yes," he whispered. Then, after a moment, "Lissa, Lissa, I'm really cold. My feet hurt."

"Shhh," she soothed. "A few hours and it will be daybreak," she lied. "And then the sun will come out and warm us. Crooked Knee will untie us and we'll go into the lodge and eat warm corn mush. Now tell me about John. You told me about the cabin, but you didn't tell me about your brother."

"John. John is big and he's strong. And he can hunt. He can run as fast as a deer."

"He can read, too, can't he, Honeek?" Lissa urged. "You said he could read."

"Oh, yes. Reverend taught him to read right out of the Lord's Bible. He's going to teach me to read as soon as my mother says I'm old enough to go to stay in his cabin with him."

"Tell me why he's coming for you," Lissa said softly. She was so tired. The baby hadn't moved in hours and she feared for the child's life. But she knew she had to keep Honeek talking. The wind had picked up and the snow was blowing even harder. If they didn't stay awake, they would surely freeze to death before dawn. They might freeze to death anyway. "Tell me," she repeated louder. "Tell me why John Eagle is coming for you."

"Because . . . because he's my *nimuut,* and I am his."

"He's your brother," Lissa whispered, "and brothers stick together."

"That time the wildcat scratched me up, he . . . he said he would never let anything or anyone hurt me again, Lissa." She heard a sob wrack his small body. "He promised. I . . . I thought he would come for me."

"And he will," Lissa insisted. The snow was settling on her face, but she couldn't move to brush it off. Her lashes were heavy with frost. Her hands were turning a deadly gray. "He will come for you. He'll ride into the camp on a white horse and cut you from this lodgepole. He'll take you home, Honeek."

"He won't."

Lissa felt him roll his head behind her.

"He will!" she insisted, trying not to panic. "Say it, Honeek. Say it for me!"

"Lissa—"

"For me," she begged. "Please?"

"He'll come for me," Honeek finally repeated softly. "And . . . and for you, too, Lissa."

Her mouth nearly pulled back in a smile. "No, not for me," she answered softly. She knew there was no hope for her. Her parents and brothers and sisters were all dead. And even if she could get home to an uncle or and aunt, what then? No decent Christian woman would dare return to her family carrying a bastard child. No one would take her in. Not her family. Not anyone.

Lissa gazed down at her swollen abdomen wishing she could stroke it. She didn't hate this baby as she knew she should. After all, it wasn't the wee little thing's fault that the man who had spilled his seed into its mother was a monster.

She thought about Crooked Knee and his rough ways. He had offered to make her his wife . . . his third wife. Lissa refused, again and again. No matter how much he bullied or how hard he made her work, she'd not marry him, not even to save her own soul. She hated the red bastard and she hoped to sweet God in heaven that someday he would burn in the pits of hell for what he'd done to her and Honeek.

Lissa tried to shift her weight from one foot to the other. Her legs were stiff and cramping. She wished she could sit down, even in the drifting snow, but the bindings at her wrists and ankles prevented it.

Lissa could see nothing of the Mohawk village now but the swirl of snow and the shadows of the longhouses. She could smell the hickory wood smoke that curled into the sky. She could hear nothing but the howl of the bitter wind and her own labored breathing.

Lissa knew she was close to unconsciousness. She was losing track of time. Her mind was drifting. The painful chill in her limbs was slowly being replaced by a numb warmth.

She thought of silly things as she tried to stay awake. She thought of her childhood rag doll that had burned in the Indian attack . . . the laughter of her dead baby sister . . . the crewel work she had never finished.

Occasionally Lissa called out to Honeek. His response was weak. She could tell that it was a struggle for him just to answer her.

They were freezing to death.

Lissa must have closed her eyes, perhaps for a moment, perhaps an hour. When she opened them again she saw a figure coming through the mist of the snow. The figure was headed straight for them. An angel? Did God send his angels in green wool cloaks? Angels with black hair that rippled down their backs and skin as red as sun-baked clay?

"Honeek!" a voice said above the howling wind. It was the angel calling Honeek! Lissa watched in awe as the figure reached the boy.

The angel was an Indian like Honeek. *How appropriate,* she mused, her thoughts seemingly detached from her body. *God has sent his Indian angel to take the boy.*

Lissa slumped against the pole, letting her eyes drift shut. The boy was safe, safe in the arms of the angel. Now she could sleep. Now she could die knowing he was safe.

A moment later Lissa felt a tug on the bindings at her wrists. Her eyelids fluttered open.

It was the angel. Honeek was clinging to him.

"Who . . . who are you?" she heard herself whisper.

"Hush," the angel answered, his voice as smooth as French velvet and lightly accented. "Save your strength."

She smiled. The Indian angel had come for her, too. For her and her baby.

The leather ties at her ankles fell into the snow and she tried to take a step but her knees buckled. She would have gone down in an icy drift, but the angel reached out with muscular arms and lifted her out of the snow. Wrapped in the warmth of his cloak, she let her eyes drift shut again. Then Lissa slept, safe and free at last.

Two

John Eagle lifted the young white woman into his arms, his gloved fingers brushing across her swollen abdomen. God help her, she was as light as a medicine bag of feathers. And she was cold, so cold that her limbs were stiff.

John took a precious moment to bring his face to hers. Honeek had insisted he wouldn't go without her, but John would carry no corpse through the snowdrifts, not even for his brother.

For a long second John felt nothing, then, finally, the faint brush of her breath against his cheek. How odd it was that she smelled of wildflowers in the dead of winter.

Shifting the unconscious woman in his arms, John held out one broad gloved hand for his little brother. "Can you walk?" he questioned in the Lenape tongue of their ancestors. "This man cannot carry you and the woman as well."

Honeek nodded, a broad smile lighting up his pallid face. "I can walk, brother of mine! I swear it," he called above the howling wind. "Please, let us go. If the Mohawks catch us, we will not die without pain."

Casting a quick glance over his shoulder at the closed hide doorflap of the longhouse, John set out through the high snowdrifts. "My pony is not far. But you must stay at my side, Brother, no matter what." Somewhere, a dog began to bark. He frowned, the snow stinging his eyes. "Do you understand me? No matter what!"

Honeek gave a nod, floundering in the deep snow. John pushed forward, the woman in his arms no burden. In her unconscious state she moved beneath his wool cloak, pressing her thin frame to his for warmth.

"Just across the riverbed is the pony," John called to Honeek.

From behind, John heard male voices. Dogs were barking and someone was shouting in the gruff Mohawk tongue. One of the sentries must have spotted them. *"Kschamehella, niimut,"* John urged. "We must hurry."

The second time Honeek stumbled and fell in the snow, John snatched him up by the thin wool blanket he wore for a cloak and dragged him along. Ahead he could hear the pony neighing in alarm at the sounds of the dogs.

John half dragged, half carried Honeek through the snow, holding tightly to the white woman in his arms. They crossed the frozen stream and turned east. There in a tangled thicket, a small, ragged-maned pony waited impatiently. The short-legged beast had carried John through the snowy foothills of the mountains where no full-size horse could have trod.

"Climb up!" John ordered, his voice terse. With one hand he reached into a saddlebag and drew out his long rifle.

Honeek shook his head in protest. "Let Lissa ride," he called above the wind.

The swirling snow was so thick that John could barely make out the outline of Honeek's thin form. "Get on," he insisted. "You must hold the white woman. I will lead the pony." John signaled for him to mount, glancing over his shoulder in the direction of the Mohawk camp.

Honeek climbed up on the shaggy pony's back and John set the white woman in his brother's lap as gently as he could. He brushed the snow from her face and pulled a thick wool blanket from his leather saddlebag. He threw the blanket over the both of them tent-fashion. "Hold on to her!" he called, slinging his long rifle over his shoulder and reaching for the reins.

Ignoring the baying dogs and the shouts of the Mohawks

sounding an alarm through their camp, John turned the pony
south. They would come after them, he knew, but most likely
not until dawn. As he forged ahead, he hoped the drifting snow
would cover his tracks. Otherwise, he realized his chances of
escaping would be slim. Traveling with a half-starved boy and
a white woman heavy with a child, it would take a miracle to
get out of these mountains alive. So John prayed for that miracle.

Lissa woke slowly to the rhythm of the pony beneath her. She
felt thin arms wrapped around her waist and she lifted her head
from the pony's mane, pushing at the wool blanket heavy with
snow. "Honeek?" she cried out, disoriented. Was she in heaven?
"Honeek."

It was Honeek's arms around her that gave her a shake. "It's
all right," she heard the boy answer in his softly accented manner.
"You are safe, Lissa. John came for us." A gurgle of laughter
bubbled up in his throat. "He came for us just like you said he
would."

Despite her exhaustion, Lissa forced herself to sit upright.
When she did, her wet moccasins nearly dragged the ground.
She pushed away the corner of the wool blanket so that she could
see the man who led the pony.

So he was not an Indian angel, after all. But close. She almost
smiled. It was John. He had to be the John Eagle she and Honeek
had spoken of for almost a year.

Just then he turned his head to look at her. When he saw she
was awake he dropped back, slipping his rifle into the opposite
hand. The snow had let up some but still swirled about his dark
head, whipping the tiny braids in his shoulder-length hair. To
Lissa, he was the most striking man she had ever laid eyes on.

"Ili kleheleche?"

She shook her head, not understanding his words, but fascinated by the sound of his voice and how it carried on the frosty

wind. He was everything Honeek had said he was. He was better. "I . . . I'm sorry. I don't understand."

"He asks if you yet draw breath," Honeek interpreted. "He means, are you all right? You fainted, I think."

She couldn't take her eyes off the man who was no taller than herself but had shoulders as broad as a blacksmith's. He walked beside the pony, his arm brushing against her leg.

"Yes. I . . . I guess I did." She blinked at the snow that fell on her lashes. "I'm cold, but . . . but I'm all right." She glanced over her shoulder at Honeek who rode behind her. "Doesn't he speak English?"

"Aye," John answered, reaching for the corner of the wool blanket. "Now cover your head and rest, friend of Honeek. The danger has not yet passed and you must save your strength."

Before Lissa could answer, he pulled the blanket over her head, once again cocooning her and Honeek.

Lissa shivered, drawing up her knees as best she could. It was warmer beneath the blanket with the snow acting as an insulation, but she was still cold to her very bones. "The Mohawks?" she questioned Honeek sleepily. "Does Crooked Knee know we're gone."

"Kihiila."

Her lower lip trembled as she threaded her frozen fingers through the pony's mane. *Yes.* That was one Lenape word she knew. "Tell me the truth. Will . . . will they come after us, Honeek?"

He rubbed her shoulder, trying to comfort her. "This boy does not know. But if they do, my brother, he will slay them all."

Lissa lowered her head to her fists, balancing herself as best she could with her protruding stomach. She could feel the pony starting a down hill decline and she fought not to slide up onto his neck.

She bit down on her lip until she tasted blood. *I won't go back to Crooked Knee and the Mohawks,* she thought bitterly. She couldn't. She would take her own life before she subjected herself to the humiliation again.

But freedom was so close that she could taste it on the end of her tongue. Thanks to John Eagle, she and her baby had a chance now, even if it was a small chance.

Lissa rubbed her swollen abdomen, barely feeling her own fingers. There was an odd tightening in her stomach. One that frightened her. "Hold on a little longer," she whispered, no longer able to keep her eyes open. "Give Mama just a little longer."

Lissa was jolted awake sometime before dawn by a voice and the feel of a firm grip on her arm. She lifted her head to see the man called John shaking her gently. Honeek had dismounted and stood beside his brother, a long, heavy skin cloak covering his shoulders.

"You must wake," John said softly. "The pony cannot carry you up the steep hill."

Lissa blinked, holding on to his arm for support. He was like an oak tree that would not yield to the force of the north wind and swirling snow.

"Can you walk?" he asked.

Lissa unconsciously lowered her hand to her middle. That tightening was still there, but it came and went. Now it hurt. She nodded, throwing one leg over the side of the pony so that she could dismount. "I can walk," she answered determinedly, ignoring the pain and the fear.

"You are certain?" John caught her with a steady hand as she swayed on her feet.

Her breath made puffs of white clouds in the frosty predawn air. "I can do it."

He tugged two leather mittens from the belt beneath his cloak. "Let me put these on your hands," he said gently. "They are very cold."

Lissa trembled as he slipped the first one over her stiff gray fingers. "But they're yours," she protested.

He flexed his fingers covered by black woolen gloves. "A man cannot shoot with mittens."

She couldn't take her eyes off him. It was as if God had sculpted his face from red baked clay. No one had ever touched her so gently. No one had ever seemed to care about her as much as this stranger seemed to at this moment. She was lost in his gaze. "Do . . . do they follow us?" she asked.

Slipping the other mitten over her hand, John nodded. "Aye." He grasped her arm and started forward. "But they will not catch us. We will disappear into the snow like the white hare of winter."

Lissa looked up into the dark sky. Snow still swirled, but she could detect the first rays of the morning light. She looked back at John as she forced one numb foot in front of the other. "Promise me you won't let them take me."

His black-eyed gaze met hers.

"Promise me," she whispered desperately.

He tightened his grip on her arm. "This man swears it. I will take your life with my own knife before I will let the enemy take you."

Relief flooded her face as she pushed another stiff leg forward. "Bless you," she whispered. "Bless you, John Eagle."

It was not until they reached the crest of the hill sometime later that Lissa heard the sound of the Mohawk dogs far in the distance. With a cry of fear, she tripped and would have gone down but for John's strong arm.

"I will carry you," he said. She could tell by the look in his eyes that he understood her fear.

"No." She shook her head. "No. I can walk myself," she said, almost shouting the words.

Seeming to understand her need to walk herself, John nodded.

"I know a place not far from here where we can rest until the storm passes."

There was no denying it any longer. Lissa knew she was in labor. Now that she was walking, the contractions were growing stronger and closer together. "But the Mohawks," she said, trying not to think about giving birth on the snowy mountainside with no woman to attend her. "They follow us. Crooked Knee—"

"I said I would not let them harm you," John answered in his lilting way. "I have given you my word, have I not?"

Lissa looked ahead, her gaze settling on Honeek's back as he struggled over a fallen log.

"Do you trust me?" John asked her, the warmth of his voice seeping through the cold fear in her heart. "Do you trust me, woman called Lissa?"

She turned her head to look at him. She had been taught that all Indians were heathens, black devils like Crooked Knee, but she knew it wasn't true. This man, this man was her savior. "I trust you," she whispered without fear. "With my life, with the life of my child."

He glanced down at her belly, leading her forward again. "The *ommamundot,* it will come soon?"

She gave a little laugh, knowing there was certainly no humor in the matter of giving birth to a bastard in the middle of a snowstorm. "Sooner than I had thought, I fear."

His grip tightened on her arm as he led her through the deep snow. "We will rest soon, this man promises you."

Later, Lissa barely recognized the coming of dawn as she trudged through the snow. Her contractions had grown so strong that now she had to bite down on her lower lip as each one came. But she kept walking, holding tightly to John's arm. He would lead her out of this hell. He would make her safe. She had to believe that. He had promised.

It was still snowing when John led her and Honeek around a

rocky, snow covered ledge and pointed. "There. There we can rest."

Lissa squinted, the snow stinging her eyes. Was that a hole in the side of the ridge? A cave? She looked to John. "They will not find us here?" she asked. She was so exhausted that she could barely stand upright. The pains were coming so hard that she feared she would cry out.

"They will not find us," he insisted. Then, carefully taking his hand from her arm, he grabbed the pony's reins from Honeek and led the beast into the side of the mountain.

Honeek and Lissa followed. They had to crouch to fit through the opening in the cave, but a short distance inside, the hollow expanded until she could nearly stand upright.

"Oh!" Lissa cried, beyond weary. It was dark, but her eyes quickly adjusted to the dim light that came through the opening in the cave. "It's so much warmer in here."

The cave smelled of musky wild cat and rodent droppings, but she didn't care. Here they were out of the wind and blinding snow. Here she could rest at last.

Lissa slid to the cold stone floor, her legs buckling as she went down. John was at her side in an instant. He thrust his hand through the darkness, boldly touching her abdomen. Lissa knew she should have pulled away, but she was too tired to care, too tired to think clearly. It hurt so much. And she was still so cold.

"The child comes?" he asked her, peering into her strained face.

Lissa didn't have the energy to lift her lashes. She was shivering violently. The pains were coming in hard waves, building in strength. "I think so," she managed.

He went down on one knee, setting down his long rifle. "How long?" he asked. He gripped her stomach one way and then another. "How long have you been having the contractions?"

She shook her head. The pain and cold and the exhaustion were clouding her reason. "I don't know . . . a few hours."

John stood. "Honeek. We must have a fire."

"No!" Lissa bolted upright, grasping her contracting abdomen. "No fire. They'll find us. Please, John, promise you won't let them take me." She was nearly hysterical. "Promise me you won't let them take my baby."

He went down on one knee to take her cold hand in his warm one. "I have already promised, my brave one, now lay back and rest."

"But my baby is coming!" she cried desperately. "Who will help me?"

His voice enveloped her with warmth. "It will be all right, Lissa," he answered calmly, squeezing her hand. "It is nothing to a Lenape brave to deliver a little baby. I will help you."

Three

Lissa's voice caught in her throat and she turned away, catching a glimpse of her own reflection in the dark, wavy glass of the cabin window. This was the part of her story that she still had difficulty telling the children. How could she explain to three small boys the agony of a woman's childbearing that mingles with the sheer joy of giving life? How could she relate to her children the fear and shame she felt at having to give birth to a bastard in a cave with no help but from a man she didn't know. How could she possibly express to them the overwhelming love she felt for John Eagle at the moment he laid her first son to her breast?

"Go on with the story, Mama," Matt insisted excitedly. "That's when I was born—in a cave in the middle of the snowstorm with the Mohawks hot on your tails!"

"Yeah," Mark chimed in, leaping up off the plank floor. "Tell us about how Papa and Uncle Honeek killed a dozen Mohawks—two dozen—and scalped 'em all!" He pulled back the string on an imaginary bow and let an imaginary arrow fly.

Little Luke threw himself backward under the impact of his brother's arrow, clutching his heart and writhing in the throes of death.

Lissa turned back to her boys, brushing away the hint of a tear in the corner of her eye as she smiled down on them. "That wasn't how it happened and you know it," she chastised warmly.

"Now, do you want to hear the rest of the story or are you all ready for bed?"

Luke popped up, coming back to life. Mark tossed aside his imaginary bow and Matt took his seat once again on the floor beside his brothers. "All right, tell us about the spider," Matt conceded. "But I still think the part about Papa killing all the Mohawks makes the story better."

Keeping a straight face, Lissa folded her hands neatly on her lap. "Now, as I was saying, the wind was still blowing and snow still coming down, but your father and uncle and I—"

"And me, don't forget me," Matt interrupted.

Lissa nodded. "—And baby Matt were safe in the cave in the side of the mountain."

"But the Mohawks came," Matt offered wide-eyed. "Didn't they? They came looking for us."

"Yes, the Mohawks came," Lissa said softly, her eyes losing focus as the memories came tumbling back. Once again she was transported back in time to the cave carved in the side of the mountain and the howling blizzard outside. Once again she could hear the soft mews of her newborn babe and she could taste the fear on her tongue like ashes. "The Mohawks came sometime mid-morning just after you were born," she murmured.

"The Mohawks!" Lissa cried out, holding tightly to her new son. She barely had the strength to hold him to her breast, but she would get up, and she would fight Crooked Knee hand-to-hand if she had to. She had a child to care for. And now that he had arrived in this world, now that John Eagle had brought him into this world with his strong, broad hands, Lissa knew she couldn't die. She had to live for her son.

"Hush," John murmured gently coming back from the opening in the cave. "Do not give us away by your voice."

He had let the small fire die out so that now there was only the light that shined through the cave opening down the short tunnel.

"The campfire. They'll see the smoke." Lissa tried to sit up, hugging the wee babe in her arm. "The Mohawks—they'll smell it."

John checked the prime on his long rifle. "You said you trusted me."

Lissa laid her head on the pillow he had made for her with one of his saddlebags. She could hear the Mohawks' dogs now quite clearly. They were close, very close. "I do," she whispered, tired beyond thought. "I do trust you, John."

"Then sleep. My young brother and I"—he motioned to Honeek, who stood closer to the opening in the cave—"we will stand watch over you and the child. We will let no harm come to you."

He was right. She knew he was right. She had to trust him. John Eagle had rescued her from the Mohawk camp. He had delivered her child. If she had trusted him this far, she knew that her trust could stretch the full distance.

Lissa let her eyes drift shut. She couldn't sleep knowing there was danger so near, but maybe she could rest a little. She knew her labor and delivery had been easy compared to many women's, but she was still exhausted beyond reason. She had to trust her instinct, and her instinct told her that John Eagle would keep his word. He would protect her and her newborn, even unto death.

For a long time Lissa lay with her eyes closed, listening to the sounds of the dogs baying. Occasionally John or Honeek spoke in their native language to each other, but their words were hasty and barely audible. As Lissa cuddled her son to her breast, wrapped warm in the wool blanket and John's heavy bear hide cloak, she tried not to think about her future. She tried not to think about where she would go with her bastard half-breed or how she would feed him and provide him with shelter. It was a miracle they were alive. For now, Lissa knew that had to be enough.

The Mohawks and their dogs came so close to the cave that Lissa saw John cock the hammer on his long rifle. She heard the guttural sounds of the Mohawk language. She was certain she heard Crooked Knee himself, and for a long moment she held her breath. The voices grew louder and angrier. She heard the men stomp their feet and shout to one another. Then, to her utter amazement, the voices began to fade. The dogs turned in another direction, and as quickly as the Mohawks had come, they were gone.

When Lissa pushed up off the floor to glance at John, she met with a broad smile and sparkling black eyes. "They're gone," she whispered, a strength in her voice she didn't recognize.

"They are gone," he repeated, still smiling.

"But why? Why didn't they look in the cave? I don't understand. They were right here. Our footprints—"

"Blown away by the father wind of the storm."

Lissa pushed her hair off her forehead in disbelief. "But they had tracked us this far. Surely they would have looked inside the cave?"

"Sometimes it is better not to question good fortune."

Lissa looked down, then back at John. "They . . . they won't come back for us, will they? I mean, when they can't pick up the trail again."

He shook his head, coming to her. "They will not. Not today at least. Now sleep, Lissa. Tomorrow we must move on." He went down on one knee to tuck a bit of cloak over her shoulder. "You will be strong enough to travel tomorrow. *Kahiila?*"

She nodded. Now it was her turn to smile. She loved him, this stranger who had come for her in the dead of night, in the midst of a snowstorm. She knew it was crazy, but she did. And no matter where she went or what the future held for her, she would never forget him.

"Good," he said. And then he brushed a stray lock of her auburn hair off her cheek. It was a simple gesture, but one strangely intimate. "The babe, he is well?" John inquired.

All Lissa could do was nod and stare up at him. "He's strong."

"Like his mother," John said softly. Then he got up. "Sleep. When it is safe I will go out and bring something back to eat. Red meat would do you good."

"It sounds like the storm has passed. If . . . if you think we should go now, I can do it," Lissa murmured. She didn't know how, considering how close to death she and her baby had been only a few hours ago. But she knew in her heart she could do it if she had to. She could do anything she had to. It was John Eagle who made her feel that way.

He smiled again. "No. Tomorrow will be soon enough, brave one. Now, sleep. Dream good dreams and we will wake you later to eat."

When Lissa did awake much later, Honeek had started a fire again and the cave was warm and filled with the scent of roasting rabbit. The young boy sat cross-legged at the campfire stirring the coals with a long stick.

Lissa sat up, yawning. She pulled back the wool blanket to check her sleeping son curled in her arm. "Where is he?" she asked, looking down at the baby, touching his small, soft cheek.

Honeek looked up.

"John," she said. "Where is he?"

Honeek got up and came to her with a water skin. "He will be right back, Lissa. He's only gone for more fire wood."

He offered her the water skin and she took it. But instead of being filled with the cold water she expected, it was a hot herbal tea. She took a sip and wrinkled her nose at the bitter taste.

"Drink it," Honeek said, squatting to have a closer look at the

baby. "My brother made it from herbs in his medicine bag. H
says the drink will make you strong for our journey."

Lissa looked at him over the lip of the leather skin. *Our jour
ney . . .* The words echoed in her head. Where were they going
Did John Eagle truly mean to include her? She took another si
of the tea. This time it went down a little easier and the tast
didn't seem quite so strong. "Where . . . where will we go?
she asked.

"I do not know exactly. My brother says he knows a trappe
a white man with a cabin not far from here. He says we can sta
with the white man until you are stronger."

And then what? Lissa wanted to ask. *What do I do then?* Sh
laid back on her makeshift pillow. Of course she couldn't expec
John Eagle to be responsible for her any longer than that.

Just then John appeared, his arms filled with snow-covere
wood. "You are awake?"

She tucked her tattered doeskin dress up over her shoulde
self-consciously not knowing what to say.

He dropped the wood near the burning fire. "How do yo
feel?"

"Warm." She smiled at him. "Good. Surprisingly good.
She glanced down at her sleeping son. "Is it safe to go out
side?" she asked, feeling awkward. "I . . . I'd like to attend t
personal matters."

"It is safe. The Mohawks grew cold and returned to thei
village, I think. Just do not wander far from the cave."

"Don't worry, I won't." She got to her knees, wrapping a woc
blanket around her shoulders. She tucked her sleeping baby be
neath the bearskin hide. He slept on contentedly. "Watch hin
will you?" she asked Honeek.

Honeek grinned. "I'll sit right here in case he wakes up."

Lissa rose to her feet, a bit unsteady. John was at her side i
a second. Lissa laughed, feeling a little silly about all this atten
tion, especially after her year among the Mohawks where he

life meant nothing to anyone. But his muscular arm was reassuring as she stood, regaining her balance. "I'm all right," she said, giving him a pat on the arm. "Really." She laughed again. "I'm not the first woman to ever give birth, you know."

John released her. "I did not mean to offend you. You are a strong woman, indeed. This man wanted only to give you his assistance."

She waved her hand, walking slowly toward the opening in the cave, ducking slightly so that her head didn't scrape the ceiling. "I'll be right back. Watch him."

Lissa reached the opening to the cave and the cold wind struck her full in the face. The last of the day's sunlight was seeping through the skeletal tree branches overhead, setting the snow afire with twinkling light.

Just as Lissa was about to step out of the cave, she noticed something sparkling hanging down in front of her. She took a step back, pulling the wool blanket tighter around her shoulders. What was it?

It was like threads—tiny, frosty threads woven across the cave opening. Lissa let out a sigh of amazement. It had not been here before, not when they had entered the cave this morning.

Lissa heard John come up behind her. "It is beautiful, is it not?" he asked.

"Is . . . is it a spider's web?" she asked in disbelief. "Is that why the Mohawks didn't come into the cave? Because it was covered by a spider's web?"

John crossed his arms over his chest. "One can never be certain what a Mohawk thinks, but that is my guess. An opening covered by a spider's web tells a hunter nothing has passed through for a long time."

Lissa stared at the glimmering threads of the web. They were like spun glass. "It doesn't make sense," she whispered. "It wasn't there when we entered the cave. But there are no spiders that spin webs in the middle of the winter." She turned to him, an eerie feeling creeping up her spine. "I don't understand, John."

He shrugged his shoulders. "As I said before, brave one, sometimes it is better not to question. It is better to simply be thankful."

For a moment the two stood side by side in a quiet moment of contemplation. Then, very carefully so as not to disturb the web, Lissa slipped through a small opening near the side of the cave and walked out into the snow.

Four

Lissa drew aside the soft leather of her tunic and lifted baby Matthew to her breast. As the child suckled, she brushed his inky black hair with her fingertips and stared into the blazing fire.

The days, the weeks, were slipping through Lissa's fingers like crystalline snowflakes. John had led her and Honeek to this cabin only a day and a half's walk from the cave where she had given birth to little Matthew. Though John's friend, the trapper, was not residing in his cabin this winter, John assured her he would be happy to extend his hospitality to them, even in his absence. So, Lissa, John, Honeek, and the baby settled into the small cabin, nestled at the foot of a mountain, to ride out the winter.

When they had first arrived at the cabin, Lissa had suggested to John that he and Honeek go on home to his place near the Chesapeake. She could take care of herself and the baby now that she had a roof over her head, she had told him. Then in the spring—in the spring she didn't know what she would do. But she didn't want to keep John from his home for her sake, not after all he'd done for her.

But John had insisted that he had planned all along to hole up in Mitchell's cabin once he had rescued Honeek. It wasn't for her that he stayed, he explained. But he was glad to help out in any way he could.

Time slipped by so quickly for Lissa in the warm, cozy cabin with Honeek and John. Too quickly. The growth of little Matthew was her proof of the passing days. His cheeks grew round and rosy, his legs plump. And the longer Lissa stayed with John Eagle, the harder she knew it would be to part from him. The truth was that she had never been so happy in her life, not even in the comfortable life she led in her father's home in Penn's Colony before the Mohawks had taken her.

It wasn't anything that Lissa could put her finger on. She couldn't say for certain what it was about John that made her so fond of him. It was just a fact. She loved him.

She loved the sound of his deep laughter. She loved the way he wrestled on the hearth with his young brother. She loved the way he treated Matthew—as if he was spun from gold and more precious.

Lissa brought Matthew to her shoulder and patted his back. The baby gurgled sleepily, and then gave a healthy burp.

She smiled to herself as she thought about John, trying to make sense of these intense feelings she had for him. It wasn't just that he had saved her life and Matthew's. It was more than that. She loved the height of his cheekbones and the color of his suntanned skin. She loved the way the muscles in his arms rippled as he dressed and undressed.

Living so close with a man in the dead of winter could be intimate at times, but never once had John made her feel uncomfortable. He seemed to sense when she needed her privacy and when she needed the encouragement of his strong voice or gentle hand. Though he told her he had never been wed, he seemed to understand the innate differences between men and women.

Never once had he made an improper suggestion or action. She slept in the single rope bed with Matthew and he and Honeek bunked on the floor near the stone hearth. There was nothing about John's demeanor that suggested in any way that he was attracted to her sexually and yet Lissa found herself thinking about him in that way. At night, when she was snuggled into her rope bed and he was bedded down on the floor, she listened to his breathing and imagined he was in the bed beside her.

With a sigh, Lissa switched Matthew to her other breast, and the baby nestled down to finish off his noon meal. She nibbled on her lower lip as she settled him in her arm. The Mohawks must have made her a wanton, she decided, because secretly, she almost wished John would make an improper proposal. She couldn't help wondering what it would be like to kiss his lips. Even after the humiliation she had suffered at Crooked Knee's hands, she couldn't stop herself from wondering what it would feel like to be touched by John.

When Matthew began to fuss, she lifted him to her shoulder, gently jiggling him. Of course she knew all this marveling over John Eagle was foolishness. He had no interest in her. Why would he? Surely a man as intelligent, as handsome, as financially comfortable as he was, even as a red man, had better prospects for a wife. He would marry an Indian woman when the time came, she assumed.

And what man would marry her now? she wondered, trying not to feel sorry for herself. What man would marry a woman who had not only been brutally raped, but had a bastard child as a constant reminder of that rape? Not even a man like John could be expected to accept her circumstances.

Lissa smoothed the small, rounded head covered in black hair that bobbed on her shoulder. It didn't matter to her how Matthew had come to this world. It wasn't his fault, and never for a moment would she associate this beautiful child with the monster called Crooked Knee. John had told her that among his people, the father of the child didn't matter. Among the Lenape there were no bastard children. Children were a gift from God belonging to their mothers. Every child had a mother.

The cabin door opened and Lissa glanced over her shoulder. An icy wind whipped through the warm room and swirling snow blew through the doorway. John stepped in and stomped his feet. Snow fell to the planked floor.

"Cold out?" she asked, thankful it was John who did the hunting and the firewood cutting. She never went outside except for necessity.

"Bitter," he answered, shrugging off his bearhide cloak.

"Where's Honeek?"

John pulled off his squirrel-skin hat and dropped it onto the peg on the wall near the door. He beat the snow from his fur cloak. "He's still working on that snare." He laughed, shaking his head. "I keep telling him it is not likely he will catch a deer with a snare, but still, he waits by the hour." He winked at her. "Just in case, he says."

Lissa laughed with him. Since their rescue, Honeek had blossomed into a young man. He still had his moment of typical child's grumbling when he didn't want to carry wood or clean rabbits, but the strength she had seen in him back in the Mohawk village was the strength of his inner personality. Here in the cabin, safe from the Mohawks, and under his brother's care, he was becoming a fine young man. He still had nightmares about the Mohawks and about his capture, as Lissa did, but even they were growing less frequent. Honeek spent most of his days exploring the nearby forest and helping his brother with the daily chores.

John came to the fireplace and stretched out his palms to warm them.

When Matthew fussed, Lissa switched him to the other shoulder, patting his bottom.

"Here, let me take him." John stretched out his hands and before she could argue, he had the baby on his shoulder and was tucking his little rabbit-fur blanket securely around him.

Matthew rolled his little round head and opened his hooded dark eyes. The corners of his kiss-shaped mouth turned up.

"You see that," John said, pointing with one hand. "He's smiled at me again. I told you he smiles."

"Oh, he did not." She laughed. "He's too young to smile."

John turned his head, studying the baby's face. "This man does not know at what age babies are supposed to smile. I know only that he smiles at me. He is very smart, this Matt. He will make a good hunter."

Lissa sat back in the wooden rocker, folding her hands in her lap. She couldn't help but smile herself as she watched John pace with her son on his shoulder, crooning words she didn't understand.

He'll make such a good father, Lissa thought. *What a lucky child he or she will be to have such a devoted man.*

After a few minutes of comfortable silence, Lissa rocking, John pacing, he spoke. "I was thinking that perhaps Honeek and I would follow the river a ways to hunt tomorrow. I do not like to hunt so much in the same place," he said, crossing in front of her.

Matthew was beginning to settle now, making those sounds infants make as they drift off to contented sleep.

"You'll be gone long?" John and Honeek hunted almost every day, but in the last two months they had never strayed far from the cabin. Lissa had not had to deal with the thought of being alone.

She pretended not to be afraid, knowing Crooked Knee was still out there within walking distance. She knew that at some point she had to begin to depend on herself and not John, not any man.

John continued to walk back and forth with the baby on his shoulder. "Just the day. We leave before light, but we will be back by dark. You and the boy will be safe. I will leave you one of my long rifles and make certain you have plenty of wood for the fire." He stopped in front of her chair. "I could leave Honeek if you would feel safer."

"No, no. That's fine. I'll take the baby back," she offered, dismissing the subject. She and Matthew had to start being more independent at some point. Tomorrow would be as good a day as any.

"No. You sit. This man likes the feel of him on my shoulder. There is nothing like a baby to remind a man of what life is all about."

Lissa picked up her sewing from the basket on the floor by the chair and started work on the little bunting she was making from the cured rabbit hides John had prepared. Inside the butter-soft rabbitskin, Matthew would be as warm as a toasted corn cake. She smiled contentedly as she rocked, keeping one eye on the sewing needle, the other on John and her son.

This was how they often spent the short winter afternoons. Lissa sewed or baked and John cared for Matthew. It gave Lissa a little time to herself, but against her will, bound her even tighter to the man who had come so suddenly into her life.

In the afternoons when Matthew slept Lissa and John talked together, often about his life or hers before they met. Sometimes he talked while he repaired weapons or made snares for trapping, telling her Lenape tales passed on from generation to generation. Sometimes they played games with or without Honeek. John taught her a Lenape game played with pebbles and a board with hollowed-out cups. Lissa found an old dog-eared pair of cards in the clothes press and taught him how to play piquet. Her father had never permitted card playing in their home, but Lissa's older brother had secretly taught her how to play.

John crossed the tiny cabin and laid Matthew down on the rope bed, tucking soft blankets around him so he wouldn't roll off. After standing there for a moment to be certain he remained asleep, John came back to the fireplace. "A game of cards?" he asked.

She looked up from her sewing. "I really should get this done for Matthew. The snow will be melting soon and—"

"Yes, yes, this man knows. There is always something to be done, isn't there, Lissa, but what of fun?"

She kept her eyes on the steel needle. "I like to have fun, it's just that—"

He took Lissa's hand and she looked up into his dark eyes. What was that she saw when he looked at her? She knew that he considered her his friend, but there was something about the way he looked at her that made her wonder if he felt something more for her. Of course the idea was absurd.

"Come on," he said softly. "Let me beat you at you piquet."

"Beat me!" She laughed, coming to her feet, his hand falling from hers. "You can't beat me."

"Hah!" He took the cards from the mantel and walked to the tiny table they used to prepare meals, eat, and do anything else that needed a flat surface, including cleaning animal carcasses. "This man beat you yesterday, if I recall correctly."

Lissa came across the cabin floor, the smooth leather of her skirt brushing against her bare legs beneath. "Luck. Naught but luck."

John took a chair, licked his thumb and began to deal. "We shall see about *that, ki-ti-hi.* We shall see."

John and Honeek left the following morning, and though it was earlier than Lissa normally rose, she stood in the doorway to wave farewell, a fur cloak thrown over the man's sleep shirt she had confiscated from Mitchell's clothes press.

She forced a smile, shivering beneath the cloak. "Don't worry about Matthew and me. We'll be fine."

John lingered near the step carved from a tree stump. The air was so cold it was brittle, but already the sun was shining down, setting the snow-covered ground and trees alive with sparkling white light. "Are you certain . . ." He ground his knee-high moccasin in the snow, making a crunching sound there. "Are you certain you don't want Honeek to stay with you?"

"No." She waved her hand. "Don't be silly. You've seen no signs of them in the two months we've been here. The Mohawks don't know where we are. And even if they did, Crooked Knee would never venture so far from his warm lodge. Not for two captives," she went on, trying to convince herself as much as John. "He likes his hot mush and new wife too much." She forced another smile.

John hesitated a moment as if he wanted to say something else to her, but then he turned away. "Keep the rifle by the door."

The wind whipped at her rumpled morning hair. "Just bring home a deer. I've a taste for roasted venison."

John held his hand over his head in farewell. Honeek was already out of sight, running ahead.

Lissa stood in the doorway ignoring the frigid temperature. When John had disappeared through the snow-laden trees, she stepped inside, closing the handhewn door behind her and leaning against it.

"So what do we do now, Matt?" she asked her sleeping son. "It's just a trial run, sweetness, but you and your mama need to learn to take care of ourselves. We can't always depend on John Eagle. You know that as well as I do."

The baby slept on as Lissa listened to the resonance of her own hollow-sounding words.

"Keep busy. That's what we'll do." She nodded with assurance as she dropped her cloak onto a wooden peg. First she'd dress and make herself some breakfast. Once Matthew had his morning meal she would prop him up in the little wooden-framed rabbitskin chair John had made for him and they would get to work. Lissa wanted to try her hand at making soap. There was bread to be baked, Honeek's tunic to be repaired, and perhaps she'd even make some gingerbread with the precious spice and flour still left in the cupboard.

That's what she'd do. She'd keep herself busy. She'd keep herself so busy today that she'd never notice John and Honeek were gone.

Five

Just after noon, several miles from the cabin, near a frozen stream bed, John brought down a large buck with a single musket shot. He and Honeek field-gutted the animal, gave thanks as was the custom, and prepared it to carry it back to the cabin.

All morning John had had an uneasy feeling in the pit of his stomach. He couldn't determine the source of his anxiety; nothing was visibly wrong. Yet now that he had meat for the table, he was anxious to get back to the cabin, to Lissa and the baby.

Dragging the deer carcass behind them through the snow, Honeek and John set a hard pace. With a little luck, they'd be back before the sun set and there would be grilled venison steaks for the evening meal.

The two talked little as they traipsed through the knee-deep snow, both conserving their energy. The trek was hard, pulling the deer carcass through the deep drifts, the bitter wind in their face, but the thought that they would soon reach the warmth of the cabin was encouraging.

John and Honeek had just followed a bend in the frozen stream when John released the rope tied to the deer's front hoof and let it fall to the snow. They were only a little more than a mile from the cabin.

Honeek was instantly at his brother's side, his hand on the hunting knife he wore in his belt over his cloak. "Brother?"

John brought his finger to his lips. The hair bristled on the back of his neck and his mouth went dry. Every muscle in his body was suddenly taut. Something was wrong, very wrong.

The howl of a war cry broke the late-afternoon stillness as John spun instinctively on his heels, letting the hatchet that had been on his belt a moment before fly off his fingertips. The blade glistened in the failing light as the hatchet flew end over end. *"Kschamehalla!"* John shouted, giving Honeek a hard shove just as the hatchet settled in their attacker's chest.

The weapon made a hollow thump as it struck the Mohawk warrior. With a cry, he went down on one knee, clutching his chest, his eyes already unseeing. Then he pitched forward into the snow.

"Run!" John shouted again as he jerked his long rifle from around his neck and threw it through the air. "Run, Honeek! The cabin."

Honeek caught the musket and took off in a dead run in that direction.

John kicked his attacker, rolling him over. Just as he dislodged his hatchet from the dead man's chest, he caught sight of the three Mohawks racing through the spruce trees toward him.

"Hurry, Honeek!" John shouted as he shifted his weight, preparing to take his stand here in the snow. Three Mohawks, one Lenape—the odds were heavy on the Mohawks but not insurmountable.

It had been a long time since John had fought another man. When he had left his people's village and taken his cabin closer to the whites, he had laid down his war hatchet, sick of the bloodshed. Red man against red man, white against red, white against white. He had had enough. But suddenly, all that he had learned as a young man about being a warrior came back to him in an instant. All the instincts, the primal urge to survive and protect loved ones, at any cost, pulsed through his body. All he could think of was that if he did not survive, Honeek would not; Lissa and the baby would not.

John mentally worked through the possibilities. He had his hatchet and his skinning knife. He slid his hand down his side, feeling for the knife, still bloody from cutting the heart and liver from the deer. Luck was with him. Mohawks were without firearms, but instead carried knives and war clubs. His hatchet would be good for one more throw, but the fight would probably come down to his ability with the razor-sharp, thin-bladed knife.

Adrenaline pumping through his veins, John threw back his shoulders, signaling with the wave of his knife. "Come!" he called to the Mohawks who moved like dogs circling their prey. "Come and meet your death, fools."

A Mohawk wearing a battered wool cocked hat stepped away from the group to approach him first. John moved slowly, forcing himself to concentrate on the fight and not on Lissa alone in the cabin. Honeek had disappeared from sight and, so far, the men had not gone after him. He prayed the boy would reach the cabin safely.

The Mohawk, losing patience with John's tenacity, lunged forward brandishing a knife with a steel blade as long as his forearm. John stepped lightly out of his attacker's reach and spun, lashing out with his own knife. He sliced through the Mohawk's dirty hide tunic and the man bellowed like a lost calf. The Mohawks behind him hooted and hollered, making such a din that John had to work very hard to keep up his concentration.

The Mohawks still thought this a game. They still underestimated their opponent—a mistake John had learned long ago could cost a man his life.

"Undach aal," John taunted, still keeping his center of gravity low, now circling the bleeding man. "Kill me or be gone with you," he dared. "Go now and I will spare your worthless life."

Without warning, the Mohawk dove at John. John managed to leap out of the way, but the tip of the enemy's knife drew blood at his chest. It was a shallow wound, but enough to remind John of the severity of his situation. The other two still stood back, watching their companion, egging him on, but John knew that if this man got him down, the others would attack like a pack of wolves.

The two men turned slowly in a circle, the Mohawk observers jeering. As John matched his opponent move for move, he kept an eye on the other two. One was a big burly man with hands like venison quarters. The other was taller, more slender, with a slight limp and a twisted smirk. Somewhere in the back of his mind John remembered something Honeek had once said about their captor—the man John assumed had raped Lissa. Could this be the infamous Crooked Knee?

John's opponent let out a shriek and once again dove at him. This time John moved his body but left one leg planted firmly. The force of the Mohawk's lunge coupled with John's well-placed foot sent the man sprawling. He hit the snow, his hat flying off as he rolled to try and bring John down on top of him. The Mohawks hooted with glee, dancing in circles around them.

John went down on one knee, his knife poised. The Mohawk let out a grunt as John's knife sank into the left upper corner of his chest. Blood spurted and John turned his head away in disgust.

The Mohawks behind him had grown suddenly quiet. They stared at their second companion laying dead in the snow. John rose, wiping his hand with the back his mouth. "Enough?" he demanded, sickened by the smell of the warm human blood and the thought that these men were here for no reason but to kill, to plunder, to rape if they could get the chance. "Do you take the bodies of your dead comrades and go home, or must this man kill again?"

The beefy Mohawk grunted something in the Iroquois tongue. A challenge . . .

The Mohawk came at John swinging a war club. Despite the frigid temperature, sweat ran in beads down John's temples. He'd lost his cloak at some point in the struggle with the last Mohawk, but still, the exertion of the fight left him heated. The palm he held the bloody knife in was sweaty; he hoped he would be able to maintain a good grip. It was possible his life would depend on it.

The Mohawk swung his club and John dipped out of the way again and again. John struck him with his knife across the cheek, at the thigh, on one shoulder, but he could not strike a deep enough wound, and the Mohawk still bore down on him. At one point, as John spun around, putting a sapling between him and his attacker, he spotted the Mohawk with the limp moving away from the small clearing where the snow was stained red with blood.

No! John's inner voice screamed. The one with the limp was skirting the fight; he wasn't coming to his companion's side. At that instant the Mohawk took off in a dead run, leaving his burly companion to finish John off, no doubt. The Mohawk with the limp was headed straight for the cabin!

Just as John turned back, his attacker hit him so hard in the shoulder with his club that John went down on his knees. As he struggled to get to his feet, fighting the excruciating pain, knowing the shoulder was dislocated, all he could think of was Lissa.

As Lissa carried the baked gingerbread away from the fireplace she breathed in the sweet, pungent aroma that filled the warm cabin. She hummed to herself as she crossed the room.

She and Matt had had a good day. Once Lissa had convinced herself that she would be all right without John Eagle, she had been able to relax. She had made her soap, she had finished her sewing, and even baked the gingerbread. The day had passed so quickly that she truly had had little time to miss John.

But she *had* missed him. She had missed him so much that she knew it would be time for her to leave here very soon. Lissa smiled a bitter smile. These last two months in the cabin with

Matthew, Honeek, and John had been magical. But it was time she got on with her life. She had thought long and hard on the matter today and she had made up her mind. When the first spring thaw came, she would leave the cabin and take Matthew with her to the nearest settlement. She would sell herself into a seven-year indenture along with Matthew. That would give them a roof over their head and food to eat. She would work her seven years and then be a free woman again. Lissa knew the plan was drastic, but it would work. The only thing was, she had to do it as soon as possible. If she didn't, she knew she would only be prolonging the pain. John had been here for her when she had needed him most, but now she had to break the ties.

Lissa had just set the iron spider with the baked gingerbread down on the small table when she heard the door latch click.

"John!" she spun around, a smile on her face. "Well, you two are certainly home early. I thought—"

The words stuck in Lissa's throat as a scream rose from her chest. It wasn't John. It was Crooked Knee.

Lissa clamped her hand over her mouth to keep from screaming out again. She didn't want to wake Matthew; she didn't want to draw any attention to him. "No!" was all she could croak beneath her hand. "Not you."

Crooked Knee threw back his shoulders, grinning boastfully. "I said, do not leave me, white bitch, else there would be trouble much for you."

"Get out of here!" Lissa screamed.

"But I have come to bring you home to my lodge." There was still that smile, that cocky smile she despised, that smile she wanted to scratch off his face.

"I'm not coming with you." Lissa felt as if her limbs were frozen. This was just like her nightmares. She had dreamed he would come for her. She had dreamed he would come and she wouldn't be able to save herself.

Sweet God, where was John?

But of course he wasn't here. He wasn't here to save her this time.

Matthew cried out from the rope bed where he napped, and Crooked Knee immediately turned his head.

"No, no!" was all Lissa could manage.

"So you did whelp? Good, another slave for my wives." He was crossing the cabin floor now, headed straight for Matthew.

Lissa was paralyzed. But she had to do something! She had to save Matthew! Her gaze strayed to the long rifle leaning against the stone fireplace across the room. She knew she could never reach it. She was too scared.

"I would have brought the Lenape boy back, but he fought me." Crooked Knee shrugged. "This man could have hit him a little bit hard. I think he is dead."

A sob rose in Lissa's throat. Honeek might be dead and now Crooked Knee had almost reached her son. She considered throwing herself on him, fighting him, but what then? He was stronger than she was. Eventually he would overpower her. He had done it that night in the lodge when he'd raped her, hadn't he?

Lissa's gaze went to the rifle once more. It was loaded and primed. John had checked it before he left. It was her only chance. No one was going to come out of the swirling snow and save her this time.

But could she kill a man? Could she pull the trigger and end a human being's life?

Lissa hesitated for less than a second before making her decision. The next moments were a blur. She made the sudden move toward the fireplace. Crooked Knee bellowed at her. She felt the comfort of the heavy, long rifle in her hand. Then, suddenly, the rifle belched smoke and the acrid scent of burnt gunpowder filled her nostrils.

Crooked Knee stared at her for an instant after the impact of the musketball struck him high in the chest. For the briefest moment his gaze met hers and she saw sheer terror. He had thought himself as always invincible. He had thought her as always the victim.

He had been wrong. Dead wrong.

Lissa threw down the discharged rifle and ran for Matthew, leaping over the dead body of the boy's father. "Son of a bitch," she muttered as she swept her son into her arms and cradled him against her breasts. "You'll not touch me again, will you?"

Just then Lissa saw John coming through the open cabin doorway with Honeek just behind him. John was covered from head to foot with snow and bloody gore. The side of Honeek's head was matted with blood. Both man and boy halted in the doorway. They stared at the dead Mohawk, at Lissa, and then at the dead Mohawk again.

"Told you I could take care of myself," Lissa said softly. "I . . . I made gingerbread. Do you want some while it's still hot?"

Lissa blinked, and John Eagle was beside her. Honeek had the baby in his hands and John was hugging her, his entire body shaking. "Ah, *ki-ti-hi,* you are safe," he whispered, a tremble in his strong voice. "This man was afraid I had lost you, my love."

Lissa didn't know what to do but to hang on to John for dear life. She didn't care that he was covered in blood. She didn't care that there was a dead man sprawled at her feet. All that mattered was John's touch and his numbing words.

My love? Had he said that or had Lissa imagined it in her shock? Was it her ears playing tricks on her? So many times she had imagined him using those words that maybe she had just conjured them up in her mind. But his lips were brushing against her temple. He was kissing her.

"John," she whispered, squeezing him tightly. "John."

"I meant to woo you as is proper, once you had regained your strength. I do not want to take advantage of you, but I realized as I ran through the snow that I could not live without you,

Lissa." He drew back so that he could look her in the eyes with his own dark ones. "Tell me. Will you marry this man?"

"M-marry you?" Lissa suddenly felt faint.

"Kehella. Yes. I know we have not known each other long. I know I have not courted you as is the way of my people. But I ask for fear I will lose you. Give this man a chance to be a good husband. Give this man a chance to be a father to your son."

The floor was spinning, and for a moment Lissa thought she might black out. But she wasn't going to miss the most important moment of her life. "You . . . you want me to marry you?" In the back of her mind she could hear Honeek as he walked to the door to close it and then to the fireplace to cuddle the baby and give them privacy.

"I . . . this man has loved you since the night I took you from the Mohawks. I cannot explain it. I only know that it is true." He lowered his head. "If you do not feel the same way—"

Lissa threw her arms around his neck, feeling the tears spring in her eyes. "I can't believe you're really saying this. You want me? You want Matthew knowing how he came into this world?"

John held out one palm. "He came into this world through a mother's labor and these hands. Does a man need to know more than that?"

Tears of joy slipping down her cheeks, Lissa's mouth trembled as John brought his lips to hers and they shared their first kiss.

Epilogue

"Oh, disgusting!" Matt rocked back on his heels, covering his face with his hands. "This is the kissy part. I hate this!"

Lissa looked up, her eyes clouded with tears. For a moment her recollections were so clear that her heart was pounding. She could still feel the touch of John's lips. She could still see the dead Mohawk on the cabin floor. But of course that was all long in the past.

Lissa's gaze settled on her unruly children. "Bedtime, gentlemen."

Mark and Luke were busy making fish mouths at each other. Matthew was rolling on the floor.

"Tell us about the Mohawks," Matt begged. "What did you do with the dead bodies? Leave 'em for the wolves to eat?"

Lissa stood, wiping her tears with the corner of her petticoat. "Hush, Matt. Now, that's how your father and I came to be man and wife, and that's how you all came to be here."

Lissa hadn't explained to Matt yet that John was not his birth father, but when the boy was old enough to understand how babies were conceived, she would tell him the truth of his birth. John Eagle was such a good father to his sons that she knew in her heart everything would be all right, even when Matthew knew he was part Mohawk by blood.

Lissa clapped her hands once to get the boys' attention. All three of them were now rolling on the floor pushing and laughing like a pile of puppies. "Enough! Enough!" she called. "I've kept my end of the bargain and now you must keep yours. To bed, boys."

"Oh, Mama," Matt groaned.

"Oh, Mama," Mark echoed.

"Mama!" Luke tugged on her petticoat. "But we didn't say g'night to Papa."

Just then the cabin door swung open and John Eagle appeared. Lissa couldn't suppress a smile as she looked up at him. He was taking off his heavy outdoor clothing and stomping the snow from his boots. "There he is," she told her boys. "Kiss your father and go to bed now."

"Mama!"

"Mama!"

"Now!" Lissa answered sternly. "Else when Uncle Honeek arrives in the morning with his surprises, I'll tell him these boys have been too bad for gifts. I'll tell him you can't go play in the snow with him because you have chosen to spend Christmas Day praying like all good boys should."

John's husky laughter filled the cabin as he took each boy in his arms and kissed them soundly. "No sense fighting a woman with red hair," he told them softly. "Go with you and I'll see you all in the morning."

It wasn't until the three boys had shimmied up the ladder to the loft that Lissa finally allowed herself to cross the room to her husband.

She reached out to take the scarf from around his neck. It was so cold out that his breath had made the wool stiff.

"You've been crying," he said, touching her cheek with one cold hand.

She smiled up at him, warming his hand in hers. "Tears of happiness."

He looked down at her with his hooded dark eyes that sparkled with the love that had grown each day between them until they were more one body than two. "Not The Christmas Story again?"

She laughed, lifting up on her toes to rest her hands on his shoulders. She kissed him soundly on the mouth. "Yes, The Christmas Story. I tell it to them every year, you know that."

He kissed the tip of her nose, the bridge of her cheek. "And they never tire of it, do they?"

"Never," she whispered, her voice warm and sensuous. "It's a Christmas Eve tradition."

He tightened his hands around her waist, pulling her even closer to him. Lissa felt her cheeks grow warm as he brushed his fingertips across the bodice of her gown. "Tradition for you and the children. What of a tradition between you and me, Wife?"

She laughed, her voice rich with the love she felt for this man, this man who had been her savior so many Christmases ago. "Oh, yes, we do have a special tradition, don't we, Husband?"

He was kissing the pulse of her neck now. She could feel the blood rushing in her veins, her heart pumping in anticipation of his touch. "But it is a special tradition. Let me lead you this way to share it with you." Taking his hand in hers, she began to lead him across the cabin toward the doorway to their tiny bedchamber.

"What of the children?" John asked.

"They're asleep. Even the baby."

"But you said you still had pudding to make. The duck—"

"The duck can wait." Lissa turned in the bedchamber doorway to face John. "But this can't." She covered his mouth with hers and all thought was lost. Suddenly there were no Christmas Eves past, not even any Christmas Eves to come. All that mattered at this moment was the two of them and a love born on a Christmas Eve so many years ago.

The Christmas Wish

by
Carol Finch

One

Lottie Dawes pulled her cloak tightly around her to ward off the crisp winter wind and turned her horse around. The shaggy gray mare was reluctant to leave the string of horses tethered in front of the schoolhouse where the "box supper" auction was in progress. Lottie nudged the mare forward, mulling over her conversation with young Oran Paine. The boy had been on the verge of tears when he'd waylaid Lottie on the schoolhouse steps a few moments earlier.

Clucking her tongue, Lottie put the mare into a trot. Her destination was a ranch two miles from town. Her thoughts clicked in rhythm with the clomp of hooves while she mentally rehearsed what she intended to say to Seth Broden. An ingenious idea struck Lottie when she was a half-mile from the ranch. She smiled in satisfaction. The solution to the problem was simple. It was a shame she hadn't thought of it months before.

In customary high spirits, Lottie tethered her mare, grabbed her box-supper-for-two that was to have been included in the bidding at the fund-raiser, and she marched up to Seth Broden's front door.

The house was as dark as the night, but the faintest glow from the hearth indicated that the master of the house was in residence—alone. Seth didn't socialize with anyone in the community if he could help it. He was a loner, a hermit, and local gossip hadn't been the least bit kind to him. But all that was about to change, Lottie decided. She was going to save this hard-bitten man from himself.

With that optimistic thought, Lottie clasped her colorfully wrapped box supper in one hand and raised her arm to rap on the door. Before her knuckles connected with wood, the door shot open wide enough for an arm to snake out and coil around her wrist. In stunned amazement, Lottie found herself jerked through the partially opened door and slammed up against a steel-hard body and naked chest. A shriek burst from her lips when a bare, masculine arm clamped over her breasts.

"What the devil—?"

The rumbling male voice came from so close to her ear that Lottie winced. She found herself released as quickly as she had been captured. Pivoting, Lottie faced the looming giant. His ominous silhouette was outlined by the dim glow from the hearth. Despite the darkness, Lottie realized Seth was fresh from the big metal bathtub that set beside the hearth. He wore nothing but breeches and it was impossible not to notice the whipcord muscles of his broad chest and powerful shoulders. Lottie inhaled a steadying breath, but it was thick with the scent that clung to him, and now to her.

"What do you want?" Seth Broden demanded gruffly.

Lottie composed herself as best she could and rearranged the blue calico gown that had been twisted sideways. "My gracious, Mister Broden, do you always greet your guests in such an abrupt fashion?"

"I don't have guests," he muttered as he strode over to retrieve his shirt and boots. "I thought you were that pesky brat I encountered earlier."

The "pesky brat" had been Oran Paine, Lottie deduced. "That's who I'm here to speak to you about, Mister Broden."

Lottie clasped her crunched box supper and cheerfully sallied forth. "Have you had supper yet?"

"No," he scowled from the darkest corner of the room.

"Good. I was on my way to sell my box supper at the fund-raiser for the Christmas celebration when I happened onto Oran."

One black brow arched inquiringly. "Oran?"

"The pesky brat," she prompted. "But Oran isn't a pesky brat a-tall. The two of you simply got off to a bad start and Oran wishes to make amends."

Seth eased a muscled shoulder against the wall and watched with curious fascination while his uninvited guest took over his home as if she owned the place. Seth wasn't in the habit of letting anyone commandeer his life. For the most part, he kept to himself and refused to let anyone intrude on his space, but this pixielike female was different. He'd seen her on several occasions while he was gathering supplies in town. He knew of her reputation as the resident saint who went about doing good deeds.

Spellbound, Seth appraised Lottie as if she were a forbidden fantasy shimmering beyond his reach. When she shed her hooded cloak, pale blond hair cascaded over her shoulders, spar-kling like starlight in the shadows that were as much a part of Seth's home as they were his life. The firelight glowed on Lottie's flawless features, enhancing what could only be described as the epitome of femininity. Seth was certain that if a host of cherubs were to dream a collective dream, it would be of this five-foot-two-inch image of visual perfection whose dimpled smile rivaled the sun.

It was said that Lottie Dawes had a heart as big as the newly formed Oklahoma Territory and a soul as pure as driven snow. The men in town and the soldiers from nearby Fort Reno fairly worshipped the ground she floated over. They invented excuses to approach her, and Seth had no doubt that the males who had attended the box supper were sighing in disappointment because the lovely Saint Lottie hadn't graced the social function with her cheerful presence.

From what Seth had heard in town, Lottie had established a laundry business at her cottage to support herself after the Land Run. Since the new territory was overpopulated with men, Lottie was doing a thriving business. According to reports, she was also averaging five marriage proposals a month, all of which she had so graciously rejected that her suitors bore not the slightest ill feelings toward her. Seth wondered how she managed it and why she hadn't taken a husband. He also wondered what it would be like to claim this enchanting nymph who . . .

Seth squelched the whimsical thought. Of all the men in the community, he was the last one who deserved this paragon. Respectable women took a wide berth around a man who was rumored to have a black soul and blood on his hands.

"Aren't you hungry, Mister Broden?" Lottie asked when the towering giant continued to stare at her from the shadows.

"Seth," he corrected in a gruff voice that was meant as a rebuke of his own dangerous thoughts. This innocent maiden was off limits. Too bad he had such difficulty convincing his male body of that.

Lottie couldn't help herself. When the powerfully built rancher strode forward with the enthralling grace of a giant jungle cat, she stared in open admiration. For a man who stood six feet four inches and weighed two hundred thirty pounds if he weighed an ounce, it was amazing that Seth could move with the silence of a shadow.

Although Lottie couldn't honestly say Seth Broden was handsome, there was something intriguing about his craggy features and imposing stature. Lottie was ashamed to admit that each time she had seen Seth in town, she felt her gaze helplessly drawn to him, speculating about him, longing to understand this standoffish man who wallowed in self-imposed solitude.

Some folks said Seth's eyes were as black as the pits of hell from whence he had come. Others claimed he had learned that prowling stalk during the dark, violent years of his life. And there were some folks who swore he was the devil incarnate who stole away lives and stripped souls . . .

Lottie's wandering thoughts trailed off when Seth's chair scraped on the wooden floor. He sank into it without a smidgen of wasted motion. Just how did he do that? It was truly impressive.

Lottie plunked down in her seat and placed the box supper between them. "You'll find no complaint with the meal, Mister—Seth," she corrected herself. "Brigit Svedberg prepared the dinner for me since I was running short on time. Fruitcake?"

Lottie stifled a smile when Seth cocked a thick brow and looked from her to the tin pan in her hand, as if he wasn't sure which one was the fruitcake.

Without a word Seth took a slice and set it on his plate.

"Chicken?" she inquired with a radiant smile.

If there was one thing Lottie Dawes was *not,* it was chicken, Seth decided. No one else had dared approach him. His infamous reputation had followed him to the new territory, working more effectively than insect repellent to drive people away, leaving him with the privacy he had come to accept—and expect. Lottie was his first house guest, and most likely his last, except for the pesky brat he'd chased off his property earlier in the evening. He accepted a piece of chicken.

"Now then, Seth," Lottie began after swallowing down a morsel of food. "About Oran Paine."

"He is that," Seth grunted. "An annoying pain in the—"

"Actually, he is a very good boy," she interrupted in Oran's defense. "The other children tease him terribly because he doesn't have a family."

"He's a bastard?" Seth supplied bluntly.

Lottie squirmed, blushed profusely, and failed to make direct eye contact. "Yes, I'm afraid he is. Oran ran away from an orphanage in Kansas and he had no place of his own. I've been caring for him, but I can't protect him from the other children's cruel jokes. They badgered Oran into serenading your home by beating on pots and pans. He obliged, hoping to become accepted by the other children. But Oran is dreadfully sorry for his prank and asked me to convey his heartfelt apology."

Seth ate the juicy chicken and waited for Lottie to continue. He knew how it felt to be ridiculed and excluded, having dealt with his share of mocking contempt the past decade.

"Since you don't socialize in the community, I'm afraid you've acquired a rather mysterious and diabolical reputation. Of course, I think it's utter nonsense and totally undeserved," Lottie hastily added. "You have simply been misunderstood and erroneously labeled by those who feed on gossip."

"So you aren't of the opinion that I'm a devil who entertains witches and warlocks in the dark of night?" he surprised her by asking.

"Certainly not! You're a peace-loving, hard-working man who has been so busy establishing your ranch and training your horses to sell to Fort Reno that you simply have not had the time to become acquainted with your neighbors."

"I haven't?" A strange feeling tugged at Seth's lips. Was it the makings of a smile? It had been so long that he wasn't sure.

"No, you haven't," Lottie assured him. "You choose to dress in black because you are a modest, self-assured man who has no inclination to call unnecessary attention to himself by wearing flamboyant clothes."

"I am?" It was *definitely* a smile that twitched his lips, Seth decided. This elf-size female amused him with her charitable explanations. In all his thirty years, no one had made such a grand display of defending his behavior or listing his admirable qualities. Hell, most folks didn't think he *had* any.

"Of course you are decent, kind, and respectable," she said

with perfect assurance. "I've found you to be very much the gentleman, except for that fiasco at the front door which, I'm certain, was nothing more than reflexive instinct after your unfortunate encounter with Oran." She lifted the gaily adorned box and smiled brightly. "More chicken?"

"Thank you. The food is delicious."

"I told you that you wouldn't be disappointed. Brigit is a marvelous cook. You should sample her Swedish meatballs. They're very much out of this world." Lottie straightened herself in her chair, prepared to present her ingenious proposition. "Now then, about young, orphaned Oran. He's just turned sixteen and he's rather large for his age, as I'm sure you noticed, being the exceptionally observant man you are."

Seth chuckled around his piece of chicken, amused by Lottie's tactic of pinpointing the qualities she expected to see in him, subtly instructing him on how he was to conduct himself.

"I've tried to instruct Oran as best I can, but he desperately needs a role model and the positive influence of a man, since he has no father to guide and train him. Oran could help you with your chores and you could take him under your wing. Since you've constructed a spacious home, you have plenty of room for—"

Seth choked on his chicken. "You expect me to adopt that brat?"

Lottie smiled her most enchanting smile. "What a wonderful idea! I'm glad you thought of it."

"I thought nothing of the kind." His dark eyes narrowed. "Do not to try to plant ideas in my head, woman."

"You give me far too much credit, but thank you kindly for the compliment, undeserved though it is," she said, undaunted by his reproachful glare. "This alliance will do wonders for Oran. You can impart your knowledge of livestock and farming practices and Oran can help you plant spring crops. No one will tease him about not having a father and none of the other boys will dare say an unkind word about a caring man who graciously took in an orphan. In addition, those preposterous rumors about you will cease circulating around town."

Seth scowled at the self-satisfied smile that captured Lottie's exquisite features. "Now wait just a damned minute, Miss Lottie Dawes. I don't know a damned thing about raising a boy—"

"Weren't you a boy at one time yourself?"

"Well, yes, but—" Seth was quickly learning that a man could get only a few words in edgewise when Lottie was on one of her persuasive campaigns.

"And don't you recall all those perplexing feelings and thoughts young men encounter at the threshold of manhood?"

"Certainly, but—"

"And would you want poor Oran growing up labeled a sissy because he's living with *me*? That arrangement can't be good for his manly image and self-confidence, now can it? There's no one else in the community that I'd want Oran to pattern himself after. You have so much to give him, so much to teach him. What boy could ask for more in a mentor?"

Seth eased back in his chair. His shuttered gaze appraised the dainty angel who took on an ethereal appearance in the flickering firelight. "And what favors are *you* willing to offer in return for training this misdirected young man?"

"Favors?" Lottie swallowed visibly when eyes as black as midnight drifted over her in silent inspection. An odd sensation tingled on her spine as she peered at the swarthy giant who was studying her with piercing scrutiny.

"Perhaps you've convinced yourself that I'm a respectable, charitable gentleman, Miss Lottie Dawes, but where I come from, debts are always repaid—one way or another."

"Just where do you come from?" she questioned.

"Some say I come from hell, and they may be closer to the truth than you would like to think. Now answer the damned question," he demanded.

Lottie frowned at the comment and the biting voice that conveyed it. "I'll do your laundry free of charge," she bartered.

"I can do my own laundry, thank you very much."

"Then I'll ensure that you receive an invitation to every social function during the Christmas holidays."

Seth shook his dark head and smiled devilishly. "I don't need invitations to go *wherever* I decide to go, *if* I decide to go."

Lottie was suddenly reminded of the gossip Brigit Svedberg had relayed to her about Seth Broden. Folks said this ex-gunslinger and bounty hunter had sold his soul to the devil to spare his own wicked life, that the money acquired to establish this ranch was blood money and that he had so many notches on the handle of his pistol that it resembled a toothpick.

Nonsense, Lottie told herself. She didn't believe Seth Broden was a spawn of the devil. He was simply mysterious, misinterpreted, and isolated. She would save him from his unseemly reputation and draw him out of the cynical shell he wore like protective armor. It would be her good deed for the holidays.

Her thoughts broke down when Seth rose from his chair and veered around the table to loom over her—and with intimidating effectiveness, she noted.

"The *favor* I expect, Miss Lottie Dawes," he said in a deceptively soft voice, "is that *you* do something for *me* in exchange for what you've cleverly maneuvered *me* into doing for *you*."

Lottie struggled to maintain her customarily cheerful composure. "I already assured you that I have no qualms about swapping favors, but—"

Her voice evaporated when Seth effortlessly drew her to her feet. Since he stood a foot taller than she did, she had to tilt her head back to meet his twinkling gaze and mischievous smile. He was going to be difficult, she predicted. But she had never walked away from difficult challenges and wasn't about to start now.

"In exchange for training Oran, I'll ensure that superstitious gossipers know what a kind, generous, decent gentleman you are," Lottie pledged. "What greater favor can I give but to restore your good name?"

Seth felt another smile quirking his lips as he stared down into Lottie's enchanting features. He wasn't accustomed to so much smiling. He wondered if his face would crack.

There had been little gaiety in Seth's life, but it amused him to be womanhandled with such cunning finesse. Jolly Saint Lottie was a rare, intelligent creature who was exceptionally good at managing people. She probably thought she could come bearing gifts of food to appease the appetite of the man who had been called by many an "uncivilized beast" and convince him to do her bidding before she walked away unscathed. But Miss Lottie Dawes, the residing angel of El Reno, had miscalculated when she pitted herself against Seth Broden.

"Do you always seek out the best in everyone?" Seth asked, studying her with an unblinking intensity that made her squirm in her skin.

"Why would I look for the *worst* in them?"

He stepped closer, intending to intimidate her with his nearness. "Because sometimes that's all you can find, no matter how you try to sugar-coat the truth."

Seth knew all about the evils of this world. He'd dealt with men who were bad to the bone while this idealistic female tried to anoint all mankind with her generosity. Admirable but hardly realistic, he mused. Miss Lottie Dawes preferred to pretend that life was a bowl of cherries, even when Seth knew for a fact that it could be the pits of hell.

"But there's not a wicked bone in *your* body," Lottie declared. "I think you have simply been misunderstood."

Seth burst out laughing, trying to remember the last time he had laughed out loud—if ever. "Oh, you do, do you?"

"Indeed I do."

Lottie felt a strange warmth course through her when deep,

resonant laughter reverberated around the room. It was a pleasurable sound that chased away the shadows that slanted across Seth's chiseled face, making him appear years younger and not quite so burdened with the oppressive weight of the world.

Lottie eyed him inquisitively. "Has anyone ever told you that you have a most unique sense of humor?"

"I've never been noted for my humor." His laughter evaporated when his gaze came to rest on her beautifully sculpted mouth. Awareness leaped through his body like a bounding jackrabbit. It had been a long time since Seth had been with a woman, and *never* had he been this close to anyone as pure and sweet as this beguiling woman who saw him through the eyes of an angel.

Suddenly, Seth knew exactly what he wanted in exchange for taking Oran Paine under his wing. The very thought caused his body to pulse with needs too long neglected. "The price for training wayward boys is steep," he said in a voice that rustled with unfulfilled desire.

"I'll gladly pay for Oran's apprenticeship," Lottie insisted without hesitation.

Seth grinned. "You are too trusting. I have yet to name my price."

"But you are a reasonable man."

"So you keep trying to convince me and *yourself.*"

"Because I *believe* it . . ." Lottie blinked owlishly when his onyx eyes darkened in intensity and his big, calloused hands framed her face. His thumbs brushed sensuously over her cheeks and parted lips and Lottie gasped at the sizzling reaction that vibrated through her body. "What are you doing!"

"I'm collecting my down payment for favors soon to be rendered."

He bent his raven head, erasing the narrow space between them, taking her lips beneath his to satisfy the craving that her alluring presence aroused in him. And sure enough, Lottie

Dawes *tasted* every bit as good as she looked. Seth savored the sampling of heaven, cherished the sweet nectar of her innocent kiss. He hungered for more than just a brief taste of forbidden fruit; he wanted to devour this feast to end all feasts!

Lottie had been kissed once or twice in her twenty-one years. Well, all right, *once,* she admitted in all honesty. Most of her male acquaintances kept a respectable distance, placing her on a pedestal for reasons she couldn't fathom, offering ridiculously dramatic marriage proposals at the second or third meeting. But the feel of Seth's full lips settling upon hers with the gentleness of a butterfly alighting on a flower petal sent a startling jolt through her nerve endings and ignited a fire in her soul.

When Seth's brawny arms encircled her, bringing her naive body into intimate contact with his lean, hard contours, Lottie knew why the touch and sight of other men had never felt quite right, why she had rejected proposals and invitations without a second thought. Now Lottie knew, without question, the difference between a kiss and a *kiss*. This, she instantly realized, was magic. Destiny must surely have brought her to Seth Broden's door.

The romantic encounter was a treat to Lottie's deprived senses. Whatever Seth Broden had been before he staked his claim in the land run, despite the cruel rumors of his association with fallen angels in fiery pits, there was a tenderness in this man's soul that called out to her in the electrified silence. The crackle of the logs in the hearth could have been her body burning on the sensual flame inside her. Lottie felt the instinctive responses in every fiber of her being. When Seth lifted his raven head, she found herself staring into those fathomless eyes that shined like black diamonds and she knew she had met her fate on this cold December night.

"You've just begun to pay the devil his due," Seth rasped as he watched Lottie's trembling fingertip trace her kiss-swollen lips. "I want your soul in exchange for training your young orphan. Are you sure you have the gumption to meet my price, little blue-eyed angel? The stakes may be higher than you think. Are you sure Oran is worth what you stand to lose to me?"

Lottie retreated a step, finding no restraint in the powerful arms that could have so easily held her captive. That they *didn't* signified a great deal about the man's true character. "I think you're teasing me to perpetuate all the ridiculous gossip that seems to amuse you. You don't really want my soul in exchange for our bargain."

One thick brow elevated and black eyes gleamed in the firelight. "No? There are those in town who are convinced I don't have a soul of my own and that I'm definitely in need of one."

No man who could hold a woman as if she were as delicate as a newborn babe and kiss her with such remarkable tenderness could possibly be in cahoots with the devil, Lottie assured herself. Her intuition rarely proved her wrong. For sure and certain, Seth Broden needed to be saved from his own dismal perspective of himself and that of his tale-bearing neighbors. It was going to take some powerful convincing before Seth stopped living down to the low expectations of the rest of the world, but Lottie had officially made this isolated man her holiday crusade. By Christmas, she vowed, Seth Broden would have a new lease on life, in addition to a well-respected reputation in town.

Lottie pushed up on tiptoe to return the gentle kiss, setting Seth Broden back on his heels. "If it's a soul you wish for, then it's a soul you shall have," she cheerfully promised him.

Both black brows jackknifed when Lottie retreated, leaving his masculine body humming like the keys on the church organ. Damn, was there no way to rattle this optimistic female? Obviously not, Seth decided. Lottie didn't frighten easily and she was entirely too trusting for her own good.

"You're in the business of granting wishes, too?" he smirked. "What in hell are you? An angel of mercy and fairy godmaiden rolled into one?"

Lottie's laughter—like jingle bells tinkling on an icy winter morning—was sweet music to Seth's ears. He hadn't realized how empty his life had been of pleasurable sights and sounds until Lottie burst in like a star beaming in the dark of night.

"Since you are such a kind and generous man I think that I will see to it that you receive far more than you even bargained for." She smiled cryptically and extended her hand, palm up. "But for now, I will accept your charitable donation for the box supper. I'll drop the money by the schoolhouse on my way home. The Christmas committee is gathering funds to purchase gifts for needy children in the community," she informed him. "I'll be sure to tell everyone how thoughtful and generous you have been."

Seth stared at her outstretched hand, muttered under his breath, then fished into his pocket. "How much do I owe you for the pleasure of your company while dining on the box supper?"

"How much would you have bid for Brigit's meal?" Lottie questioned his question.

Seth peered into those eyes that sparkled like sapphires in the firelight and paid the price he knew any man would have paid to share a meal with this delightfully entertaining angel whose smile defined the boundaries of paradise.

When he pressed ten dollars into her hand, Lottie gasped in amazement. "My gracious! You *are* a most benevolent man! And I can give Oran no greater gift for Christmas than the benefit of your skillful expertise."

Seth stood there like an immovable mountain when Lottie grabbed her cloak and swept out the door to disappear into the night. He was still standing in the shadows when he heard the thunder of hooves fading into silence. He glanced around him, wondering how the room could be doused in a darker shade of black the instant that angelic vision vanished from sight. It was as if the shadows that had been his life had returned, more defined and noticeable than ever before . . .

When the hypnotic spell wore off, Seth grumbled to himself. He had let Lottie persuade him to raise a half-grown boy who didn't know beans about ranching. Seth had sacrificed his privacy for the slightest whisper of a kiss from a cherub bearing a box supper. Good Lord! That woman would play havoc with his regimented lifestyle if he let her. Besides, her cheerfulness and bright-eyed honesty unhinged him. He wasn't used to it, considering the kind of individuals he had known in the past. He must have been out of his mind to take such bold privileges with that innocent maiden! God, what could he have been thinking?

Seth pulled off his clothes and climbed into bed. He'd let himself be talked into becoming a damned nanny for an orphan. He must've suffered a momentary lapse of sanity when he'd stared into those spell-binding blues eyes. And he was every kind of fool if he deluded himself in thinking that something could come of this ill-fated infatuation for cheerful Saint Lottie.

Lottie only saw in him what she wanted to see, Seth reminded himself sensibly. She didn't want to accept the truth about his jaded past—a past that would always be a barrier between them, no matter how much he found himself craving another taste of heaven. Seth had spent too much time in hell, doing the kind of things a woman like Lottie would never approve or understand. If Seth had a lick of sense, he would keep his distance from that blond-haired goddess. Lottie could do better than a man like him and Seth had better not let himself forget that. He had accepted his sequestered life and he was comfortable with what fate had dealt him. This was the price he had to pay after seeing vengeance served.

On that realistic thought, Seth fell asleep . . . and found himself dreaming dreams that could never come true.

* * *

"You did *vhat!*" Brigit Svedberg chirped in disbelief.

Lottie glanced up from the scrub board to survey the shocked expression that claimed Brigit's fair features. The middle-aged widow gaped at Lottie as if she had mistletoe sprouting from her wooden skull.

"I said I made arrangements with Mister Broden to take Oran under his wing."

"Yah, I heard vhat you said. I yust can't believe vhat I'm hearing! You vent alone to Devil Broden's ranch and turned poor Oran over to him? Vhat could you have been dinking?"

Lottie smiled at Brigit's heavy Swedish accent and her bewildered tone of voice.

"There, Brigit doesn't think this is such a good idea, neither," Oran Paine piped up.

"Either," Lottie automatically corrected.

Lottie twisted the army uniform, squeezing out the excess water, before hanging the garment over the line to dry. "Now, Oran you know you can't stay here with me indefinitely," she reasoned with the brooding boy who was hunkered over the wash basin beside her. "You can learn things from Seth Broden that I can't teach you. And besides, you'll be doing him a tremendous favor. He needs your help with his chores, as well as your companionship. The townsfolk have treated him like an outcast, when, in truth, he is every bit the gentleman. You'll like him immensely, if only you give him a chance."

"A yentleman? Ha!" Brigit hooted.

"A gentleman," Lottie confirmed before focusing a reassuring smile on Oran. "Seth Broden needs you, Oran, and you need *him* to teach you the responsibilities of becoming a man."

"More dan likely our poor Oran vill find himself sacrificed to de devil!" Brigit harrumped. "De very idea!"

"Would I make these arrangements if I weren't thoroughly convinced Oran will be in competent hands?"

"Vell—"

"Of course not," Lottie said with her usual optimism. "Oran is like a brother to me. But the greatest kindness I can bestow on him is to apprentice him to a successful, self-reliant rancher. Oran will only be two miles away, after all. Would you prefer to see Oran scrubbing clothes when he could learn to train horses and mules and tend a herd of cattle?"

"Vell—"

"I knew you would understand once you had time to warm to the notion."

Brigit settled her ruffled feathers and strolled over to straighten the second uniform Lottie had draped over the line. "Yah, I suppose it vould be good for de boy, *if* you're sure Seth Broden is dependable."

"Very dependable," Lottie affirmed. "Come Christmas, Oran will have made great strides in securing his future."

Oran stamped into the house to gather his belongings. Lottie was one step behind him, offering last-minute instructions. Brigit brought up the rear of the procession, mumbling in Swedish.

Lottie waved Oran on his way with an encouraging smile while the reluctant lad slung his knapsack over his slouched shoulder and trooped off. Oran glanced back at irregular intervals, just in case Lottie changed her mind. To his dismay, she didn't call him back . . .

Two

Seth Broden glanced over at the bulky form of the young man who rode silently beside him. After three days, Seth had adjusted to having Oran Paine underfoot. Whether out of fear or growing respect—*fear* was Seth's guess—Oran had attempted to master every task Seth requested of him. When Seth instructed Oran on the techniques of breaking green colts to the halter and saddle, Oran listened attentively. The boy also scraped himself and his bruised pride off the ground, dusted himself off, and climbed back in the saddle after being unseated countless times. The boy's determination impressed Seth. Much to Seth's surprise, he had already become accustomed to the sounds of someone else in his domain and accepted sharing his private space with the lad.

"Seth?" Oran questioned his mentor as they rode toward the house after checking the cattle and repairing sagging fences. "I was wondering if . . . that is . . . if you don't have chores for me to do tonight if . . . well . . ."

Seth slanted the self-conscious lad a frowning glance. "Spit it out, Oran. Men don't hemhaw. If you have something to say, just say it."

Oran inhaled a deep breath and expelled the words that teetered on the tip of his tongue. "I'd like to ride into town to visit Molly."

"Who in hell's Molly?"

"A girl." Oran's face turned the color of a sand plum as he

squirmed in the saddle. He stared every which way except at Seth.

A smile twitched Seth's lips. "I could've figured that much out for myself." Having Oran around had put Seth back in touch with the innocence of life—a time of dreams and visions of the future. He recalled his own awkwardness with the female of the species and wondered just exactly how much Oran knew about women. "What do you plan to do with Molly?"

Oran's freckled face flushed with another wave of embarrassment. "Just talk, of course. Miss Lottie says ladies should be treated with consideration and respect. And Molly is the sweetest, prettiest—" He halted his words abruptly and stared at his clenched fist which was clamped on the reins. "I wanted to invite her to the Christmas celebration before somebody else beats me to it."

"I see." Seth stared straight ahead, allowing Oran to wrestle privately with his uneasiness.

"Seth?"

"Yes?"

"Have you ever . . . er . . . I mean—"

"You're stammering again. Spit it out."

"Kissed a girl?" Oran blurted.

Seth clamped down a chuckle. "Once or twice."

"Do you think it'd be all right if I kissed Molly?"

"For practice?"

"No! I get these funny feelings when I'm around her and something inside me keeps telling me I ought to do something about it . . ." He glanced up from beneath thick lashes. *"Should* I?"

Now it was Seth's turn to squirm. He'd never been involved in this sort of conversation, but he had the feeling Oran was angling for information about sex. "Are you in love with this Molly?"

"I don't know. My heart nearly beats me to death when she

smiles at me. My palms sweat so badly I'm afraid to hold her hand," he confided in mortification. "Nobody else has ever affected me that way. Is that love, do you think?"

"Could be rioting lust," Seth diagnosed.

"Lust?" Oran frowned, bemused.

"That's the man in you hungering for the touch of a woman, Oran."

"You mean like those drifters who visit Sally's Pleasure Parlor?" Oran squawked indignantly. "That's not what I want from Molly! Not a girl for just one night. I'm talking about having someone to call my own who cares for me the way I want to care for her. Miss Lottie says that's most important—sharing, caring, and giving unselfishly."

"And what does Miss Lottie Dawes have to say about lust?" Seth questioned.

"She doesn't know diddlysquat about it. That's why I'm asking *you*," Oran replied. "Miss Lottie said you'd tell me everything I needed to know because you know everything about being a real man since you are one."

Laughter rumbled deep in Seth's chest. "And you believe everything Jolly Saint Lottie tells you, do you?"

"Miss Lottie never lies," Oran declared. "She said you were a good and decent man, and she was right about that. She said you were the kind of man a boy would be proud to pattern his life after, and you are. I was afraid to come here because of the rumors, but Miss Lottie said I would be glad I did, and I am. Now, what about kissing Molly?"

Seth's nose suddenly caught a whiff of an unexpected aroma floating on the cool evening air. A wary frown plowed his brow as he stared at his two-story cabin. No doubt about it, somebody had been cooking in his house.

"Seth? Should I kiss her or not?" Oran demanded anxiously.

Seth swung from the saddle and grinned at Oran. "If it feels right, then kiss her. And tonight when you come home, we'll have a long talk."

"Home?" Oran stared pensively at the house before refocusing on Seth.

Seth muttered under his breath when he realized what he'd said. He'd unwittingly made room for Oran in his life when he hadn't thought he needed *anyone* in his private domain. Having Oran following in his footsteps was beginning to feel . . . natural, comfortable.

"Home," Seth affirmed. "Now go unsaddle our mounts and haul in some water for a bath. Proper ladies like Molly don't care for men who smell like lathered horses."

When Oran trotted toward the barn, Seth strode onto the stoop. There was *definitely* a tantalizing aroma seeping through the woodwork and windows. Not knowing who or what to expect, Seth clamped his hand around his pistol and barged inside, pointing in every direction at once. If claim jumpers were attempting to steal his property, they would have one helluva fight on their hands!

A high-pitched squawk blasted Seth's eardrums. To his shock and disbelief, a hefty raw-boned woman of forty or thereabouts clutched her wooden spoon to her bosom and half collapsed against the table. Wide, rounded eyes focused on the six-shooter that was pointed at her heart.

"Who the hell are you and what are you doing in my house?" Seth demanded to know that very second, and not very nicely, either.

Brigit Svedberg breathed a shaky sigh of relief when the ominous gunman slid his pistol into his holster. "I'm Brigit Svedberg," she introduced herself in a croak. "I've come to cook for you and de boy."

"By whose proclamation?" As if Seth couldn't guess. This had to be more of Saint Lottie's handiwork. The woman had become too damned presumptuous! Not even to politely ask permission before dropping another body in Seth's lap!

"Miss Lottie sent me o'course." Brigit turned back to the stove to stir the potatoes and onions that crackled in the skillet.

Seth surveyed the table that was heaping with pastries, mincemeat pies, raw vegetables, and several other dishes that were unfamiliar to him. He had the feeling he'd just discovered what a Swedish smorgasbord was. His gaze swung to the trunk beside the spare bedroom door. He scowled sourly. From all indication Brigit was here to stay.

Damn that Lottie Dawes! Seth did not need extra mouths to feed and more folks crowding him. He'd just begun to adjust to Oran's presence and wham! The chief cook and bottle washer showed up.

"You vill like Svedish meatballs, yah," Brigit declared. "Dey are my specialty. Oran can eat a pot of dem all by himself. A man and growing boy need plenty of food to keep up deir strength. Yah, I vill see dat you and Oran have a clean home and proper meals."

Although his stomach growled at the sight and aromas of the waiting feast, Seth silently fumed. Lottie was trying to run his life, and Seth wasn't about to let her. Damn it, there was no telling who would arrive on his doorstep next if he didn't put a stop to Miss Lottie Dawes's interference—and quickly!

"De invitation is on de table," Brigit informed him, gesturing her wooden spoon toward the envelope.

"Invitation to what?" Seth muttered in question.

Brigit half turned to peer at the giant hulk of man dressed in black. "Miss Lottie said she vould see dat you vere velcome in every home. De pound party vill be held at de Adams's house tonight."

"Pound party?" Seth queried as he munched on a pastry that melted in his mouth.

"Every yentleman brings a pound of crackers, candy, or

someding edible to share wid de young ladies," Brigit explained. "You vill take a pound of strudel and mingle wid your neighbors."

Seth gnashed his teeth. He definitely did *not* need a cook and housekeeper bossing him around. Jolly Saint Lottie wasn't going to get a piece of *strudel* tonight; she was going to get a piece of his *mind!*

When Seth wheeled toward the door, Brigit's shout froze him in his tracks. "You vill eat first and den you vill bathe." She indicated the huge pot boiling on the stove. "I've already prepared your vater."

"Brigit?" Oran suddenly appeared in the doorway. "What are you doing here?"

Brigit gave Oran the once-over twice. "Vell, you can yust guess who sent me! You look real fine, boy, just as Miss Lottie said you vould."

Seth watched the unlikely pair smile broadly at each other before Brigit scuttled across the room to hug the stuffing out of Oran and ruffle the boy's crop of brown hair. "Dis life on de farm *is* good for you, yah. Yust as Miss Lottie said it vould be."

"I'm learning to ride and rope," Oran told her proudly. "Seth even gave me my own cow and calf to start a herd when I have a place of my own."

Brigit swiveled her blond head and gaped at Seth in amazement. "You did dis for de boy? You are druly a good and decent man, yust like Miss Lottie said." She nodded affirmatively. "Yah, I vill like it here, too, yust like Oran."

Seth noted the porcelain crock beside the stove and frowned. "What the blazes is that?"

"Julgrot," Brigit informed him as she shepherded Oran to the table to enjoy the smorgasbord she'd prepared. "In Sveden ve make a rice pudding wid a single almond at Christmas. Whoever gets the almond vill have good luck all year. De pudding has to ferment before it's prepared."

Seth watched Brigit scampering around, alternately fussing over the food cooking on the stove and Oran. Seth was ordered to the bathtub that had been dragged into his bedroom so he could spruce himself up for the pound party. The only *pounding* Seth wanted to do was on Miss Lottie Dawes's head! Damn it, whose house was this anyway? His or Miss Lottie's? The nerve of that woman!

"Ve vill celebrate St. Lucia Day dis weekend," Brigit announced after Seth appeared from his bath, still steaming—figuratively and literally. "In de old country dere is no vorking on St. Lucia Day. Yah, ve vill observe the holiday custom."

Seth scooped up another mouthwatering morsel of mincemeat pie on his way to the door. He was bound and determined to have a talk with Saint Lottie. That woman would *not* rule his life and he was going to tell her so the minute he laid eyes on her.

"Don't forget your pound of strudel!" Brigit called after him.

Seth reversed direction and snatched up the package, vowing to extract a pound of Lottie's flesh instead of passing out a pound of strudel.

Lottie was munching on a pound of nuts and chatting with the soldier who was seated in the chair beside her when Mrs. Emily Adams announced it was time to change conversation partners at the set-to party. At fifteen-minute intervals, Emily requested that the single ladies and gentlemen in attendance find a different companion. The young doctor who had been paying Lottie considerable attention from across the room had just planted himself beside her when a firm rap caused the front door to vibrate like chattering teeth.

Emily gasped audibly when she opened the door to find a man dressed all in black looming over her like a thundercloud. All conversation in the parlor died a quick death as anxious faces focused on the brooding giant who was known by sight and by notorious reputation.

Lottie had spent the past three days doing her best to polish Seth's tarnished credentials. In a matter of seconds he was undoing all her handiwork. His smoldering glare burned like black fire in his slitted eyes and his very stance spelled trouble for anyone who dared to cross him.

Lottie bounded to her feet, determined to soothe the savage-looking beast. "Seth! I'm so glad you came." She surged across the room to grasp his hand. It was like grabbing steel. She ignored that. "Let me introduce you to everyone."

"I'm not interested in introductions," Seth hissed in her ear.

Lottie ignored that, too. Instead, she cheerfully made the introductions to the leery congregation who looked as if they expected the formidable dragon to breathe fire on them at any moment.

Seth stalked over to the young doctor who was peering wide-eyed at him from behind wire-rimmed spectacles. Seth doubted this pathetic excuse for a man possessed the medical skills to cure a Christmas ham, much less patch up an injured patient. And worse, this meek physician wasn't Lottie's type. It would take an extraordinary man to handle the likes of Lottie Dawes.

"Go find another seat unless you want to—"

"Seth!" Lottie tugged on his arm. "You're not winning friends with your bullying behavior. I've been telling everyone how charming and gracious you are."

"And I keep telling you—" Seth clamped his jaw shut when Lottie discreetly ground her heel in the toe of his boot.

"Go sit in the empty chair beside Melody Prickle and mind your manners," Lottie instructed before returning to her designated seat beside the physician.

Seth plunked down next to the timid brunette who shrank away from him as if he were a coiled rattlesnake. "Strudel?" he questioned gruffly, shoving the package under her nose.

Melody Prickle winced as if Seth had lashed her with a whip. "N-no, s-sir. Suddenly I'm not v-very h-hungry," she stuttered before getting up and scuttling away.

Forty-five minutes later, the chair beside Seth remained unoccupied. Seth and his strudel had no takers. Not that he cared or noticed. He was too busy glaring at Lottie Dawes who was never without an eager, fawning male companion. When the social torture finally ended, Seth made a beeline toward Lottie who, as usual, was surrounded by a crowd of rapt admirers drooling over her like teething babies.

Lottie blinked curiously when the men who formed a semicircle around her stepped back apace and stared apprehensively at the air over her head—or whatever loomed there. She knew without turning around who had put a damper on the conversation. She sensed Seth's presence behind her, inhaled the fresh, clean scent that she had come to associate with him.

"Excuse me, gentlemen," Seth said as politely as he knew how. "I have a matter to discuss with Miss Dawes." With that, he clamped his hand around Lottie's elbow and towed her across the room.

"Thank you for an enjoyable evening, Emily," Lottie called to her hostess before Seth shoveled her out the door. To Seth she said, "Good gracious, how do you expect me to improve your reputation when you behave like an irascible bully? Poor Melody Prickle never recovered after her conversation with you. She sat there looking peaked the remainder of the night!"

"I didn't say a damned thing to her," Seth muttered.

"My point exactly. You were too busy glaring at me from across the room," Lottie replied while she was being shepherded to her gray mare. "The idea of a set-to or pound party is to engage in conversation to develop close acquaintanceships with other members of the community. You can't make friends when you're scowling."

"The only reason I came at all was to talk to you," Seth growled as he scooped Lottie up and deposited her in the saddle.

"And after you showed up looking like black thunder it will take me three days to undo the damage. You would've made a better impression if you'd have stayed home and let me sing your praises."

Seth stepped into his stirrup and grabbed the reins to Lottie's steed, leading her toward her cottage. "I can't stay home," he snapped. "Thanks to you, my house is suddenly overcrowded."

"You are upset with Brigit?"

"No, I'm upset with *you,* as if you don't know. I'll not have you stocking my home with orphans the way I stock my pastures with cattle and horses," he all but roared.

"Keep your voice down. You'll ruin your repu—"

Her words evaporated when an all too familiar voice erupted in a yelp. To Lottie's dismay, she saw Oran Paine cartwheel off the boardwalk and skid in the street after a drunken gambler delivered a right cross to the boy's jaw.

In the batting of an eyelash, Seth was off his horse, striding purposefully toward the gambler who'd grabbed Molly Simpson's hand. When Molly wailed Oran's name, every citizen within hearing distance poured out of doorways to determine what the commotion was all about. They stopped stock-still when the ominous black shadow passed beneath the streetlamp.

The stumbling gambler found himself slammed up against the wall of the dance hall. His breath came out in a whoosh when Seth's elbow mashed his belly into his backbone.

"Apologize to the young man and his young lady . . . *now,*" Seth demanded with deadly menace.

"I'll do no such—ooff!" The gambler gasped for breath when another blow plowed into his midsection.

"The good people of El Reno are waiting," Seth growled. "I'm told this is the season of peace and good will, *friend.* A gentleman never interferes when a young man has a lady on his arm. It isn't polite."

"I'm . . . sorry," the gambler muttered when he felt a cold steel pistol barrel threatening to pry his ribs apart.

Seth swiveled his head around to see Molly blubbering all over Oran, who had scraped himself out of the dirt the same way he'd hauled himself to his feet after being unhorsed by a wild bronc. A sense of pride channeled through Seth as he watched Oran recover his poise and brush the blood from his lips as if it were nothing but a raindrop.

"Oran, do you have anything you want to say to our friend before he goes on his way?" Seth questioned.

Oran strode forward, his determination and dignity restored. "Indeed I do. The apology should be directed to Molly. Ladies are to be treated with courtesy and respect. Apologize to Molly—nicely."

"I'm sorry," the gambler said humbly when the barrel of Seth's pistol dug a little deeper in his ribs.

While Oran wrapped a protective arm around Molly and she huddled against him, the gambler wobbled back into one of the twenty-three saloons that lined the streets of El Reno.

A smile of satisfaction brimmed Lottie's lips as she surveyed the silent crowd. She'd heaped glowing verbal accolades on Seth Broden the past few days, and now this bold intervention had clinched it and earned him instant respect with the townsfolk.

"It is ever so comforting to know there is a man in town who is willing to step forward to see justice served when the sheriff is unavailable," Lottie declared loudly enough to catch the attention of everyone on the street. "I know I shall feel safe and protected while Mister Broden is in town. He's a godsend."

Seth blinked in amazement when he noticed the tentative smiles that claimed the faces of the bystanders. Damn, the fairy godmaiden had waved her magic wand and given him respectability. She had planted kind thoughts in everybody's heads. The woman's persuasive skills were impressive.

Before Seth knew it, Lottie had scurried toward him, pumping his hand, proclaiming that his act of bravery was greatly appreciated by one and all.

Lottie turned to Oran. "Are you all right?"

Oran massaged his jaw and nodded his tousled brown head. "Yeah, thanks to Seth." He smiled gratefully out of the side of his mouth that wasn't quite so swollen. "After we have our talk tonight, maybe you should show me how to defend myself. I think I could use some pointers."

"What *talk* are you referring to?" Lottie inquired interestedly.

"Never mind." Seth grasped her hand and ushered her to her mount. "I have a bone to pick with you first."

Lottie found herself led to her cottage. The minute she and Seth were in the privacy of her home, he rounded on her, his thundercloud expression back in full force.

"I want to know why in hell you sent Brigit Svedberg to my house without asking my permission. Damn it, Lottie, I'm still the master of my own home!"

"You didn't enjoy Brigit's cooking?"

"That's not the point—"

"She didn't have the floor swept clean and the house dusted to your satisfaction?"

"Of course, she did, but—"

"And Oran wasn't delighted to see her?"

"Hell, yes, but—"

"I knew she'd make a fine addition to your home," Lottie declared as she removed her cloak and hung it on the hook beside the door. "You're very kind to allow Brigit to become a part of your family. I know she'll be happy there. Brigit has been living at the boardinghouse since claim jumpers killed her husband after the land run. She has no other family in this country and her small savings are nearly depleted. She needs someone to fuss over, a woman who has such strong maternal instincts and no children of her own. And she does love to cook. I was paying her to cook and clean for Oran and me, but now that Oran is under your capable care, Brigit didn't feel needed to the same gratifying degree."

Lottie lit the stove and brewed a pot of tea. "Brigit has become very fond of Oran and he of her. Knowing how busy you must be training Oran and tending your chores, I knew you would appreciate returning home to succulent meals, clean laundry, and a tidy home." She smiled elfishly when Seth leaned against the doorjamb to study her with those penetrating black eyes. "I can certainly understand that a man who desires to be the *master* of his own home has little time to be his own *servant* as well."

"You're doing it again, damn it," Seth grumbled.

She blessed him with her most angelic smile. "Doing what?"

"You know damned well what. You're planting ideas in my head like a farmer sowing seeds. I'm sure you convinced Brigit that she was needed at my ranch. Then you sat at that damned pound party tonight, telling your various companions what a good and decent man I was—'despite those preposterous rumors,' " he quoted. "I could hear my name being bandied about all the live-long night. And after I rescued Oran from being humiliated and beaten to a pulp in front of his young lady, you announced to the whole cursed town that I was some sort of guardian angel who had been sent to keep the blessed peace! Now you're trying to persuade me that *I* need Brigit as much as she and Oran need *me*."

"I knew you would understand." Lottie retrieved two mugs from the cupboard.

"Understand what?"

"How much you need Brigit and Oran."

"I didn't say that; *you* did!" Seth blared in exasperation. "And what favor are you granting me to compensate for this new mouth I'm expected to feed this time?"

Lottie strode over to press a light kiss to his thinned lips. "Another kiss of gratitude—"

His arm curled around her trim waist, bringing her petite body into familiar contact with his. Wild heat pulsated through him as he stared into those expressive blue eyes that danced with irrepressible inner spirit. "Damn it, woman, you're turning my life upside down. Do you think a simple kiss is going to satisfy me after all your meddling?"

Lottie felt her feminine body respond when Seth's sinewy physique molded itself so perfectly to hers. His alluring scent instantly saturated her senses and she surrendered to the elemental pleasure of his touch.

Lottie recognized the problem immediately. She was falling in love for the first time in her life, and with a man who was so busy trying to keep himself isolated that he hadn't noticed how much she enjoyed sharing his company, even when he wasn't in the best of moods—which he definitely wasn't at the moment.

Lottie tipped back her head and met those troubled obsidian eyes. "I can only offer you a simple kiss," she murmured. "Truth be told, I'm not sure you can handle a complicated kiss."

"A complicated kiss?" he repeated dubiously. "What the hell's that?"

"*This* is what the hell *that* is . . ."

Lottie looped her arms around his broad shoulders. Pushing up on tiptoe, she kissed him full on the mouth, employing the techniques she'd learned from him. Aware of her lack of experience in kissing, she waited for Seth to respond and then followed his masterful lead. When his tongue stabbed sensually into her mouth, she emulated the gesture. When his arms tightened around her, pressing her closer, she melted against him. When his hands glided downward to explore the curve of her hips, her fingertips measured the massive expanse of his chest, monitoring his accelerated pulse beneath her questing palm.

Fire sizzled through Lottie when adventurous caresses cruised up her rib cage to trace the underswell of her breasts. When his thumbs grazed the taut peaks that strained against the fabric of her wool gown, Lottie swore the floor had tilted beneath her feet. When his knee insinuated itself between her legs, she could feel delicious heat coiling deep inside her and fanning out in all directions.

My gracious! Kisses could be even more complicated than *she* had imagined! Wanting this sensual wild man had become a tangible desire that touched every part of her being, urging her to experiment with these wildly compelling sensations he had instilled in her.

With that erotic thought, Lottie realized her hands were drifting in curious exploration, aching to investigate the hair-covered flesh and washboard muscles without the hindrance of his shirt.

A muffled groan rumbled in Seth's throat when he felt untutored caresses spanning his chest. His arms contracted with the same urgency that hammered through his aroused body. His kisses trailed across the soft texture of Lottie's cheek, relishing her tantalizing scent, cherishing the feel of her satiny flesh beneath his lips.

Lottie gasped when his moist breath whispered over the pulsating column of her throat. The pearl buttons of her gown must have melted in the intense heat that radiated between her quivering body and Seth's. She could feel his fingertips and lips swirling over the swell of her breast, leaving her wild and desperate to satisfy a need she couldn't define.

"Seth . . . ?" Lottie rasped when his tongue flicked out to tease one throbbing crest and then the other.

The sound of his name on her lips was like a hypnotic incantation, luring him deeper into her beguiling spell. Touching her was another precious glimpse of forbidden paradise. Seth couldn't get enough of the taste and feel of her sweet, responsive body trembling in his arms, on his lips, his fingertips.

His free hand glided downward to tunnel beneath the hem of

her hiked gown. God, her skin was like warm silk! He had never known such exquisite softness, such innocence. He wanted to memorize every curvaceous inch of her body, to explore the satiny heat of passion he'd called from her and share each unprecedented sensation that claimed her, as if it were his own.

His male body clenched with overwhelming need as his fingertip stroked the soft texture of her inner thigh. Her breath caught in a rippling cry as he intimately caressed her sensitive flesh. When his fingertip carefully penetrated the shimmering fire that he'd ignited, her body answered each daring caress. Need exploded inside Seth with devastating force. He could feel Lottie's nails digging into his forearms, hear her whispering his name in ragged refrain. He ached to be the living flame burning inside her. He wanted to feel her come apart in his arms. to take her with him to heaven for just one glorious moment in a space out of time . . .

"Miss Lottie says ladies should be treated with courtesy and respect."

The words Oran Paine had spoken twice in the course of the day struck Seth like a lightning bolt. His eyes popped open when he heard the tea kettle hissing at him in steamy reprisal. The lantern light flickered, casting shadows that seemed to shake their dark heads in disapproval.

Good Lord, what did he think he was doing? Lottie Dawes wasn't some harlot who catered to men's basic cravings. She was two wings short of an angel, for heaven's sake! Everybody in El Reno said so! And if she hadn't offered herself up so generously in a kiss that was definitely more complicated than Seth could handle, he wouldn't have lost the good sense he'd spent three decades cultivating. This lovely elf was becoming the tormenting curse of his life. She was all wrong for him and he knew it. He was torturing himself and it had to stop—now!

Lottie inhaled a fortifying breath and covered her bared breasts when Seth set her away from him. Her thick-lashed blue eyes focused on the haunted expression that captured Seth's face. Sweet merciful heavens, she'd never dreamed passionate love could be so demanding and consuming. She never realized she could desire a man so fiercely, could want to share so hungrily the intimacy that this ruggedly handsome giant had unveiled to her.

Seth scowled and fumbled with the buttons of his shirt that Lottie had unfastened. He swore he could still feel the imprint of her innocent caresses burning the flesh each place she'd touched. He was swamped by unruly desires that he was nobly trying to hold in check, hounded by the knowledge that this bewitching nymph deserved better than a man with a disreputable past. And yet, he could feel himself wanting her as he'd never wanted anything in his life! He was losing control, and the vulnerable feeling was as awkward as it was unnerving.

"Damn it, woman, what are you doing to me?" Seth growled in frustration.

Lottie was highly amused by his stubborn attempt to deny the compelling bond that had developed between them. She had sensed it at their first kiss, but as cynical as Seth Broden had become through years of hard living, he refused to accept what seemed to Lottie as natural and inevitable as sunrise.

"You asked for a soul in exchange for our bargain, did you not?" she questioned his question. "I'm simply giving you what you requested."

Giving him a soul? Seth didn't think so. It felt more like she was *stealing* the soul he wasn't even sure he had left after the years he'd spent doing the kind of things that would shock this veritable angel out of her halo!

"No more complicated kisses," Seth said gruffly. "And no more homeless orphans better show up on my doorstep. And don't send me any invitations to chitchat with the unattached females in town, either. You're messing with my life and my mind and I don't like it. I won't tolerate it! I just want to be left alone!"

Seth wheeled around and stalked off, only to hear Lottie calling his name like a voice from his elusive dreams.

"You forgot your hat, Seth." She scooped up the black hat that had fallen to the floor when she had succumbed to the urge to comb her fingers through his thick ebony hair.

Seth snatched his hat away, mortified to note that his hand was still shaking with unappeased need. "Damn it all, I've dealt with outlaws and cutthroats who look like tooth fairies compared to you, woman. They only tried to tear my life up from outside in, but you're going about it from inside out. Just stay the hell away from me. I like my life just the way it is. Do you hear me!"

Who couldn't? His baritone voice boomed in the night like an exploding cannon. Lottie grinned in amusement when Seth stamped out. The man truly did cherish his freedom, didn't he? Or at least he thought he did. Lottie rather suspected Seth Broden had only grown accustomed to loneliness, because he'd decided that was all he deserved after the less than respectable life he'd once led. All that snapping and growling was just an act to drive her away from him. Somehow, Lottie had to make him believe in himself—as strongly as she believed in the goodness and tenderness that was buried beneath that callous shell he'd constructed around himself.

There were two weeks left before Christmas, Lottie reminded herself as she poured two cups of tea and propelled herself toward the back door to powwow with the wise old half-breed who had camped out in her washshed.

Lottie had a fortnight to convince the brooding Seth Broden that he *was* worthy and deserving of the gift she had waited a lifetime to give—her heart.

Three

Three days after Brigit's arrival, Seth began to adjust to being pampered and having his laundry smell like Swedish rose-scented soap. And his stomach certainly had no complaints about the appetizing meals that appeared on his table morning, noon, and night.

Brigit, however, hadn't adjusted to seeing Seth automatically grab for his pistol at the slightest unidentified sound. Seth's mistrust of everything that moved confirmed Brigit's belief that he was no stranger to danger and violence.

On St. Lucia Day, Brigit followed Swedish tradition by dressing in white and placing an evergreen wreath on her blond head. She entered Seth's bedroom at daybreak to serve him a breakfast of coffee and fresh-baked buns. Although Brigit was cheerfully and faithfully carrying out the old country's holiday customs, she found herself staring down the barrel of a loaded Colt .45—again.

Shakily, Brigit set the tray on the nightstand and then breathed a mite easier when Seth tucked the deadly weapon under his pillow. "December thirteenth marks de beginning of de celebration of de twelve days of Christmas," she announced. *"God Jul* Mister Broden."

"God Jul to you, Brigit." Whatever *that* meant. Seth presumed the phrase was "Merry Christmas" in Swedish. "I'm sorry for scaring ten years off your life. Old habits are difficult to break."

"Vell, don't expect *Joltomten,* the lively elf who brings gift from Santa Claus on Christmas Eve, to grace your doorstep if you plan to meet him wid a loaded six-shooter," she said with a disapproving sniff.

When Brigit paraded off to deliver breakfast in bed to Oran, Seth downed his meal and dressed. Yawning, he strolled outside to tend his morning chores. His astonished eyes gazed upon a tepee pitched beside the grove of cottonwood trees that formed a windbreak on the north side of his corral.

Before the shock wore off, Seth spied an aged Indian, dressed in fringed buckskin, pacing around the stock pen where the wild-est bronc in Seth's herd lay on its side in a tangle of rope. The roan stallion had been gelded and was snorting in outrage. The old Indian was gently slapping the contrary colt with an empty feed sack, murmuring to the animal in what Seth presumed was the Cheyenne tongue.

"Who the blazes is that?" Seth growled in question when Oran emerged from the house to join him on the stoop.

"Standing Bear," Oran informed him. "Miss Lottie be-friended the half-breed shaman because she says he's wise in the ways of the world. Some of the riffraff in town tried to run Standing Bear back to the Cheyenne-Arapaho reservation at Darlington, but she wouldn't hear of it. Standing Bear set up housekeeping in the wash shed behind Miss Lottie's house."

Seth swore under his breath. Another damned mouth to feed, compliments of Jolly Saint Lottie. Curse that meddling woman! He'd told her to stop trying to rearrange his life, but did she listen? Hell no, she just forged ahead, doing her misguided good deeds in spite of Seth's orders to cease and desist. What the devil did she think she was doing? Foisting off all her homeless house guests so she could gather a new batch of orphans for herself?

Seth stalked off the steps and hopped over the corral fence. Before he could tell the old half-breed where he could take his tepee and what he could do with it when he got there, Standing

Bear gestured toward the colt that was wrapped in so much rope
that it looked like a Maypole.

"Come, Seth Broden, I will teach you to break the colt without
breaking your bones, or those of young Oran. Miss Lottie says
there is much for you to learn."

If Seth heard any more of what "Miss Lottie says" he was
going to shoot somebody—starting and ending with her! Wasn't
it enough that thoughts of her generous, passionate responses
to his touch were burning him up in midnight dreams? Hadn't
he paid his due for taking daring privileges with her by adopting
this brood of a family he hadn't wanted or needed?

Seth shook off his resentful thoughts when Standing Bear
impatiently waved him closer.

"Kneel before the colt," Standing Bear instructed. "Blow
your breath in the colt's face until it adjusts to your scent and
comes to accept you as its master. This is the way of the Indian
in training horses to obey commands."

Feeling ridiculous, Seth got down on his hands and knees. He
blew into the colt's nostrils until the frightened animal no longer
widened its eyes in alarm and quivered at the touch of Seth's
hand stroking its neck.

"Now you must introduce yourself, Oran," Standing Bear
commanded. "The colt will learn your scent, your touch, and it
will remember that it is to obey those who are its master."

While Oran was taming the colt, Standing Bear nodded his
silver-gray head. "When this phase of mastery is complete, you
will harness the colt to your gentlest mare and turn them both
out in the pasture for a week. The green colt will be halter-broken
without the task consuming all your time. When you break the
colt to ride, do not use the trodden ground in this corral. Take
the horse to the stream. It will be more difficult for the horse to
buck and rear up when it is wallowing in wet sand and mud.
The spills the rider takes will also be less painful."

Standing Bear stared northwest. His buckskin-clad arm swept

n an all-encompassing gesture. "I heard the coyotes howling at
unset." He directed Seth's attention to the birds that fluttered
verhead. "When the birds begin to flock together to provide
varmth, it is a sign of bad weather approaching. The animals
an teach you much about the Earth Mother. While you train
he boy, Seth Broden, I will teach you the ways of my mother's
eople and you will prosper."

"Why? Because Jolly Saint Lottie commands this to be so?"
eth grunted sarcastically.

Standing Bear regarded the towering giant who dressed like
shadow. "You are a stubborn man, Seth Broden, but Miss Lot-
ie has asked me to grant you the gift of my wisdom. Come,
here is much for you to do before the white man's Christmas
s coated with a blanket of snow."

Seth found his arm in the old half-breed's fierce grip. While
)ran breathed on the colt, Seth was towed off to learn only the
Great Spirit of the Cheyenne knew *what!*

Miss Lottie Dawes's interference in his life was really getting
eth's goat. He wanted to chew her up one side and down the
ther, but if he went near her again he would probably lose his
elf-control, the same way he did the night of the pound party.
Ie'd already proved he couldn't get within two feet of that lovely
ngel without his unruly desires running rampant. When he
tared into those luminous blue eyes fringed with long, sooty
ashes, he was hounded by the same forbidden dreams that in-
errupted his sleep. She was already becoming an obsession, an
che that would demand constant appeasing, a fire that would
eed upon itself until it was thoroughly consumed. Seth already
ad a family of orphans depending on him, restricting his free-
lom, interrupting his privacy . . .

"Pay attention, Seth Broden," Standing Bear barked. "You
ave to prepare for the coming storm. There is much for us to
lo."

Seth tucked his frustrated thoughts in the closet of his mind and focused on the weather-beaten old half-breed who was rattling off instructions to foretell the coming of storms and the Indians' ways of protecting the livestock from harm. It was only when Brigit appeared on the porch to announce lunch that Standing Bear ceased his yammering.

Seth found his table heaping with more foreign dishes, his chairs occupied by an adopted family. Thanks to Lottie Dawes, his private space was shrinking by the day, damn it!

Another social invitation arrived shortly after noon, provoking Seth to gnash his teeth and swear under his breath. He was *not* going to join the *charivari* being held in honor of Gerald and Amy Foster who'd tied the matrimonial knot that morning. He wasn't going to be caught dead clanging on pots and pans in an idiotic mock serenade under the window of the honeymoon quarters. And that was that!

Seth scowled at the metal ladle and iron skillet Brigit thrust at him after she had herded him through the bushes to join the rest of the *charivari* serenaders on the secluded Foster farm. He did *not* wish to be lurking under anybody's bedroom window, waiting for the mischievous orchestra leader to give the signal to commence playing their makeshift instruments. But damned if he wasn't there, and so was his newly acquired family, minus Standing Bear, who was still decorating the interior of his tepee with thick animal skins to ward off the chill of the supposed blizzard he'd predicted.

When Gerald Foster's younger brother—the maestro of the motley musicians—signaled for the serenade to commence, Seth half-heartedly clanked the ladle and skillet together, but he refused to sing off-key. The orchestrated choir sounded bad enough without his contribution.

The minute Seth spotted Lottie on the far side of the crowd,

howling like a wounded wolf and pounding on her tea kettle, he
thrust his skillet at Oran and stalked toward her.

Lottie was yodeling her first chorus of "Jingle Bells" when
a hand curled around her forearm, yanking her back into the
bushes. She didn't have to glance over her shoulder to know
who was breathing down her neck. She would recognize that
masculine scent anywhere.

"I told you I wanted no more interference from you, woman,"
Seth snarled.

Lottie straightened her bonnet and pivoted to face the lurking
shadow. "I presume you're referring to Standing Bear."

"You presume right," Seth snapped. "The next thing I know,
there will be an entire war party of Cheyenne camped beside
my corral. Damn it, don't you know when to quit?"

"Don't you think you're reacting a bit too strongly?" she questioned calmly.

"No, I do not!" Seth fumed.

"There are things you don't know about Standing Bear that
will change your mind about him."

"And I'm sure you're going to tell me his teary-eyed tale."

"I knew you would want to know."

"*I* didn't say I wanted to know. *You* said—"

"Standing Bear needs you desperately," Lottie interrupted as
she had a tendency to do when she was on a convincing crusade.
"He's like a lone tree rooted on the boundary between two con-
trasting civilizations. He's spent fifty years swaying back and
forth between the Indian and the white man's way of life. According to Standing Bear, he is living inside a skin that doesn't
quite seem to fit, searching for life's deepest truths. The reservation at Darlington is no place for him and the jeering crowds
in town don't understand him. He is constantly seeking his own
niche, craving inner peace. He will be content with you."

"Well, there's no peace to be found on my ranch," Seth muttered. "Not with a young man wanting to know the how-to's and what-for's of dealing with females and learning self-defense, not to mention that Swedish hen who clucks around the place."

"Brigit and Oran are happy," Lottie said with firm conviction. "One look at their smiling faces testifies to that. Do you begrudge them contentment, especially at this special time of the year?"

"No, but—"

"They are delighted to be under the local hero's competent care."

"I'm *nobody's* hero, damn it. I'm tired of you playing on my sympathy. I just want to be left alone!" Seth blared over the racket of the off-key choir. "I—"

He slammed his mouth like a crocodile when the newlyweds' door opened and the guests were invited inside. He no longer had to yell to be heard, so he continued in a quieter voice. "I can't even walk down the streets of town these days without exchanging a hundred pleasantries. People who used to take a wide berth around me are respectfully tipping their hats and pausing to pass the time of day because *you* have convinced them I'm some sort of do-gooder, which I'm *not!*"

"You disapprove of doing good deeds, do you?"

"Hell, no, but—"

"Then what seems to be the problem?"

"You are the problem!" Seth exploded.

Lottie blinked. "Me? What have I done besides restore your sterling reputation and respectability? Is that a crime?"

"Of course not, but—"

It exasperated Seth that he couldn't complete a sentence before the crusading angel interrupted. There was only one surefire way to shut her up.

"If not for your endearing qualities—"

Lottie's words evaporated when warm, full lips swooped down

on hers. She surrendered without hesitation to the streams of pleasure that rippled through her. Her arms glided around Seth's neck, inching familiarly closer to savor the taste and scent of him. He could bark and growl and object to his heart's content if it got her in his arms to feel his anger transforming to ardent passion.

When Seth let go of his bottled emotions, that's when Lottie loved him best of all. And when he kissed her with hungry impatience, she surrendered body and soul.

Lottie heard Seth groan and felt his body harden with unmistakable need as he guided her hips into his lean contours. She knew he shared the fervent need that was becoming more demanding with each heart-stopping kiss, each nerve-tingling caress. Even if Seth was determined to shut her out of his life, he couldn't deny this volatile passion that simmered between them. When she was in his arms those invisible walls he built around himself came tumbling down. Lottie could feel Seth surrendering against his will, despite his attempt to remain emotionally detached. She moved sensuously against him, returning each hungry kiss and bold caress until they were both panting for breath and trembling with ungovernable desire.

"No, damn it!" Seth flung himself away from tormentingly sweet temptation and cursed his failing willpower.

Lottie struggled to prevent laughing out loud. For a man who had cultivated a bad reputation and was afraid of next to nothing, he was behaving comically. Seth Broden, for all his hissing and snarling, had turned out to be quite the gentleman—more than Lottie would have preferred now that she had her heart set on him.

"Proper ladies are *supposed* to object when a man takes liberties," Seth lectured in a grouchy voice.

"Fine. I object," she playfully patronized him. "Don't kiss me again if you don't want me to respond. We already established the fact that you can't handle complicated kisses. You're simply too much the gentleman."

"I am *not* a gentleman and I have no aspirations of becoming one, damn it!"

"Then why are you offended when I kiss you back, as if I'm enjoying it? I do, you know. Would you prefer that I stand here like a slab of stone?"

"No."

"Then you *do* want me to kiss you as if I'm enjoying it?"

"No!"

Lottie shook her head and chortled in amusement. "Then exactly what do you want, Seth. Or don't you even know yourself?"

Confound it! Dealing with this impossible female was making him crazy. Seth didn't know his own mind these days and he could barely control the lusty demands of his body. She was tying his emotions in knots. He shuddered to think what this cunning female could do to him if he entrusted her with his heart—that is, if he still had one.

"This is the very last time I'm coming near you," Seth vowed determinedly. "And no more orphans better clutter my doorstep."

Lottie peered up into his shadowed face. She could see him backing away from her again, just as he always did when he felt her getting too close to his private emotions. She wondered if she was deluding herself by thinking she could teach Seth Broden to love her when he was fighting her tooth and nail.

Perhaps it was true that love couldn't grow where it had never been planted. And perhaps Seth would never learn to love her, even after he had come to appreciate the company of the orphans she had entrusted into his care. She had hoped to change his life completely by Christmas. But Seth Broden was a tough one. This could take years!

"And don't invite me to any more of your holiday celebrations," Seth demanded, retreating another step.

"Whatever you wish, Seth."

"Whatever *I* wish?" he smirked sardonically. "Now, *that* would be a first."

Lottie knelt to retrieve the tea kettle she had dropped. For the first time in years, her optimistic enthusiasm deserted her. She had convinced herself that, given time, Seth would come to care for her and her unusual collection of friends. Perhaps she had deluded herself. Though she had finally met the man she wanted to love for all eternity, there was unfortunately no hard and fast rule stating that a man had to love the woman who had lost her heart to him.

Slowly, Lottie unfolded herself from the ground to stare up at the looming shadow who seemed to prefer his dark past and cloudy solitude to the radiance of love she wanted to offer him.

"This is your Christmas wish then? That I permanently remove myself from your life?"

"Yes," Seth insisted. "I don't want or need any complications."

Lottie stated into those onyx eyes and forced herself to face the fact that she wasn't wanted or needed. "Then you shall have your wish, Seth Broden. I will never bother you again." Lottie brushed a parting kiss over his lips and smiled tremulously. "Merry Christmas . . ."

Without a backward glance, Lottie strode toward the steps and disappeared inside Gerald and Amy Foster's cabin. Seth stood in the shadows, listening to the drone of voices and the occasional outbursts of laughter. He'd become an outsider again, living on the edge of civilized society—where he belonged.

That's what he wanted, wasn't it? Of course it was, he convinced himself. When a man came to need and depend on others for his happiness, he lost his individuality, his identity. He was capable of being hurt then, was no longer the captain of his own soul, the master of his own fate.

Seth wheeled around and aimed himself toward his tethered

horse. All he had ever wanted was to be left alone. He was glad that meddling female had given him up as a lost cause. He didn't want Lottie to become such an integral part of his life that losing her would tear him into agonized pieces, just as he had been tormented by the loss of his younger sister to a band of brutal outlaws.

Seth squeezed back the hellish memory of what his sister had suffered before she died. Bitter revenge had eaten at him like a poison until he had finally seen justice served. By that time, hunting down fugitives of justice had become a way of life and he had come to expect no more for his future than disposing of the evil forces in this world. He had packed his emotions in cold storage and vowed never to let anyone close enough that he could actually feel pain when they vanished from his life. If a man didn't care, then he couldn't be hurt, and Seth could do without that kind of soul-wrenching torture, thank everybody—especially Jolly Saint Lottie—very much!

True to her word, Lottie disappeared from Seth's life. No other homeless orphans showed up on Seth's doorstep. The invitations that arrived for Oran and Brigit, announcing the Yuletide activities that were scheduled at the church and schoolhouse, excluded Seth's name, just as he had demanded.

Seth was spending another quiet evening at home—too quiet, he begrudgingly admitted to himself. Oran and Brigit had ridden off to the "literary" held at town hall. *A Christmas Carol* by Charles Dickens was being read for the enjoyment of the community by none other than Lottie Dawes. That was reason enough for Seth not to attend the festive social function.

Standing Bear had wandered off earlier in the afternoon to consult with Indian spirits, leaving Seth to lounge in his chair beside the hearth. He took a bite of *Julgrot* and felt the crunch of the single almond Brigit had placed in her Christmas pudding.

Seth chewed on the nut that supposedly signified he would be blessed with good luck during the coming year. Bah, humbug, that would be the day! he thought to himself.

Seth focused his attention on the shiny tinsel and wood-carved decorations Oran had strung around the monstrous cedar tree that stood in the corner of the room. It was beginning to look a lot like Christmas around here. Ho, ho . . . hum.

Under Brigit's supervision, Oran had hung mistletoe above every doorway and fastened a decorative evergreen wreath on the front door. The aroma of baked foods clung to the house to such extremes that Seth had difficulty remembering what his home smelled like before it had been besieged by the thick scents of holiday pastries.

The shadows that had been Seth's life loomed in the corners, untouched by the glow of the hearth where stockings hung, awaiting the arrival of the fabled elf *Joltomten*—the delivery boy in Saint Nicholas's service. Fat chance that Swedish gnome would show up here.

Seth took a sip of the *glogg* that Brigit had prepared before she traipsed off to the "literary." The hot punch—flavored with spices, sweet liquor, raisins, and nuts—did nothing to warm the cold, vacant place deep inside Seth.

Restlessly, Seth climbed to his feet and paced the confines of the room. Something vital was missing these days. He felt uneasy and discontent. It was more than just the absence of both the ever-inquisitive Oran and Brigit, whose overbearing maternal instincts occasionally left Seth shaking his head in disbelief. It wasn't because Standing Bear—who talked Seth's ears off, quoting Cheyenne legends and teaching Seth more than he'd ever wanted to know about the spirits that inhabited the bodies of animals—wasn't in residence. No, Seth had adjusted to the habits and idiosyncrasies of his adopted family. He had learned to cope with them and had made room for them in his life . . .

The creak of the front door caused Seth to spin around, reflexively reaching for his pistol.

Standing Bear grinned wryly at the powerful hulk of man who was prepared to fill the unannounced intruder full of lead. "You still have not put the ghosts of your past to rest," he observed. "Do you think they will come for you sooner or later, Seth Broden?"

Seth replaced his weapon and turned away. "No, those lost souls are serving their well-deserved sentences in hell."

The old half-breed nodded thoughtfully as he gravitated toward the warmth of the fire, sinking down Indian-style. "It is difficult to know whether to cling to past habits or reach out to the future, is it not? Eyes that have seen too much darkness fear they cannot adjust to the blinding radiance of light—"

"If this is going to evolve into one of your philosophical lectures, I'm not in the mood," Seth grumbled as he went back to his pacing.

"I am only trying to understand why you refuse to accept Miss Lottie's love," Standing Bear replied.

Seth stopped in his tracks and pivoted toward the Indian who sat beside the fireplace. "Who says Lottie loves me?"

"I do. I hear it in her voice when she speaks your name to me. I see it in her eyes, feel it in the sadness that betrays her smile. She shows all the signs of a woman in love."

"Well, she *shouldn't* love me," Seth declared, valiantly fighting the tender feelings that had been trying to take root in the cold depths of what had once been his heart.

Quiet laughter rumbled in the old Indian's chest. "I did not say she *should* love you," he corrected. "I said she *does* love you. The heart sometimes aches to feed the fire, in spite of—"

"If you don't mind, I'd rather not discuss *that* subject, either," Seth cut in brusquely.

Standing Bear shrugged his shoulders. "As you wish, Seth Broden. I only came to tell you that the storm approaches. The first snowflakes are dancing on the wind. Your family might have difficulty making their return trip from town." He paused to fling Seth an assessing glance before refocusing on the leaping flames in the hearth. "But then, maybe you do not wish for them to find their way back to your home. Perhaps you prefer that they perish in the howling blizzard and vanish from your life as Miss Lottie has."

"What howling blizzard? I haven't heard—"

Seth's voice trailed off when the wind roared across the prairie like a runaway locomotive. Frigid drafts swept under the door and rattled the windowpanes. Seth drew back Brigit's colorful new curtains to see gigantic snowflakes beating against the panes like rioting white butterflies. He could barely make out the rails of the corral fence in the gray darkness that descended on the ranch. The temperature seemed to be dropping a degree with each passing minute, coating the window with a hazy fog and sending chills rippling all the way to the hard-rock bottom of his heart.

"There is no need to worry about the two cows that show signs of birthing," Standing Bear assured him. "I locked them in the barn for safekeeping. By morning you will have new additions to your herd. Drastic changes in weather always bring on new life . . . or strip it away—" He frowned when Seth lurched around to grab his coat. "Where are you going, Seth Broden?"

"To make sure Oran and Brigit don't get lost in the blizzard."

Standing Bear climbed to his feet and smiled to himself. "So you *do* care about this family Miss Lottie gave to you for Christmas."

Seth scowled. "Of course I care. Do you think me completely heartless?"

"No, Seth Broden, not heartless, only stubborn and foolish."

Seth flashed Standing Bear a disdainful glance as he reached for the doorknob. "There is, however, a certain member of this family who I might be willing to *lose.*" His sententious glance indicated who the "certain member" was.

Standing Bear chuckled, undaunted. "You need me, Seth Broden, just as you have come to need Oran and Brigit in ways you refuse to admit to yourself."

"Oh, really? How do you figure that, Chief Know-it-all?" he snorted before whipping open the door to be slapped in the face by wind-driven snowflakes.

"I am the one who will prevent you from getting lost in this deadly blizzard," Standing Bear promised. "Blind fools must always be shown the way."

Seth gnashed his teeth and followed the outspoken half-breed outside to retrieve their mounts from the barn. The wind burned against Seth's cheeks and he wrapped his bandana around his face like a bandit's mask. The old Indian pulled the hood of his buffalo robe over his head and trotted off, seemingly unaffected by the icy blasts that chilled skin and bone . . . and soul.

Four

By the time Standing Bear and Seth reached town, the blowing snow and wailing wind had transformed the black of night into a treacherous maze, distorting all sense of direction. It was impossible to tell unfenced prairie from crude paths in the blinding blizzard. At Standing Bear's instruction, Seth had wrapped a lantern in the oiled paper he had first used for windows before the glass panes arrived. The dim glow had helped to orient two lost travelers Seth and Standing Bear encountered en route to town. Still, there was no sign of Oran and Brigit.

Town Hall had been abandoned. The tinkling of piano music could faintly be heard above the wind as Seth and Standing Bear passed the saloons where stranded travelers had congregated to warm their innards with whiskey and wait out the brunt of the storm.

Seth aimed himself toward Lottie's house, hoping Oran and Brigit had had the good sense to take shelter in town. To his relief, his adopted family was waiting at the small cottage. But to Seth's dismay, Lottie—invincible angel of mercy that she obviously believed herself to be—was braving the howling storm instead of nestling beside the hearth.

Seth irritably brushed the snow from his coat and warmed himself by the fire. "Doesn't that woman have the sense God gave a mule?"

"Vell, Miss Lottie didn't vant to go out," Brigit explained in Lottie's behalf. "But Amy Foster, de newlywed we serenaded at the *charivari,* vanted to be wid her new husband." Brigit nervously wrung her hands and peered out the window every other second. "Miss Lottie volunteered to accompany Amy home."

"Damnation," Seth grumbled. "I don't suppose she'll take the precaution of staying put once she reaches the Foster's farm."

"Spend de night wid newlyweds?" Brigit asked incredulously. "Vould *you?*"

Seth cursed under his breath, tied his bandana around his face and wheeled toward the door. "Standing Bear, you stay here in case Lottie comes back. You can lead Oran and Brigit back home when the wind dies down."

The old Indian nodded in compliance as he watched Seth disappear into the swirls of blowing snow and engulfing darkness.

Lottie was faithfully following the instructions Standing Bear had given her the last time he'd come to town to warn her that a winter storm approached. The old half-breed had told Lottie then to follow fence lines if they were available. If she lost her sense of direction, she was to drop the reins to her mount and let the animal guide her by its homing instincts.

Lottie had done exactly that when the fence row ended and she could no longer distinguish prairie from trodden path. But she never dreamed she could be so disoriented that she could barely tell which direction was up, much less where *south* was. The wind was swirling to such confusing extremes that snowy gusts hammered at her back and then suddenly switched around to pelt her in the face. Her skin felt like ice beneath the three layers of clothes she'd donned to escort Amy Foster home. Lottie couldn't remember being so cold in all her life!

Things were going as well as Lottie could expect during her return journey. The gray mare plodded through the rising drifts, seemingly aware of its destination while Lottie shivered in her frosty skin. When a branch from the overhanging tree snapped above her head, Lottie instinctively ducked. The horse bolted in alarm when the limb shot down like a lance spearing the darkness.

Since Lottie had given the mare its head, she was unable to clutch the reins to steady herself when her mount reared up and whinnied in fright. The falling branch slammed against Lottie's shoulder, knocking her to the ground.

A dull groan tumbled from Lottie's blue-tinged lips as the mare thundered off. Lottie tried to scramble to her feet to give chase, but she was pinned beneath the limb that covered her like a bony hand. She had the faintest sensation of pain in her right leg, but she was so numb with cold that it was difficult to tell how seriously she'd been injured. Struggling, Lottie wedged her shoulders through the spiny branches to sit upright. She tried to drag her right leg out from under the heavy limb that weighted her down like an anchor, but the leg wouldn't budge.

Despite her attempt to remain cheerfully optimistic, Lottie had grave doubts about surviving. She could be frozen solid, buried beneath one of the drifts that surrounded her like igloos. She knew better than to let herself fall asleep because she might never awake. She had to bundle her clothes around her to insulate herself . . . and she had to find a distraction from the cold.

Lottie inhaled a courageous breath and began singing every Christmas carol she could remember, in as loud a voice as she could muster. If by some miracle there was another traveler in the area, she might be heard and rescued. Otherwise . . .

She refused to consider *otherwise*. She would sing her heart out and pray for all she was worth. That was all there was to it!

Sickening dread settled in the vacant cavity inside Seth's chest when he heard the clomp of the riderless mount. Seth lifted his oiled-paper-covered lantern and cursed colorfully when he recognized Lottie's gray mare.

When the horse stopped to rub its muzzle against Seth's mount in greeting, Seth grabbed the reins and stared apprehensively into the darkness. He could only guess what direction he was traveling now that he'd lost the ability to trek along the row of fence posts. He didn't even know long he'd ridden after encountering Lottie's mare. His heart was pounding too furiously to count the passing seconds that evolved into nerve-wracking minutes.

A strange sound reached Seth's ears and he reined his steed to a halt, listening intently. He couldn't tell if it was only the wailing wind or if . . .

Instinctively, he found himself nudging the horses forward, following the faint sound. If he wasn't mistaken he swore he was hearing the croaking chorus of "Hark! The Herald Angels Sing." Seth only knew of one angel who would brave such a night as this to see her good deeds done and lift her voice in song while she was doing it.

Seth trotted through the swirling darkness toward the feeble sound. When he lifted the glowing lantern, he spied the snarled branches of the fallen tree and spotted the hunkered form trapped like a half-frozen fish in a tangled net.

"Hark! The Herald—"

"Lottie!"

Lottie's snow-caked lashes swept up to see a strange light hovering above the ground. "Is that you, Lord?"

"No, it's me, damn it!" With lantern held high, Seth swung from his saddle and stepped over the branches.

Relief washed through her chilled body. "A guardian angel, thank goodness!"

"I'm nobody's angel. I'm only guarding the angel who obviously considers herself indestructible," Seth muttered. "Of all

he nights you *should* have stayed home, *this* is it! You could
ave frozen to death."

"But Amy Foster wanted to— Ouch!" Lottie sucked in her
breath when Seth tried to yank her up as if she were a cork
opping from the neck of a bottle.

Seth released her immediately. "You're stuck."

"I realize that. Don't you think I would've gotten up by myself
f I could have?" Lottie questioned reasonably.

"I'll have to tie a rope to the horses and pull the limb off.
Cover your face and curl under the branches," Seth instructed.

Lottie wormed her shoulders between the prickly limbs and
covered her face with her arms to prevent being scratched be-
ond recognition. Minutes later, she felt the heavy weight scrap-
ng across her body until she could no longer restrain the yelp
f pain. Cold though she was, she could still feel the slash of
ough bark and snagging limbs digging into her flesh. Tears
roze on her cheeks as she bit back the pain and struggled to sit
p after Seth had freed her.

Lottie found herself hoisted into strong arms and cuddled
protectively against the warmth of Seth's body. It was pure
eaven.

"And Standing Bear calls *me* a fool," he murmured as he
arried Lottie to the horses.

"I'm really sorry about this," Lottie apologized through clat-
ering teeth. "I promised not to interfere in your life and—"

"Forget your promises and my reckless wishes." Seth set Lot-
ie on his saddle and swung up behind her.

"But you said—"

"Curse it, woman, for once in your life clam up. I'm going
o try to find the fence posts that lead to my ranch house. It will
e closer than riding back to town. Now, hold on to the lantern
nd don't let too much wind sweep through the hole in the oiled
aper or the flame will go out."

Lottie clamped her mouth shut and did as she was told. The

glowing lantern provided a warmth Lottie feared she would never feel again. But she would survive, she assured herself. She was in the arms of a guardian angel, even if he had become too soured by life to consider himself as such. Seth Broden was simply too modest to toot his own horn, that was all. But that was all right, Lottie mused as she snuggled closer. She would toot Seth's horn for him.

After what seemed a century of trekking through the icy darkness, Seth reached home and deposited Lottie on the braided rug in front of the hearth. He tossed more logs on the fire and pulled up the hem of Lottie's gown to examine her injured leg. She had been badly bruised but no bones appeared to be broken. Jolly Saint Lottie was lucky to be alive and Seth breathed an enormous sigh of relief that he'd reached her before those gorgeous legs suffered severe frostbite.

"Thank you," Lottie murmured. "I'm really sorry about all the trouble I've caused you." She took a sip of the *glogg* Seth offered her, lubricating her vocal chords. "I'm sorry about tonight and the entire month of meddling. You saved my life and I shall forever be in your debt. To repay you, I promise never to come near you again since you have a strong aversion to me—"

"Lottie?"

Luminous blue eyes lifted to the man dressed in black who leaned leisurely against the mantel where empty stockings hung in anticipation of the coming of the elf Brigit called *Joltomten.*

"Yes, Seth?"

Seth peered down into the flushed, pert face and felt the cold dark cavity that had been his heart fill with indescribable warmth. He remembered what Standing Bear had said about those who had lived so long in the shadows that they were afraid to reach out for fear they weren't meant to survive in the blinding light. But this spirited female who had the remarkable knack of seeking and finding the good in all mankind had shown him the light in her hypnotic eyes. She was his source of warmth, the new beginning he wasn't certain he deserved.

But there was no going back to the darkness again. Seth had known that for a fact when he heard Lottie singing Christmas carols to ward off the cold silence that lurked in the jaws of the deadly storm. He had experienced more than a sense of relief when he found Lottie. He had discovered that part of himself that had shriveled up and died when he lost his sister to butchering marauders almost a decade earlier. He had found hope and pleasure . . . and purpose.

Seth squatted to trail his forefinger over Lottie's heart-shaped lips. "Do you remember when you promised to give me a soul in exchange for assuming responsibility for the family of orphans you sent to me?"

"Yes," she murmured, relishing his gentle caress, aching for the sensual warmth of his masterful kiss.

"You didn't give me a new soul in the bargain," he softly accused.

"But I did. Or at least I tried, really I did," she protested. "I—"

"No," he interrupted the way *she* usually did. "You breathed new life into my lost soul and then you stole it away from me."

"I did?" Lottie studied the unfamiliar sparkle in those black diamond eyes.

"You did," Seth confirmed huskily. "And then you chased away the shadows until I was no longer comfortable living with them."

Lottie smiled, causing becoming dimples to bracket her lush mouth. "Well, I'm glad I did *something* right."

"And then you made me fall in love with you when I was certain I wanted no one in my life, certain I could never be the man you deserved. Now, what are you going to do about *that?*" Seth questioned with a rare grin.

Lottie blinked in astonishment, afraid to trust her frostbitten ears. "You love me?" she parroted.

Seth brushed his mouth over her petal-soft lips, feeling the shimmering emotions he'd battled until they utterly defeated him.

"Mmm . . . yes . . . and I'm tired of pretending I don't love you," he whispered with great certainty. "Trying *not* to care is wearing me out."

Lottie graced him with an impish grin of her own. "Well, it took you long enough to say so. I almost froze to death before you got around to admitting that you love me, too. Now, what are *you* going to do about *that?*"

Seth chuckled when she tossed his words back in his face. "I'm going to give you one of those *complicated* kisses and see if *you* can handle it, Miss Lottie Dawes."

Lottie beamed. "And then?"

"And then I'm going to make one last Christmas wish and hope you'll say you'll marry me, even if you could do better than a man who wasn't always the good and decent gentleman you believe him to be." Seth heaved a fortifying breath and stared at the far wall. "There was a time when I was so poisoned with the need for revenge that I became a gun for hire—"

Her index finger settled on his lips to shush him. There would be time enough later to explain the reasons for the cynical darkness that had once ruled his life. There would also be time enough for Lottie to confess that young Oran Paine had followed *her* from the orphanage in Kansas where her mother had abandoned her unwanted child. Lottie and Oran had *both* grown up without families to call their own, one day hoping to find their special niche, longing to find someone to love and cherish for a lifetime and the eternity beyond. This was not the time to unveil unpleasant memories, but rather a time to embrace the promises of the future.

"I love you, Seth Broden," she murmured with heartfelt hon

sty. "And I didn't lie to you. I did give you a soul, just as I
romised to do. It was my own. It was the one gift I longed to
ive you for Christmas, but I was afraid you wouldn't accept it,
fraid I wasn't woman enough to please you. Everything I tried
o do in the name of love always turned out wrong."

Seth glanced at the tinsel sparkling on the evergreen tree that
raced the corner of the room. "You know, Lottie, there's only
ne thing missing on our Christmas tree. Lovely though it is,
ere's no angel perched atop it to watch over us. We really
ould do something about that, don't you think?" He curled
is hand beneath her chin to peer into those pixielike features.
My new family is missing one final link. I *wish* I had an angel
ith hair of gold and eyes of blue to hold near and dear, now
nd forevermore."

He stared longingly at the enthralling vision of beauty and
enerous spirit who was spotlighted by the leaping flames of
e hearth. "Will you marry me, Lottie? I have a wise half-breed
entor to teach me the truths of the world, a housekeeper whose
atural instincts would suit the necessary requirements of a pro-
ctive grandmother, and an adopted son to watch over a brood
f younger brothers and sisters. But I need a wife to nurture all
e good and decent qualities she sees in me."

Lottie looped her arms around Seth's broad shoulders and
iggled at his attempt to emulate her technique of convincing
ersuasion. "Are you certain that's what you *wish* for Christ-
as?"

Seth met her incandescent smile and he knew beyond all doubt
at he needed this lively little elf as much as he needed air to
reathe. "Very certain," Seth assured her as he wrapped her in
is arms and held her to his heart. "Please don't ever leave me,
ottie, even if you are more than I deserve. Don't ever stop
ving me. I don't think I could bear it. I need you . . . want you
ith me always . . ."

He kissed her with all the love and affection that had been

bottled inside him, and Lottie responded as sweetly and generously as she always had . . . until the door banged open and three snow-covered forms scurried inside, accompanied by a blast of arctic wind.

Seth cuddled Lottie close and surveyed the pleased smiles that lighted the faces of his newly acquired family. Then he stated the obvious. "I found her."

Standing Bear chuckled as he appraised the two halves of the hungry soul that nestled in front of the dancing flames of the hearth. "Or perhaps when you went out to rescue Miss Lottie tonight, it was *she* who saved *you* from the cold darkness, Seth Broden."

The old half-breed could feel love radiating across the room. For the first time ever, Standing Bear felt a deep sense of inner peace whispering through him, assuring him that, at last, he, too, had come home where he belonged.

He glanced at Oran and Brigit, noting the same contented satisfaction on their smiling faces. This had become a true family, unusual in its own origin but a family nonetheless. The little elf whom Brigit promised would come bearing gifts on a snowy, winter night had arrived, granting secret wishes and enriching the lives she had so lovingly touched with her kindness, warmth, and generosity.

Seth's attention shifted from the wise old Indian to the flawless face that had become the vision of his every dream. In Lottie's sky-blue eyes he saw the sweet reward of life, the answering need to be needed, a promise of enduring love. Seth had staked his claim on this wild prairie that had become Oklahoma Territory and he had made more than a new beginning. He had acquired a family who needed him as much as he had come to need them. In addition to those treasured blessings, he had earned the love and respect of the one woman who was gentle enough to draw out the tenderness buried deep inside him, strong enough to make him believe in the goodness within himself again.

More than anything, Seth wanted to sweep Lottie away to the privacy of his bedroom and cherish her like the precious gift she was. But his new family was inching ever closer to the fire to fuss over this beguiling angel he had rescued from the storm so she could save *him* from the shadows of his past life.

"Lottie, I wish—" he whispered longingly.

Her eyes twinkled as she peered up at Seth's rugged features, knowing he was wishing for the very thing she desired—the chance to fully express the love that had blossomed between them.

"You shall have your Christmas wish," she assured him softly. "And I shall have mine. I'll be waiting at the darkest hour before dawn, when shadows evaporate into sunshine . . ."

A jolt of hungry need sizzled through Seth as he sealed her promise with a kiss that carried enough heat to melt a blizzard.

Seth was to remember this particular Christmas well. It was to be the glorious new beginning that spanned all the years of his life, shimmering with the generous and unfaltering love of a blue-eyed angel who could—and did—make his hopes, dreams and wishes come true.

Holiday Tradition

by
René J. Garrod

One

1854
Aboard the Clipper Ship Guillemot

"You, sir, have no passion for living," Maggie Danton announced, after restlessly listening to Captain Nathan Garrett lecture her for the better part of a half hour.

"I beg your pardon." He glared at her. Maggie met his stern mien without flinching.

Ignoring the certain knowledge he had heard her perfectly well the first time, she repeated, "I said, you have no passion for living."

"And you, ma'am, have not a whit of sense, common or otherwise," the captain growled. "You seem not to realize how close you came to forfeiting your life. The sea is nothing with which to toy, and *I* have better things to do with my time than rescue passengers who insist on throwing themselves overboard."

Maggie wrinkled her nose. "I didn't throw myself overboard. If you will only allow me to explain . . ."

"Spare me your explanations. In the seven weeks you have been on my ship, my sensibilities already have been abused by far too many of them. Your brother claimed his willingness to pay me triple my usual fare was borne of anxiety for your well-being. How elegantly he waxed about your angelic qualities and the need to protect you from those who would take advantage." Captain Garrett glanced about his starkly utilitarian cabin as if his eyes preferred any other sight to that of her. Maggie followed their path. When his gaze reluctantly returned to her, she met it. The furrows in the captain's forehead deepened, and he raked his fingers down one sideburn and through the fringe of charcoal-black beard outlining his tightly clenched jaw. "I can see now I was cheated," he proclaimed with distaste. "You are no angel. You're a she-devil. He could have paid me ten times my rate, and still I would not be fairly compensated for putting up with the inconvenience you have caused me and my crew."

Tilting her head to one side, Maggie wrung a bit of saltwater from her golden-brown hair. Her green eyes twinkled as she smiled up at him. "I think you wrong your crew when you claim they have no regard for me. As for my brother, I'll admit James's assessment of my virtues may be a trifle overgenerous, but you mustn't blame him for loving me too dearly. He can't help himself."

"A trifle overgenerous?" he challenged.

Her grin broadened. "Yes, only a trifle."

Maggie knew she was annoying the captain by refusing to take offense, which was precisely why she refused to take it. She deemed herself an excellent judge of character, and she judged Captain Garrett a good man, but he was so straitlaced it was a wonder he didn't strangle on his own rigid code of conduct. He was a humorless tyrant. It was a pity, too. With his fine stature, thick dark hair, and deep-set brown eyes, if he ever wiped the dour expression off his face, he might come close to handsome.

Her favorable measure of his physical person was purely an observation. The mere notion of her developing a romantic attachment to their stiff-necked captain was enough to force her to clamp her hand over her mouth to hold back a guffaw. She would sooner have the crew of the *Guillemot* hoist her up one of the masts and let the sea gulls peck her to death.

The captain continued to sermonize. "I should have listened

to my instincts and refused to be persuaded by your brother's pleading or his purse. A young, unmarried woman has no business traveling alone in the first place. If your brother truly valued you, he would never have allowed it."

"But he had no choice," Maggie submitted. "Before he left for the California gold fields we struck a bargain. At the time, we couldn't afford to buy passage for both of us, and in exchange for my agreement to stay behind, he promised to send for me as soon as he struck it rich. It took far longer than we'd reckoned—two years, five months, three weeks, and six days to be precise," she supplied without pausing for breath, "but at long last I am able to share in the adventure."

"Yes, your brother told me much the same." A muscle in his neck twitched. "He struck a bad bargain, but having given his word, he *was* honor bound to keep it. If he had not been so bound, no amount of gold would have induced me to bow to his wishes."

Maggie didn't doubt the sincerity of the captain's words, but she wasn't about to let his disagreeable mood ruin her own high spirits. She was delighted to be on her way to California and delighted she would remain. Her agile mind flitted to a new progression of thoughts. "James says we're so rich it's positively sinful. I've never been sinfully rich, or any kind of rich at all, but I'm certain I'll get used to it."

"I'm sure you are up to the task."

"Of course, I really don't believe it is sinful to be rich. Unless, one's riches were acquired through nefarious means. Which ours weren't. So, I prefer to think of us as pleasantly rich."

"Your family finances are none of my concern. My concern is the efficient captaining of this ship."

"Then, I think you should smile more," she blithely offered. "Aunt Sophie says a request accompanied by a smile is far more likely to—"

The captain cut her sentence short. "Is it possible for you to stay on one subject for more than five seconds at a time?"

Maggie met his glower with tinkling laughter. "I don't know. I've never tried."

"Well, attempt to do so now," he commanded. "We are not here to discuss your brother or your aunt or the religious significance of wealth. We are here because of your blatant disregard for the rules of this ship."

Assuming a soldier-stiff stance, she waggled her eyebrows. "I thought I was here because I took an unintentional swim."

"I do not believe you are taking this matter seriously enough!"

"And you are taking it *too* seriously. I leaned over the rail a little too far while watching a school of porpoises—they are such winsome creatures, anyone with an ounce of curiosity couldn't help but be fascinated by them—and I fell into the ocean. You pulled me out. I thanked you." She shrugged. "It isn't worth puckering your brow over. You'll give yourself a headache."

"You could have drowned."

"But I didn't."

"I promised your brother I would deliver you into his hands unharmed."

"And you will."

"Yes, I will, provided I can prevent you from doing yourself some grave bodily harm . . ." Lowering his voice, he finished the sentence with a muttered, "and myself from flogging you." Reverting to an authoritative timbre, he continued. "If I were not a man of honor, I would put to port in the next village and exile you from my ship."

"But you *are* a man of honor," Maggie stated with utter conviction and an unrepentant grin. "Besides, if you really wanted to rid yourself of my company, I think a man as enamored with efficiency as yourself would have simply left me in the sea."

"I did not rescue you out of fondness for your company. I rescued you because it was my duty."

"Are you sure?"

"Yes, I am sure! I am also sure that if you give me or my crew any more trouble, I will take great pleasure in clapping you in irons and confining you to your cabin for the remainder of our voyage. Have I made myself clear?"

"You have made yourself loud. This is a very small cabin, and if you insist on booming like a cannon, we shall both be deaf before long."

Sighing out an exasperated breath, Captain Garrett spoke in deliberate tones. "Why is it the other passengers can behave and you cannot?"

"Surely, you don't prefer their company to mine?" Maggie was genuinely perplexed.

"I do."

"But Mrs. Kendall hasn't stopped complaining since she stepped foot on this ship. All she does is lie abed while her husband waits upon her—though from my observation, he seems to find contentment in the role of her toady. I don't mean to make light of the woman's discomfort, but I cannot help but believe the dear lady exaggerates her misery. Anyone with the strength to moan as incessantly and robustly as she cannot be at death's door as she claims. Then, there is poor, melancholy Mr. Bews. He keeps to himself so much it's no wonder he is so sad. I can barely pull three words out of him at a time."

The captain acknowledged the accuracy of her appraisal with a curt nod. "Therein lies their appeal. They keep to their cabins and are not given to wasting my time with asinine conversations."

"But it was you who ordered me to your cabin."

"You would prefer I reprimand you in public?"

"I would prefer you didn't reprimand me at all."

The captain flexed his hands against his thighs. "This is a

cargo ship, Miss Danton. I only have three cabins to accommodate passengers. If I wanted to spend my days playing nursemaid, I would have more. It is a privilege to be on this ship—"

"Yes, it is," Maggie interrupted. "I have written those exact words in my journal. I have explored her from stem to stern and from spar deck to hold and the *Guillemot* is a lovely ship. You have every reason to take pride in her."

"You need not remind me, you have wreaked havoc on every inch of this ship. I know only too well you are wont to go where you have been forbidden."

"You act as though I spend my days menacing your ship, when all I have done is seek to entertain myself. I defy you to name one person or part of this ship I have damaged." She started to tap her foot. The water in her shoe produced an audible *squish,* and she halted in midtap. "I'm waiting, Captain. What harm have I caused?"

"You distract me and my crew from our duty," he answered succinctly.

"What harm is there in that? There is more to life than duty. A little distraction is good for the soul."

"Are you saying I should confine you to your cabin now and save myself the irritation of your next offense? Do not tempt me, for I would like nothing better. In fact, now that I think about it—"

"You cannot chain me in my cabin. It's almost Christmas."

The captain blinked at her. "What does one have to do with the other?"

"Christmas is a time for celebrating. I have plans," she declared.

"Whatever they are, I'm sure I will not approve. A ship is no place for frivolity. Order and strict discipline, those are the standards of a tight ship."

Shaking her head, Maggie assessed him from head to toe. "How old are you, Captain Garrett?"

"Not that it is any of your concern, but I am thirty-three years."

"I would have guessed you at least a decade older," she disclosed. "I daresay your prematurely fading countenance is caused in no small measure by a lack of frivolity. You may ignore the holidays if you wish, but I . . ." She abruptly abandoned her speech and stared at the captain. Her lips slowly curved upward, and her eyes took on an emerald gleam. "I can't believe I didn't think of it before! What is that saying? Something about not seeing the tree for the forest. Or is it the forest for the trees? Whatever. I have thought of it now, and that's what's important, isn't it? You're perfect!"

"What are you babbling about now?" the captain demanded.

"Our family tradition," Maggie excitedly explained. "Each year at Christmastime we choose someone—sometimes a family, sometimes a widow or orphan, once when we had next to nothing to eat ourselves we chose a half-starved stray dog—anyway, we choose someone who is worse off than we are and we help them. It is a yearly reminder that no matter how burdensome we think our own difficulties, we are lucky compared to some." She paused for dramatic effect, enjoying the confounded look on his face. "I have decided you shall be my project this year."

Though Maggie had not thought it physically possible, he stiffened his already rigid posture. "I am not in need of your charity. Your brother may be rich but—"

"I'm not talking about money, silly man. I'm talking about teaching you how to smile. I'm talking about teaching you there is so much more to life than doing your duty. I'm talking about saving you from the drab existence you have inflicted upon yourself." With each statement Maggie grew more inspired.

"You are out of your mind."

Laying her fingers against her temples as if to test his statement, she remained cheerfully determined. "I must admit it is a daunting task, but think of the satisfaction I shall have in the end when I have saved you from yourself. I'm sure you'll be worth the effort."

"I neither want nor need to be saved from anything, especially not myself."

"Oh, but you do. Honor and duty are well and good, and I could never esteem a man who didn't pay homage to both, but what about compassion and whimsy and pleasure for the sake of pleasure? You live your life as if you're only half alive." Her hands danced to the rhythm of her words. "You needn't worry I expect anything in return. I don't. That would spoil the spirit of the tradition."

"Miss Danton, I realize your mind is wont to travel down misguided paths, and I have done my best not to lose patience, but this time you go too far. I am captain of this ship, and I absolutely forbid you to pursue this ridiculous ambition of yours. Not only is it bad manners, it is . . ."

Maggie pursed her lips in vexation. Another lecture. From the starch of his shoulders and his stern tone it promised to be a long one. It was not to be endured. She rummaged her mind for an avenue of prompt escape.

Pleading for mercy would have no more effect than it had when she tried the tactic on other occasions. Feigning tears was beneath her dignity. Clapping her hand over his mouth held much appeal, but a consideration of his superior size and strength caused her to quickly discard the notion.

A bold idea entered her head. At first, she rejected it outright, a little shocked she had thought of it at all. But, slowly, the certainty the stratagem would work overcame her initial reluctance. From there it was only a small step from hesitation to resolve.

Standing on tiptoe, Maggie cradled the captain's face between her hands and pressed her lips to his.

Ending the silencing kiss with a resonant smack of triumph,

she nodded in satisfaction at the captain's startled expression, lifted her soggy skirts, and marched from the cabin.

Maggie absently reached to stroke the head of the tawny cat pacing the length of her bunk while she stripped herself of her sodden garments and exchanged them for dry clothing.

"You should have seen his face, Pounce," she chortled. "I thought his eyes were going to pop out of his head. I know it was mean of me, but I'd kiss him again if I had it to do over again. It certainly shut him up, and I judge the result well worth the price."

Pounce meowed.

"You think so, do you?" Maggie cocked a brow. "Well, I must admit kissing him wasn't all *that* unpleasant. In truth, it was rather nice. His lips taste slightly salty, and they are quite warm." Recalling the fiery surge of delicious sensation the fleeting kiss had evoked, she touched her fingertips to her lips. "Who would have guessed such a cold man could . . . Never mind. I only kissed him because I had to, not because I wanted to, and I won't do it again unless it's absolutely necessary. At least, I don't think I will. It was really quite audacious of me, and I only dared do so because I am absolutely confident the man's sterling sense of honor will protect me from any untoward consequences. If he were any other man . . ."

Pulling on her petticoat, she changed the subject. "What do you think of my plan to cheer our captain? Divine inspiration, that's what I judge it to be." Her eyes sparkled. "He's such a grump. Heaven knows, even if he doesn't thank me for improving his disposition, the rest of the crew will be grateful."

She plopped down on the edge of the bunk to tend to her stockings and shoes. Pounce filled her lap, rubbing her head against her mistress before curling into a purring ball of fur.

Temporarily forsaking her stockings, Maggie gave her full

attention to the cat. Her hands continued to stroke her pet, but her thoughts returned to the captain of the *Guillemot*.

Her strategy for dealing with the stringent captain the last seven weeks had been to avoid him whenever possible. Now all that must change. She didn't really mind. In retrospect, she could see her behavior had been rather spineless and she had been overlooking a golden opportunity to do the poor man a service. Too, she was growing bored of the routine of ship life, and the prospect of a challenge was most welcome.

Lifting her cat from her lap to her face, Maggie rubbed her nose with hers. "So, what should I do to coax our captain out of his perpetually somber mood? Tell him jokes? Point out the beauty of a sunset? Engage him in witty conversations?" She frowned thoughtfully as she continued to conjure ideas. "Perhaps I should make a list. I have a suspicion, with our crusty captain, I may need to employ every resource at my disposal."

Captain Garrett opened the ship's log and, as was his habit, reread the previous day's entry to reassure himself of its accuracy. Satisfied, he picked up his fountain pen to record an account of today. He did so with cool efficiency until he wrote the words: "Passenger, Margaret Danton, overboard." Laying his pen aside, he combed his fingers through his hair.

All through supper she had stared at him, her eyes gleaming while she gaily carried on conversations with everyone at the table. He wasn't used to the attention, and he didn't like it one bit. The woman was sadly lacking a sense of propriety.

At least he could be grateful she hadn't disclosed to all present her plans to ruin his life, and even more importantly, she had not seen fit to regale the company with the tale of the impetuous kiss she had bestowed upon him. Considering Miss Danton's fondness for incessant chatter, he judged her restraint close to miraculous.

What he did not judge with a sense of gratitude or blessedness was the fact she had kissed him in the first place. Why she had done it was a question he didn't care to contemplate. He was convinced she had no more affection for him than he had for her. So, why would she do something so outrageous? Having no ready rational answer, he turned away from the question.

His participation in the kiss was less complicated to catalog. He had been embarrassed by it. So much so, his blood had run hot with mortification. For the briefest of moments he had feared the heat of his blood might have another, less acceptable, cause, but he had quickly rejected the idea as ludicrous. He was embarrassed. What gentleman wouldn't be embarrassed? Polite women did not throw themselves at men.

Not that he judged Miss Danton a wanton. There was an air of childlike innocence about her misdeeds that forced him to conclude she was guilty of the lesser sin of being imprudent. Whereas he had had the benefits of a firm, guiding hand during his youth, from the comments she had made about her family, he was certain her high spirits had been woefully overindulged.

That didn't excuse her behavior. Never in his life had he met a more exasperating and irresponsible human being. It only made him willing to concede she didn't possess the morals of a harlot. The kiss had been an impulsive act of a twitter-brained female.

The urge to confine her to her cabin for the remainder of the voyage was fierce; however, her assessment of his crew's estimation of her was unfortunately accurate. From his first mate to his cabin boys she had charmed all his crew with her headstrong antics and relentlessly sunny disposition. Any perceived harsh treatment of her on his part—even though he would be well within his rights as captain—would likely incite a mutiny.

Captain Garrett scowled. A mutiny might amuse Miss Danton, but there was no place on earth more dangerous than a captainless ship. Whatever his opinion of her, he had made a solemn vow to her brother he would give her his protection, and he was a man of his word. A more onerous task he had never set for himself, but he would persevere.

A knock at the door interrupted his thoughts, and he rose to answer it.

"Miss Danton, what are you doing here?" he stiffly greeted her.

"I thought you might like to go for an after-supper stroll," she cheerfully replied.

"No thank you."

"The stars are sparkling like diamonds tonight. I'm sure it would do you good to see them."

By dint of will he checked the impulse to curse aloud. "I'm busy."

She craned her neck to look around him into the cabin. "You don't look busy, and even if you are, you should come anyway. You work far too hard. It's not healthy."

"I am in excellent health," he countered. Firmly setting his feet in place, he attempted to quell her enthusiasm with a stare. She answered it with a grin.

"Today, yes, but what about tomorrow? We had a neighbor, Mr. Foster, who worked himself into an early grave. It was so sad because he was such a nice man. He owned the hardware store on the corner. His wife warned him. His neighbors warned him. Even his customers warned him. But he wouldn't listen because he believed himself to be in 'excellent health.' Fell over dead, just like that one day as he was walking out the door. wouldn't want something like that to happen to you." Though her face transformed into the picture of heartfelt sympathy, she could not suppress the twinkle in her eyes.

"You are here to forward your misbegotten plan, aren't you?"

"If you mean am I here because of my desire to celebrate the sentiment of the season by looking after your welfare, then my answer is: yes. I congratulate you on your keen sense of perception."

Captain Garrett clenched his teeth and prayed for patience. "Miss Danton, I told you quite plainly I don't want you—"

"Yes, I know, you don't want my charity." She swept away his objections with a flutter of her hand. "Don't think of it as charity. Think of it as an education."

He could feel the frustration and fury boiling up in his chest, but he refused to give in to it. This afternoon her comments had caused him to lose control of his temper, and he was determined it wouldn't happen again. His was an iron will. It would not be defeated by this wisp of a woman. With forced politeness, he responded, "My parents saw to my education, thank you."

"Education should be a lifelong endeavor, don't you think? *I* do, and I'm certain your parents would, too, if they were here for me to ask." She tugged at the lace of one sleeve. "But if you're not in the mood for a stroll, we can do something else. James writes me poker is all the rage in California. You could teach me to play it. That way we can both learn something new."

"I don't gamble."

"Yes, you do." Though she impudently contradicted him, her tone remained maddeningly amiable. "Every time you set sail you're gambling the winds will blow in your favor and you won't run aground or be capsized by a storm. You're gambling your competition won't arrive ahead of you with a hold full of the same cargo you carry and that prices will remain steady. Your entire life is a one huge gamble. Why—"

"Point made," he interrupted. Drawing his hand across his beard, he grimly amended, "I don't play poker."

"What about cribbage? Dominoes? Backgammon?"

He shook his head negatively to each suggestion.

"Checkers? Everyone has played checkers at least once in their life. Surely you've played checkers."

"Yes, I have played checkers."

"Wonderful. I'll be right back."

Before he could protest, she was gone. Just as quickly, she returned, board and playing pieces in hand. Without waiting for an invitation, she stepped past him into his cabin and began to set up the game. "Would you like to be red or black?"

"I would like to be left alone."

"That's because you're confused. You'll just have to trust that I know what I'm doing."

"What you are doing is wasting my valuable time."

"A person's time is only as valuable as the activities with which one chooses to fill it."

"I agree. Might I suggest you fill your time with reading, knitting, praying . . ."

She didn't even pause to consider his counsel but continued to set up the game board. "I'm afraid I have no talent for activities that require me to sit still. Besides, I enjoy the company of my fellow man too much to be tempted to engage in such solitary pastimes."

"If you do not like to be alone, spend your time with the other passengers."

"I cannot ignore my family's Christmas tradition."

"Then kindly inflict it on someone else."

"Who?"

Though his conscience tweaked him for shifting his burden to another's shoulders, he offered her the most logical choice. "I suggest Mr. Bews. You said yourself, he is a melancholy man. If you insist on 'saving' someone, he seems a more likely candidate than I."

Raising her head, she gazed directly into his eyes. Golden flecks glittered in her green eyes. "I'll save you both."

He closed his eyes, then slowly opened them again. "Miss Danton."

"Yes," she answered sweetly.

"Go away."

She didn't budge. "Let's strike a bargain, Captain. You will agree to play checkers with me, and I will agree to leave your cabin the moment you best me."

He took a step toward her in preparation of forcibly escorting her from his quarters. "Why should I strike a bargain with you when I can order you to leave now?"

"Because left to my own devices there is no telling what sort of trouble I might get into. I wouldn't mean to, but you know how I am." She shrugged her shoulders and pouted prettily.

Her words rooted him in place. "Does your brother know of your willingness to stoop to blackmail to get your way?"

"Is that what you think I'm doing? Blackmailing you? I do apologize if I gave that impression. I would never try to coerce you into doing something disagreeable. I was only stating the sad truth, or at least your version of it."

"I intend to inform your brother of your abominable behavior before turning you over to his care in San Francisco."

She smiled. "Feel free to do whatever pleases you. Now, come sit down. The board is ready."

Though he was loath to give in to her artless finagling, Captain Garrett sullenly concluded it would waste far less of his valuable time if he cooperated with her request than it would rescuing her from and punishing her for whatever misdeed she was sure to engage in if he insisted she leave. He had no doubt he would best her the first game. Miss Danton's mind did not possess the capacity for the kind of logic required to win games of strategy. Notwithstanding, in exchange for his cooperation, she would have to agree to give him more than his solitude. He cleared his throat and curtly declared, "I will accept your bargain with the addendum that once I win the game you will not only leave me in peace but return to your cabin and remain there until seven o'clock tomorrow morning."

"Agreed." She pulled up a chair and arranged herself upon it. "Red or black?"

"Black."

They were only four moves into the game when Captain Garrett realized he had underestimated the skill of his opponent. By the ninth move, he knew he had done so seriously. He was surprised, but he remained undaunted.

The first game ended in a draw. Miss Danton won the second match. She was well on her way to winning the third. How she did it he couldn't fathom, as she seemed to be far more interested in carrying on animated conversations about anything and everything under the sun than she was in the game. When her turn came, she moved her pieces with what appeared to him casual indifference to the outcome. He glared at the checkerboard. "Is it possible for you to still your tongue? I find it impossible to concentrate when my ears are being bombarded with idle chatter."

"Tsk, tsk, Captain. Grasping at excuses to explain your poor performance. I thought you would be above that sort of thing. From this moment forward, I shall be as silent as a mouse." She pinched her lips together.

"Thank you. I hope you are having fun, because I am not," he grumbled.

She ran her forefinger over her compressed lips to remind him of her inability to respond.

Captain Garrett's gaze followed the trail of her finger. Her lips were full and pink. He shifted his gaze to the game board and adjusted his collar. He made his next move. She did likewise.

It seemed unusually stuffy in his quarters tonight. He drew in a deep breath and was dismayed to find it carried the hint of lilac perfume. Rebuking himself for failing to concentrate fully on the game, he hastily picked up a checker and jumped two of her pieces. Miss Danton grinned and promptly jumped three of his.

Studying the board, he realized there was no way he could recover from his blunder and win. Another draw was the best he could hope to attain. In either case, the result was the same. He would be obliged to play another game.

The temperature of the cabin was definitely too warm for comfort. Though he would have preferred to lay the blame on the heat of the contest, he knew that explanation to be false. He should never have allowed *her* to inveigle her way into his cabin.

Being older and wiser, he should have realized a man and woman, even a man and woman who had no use for each other, should not be alone in such close confines. Man was not so far from the animals as he liked to believe, and though it galled him to admit it—especially when he considered the woman involved—he was subject to the same weaknesses of all men.

"I believe I am in a mood for that stroll after all." He abruptly rose to his feet. "Would you be willing to exchange it for our earlier bargain?"

He cursed under his breath when she again brought his attention to her too provocative lips by laying her finger on them and remaining speechless. "I release you from your vow of silence," he brusquely notified her.

"Are you conceding the game?"

"Yes." He took a step toward the door.

"Then I would be more than happy to take a stroll with you." She allowed him to usher her out the door and into the moonlight. "Actually, I would be happy to do so whether or not you named me the winner, but I do admire a good sport."

The crisp night air filling his lungs as they promenaded across the deck was reviving, but not nearly as helpful as he had hoped it would be. Captain Garrett was not pleased. In hopes of distracting himself, he commanded, "I can't imagine why walking with me would make you happy. Kindly explain your reason."

"I don't have one," she replied without concern.

"Then you cannot be happy."

"Yes, I can. I feel what I feel because I feel it."

"Gibberish."

"To you maybe, but it makes perfect sense to me."

Since it was impossible to argue a point of logic with someone who sincerely believed absurdity carried as much weight as reason, he dropped the subject.

Before he could propose another of his own choosing, she was grabbing his hand and excitedly exclaiming, "Oh, look at the moon! Isn't it beautiful? The moon never looked so beautiful back home."

"There is only one moon. This is the same one you have seen all your life."

"Perhaps it is, but you must admit it is lovely tonight."

"It is the moon," he answered noncommittally.

"Did you know moonlight softens the harsh angles of your face? In fact, it makes you look positively comely."

He grunted.

"What about me?" She presented her profile for his inspection. "Does moonlight favor me as well?"

He turned away from her, staring morosely at the sea. "If you are seeking compliments, Miss Danton, seek them elsewhere."

"I would if that was what I was looking for," she assured him. "But what I am seeking is unbiased information. It might be a useful thing to know in the future."

"Thinking of snaring yourself a husband when you reach California?" he acidly commented.

"No. The man I marry will have to fall madly in love with me of his own accord or I won't have him."

"A man would have to be mad to want to marry you."

"True. I don't think I would make a very good wife."

He wheeled from the ship rail to face her. "Don't you take offense at anything?"

"I'm sorry. Were you trying to offend me?" Her guileless gaze met his piercing stare as she answered his question with one of her own.

"Yes! Of course I was. It was extremely rude of me to say such a thing."

"But it's true," she argued. "I don't like to clean or cook or sew. To love and honor are vows I could make in good conscience, but we both know a vow to obey my husband would make me a liar. I'm just not the obedient sort."

As he listened to her make her speech, he couldn't help but notice that moonlight did indeed favor her. It spun her hair into a golden halo and bathed her finely chiseled features in ethereal light. He had been so preoccupied with being annoyed with her, he had never noticed Miss Danton was an uncommonly attractive woman. He wasn't happy to have noticed it now. "I applaud your honesty, but I cannot approve of your willingness to accept your failings without distress," he gruffly stated.

"Your brow is wrinkled again, Captain," she observed, reaching up to smooth away the lines.

He took a step back, but the rail prevented further retreat. He grimaced.

"You're afraid of me, aren't you?" she declared with both astonishment and sympathy.

"I most certainly am not," he denied.

"Yes, you are. You're afraid to let me touch you. The question, of course, is why?"

He refused to look at her, but he could feel her speculative perusal of his person and hear the note of bemusement in her voice. He assumed an authoritative stance. "The *question* is where you get these idiotic notions that are wont to pop into your head without reason or warning."

"Then you won't mind if I kiss you again." She advanced upon him.

"I most certainly *do* mind."

"Because you're afraid you might like it."

"Because propriety demands . . ."

She cut off the rest of what he was about to say with her

warm, rosy lips, moving them against his tentatively at first. But the kiss soon escalated in intensity. She wrapped her arms around his neck, leaning against him, lighting a fire in his loins. He tried to douse it by forbidding his body to react. He failed.

Not only did his loins refuse to obey his will, his arms refused his command to rise and set her away. It had been a long time since he had been kissed by a woman—any woman—and he didn't remember the sensation being so pleasant or overwhelming.

When at last she stepped away, she looked as flustered and flushed as he felt. She stared at him with round, overbright eyes. "You're right. I shouldn't have done that," she breathlessly whispered.

"No, you shouldn't have," he wholeheartedly agreed.

Lifting her skirts, she turned on her heels, and beat a hasty retreat.

Two

Christmas was Maggie's favorite time of year. If she were home she would be going to parties, caroling, sipping hot cocoa by the fireside with good friends. A ship offered far fewer opportunities for entertainment, but she was not disheartened. The passengers and crew of the *Guillemot* made fine friends, and a little improvising could supply the rest.

The only element of her ambition to orchestrate a merry Christmas that gave her pause was Captain Garrett. Unless she was willing to forsake her plan to brighten his spirits, he had to be included—which meant spending much of her days and evenings in his company.

Originally, the knowledge of this necessity hadn't daunted her in the least, but that was yesterday before she had kissed him twice in one day. The first time was justifiable. The second was not.

She had been so sure she knew exactly what she was doing. Now, she wasn't at all certain. Though she honestly had his welfare in mind, initially she had conceived his salvation as a game, something to divert her from the tedium of the voyage. She wasn't supposed to feel anything for him but pity. And what she was feeling was definitely something more than pity. She wasn't sure what it was she *was* feeling, but whatever it was, it made her restless—and curious. Once something piqued her curiosity she knew there was no turning back. She would never be satisfied until she found out just exactly what kind of man she had taken on and where it might lead.

Since she wasn't going to change her mind, she was faced with a choice. She could sit and fret about this unexpected turn of events or view it as an intriguing new dimension to the original game. She chose to do the latter.

"Miss Danton, just exactly what do you think you are doing?"

"I'm decorating the ship for Christmas."

Captain Garrett perused her through narrowed eyes. His question had been rhetorical. He could see the wreath in her hand. It appeared to be made of holly, but on closer inspection he could see it was constructed of stiff green fabric cut in the shape of leaves and red beads. He couldn't place the fabric, but he recognized the beads from a necklace he had seen her wear. Murmuring a caustic comment about presumptuous passengers beneath his breath, he starched his posture and sternly stated, "You have not sought my permission to do so."

"Would you give it?"

"No."

She turned her palms upward as if his answer made any further explanation on her part unnecessary. His brow knit when she presented her backside, giving her full attention back to the task of deciding the proper location for her wreath.

It had been two weeks since Miss Danton had announced her scheme to make a light-hearted man of him and the woman was relentless. It didn't matter what he said or did, not a day went by that she didn't show up at his cabin door requesting he join her in some game or another. She was up at dawn to point out the colors of the sunrise. She insisted on reading him poetic passages describing their voyage from her journal. She followed him about on deck asking questions about everything he did, responding as if his answers were the most fascinating thing she

ad ever heard and invariably seizing upon some word or phrase
nd discoursing on it until, moments later, some other subject
aught her fancy. The convoluted progression of her mind ex-
austed him.

What left him even more exhausted was the constant battle
e fought against his own prurient propensities whenever he was
n her company. At this very moment he was noticing the fetch-
ng way her trim waist curved into her round hips. He was re-
nembering how it had felt when she kissed him.

He had been successful in his efforts to make certain she was
given no opportunity to repeat the misbehavior. So why couldn't
e banish the memory of her welcoming lips from his mind?
Why, instead of abating, did he find his physical attraction to
er intensifying? Why, instead of feeling grateful she had made
no attempt to kiss him again, did he find a part of himself wish-
ng she would?

He didn't want to be physically attracted to her. She was a
passenger on his ship. She was nothing to him. When they
eached California, they would go their separate ways, and he
would be glad of it.

He had a duty to Miss Danton and her brother. His duty was
o protect her as "he would his own sister." That was the promise
he had made her brother James. It had never occurred to him
he person from whom she needed the most protection might be
himself.

All his life he had taken pride in performing his duty with
honesty and honor. He had followed his father's footsteps to the
sea without resistance. Since his father's death, he had provided
for the financial well-being of his mother and sister. Though he
brooked no sluggards, he had earned his crew's respect by being
a scrupulously fair man. They could depend on him to see them
through the fiercest storm and always to pay them in full and
on time. He couldn't understand why God had seen fit to test
him with Miss Danton.

She might not intentionally be trying to corrupt him, b
she kept herself underfoot day and night, constantly tempti
him with the sight of her beguiling figure and the scent of h
femininity.

The notion he might have been chosen as some modern-d
Job entered his mind, but he banished the thought as borderi
on sacrilegious.

His gaze drifted across the deck over various members of I
crew. They were all hard at work, performing their assigned tas
with the diligence they knew was expected of them. He shou
have taken pleasure in the sight of their industry, but he didn
Though they were careful never to let him catch them in the a
he knew his crew watched with amusement as he tried to nav
gate the choppy waters Miss Danton's constant presence visit
upon him. He was certain they only saw his frustration at h
lack of obeisance to his authority as captain and they had
inkling of the internal war he waged, but still . . .

His gaze shifted back to the object of his ruminations. T
instant he realized it had done so, he forced it away from h
focusing on a distant point out at sea. His thoughts were not
easily redirected. He grimaced.

His present predicament really was more Miss Danton's fav
than his. She was the one who had decided to make a project
him. She was the one who had initiated the kisses that had i
nited his unwelcome lust. He had no idea why he tolerated h

It was little consolation she had taken his advice and decid
to "save" Mr. Bews as well. If only she would confine herse
to Mr. Bews, he might survive this journey with his peace
mind intact. In that gentleman's case her efforts were appreciat

He had overheard the man tearfully confessing his failings
Miss Danton shortly after she had taken him under her win
Mr. Bews, an accountant, had made an addition error, resulti
in his employer losing a considerable sum of money. Upon di
covering and apprising his employer of the error, he had be

red. Now, he was running away to California because he uldn't face the shame. Miss Danton informed Mr. Bews with er usual unwavering confidence in her own opinion that his nployer was an ogre, he himself was a gentleman among gen-emen, and that mistakes were what made life interesting. The llow still was more mouse than man, but every day he seemed walk a little taller.

A smile tugged at the corners of the captain's lips. Margaret anton had a way of treating everyone as if they were the finest f human beings, and she valued their acquaintance as she would member of her own family. His chief mate, Jonas Taylor, lit like a lantern and stayed that way all day whenever she ex-anged more than a half dozen words with him. Brian Moll, e ship's carpenter, strutted about like a soldier. Charley and y, his two cabin boys, had taken to inventing excuses that al-wed them to perform their duties in her company, working vice as hard whenever she was near.

Captain Garrett's half-smile sagged into a thoughtful frown. t first he had believed her behavior a sham, but it wasn't. She stinctively found the good in every person and situation she acountered and was not shy about sharing her discoveries with ιyone in hearing distance.

Perhaps that was why he found himself tolerating Miss Dan-n when good sense counseled him to exercise his dominion ver her and banish her from his sight. She truly believed her uixotic view of the world. He neither agreed with nor approved f her carefree approach to life, but in some core part of his ɛing he couldn't help but admire and feel a twinge of jealousy r her ability.

"Will you hand me that ribbon?" Her voice jolted him out of is musings.

"What?" Turning to face her, he tensed upon discovering her alancing on a water barrel.

"The ribbon." She leaned over and held out her hand. "W you please hand it to me so I can tie my wreath in place?"

"Correct me if I'm wrong, but didn't I just forbid you decorate my ship?"

"You're wrong." She climbed off the barrel and fetched t ribbon herself. "You said, *if I had asked* you would have forbi den me. I didn't ask." Gifting him with a broad grin, she turne to climb back on the barrel.

"Miss Danton!"

Sighing, she faced him. "Before you say something you w only regret, why not give me permission instead? It is after Christmastime. A wreath and ribbon or two will remind you home."

"My family does not celebrate Christmas with trimmings ar trappings."

"How do they celebrate?"

"We attend church services and spend the day quietly med tating on our blessings."

"Oh, dear, how very boring for God. I'm sure He appreciat your gratitude, but He prefers a more lively observance of H Son's birth."

"And how do you know that?"

"My father told me so when I was a little girl."

While negotiating for her passage, Miss Danton's brother ha apprised him that both their parents had died during an influenz epidemic when their children were in their early teens, and r spect for the dead prevented him from calling her father a lia He decided to try a different tack. "Last night when I calculate our position, I confirmed we will begin rounding the Horn b fore Christmas. The winds and currents there are called the Roa ing Forties for good reason. All your decorations will be blow away."

"I'll nail them in place," she offered a solution to the problen "With your permission, of course."

The fact she was asking permission at all was so surprising, e considered giving it. He thought her efforts a waste but they vouldn't do him any harm, and they might keep her busy and ut of his hair. He cleared his throat. "All right. You have my ermission to decorate the ship as long as you use your own esources and stay out of the way of my crew and myself. Any- hing that causes us inconvenience will be removed and you will ot voice complaint. You will not decorate anything that cannot e reached by standing with both your feet firmly on the deck. f you violate my rules, everything will be torn down. Do I have our word you will abide by these regulations?"

After raising her eyes and hesitating a moment, she replied, 'Yes."

Three

Captain Garrett stood on the spar deck shaking his head i amazement both at the very fact Miss Danton had talked hi into allowing her to hold a Christmas Eve dance and the tran formation she had wrought upon his ship.

Recalling their conversation, he still wasn't clear how she ha managed to wheedle his permission. He had given her a lengt list of reasons her scheme was impossible . . .

"Miss Danton, surely you have noticed the *Guillemot* suffe from a severe shortage of females to serve as dance partners.

"Yes, I have, but it is of absolutely no consequence." She ha apprised him, her green eyes twinkling with joyful anticipatio "James writes that in California the lack of women at dances solved by having half the men tie a ribbon around their arm an dancing the female part. Nobody minds in the least and everyor has a lovely time. We'll do the same."

"And the weather. How will you arrange that to your liking?

"Despite your dire predictions, a brisk breeze is the wor we've seen. I'm willing to gamble our luck will hold."

"And if you're wrong?"

"I'll be disappointed, of course, but no harm will be don I'll not be asking you to lift a finger, so any time and effo squandered will be my own."

The conversation had gone downhill from there.

So here he stood within the circle of light of a dozen lantern staring at a garland crocheted from yarn unraveled from he shawl, brightly colored bows made of material that had once been a dress or blouse, and a Christmas tree fashioned out of a wooden frame and a green velvet skirt.

Of all her creations, she was most proud of her "tree." He had never heard of such a thing as a Christmas tree and told her so. Smiling her indomitable smile, she had explained the story behind the tradition of bringing a fir tree into the house and how her family had adopted the custom from a German neighbor. Her family habitually embraced customs that were not their own if they took a fancy to them, or so she gaily informed him, in the same breath counseling him to do the same.

Despite his objections to the waste of lantern oil and good clothing, he had to admit she had done wonders with her limited resources.

He shouldn't have been surprised. It was beyond his ken why, but *everything* she did had a way of turning out well for her. It was as if she had been born into the world determined to enjoy herself, and fate felt obliged to lend a hand. Even the weather was cooperating. A few clouds had been gathering in the sky since midafternoon, but they didn't appear imminently stormy. In all his voyages around the Horn, he had never seen the weather so calm. By now they usually had experienced two or three major squalls.

"So, what do you think?"

Recognizing the voice beside him, he turned to greet her. She was wearing an off-the-shoulder, claret-colored, broché silk gown with a pointed waist and a profusion of creamy lace. She had pulled her hair up off her neck with a matching ribbon, fastening it on one side. Her bared skin glowed golden in the lantern light. His mouth went dry. "About what?"

"My decorations."

"I think the crew will appreciate your efforts."

"What about you?"

"You know I do not approve of frivolity."

"Or me," Maggie supplied, making no attempt to hide her disappointment at his less than enthusiastic reaction to all her hard work. She hadn't expected him to respond any differently, but that didn't mean she hadn't hoped she was wrong.

"Don't frown," he brusquely ordered.

"Why not?"

"It is at odds with your nature."

"Then you should be pleased."

"Miss Danton, I only object to your nature when it interferes with the efficient discharge of the responsibilities of my ship; the rest of the time I am merely confused by it. You are very different from other women who have peopled my life. I don't understand you at all. But that doesn't mean I can't appreciate your unique 'qualities.' "

Her brow quirked as she tried to decide if he meant his words to be a compliment. Regardless of his intent, she elected to accept them as such. She smiled. "Then you'll join in the dance?"

"I didn't say that."

"Please." Lifting her skirt ankle-high, she rustled the fabric and performed a jaunty two-step to entice him. The captain looked away.

"What would my men say?"

"That it is Christmas Eve, and it is good to see their captain joining in instead of standing off at a distance glowering at them for engaging in a little holiday recreation."

He stiffened his posture. "My men respect me."

"Yes, they do, but sometimes don't you wish they liked you as well? I know I do."

Despite his desire to remain aloof, his gaze gravitated back to her. "Why should what my men think of me concern you at all?"

"Because it does." The answer seemed satisfactory to her, but by the perplexed expression on his face, she knew the captain required more. Forcing herself to analyze her reasons, she elaborated. "Since I have taken the time to get to know you better, I count you as a friend. Friends care about friends."

"It is better a captain has his crew's respect than their affection," he contended.

"Why not have both? One does not exclude the other. I for one don't believe you will lose a whit of your crew's respect if you let them see you have a little fun."

"You are assuming I think dancing is fun."

"We won't just be dancing. We'll be decorating the tree."

"And what makes you think I'll enjoy that activity any more than dancing?"

"You will enjoy them both if you will only let yourself." Her eyes met his and she willed him to comprehend both the strength of her conviction and how important it was for him to take an active part in the festivities. If he didn't, it would put a damper on the whole evening. Didn't he understand she had done all this for him? Every wreath and ribbon had been fashioned for him—for the man she intuitively knew him to be under his rigid hide. She touched his hand.

As he gazed into her hope-filled eyes, it occurred to Captain Garrett how mean-spirited his arguments must sound to her ears. Though on innumerable occasions he had commanded her to take a situation more seriously, now that she was showing him she was capable of being serious, he didn't like it one bit. It made him feel like a villain.

To blame her for his unsettling feelings and abiding lust was unfair. She spent more time in his company than she should, and sometimes he imagined she looked at him as though she might kiss him, but not once in the weeks since she had stated she regretted her impulsive behavior had she tried to throw herself into his arms. As far as he could discern, she had forgotten the incident completely. *He* was the one having trouble forgetting.

She had gone to a lot of effort to make this evening special. It was only a few hours of his time she asked of him.

He found himself wanting to please her.

He wasn't going to dance with *anyone,* but that didn't mean he couldn't be polite and feign a little enthusiasm for her sake. He took a deep breath. "Tonight, *and tonight only,* I will test your theory concerning my men. I'm not saying I agree with you, but what damage I do my image—if there is any—can be mitigated by strictly enforcing my command for the remainder of the voyage. Any crew member who persists in questioning my authority can be permanently put to shore in San Francisco."

The instant he acquiesced, her vibrant self returned. "I'm glad that's settled. Look, here comes Mr. and Mrs. Kendall. I'm so glad Mrs. Kendall bestirred herself. The fresh air will do her good. And Mr. Bews is right behind them."

Assuming the role of hostess, Maggie threw herself wholeheartedly into the task of greeting her "guests." Not all of the crew could come at once, but she previously had persuaded the captain to allow a temporary adjustment in the usual schedule of duties so no one would be completely left out.

"Here's them plum puddings you asked me to make," Donald Kelly, the ship's cook, called to her, tray in hand. "I didn't have all the ingredients, but I stuck to the recipe you wrote down for me close as I could."

"Whatever you left out can't have mattered much. They smell heavenly."

"Thank you, ma'am."

It wasn't long before everyone arrived.

"What shall we do first, eat our pudding or decorate our tree?" Maggie queried the crowd. Opinion was evenly split. Her eyes sparkling, she stated, "Looks like we'll have to do both at the same time."

Mr. Kelly manned the pudding tray, while Maggie manned the tree. Though some men filled their bellies with the steaming pudding first, no man came empty-handed, and a flurry of activity surrounded the Christmas tree. The captain silently watched from a safe distance from the bustle.

Some men contributed polished buttons. Charley brought tiny dolls fashioned from scraps of rope. Mr. Bews brought bits of paper cut in the shape of bells and stars. Mr. and Mrs. Kendall placed three balls stitched of blue-and-yellow fabric in her hand. Several ordinary seamen offered their gold and silver earrings. Brian Moll had carved a half dozen tiny wooden animals, fashioning them with leather laces to hang them. Maggie contributed her earbobs, necklaces, and bracelets to the cause.

When all the decorations were fastened to the tree, Maggie stepped back to admire their handiwork. "It's the finest tree I've ever seen," she declared.

She glanced in the captain's direction. His lips formed a straight line, but his eyes were smiling.

Maggie brought him a plate of pudding and stationed herself by his side while she ate her own dessert. "Do you like the pudding?" she asked after he had taken a bite.

"It's quite pleasant."

She nodded her approval. "The recipe was my mother's. There was no one on earth who could make a tastier plum pudding."

He told himself he was merely making polite conversation, but the question formed on his lips to satisfy an earnest curiosity. "Was your mother like you?"

Swallowing a mouthful of pudding, Maggie replied, "In some ways, yes. Our looks are similar, and she was almost always happy. That's what I remember most about her—her laughter."

"It must have made you sad that she died so young."

"I was sad that she had to leave her family, but by my reckoning she'd lived more life in the years she was given than most people do in a lifetime, so I didn't feel like she was cheated."

"And you are determined to follow in her footsteps," Captain Garrett observed.

"No. I'm forging my own path. She told me never to try to

be like anyone but myself. My mother believed if everyone listened to their own heart instead of trying to be who they thought they ought to be, it would eliminate ninety percent of the misery in the world."

"An interesting philosophy."

"She was an interesting woman."

"But you don't believe her advice applies to me."

Maggie gave him a quizzical look. "Of course it does."

"Then why have you made it your project to change me?"

"I'm not trying to change you."

The captain eyed her skeptically. "You're not?"

"No."

"Then what am I doing here eating pudding with you and my men?"

Maggie searched her mind for the right words to explain her conduct toward him. When she hit upon them, her face lit up. "I'm not trying to change you; I'm trying to unwrap you." His countenance tensed, and she quickly clarified, "You know, like a Christmas present. A body knows what's inside is delightful, but until you take off the paper and open the box, the contents give little pleasure. You keep yourself confined inside an austere box where no one can appreciate you. I want to let you out."

"Maybe there is nothing in the box, and austere is what I am," he challenged.

"No."

"How can you be certain?"

Standing on tiptoe, she whispered in his ear. "I've kissed you."

He nearly choked on his own breath. So, she hadn't forgotten kissing him. He was vexed and unaccountably gratified in equal measure. Both emotions were overwhelmed by the voice shouting in his head to put some distance between himself and Miss Danton without delay. "Everyone has finished their pudding.

roceed with your party or dismiss us," he hoarsely commanded. I do not intend to stand here all night humoring you."

Maggie was aware of his discomfort, but rather than seek to mitigate it, she was inspired to do the opposite. It was time. For several weeks now, she had been denying herself permission to explore the delicious longing the captain kindled in her breast. She'd lost count of the times she'd passed up an opportunity to hold his hand or give him a hug or kiss. This was Christmas Eve. As a present to herself—and him—tonight, she would discard the constraints she had put on herself and let fortune lead them where it may.

Clapping her hands to gain everyone's attention, she announced, "The captain is eager to begin our dance. Mr. Riley has kindly consented to provide our music with his tin whistle. If those of you who drew the long straw will tie the ribbons I have provided on your left arms, we can give the captain his wish."

"What do you think you're doing?" he hissed.

"Obeying orders," she calmly replied.

"I don't dance."

"You will tonight." Grabbing his hand, she tugged him toward the open space of deck the men had cleared for a dance floor. The crew erupted in spontaneous cheers.

Captain Garrett gritted his teeth. She had trapped him. If he refused to dance with her, he would call more attention to himself than she already had. He would appear a donkey before his men.

"Do you know a waltz, Mr. Riley?"

"Yes, ma'am." He lifted his flute to his lips and began to play.

The captain stoically led his partner through the steps of the waltz with skill and grace. He watched her under hooded eyes. She didn't appear the least bit guilty for maneuvering him into his uncomfortable position. She appeared contented and far too attractive for his peace of mind. Her dress was too revealing,

her perfume too intoxicating, the flesh of her hands too warm
and soft. Beneath his dispassionate exterior, he cursed both him
self and her.

"I thought you said you didn't dance," Maggie commente
as he smoothly guided her through a turn.

"I don't, but that doesn't mean I don't know how. And don
look so pleased with yourself. I'm furious with you."

"You don't have to be. You could choose to relax and relis
the dance."

"Unlike you, I find no pleasure in making a spectacle
myself."

"If that's what's bothering you, I can fix it." Disengaging or
of her hands, she motioned for the others to join them on th
dance floor. As soon as they complied, she gave her hand an
her attention back to the captain. "Better?"

"No."

"You find me lacking in skill?"

"No."

"Your boots are too tight?"

"No," he muttered. "Stop talking and dance."

Maggie happily complied, casting her gaze over the crow
The other dancers were a rowdy, clumsy lot, inclined to hagg
over who was leading who, but they were clearly enjoying then
selves. She was glad. She liked to see people make merry.

She also liked dancing with the captain. It was nice being th
close to him, to feel the firm pressure of his hand on her bac
She felt sheltered in the circle of his strong arms. His brea
tickled the fine hairs at her temples. His masculine scent titi
lated her nostrils. She knew she couldn't dance with him ar
him alone all evening, but if she had her way, that's exactly wh
she would do.

When Mr. Riley blew the last note of the waltz, she reluctant
let go of her hold on the captain's hand, turning toward the oth
dancers as he walked away.

Next, Maggie partnered Mr. Bews. After Mr. Bews, she danced one dance with every member of the crew, beginning with Charley and working her way up the ranks to Mr. Taylor. Each man received her full attention and was treated as a gentleman nonpareil.

It took several attempts, but between dances Maggie eventually was able to convince Mrs. Kendall she possessed the strength to partner her husband. The first dance led to another, then another. Maggie could not have been more pleased.

When she finished her dance with Mr. Taylor, Maggie presented herself before the captain. "It's your turn again." She reached for his hand. He tucked both hands behind his back and clasped them together.

"I believe I shall do you the favor of allowing you to sit this one out."

Her heartbeat quickened. He hadn't refused her outright. Was this progress? She covertly scrutinized him from head to toe. Yes, it was! It was written plainly on his face. He wanted to dance with her. He just didn't know how to admit it. "I'd rather dance," she ardently declared.

"Aren't you exhausted?" he protested.

"No."

"You should be, and I'm surprised you aren't limping as well. I've lost count of how many times your feet have been stepped on."

Another good sign. He had been paying close attention to the revelry—most likely stiffly standing here wishing he knew how to become a part of it while some dreary demon in his head told him if he did, it would undermine his authority and dignity. She'd seen the look on his face before, when his lips were telling her to leave him alone but a twitch of a muscle in his cheek or a faint glimmer of light in his eyes pleaded with her to stay and make him play whatever game she had devised to distract him from his duty. Well, she knew exactly what needed to be done, and she was more than willing to help him solve his dilemma.

"What your men lack in skill, they make up for in enthusiasm. Everyone is having a wonderful time, don't you think?" Maggie offered the opinion, curving her lips into a generous smile.

"Yes."

"Even you?"

After a moment's pause, he replied, "Yes. The festivities have not gotten out of hand, and the opportunity to observe my men's behavior in these informal circumstances is educational."

"And to thank me for providing this 'educational opportunity,' you will dance with me again." Laying one hand on his shoulder and snaking the other behind his back to capture his hand, she assumed an approximation of the classic dance position.

He scowled, but he didn't pull away. "You are nothing if not persistent."

"Thank you, Captain."

Captain Garrett appeared to take more pleasure from his second dance than he had the first. Maggie was inclined to stay by his side and persuade him to dance another, but she had enough sense to know the captain would retreat behind glacial walls if she pushed him too far. Still, she cajoled him into dancing three more dances with her before the evening was over.

Though she was certain he would never confess it if she asked, he liked dancing with her. She could see it in the depths of his dark-brown eyes and feel it in the muscles of his arms. He fought it, but more than once his lips quivered into a satisfied smile.

Those smiles warmed her heart like nothing on earth ever before had.

With each dance they shared he seemed to her to become less the captain and more a warm-blooded man.

When the other passengers and members of the crew began to wend their way to their bunks, Maggie was tempted to call them back. She wanted the night to go on forever so she could coax more smiles to the captain's lips.

After the last man had offered his thanks, she lingered on the deck, soaking up the last moments of an extremely agreeable evening.

The captain touched her shoulder. "You should go to your cabin. The wind is picking up, and you'll catch a chill."

She turned to face him. He was staring at her with a strange light in his eyes. It sent trills of anticipation coursing up her spine. "After all that dancing, the breeze feels nice against my skin," she murmured.

His gaze fell upon her flushed skin and he frowned.

"Is something wrong?"

He continued to stare at the gentle swell of flesh just above the lace trim of her neckline. "Though you feign náiveté, I believe you know exactly what my problem is, Miss Danton."

Their gazes met and fused. "I suppose I do. *I* am your problem just as *you* are mine. The difference between us is, I wish to face my feelings, try to understand them. You wish to run away from yours."

"Avoiding disaster is an act of wisdom, not cowardice."

"True."

"Then we are agreed we will avoid each other's company for the remainder of this voyage."

He was standing so close she could feel the heat of his breath on her skin. She could hear his racing heartbeat, or was it her own heartbeat drumming in her ears? "No. I will not avoid your company."

"Why not? It is the sensible thing to do."

"Don't you ever get tired of being sensible?"

"No. I like being sensible."

"Possibly. But if you like being sensible as much as you claim, you would wear a smile more often, and you rarely do. I doubt very much if dancing falls within your definition of being sensible, but tonight I couldn't help but notice the ravishing smiles gracing your lips when you danced with me. Perhaps you have merely acquired the habit of being sensible."

"Obviously, *you* have not."

"No, I haven't. Sometimes, I like being sensible, but sometimes I like to take the path that makes no sense at all just to see where it may lead."

"I know what lies at the end of this particular path."

"What?"

"Disaster."

Maggie nervously licked her lips. "You may be right, but I can't help wondering if denying our feelings wouldn't be a worse disaster. Right now, I know you want to kiss me. I want you to kiss me. If you don't I shall lie in my bunk all night wondering what it would have felt like if you did."

"You should not think about such things."

"Why?"

"We are not at all suited to each other."

The heat of a blush stained her cheeks. "I know."

"Miss Danton."

"Yes."

"Ah, damn!" Gathering her in his arms, Captain Garrett pulled her against his chest and covered her lips with his. The hunger in him startled Maggie, but she did not resist. Melting into his arms, she surrendered herself to sensation.

His lips were soft and warm and moist as they moved over hers, kissing her again and again. One hand kneaded her back while the other cradled her head. His tongue slipped into her mouth, igniting a fire in her belly with each delicious stroke. Tentatively, she tested her own tongue's power over him. He groaned, clinging to her so tightly it stole her breath away.

The kiss went on and on, becoming more pleasurable and overwhelming by the moment. His hands would not be still. Everywhere they touched her they set her flesh on fire.

The tingling heat his hands evoked was unfamiliar, but it didn't frighten her. It felt right to be here in his arms.

A hand slipped inside her bodice. His thumb stroked her breast through the fabric of her chemise. When it brushed across her nipple, the surge of hot sensation jolted her back to her senses. She didn't want to make him stop, but she knew she must.

"Captain," Maggie whispered.

"What?" He was not deterred.

"I believe we've both had enough for one night," she gasped between panting breaths.

"I don't think I can get enough of you," he mumbled against her neck.

"If the night watch discovers you trying to bed me on the deck, we'll have a devil of a time explaining ourselves."

He released her so abruptly, Maggie staggered before regaining her balance.

"My God! What am I doing?"

"Kissing me," she sighed. "And making a thorough job of it. I had no idea you were capable of such passion."

"Miss Danton, I do apologiz—"

"Don't you dare." Maggie clamped her hand over his lips. "I liked what you did to me, and I'll not have you spoil it. Before you do, I'm going to my cabin and pulling the covers over my head." Replacing her hand with her lips, she gave him a lingering kiss. "Merry Christmas, Captain . . . *and sweet dreams.*"

Four

Captain Nathan Garrett punched his pillow, rolling first to one side, then the other. With a woeful sigh, he flopped to his back. The wind howled outside his cabin, promising a full-fledged storm by morning.

A storm was already raging inside his head and in his loins. His lust for Margaret Danton could no longer be ignored in hopes it would vanish. He must face it head on.

He had lost control of himself this evening.

He had promised her brother he would guard her virtue, and he had—from every man save himself. The memory of the lascivious kiss still caused the blood in his veins to burn. He wanted to leap from his bed, march to her cabin, and kiss her again. He wanted to do much more than kiss her.

He was appalled with himself.

The worst of it was he couldn't even say why he had so flagrantly violated his own standard of decency. True, his opinion of Miss Danton had undergone a change to her favor these past few weeks. He was willing to concede she was fair of face. On occasion, he found her fleet sense of humor charming. He still thought her scatterbrained, and her tendency to act first and contemplate the consequences later was as entrenched as ever; but her joy for life and the generosity of her heart were so earnest they made these failings seem trifling.

But that was no excuse. He had been in the company of other women who possessed physical beauty, ready wit, and pleasant dispositions, and not once had he lost control of the situation. He never even had been tempted to step beyond the bounds of propriety. So, why was his reaction to Miss Margaret Danton different? It shouldn't be. *But it was.* He let loose a moan and punched his pillow again.

The whys and wherefores of his behavior tonight were not nearly as important as making certain it never happened again. He must ride out this storm of emotion. It was his moral duty. If he could not trust himself to behave rationally in Miss Danton's company, the logical solution was to give her wide berth until she left the *Guillemot* and his life could get back to normal. It might not be easy, but it could be done. He was, after all, captain of this ship.

By dawn the wind had whipped itself up to gale-force fury. Having sailed this route many times, Captain Garrett knew they were in for the worst the Roaring Forties could offer.

He stood upon the deck of the *Guillemot,* drenched to the skin despite his slicker, shouting orders to his men and inspecting their preparations for the storm. It was difficult to make himself heard above the howling wind and pounding rain, but he was unwilling to delegate the task to his chief mate.

A captain's steady presence had a calming effect on a nervous crew. Most of his men had been through these storms before, but that didn't eliminate his responsibility to them.

Too, he was glad for the distraction. He had been awake most of the night trying to sort out his feelings for Miss Danton and had made little or no progress. The passengers had all been advised to remain in their cabins until given further notice. He welcomed the respite.

* * *

Maggie clutched the edge of her bunk as the ship roiled to the starboard side before setting itself upright again.

Pounce arched her back and retched for the third time that morning.

"Poor baby, I wish I knew how to make you feel better," Maggie commiserated. Pulling a blanket from the bunk, she made a soft bed for her pet, tucking her in as she would a child.

Though she possessed an iron stomach, Maggie feared it wouldn't be long before she joined her cat and cast up her own accounts if she didn't occupy her mind with something besides the storm. The subject that immediately sprang to mind was Captain Garrett.

A wry smile curved her lips. Just thinking about last night's kiss brought a fiery blush to her cheeks. She supposed she should be embarrassed. After all, she never had been kissed like that before. But she *wasn't* embarrassed. The flush of her cheeks was caused by pleasure, not chagrin.

She might as well accept the fact she was wildly attracted to the captain of the *Guillemot* because pretending otherwise served no purpose other than to confuse matters further, and she was already confused enough, thank you.

She judged her attraction to the captain the strangest turn of event imaginable. Never had two people with such opposite natures been born.

Maggie fingered the hat she had knit for his Christmas present. It was a sorry-looking hat, but she hoped he would appreciate the effort she had made to please him. She liked him. She wanted him to like her.

Not that she believed anything lasting would ever come of it, no matter how keen their liking might be. The captain was too sensible to ever fall in love—especially with her. As for herself, she imagined she might be persuaded to throw caution to the wind and fall in love with him with the least bit of encouragement. Luckily, there would be no encouragement and she would be saved from her own foolish heart.

She was going to California to find adventure, not a husband. Of course, a husband could be an adventure . . . She slammed the door on her train of thought before she could carry it to its logical conclusion. Still, she could not stifle a fervent longing in her breast.

"Captain Garrett is right. I am sadly lacking in common sense," she confessed to Pounce. "What I feel for Captain Garrett is friendship, nothing more. One lusty kiss does not a lover make!"

Rising to her feet, Maggie yanked on her cloak. She couldn't stand sitting here with nothing but her wayward thoughts to occupy her mind a moment longer. She was going to find something to do to make herself useful.

It was a struggle to navigate the companionway, and a gust of wind snatched her first breath away, but the air on deck was a vast improvement over the stale air of her cabin.

The deck pitched beneath her feet. Overhead, clouds formed a black shroud. Huge gray waves rose from the sea like mountains, crashing with earthquake force over the bulwark onto the deck. The sails had been trimmed, but the ends of the wet canvas slapped against the masts, whose timbers creaked ominously. The fury of the storm was both magnificent and alarming.

Squinting against the rain, Maggie spied the captain. She covered half the distance between them before he noticed her. With rapid strides, he closed the gap.

"Didn't I send word all passengers were to remain in their cabins?" he shouted over the wind.

"Yes," Maggie shouted back. "But I thought there might be something I could do to help."

Both continued to converse with shouts to make themselves heard.

"There is! Go back to your cabin!"

"Something besides that!"

"No!" He grabbed her elbow to steady her as the ship rose on a wave. "Your cabin is the safest place on the ship for you!"

Cupping her hands around her mouth to amplify her voice, Maggie replied, "But I really do want to help!"

"I'm sure you do, but for once in your life be sensible. If you're blown overboard in this storm, no one will be able to save you. They will, however, be compelled to risk their own lives trying. Do you want the deaths of men you call your friends on your conscience?"

"No."

"I didn't think you would. Riley, escort Miss Danton back to her cabin," he directed his third mate. Maggie started to follow Mr. Riley, but her progress was momentarily halted by the captain's voice. "And Miss Danton, *stay there.*"

Back in her cabin, Maggie scolded herself for going on deck. Though her desire to help had been sincere, her desire to avoid thinking unsettling thoughts had been equally as great. It was wrong for her to put her own needs above the welfare of the crew.

She knew nothing about handling a ship, and the middle of a raging storm was not the time to take up the profession of sailor.

Pounce was now sleeping peacefully; for that she was grateful. Crossing the floor of the cabin with a drunkard's gait, Maggie held on to whatever was handy to keep herself upright. She peered through the porthole but could see nothing.

The trip on deck may have temporarily distracted her from one concern, but witnessing the force of the storm caused a new concern to afflict her. The wind and waves were just as capable of sweeping the captain overboard as her. What if something happened to him? Her heart constricted and her eyes filled with tears even as she assured herself of the captain's competence.

he man didn't make mistakes where the safety of his ship and ew were involved. He would see all of them through the storm.

Despite her assurances, Maggie could not prevent her imagiation from conjuring harrowing images of the drama being layed out above her head.

After changing into dry clothing, Maggie sat huddled on her unk, her knees drawn up under her chin. The ship careened om one side to the other, its bow rising to a dizzying angle, en crashing downward. The timbers of the *Guillemot* groaned nder the strain. Wind buffeted the ship in great howling gusts. he rain turned to hail, adding to the cacophony of nerve shatring sounds. Again and again, the savagery of the storm comelled her to clutch the frame of the bed to prevent herself from eing thrown off the bunk.

It seemed she sat for hours, and the longer she sat, the more gitated she became. She wasn't frightened, at least not for herelf. She was sheltered in her cabin. Her brother's account of is experience rounding the Horn told of a similarly fierce torm. It was the captain and crew for whom she was frightened. xposed to the full impact of the storm, they were the ones at eril. A mast could break or an unexpected wave wash over the eck and . . .

She stifled a scream of frustration. Sitting and fretting herself to a dither was not to be borne! She had to do something. She ould check on the other passengers to see how they were faring. here were less than ten steps between their cabins and hers. he rose to her feet, staggered her way to the door, then stopped. aptain Garrett had told her to stay in her cabin. No matter how reat the temptation, she would not disobey him without good ason. If one of the other passengers needed her, she would be ble to hear their call for assistance through the walls.

Returning to her bunk, Maggie tried to read. She tried to write her journal. In desperation, she even picked up the stitchery Irs. Kendall had given her. However, the world was too unstable

to allow for these or any other activity, and her lantern blew ov
so many times, she gave up relighting it.

Maggie had no idea how long she sat in her cabin. It wa
impossible to tell whether it was day or night. When she squinte
at her watch, she discovered she had forgotten to wind it.

The storm showed no sign of abating.

The ship rose and plunged down another enormous wave
Seconds later, Maggie heard a loud crack and a cry of pain. Th
sound came not from above her or beside her but from belov
She listened carefully to be certain her ears hadn't deceived he
The cry came again. This time she recognized the voice. It be
longed to Charley. He was calling for help.

Instantly, Maggie was on her feet and out the door. For
moment she paused in indecision, wondering if she should g
on deck to seek assistance or handle the matter herself. Sh
decided on the latter, reasoning the men on deck already ha
more than enough to do and that as long as she remained belov
deck she was in no danger of being swept overboard.

Stepping back inside her cabin, she relit her lantern an
stuffed the match tin in her pocket. Assuring Pounce she wou
be back in a few minutes, she set out to find Charley.

His cries for help continued, and Maggie used them as a bea
con to guide her down the companionways. Her lantern re
mained lit more often than it went dark and she was able t
utilize the walls of the passageways to brace herself against th
roil of the ship, but still her progress was maddeningly slow.

By the time she found Charley lying in the hold amongst th
cargo, a heavy piece of dunnage lying across one leg, Maggi
had fallen twice, filled her hands with countless splinters, an
bruised her right shoulder. However, her concern for Charley
injuries made her unaware of her own.

"Miss Danton, you shouldn't be here. The captain'll have you
hide . . ."

"Shush! I'll deal with the captain later. Right now my only concern is you."

Despite his pain, Charley grinned. "I think my leg is broke."

Gingerly examining his bloody leg, Maggie confirmed his suspicion. "You're right, it is." She sat back on her heels while she thought out a plan of action. "I'm going to get this board off you, wrap your leg so you don't lose any more blood, and make you as comfortable as possible. After that, I'm afraid I'll have to go for help. If I try to get you out of here by myself, likely I'll do your leg more harm than good."

"The board is too heavy," Charley warned. "If it weren't, I would've got it off myself."

"I'm stronger than I look. At least, I hope I am. In any case, we'll soon find out."

Charley nodded and closed his eyes. Maggie took in his pale complexion with a worried gaze and immediately set to work.

It took every ounce of her strength, but Maggie succeeded in lifting the heavy board high enough to clear his toes. She let out her breath in a whoosh of triumph.

Without pausing to catch her breath, she hefted her skirt and began tearing strips of cloth from her petticoat. When she had several strips ready, as gently as she could, she wrapped Charley's injured leg. He bit his bottom lip and a cold sweat broke out on his brow, but he didn't so much as whimper.

"You're a brave boy, Charley," she admired.

"Not half as brave as you," he whispered.

She brushed a lock of hair from his forehead. "Save your strength for your leg. You can turn my head with flattery when you're feeling better."

Even before she finished tying them in place, Maggie could see Charley's blood seeping through the first bandages. She stood to tear more strips of cloth.

In that same moment, the ship lurched sharply port side. Maggie was lifted off her feet and thrown violently backward. A deafening pop assaulted her ears as the back of her head hit a solid surface; then, she was surrounded by nothingness.

"I think we're in for a break in the storm, at least for an hour or two," Captain Garrett informed his steward. "Go below and see how our passengers have fared."

"Yes, sir."

A few minutes later the steward returned, a worried expression on his face. "They're all white as ghosts but otherwise fine, Captain. Except Miss Danton."

"Don't tell me. She is wearing a grin and deems this tempest great sport."

"No, sir. She's nowhere to be found."

"What!"

"She ain't in her cabin, sir. I asked the other passengers and none of them has seen her since early this morning."

The captain's face blanched. "Organize a search party! I want every man questioned and every inch of this ship combed and I want it done now!"

"I'm sure she'll turn up, Captain."

"So am I," Captain Garrett replied, refusing to let his voice waver from his lack of conviction. They had all been so busy battling the storm, she could have easily slipped back on deck and just as easily been swept overboard, her screams lost in the wail of the wind. He felt sick at the thought, but he forced himself to face the possibility.

The sickness spread to his limbs and seized his chest, making it difficult for him to breathe. Her death might be a possibility, but he didn't have to accept it until he had no other alternative. He *wouldn't* accept it. Stiffening his spine, he shouted, "I said *now*, Mr. Hiller!"

"Yes, sir."

Every hand who could be spared was enlisted in the search.

It wasn't long before they discovered that not only was Miss Danton missing but the cabin boy, Charley, as well.

Captain Garrett, who had given over command of the deck to his Mr. Taylor and joined the search from the beginning, grimly digested the news. "Where was the last place anyone saw him?"

"On deck," his steward supplied. "Knowing how he fears storms but ain't about to admit it, I sent him down to check the dunnage in the hold so he'd have a few private minutes to screw up his courage."

"Has anyone checked the hold?"

"Not yet."

"Then let's go!"

The sight that greeted him when he stepped into the hold caused both relief and agony to contort the captain's features. They were both here, but Miss Danton was slumped motionless against a wooden crate. Charley lay still as death, his leg crusted with blood.

Motioning Mr. Hiller to tend Charley, the captain rushed to Maggie's side. He pressed his hand to her chest.

"Thank God!" he exclaimed when he felt her heart still beating within her breast. The rush of elation was so overpowering it caused his entire body to tremble. He took a steadying breath, struggling to regain his composure. Laying his ear to her lips, he was further reassured when he found her breath shallow but consistent. He surveyed her from head to toe. At first he found no visible signs of injury, but a more thorough examination revealed a large knot on the back of her head.

It worried the captain that she didn't stir when he gently called her name and squeezed her shoulders, but for the moment the fact she was alive was enough.

He turned his attention to his cabin boy. "Is he . . ."

"No, he's still with us. His leg is broke, and he's lost a lot of blood, but I figure we can pull him through. He's a tough lad, ain't you, Charley?"

The sound of voices roused Charley back to consciousness. He blinked his eyes open. "Tell the captain it ain't her fault," he mumbled to Hiller. "It's my fault. She was only trying to—" Closing his eyes, he drifted back into darkness.

The captain glanced down at the face cradled in his lap. His mind was still giddy with relief she wasn't dead, but habit allowed him to seize command of the situation. "Let's get them out of here to someplace warm," he ordered.

Together Hiller and Captain Garrett immobilized Charley's leg with boards pried from a crate. The captain then returned to Maggie.

After a second check to be certain he hadn't overlooked some additional injury that might be worsened by moving her, he lifted her into his arms. "I'll let the others know they've been found and send someone down with a stretcher to help you move the boy. I want hourly reports on his condition."

"Yes, sir."

The captain's years at sea stood him in good stead as he carried his precious burden to his cabin. Carefully laying her on his bunk, he stripped off her damp clothing and bundled her in his blankets. As he did so, he couldn't help but notice the loveliness of her breasts and the alluring curve of her hips and thighs, but at the moment bedding her was the furthest thing from his mind. All he wanted was for her to awaken. He wanted to gaze into her mischievous green eyes while she offered some artful explanation for why she hadn't remained in her cabin as he had ordered.

She had not murmured so much as a sigh since he'd found her, and the longer she was silent the more it worried him. He had no idea how long she had been unconscious before he located her, and that worried him, too. Head injuries were unpredictable, but past experience told him the longer she remained unconscious, the less likely her recovery. She was too bright a candle to be snuffed out so soon.

"I order you not to die," he whispered in her ear as he tucked the blankets tighter. Straightening, he looked down on her, his face wrenching with dismay.

"You idiot," he cursed himself. "You know she never obeys your orders. She goes out of her way to disobey them. If you want her to recover, you should order her to die."

Though he embraced the logic of his reasoning, he couldn't bring himself to say the words. He didn't want her to die. He wanted her to live. He needed her to live.

His last thought gave him pause, but he didn't recoil from it. Popular wisdom said a man never appreciated what he had until he lost it. He was terrified he was about to learn that lesson firsthand.

Margaret Danton would make him a most unsuitable wife. They were polar opposites. She kept him so off-balance ofttimes he didn't know if he was standing on his feet or his head. But staring at the too still woman in his bed, he suddenly realized how much he would miss her company when she left his ship. Their daily battles kept his mind sharp; they made him see the world through different eyes. Life would be flat without her. Already the absence of her interminable chatter tortured him.

Against all reason he loved her. Even more startling, he loved her for all the reasons good sense told him he shouldn't.

The realization didn't bother him nearly as much as he thought it should. He was, after all, a rational man. Or at least he had been when he started this voyage.

If he married her, it would certainly solve the problem of his unbridled lust for her. A married man could lust after his wife without compunction. By bringing her to his cabin and disrobing her himself, he had compromised her, so she *had* to marry him. He started to smile at the prospect.

If she lived she had to marry him, he reminded himself.

For three days she lay on his bed like a sleeping angel, alive but her mind beyond his reach. Captain Garrett ignored every other duty and sat vigil by her side. He could rouse her enough to swallow when he spooned broth down her throat, but he could coax no other response from her. It killed him by inches to see her so still for so long. In anyone such stillness was unnatural, but with her it was doubly so.

He raked his fingers through his hair. He was exhausted. He knew he needed to sleep, and he had tried, but he couldn't.

The other passengers and his crew had given up hope, but he would not. As long as she was alive, there was hope. He had been practicing in his head what he would say to her when she awoke, practicing what he would say to convince her she should marry him. Leaning back in his chair, he closed his eyes. Practicing helped pass the time. . . . Practicing kept his hope alive. . . . His head fell against his chest and he dozed fitfully.

"Captain Garrett, you look dreadful. Surely, your crew can handle the storm while you rest yourself."

Captain Garrett stared at the woman in his bed. Her eyes were open and she was frowning at him.

"You're back!" he shouted for joy.

"Back from where?" Maggie asked, attempting to push herself to a sitting position. The captain was instantly at her side, slipping his arm around her shoulders to assist her. The blankets slid to her waist, and her gaze fell upon her arms and chest. They were clad in a man's shirt. Her eyes widened with consternation. "What is going on here? These aren't my cl—" Her gaze darted about the room, ". . . and this isn't my cabin."

He stroked her cheek. "I'll explain everything in due time. The important thing is you're back."

"Back from where?" she plaintively repeated.

"You've been unconscious for three days. I had begun to despair you would ever wake up, but you have." His lips stretched into a beaming smile. "I've been praying day and night you'd be too stubborn to die ."

She gaped at him. Her head did feel fuzzy, but . . . "How did I . . . ?"

"You fell and hit your head against a crate in the hold while you were rescuing—"

"Charley," Maggie supplied the name as her memory returned. "Is he all right? I hadn't finished bandaging him when—"

"You bandaged him well enough he didn't bleed to death before we found him. He's still weak, and he won't be walking without crutches for a long time, but there's no reason to believe he won't fully recover."

"Pounce?" Anxiety suffused her voice.

"Mr. Bews has been feeding her."

She immediately relaxed, but continued to question him. "The storm?"

"It's over."

"So is Christmas Day, isn't it?"

He nodded.

Maggie pursed her lips. "I never had a chance to give you your gift, and I did so want to make the day special for you. I'm sorry I disobeyed your orders and spoiled it."

"Don't be. If you hadn't disobeyed me, I doubt Charley would still be alive. As for my gift, the moment you opened your eyes, you gave me the best Christmas present I could ever hope to receive."

She fell silent, leaning against his arm, as if satisfied to absorb the information he had given her. Abruptly, she lifted her head and stared into his eyes. "How did you say I got into this shirt?"

"I didn't say."

"Tell me."

"I put you in it."

"You, not Mrs. Kendall?"

"Me," he confirmed. "When she discovered what I had done,

Mrs. Kendall fussed and fumed, but I insisted she leave you to me."

Maggie blushed, bringing much needed color to her cheeks. The fuzziness in her head had completely cleared. She skewered him with a jaundice eye. "What else have you done to me while I was unable to defend myself?"

"Held your hand, brushed your hair, decided to marry you."

Wondering if she still might be suffering the effects of her injury after all, she peered at him. "You decided what?"

"I decided I want to marry you," he responded.

"Why on earth would you want to do that?"

Nervousness caused the romantic speech he had rehearsed to fly from his head. He seized upon the practical reasons that entered in its stead. "What does it matter? I have seen you naked. Even if I hadn't, the mere fact you have lain in my bunk in my cabin these past three days has compromised your reputation beyond repair."

"Ah, for my reputation's sake you are willing to sacrifice yourself." Abandoning the support he provided, Maggie scooted an arm's length away. She threw him a sulky look. "I should have known. You are a man who always does his duty."

"Duty has nothing to do with why I want to marry you. It is just a convenient circumstance that allows me to compel *you* into marrying *me*."

"What makes you think I need to be compelled?"

"I am not an easy man to live with," he stoically stated.

"That is true."

"Regardless, you have to marry me."

"I don't *have* to do anything I don't want to do, and you have yet to give me a good reason to marry you."

His eyes begged for compassion. "I can't give you a good reason. Reason says my desire to marry you is absurd. You have never shown any affinity for reason before. Why require it now?"

The corners of Maggie's lips twitched. She turned her head so the captain wouldn't see. "You do not plead for my hand very prettily, Captain Garrett."

"Nathan, I would like you to start calling me Nathan. And I am sorry I cannot woo you with poetic phrases, but I have no experience with such things, which is all the more reason you should marry me. Did you not promise to save me from my drab existence?"

Feigning reluctance, Maggie admitted, "Yes."

"And I intend to hold you to your promise. I need you. Would you desert a man in his hour of need?"

"Marriage lasts more than an hour. Marriage lasts a lifetime."

"Is there nothing I can say to convince you?" he beseeched.

"I require only three words."

"You are asking me to tell you I love you? If that is all it will take, I will say the words a hundred times over."

The poor man sounded so desperate, Maggie relented, "Once will suffice, thank you, but the words must come from your heart not your head."

"I love you, Margaret Danton."

"Madly? You will recall I require the man I marry to be madly in love with me."

"Yes, madly."

She smiled at him. "I believe you."

"Then it's settled. We will put into port at Talcahuano and be married."

She took his hand. "Don't you want me to tell you I love you?"

"I know you do not, but I am hoping over the years I can earn your love."

"You know, Captain Garrett . . ."

"Nathan," he corrected.

"Nathan," she amiably amended. "You really are the most arrogant of men, either that or you think me some kind of saint, which I hope isn't true, because I'm not. Do you really think I would sacrifice my future for a man I didn't love? You're the one with a exaggerated sense of responsibility, not me."

His brows knit. "You love me?"

"Of course I do."

"You're sure this isn't the bump on your head speaking?"

"I'm perfectly lucid."

Pulling his hand from hers, he folded his arms across his chest. "Then why didn't you immediately accept my proposal of marriage?"

Maggie laughed at his affronted expression. "First, because you took me by surprise; then, because I couldn't resist the opportunity to twit you."

"I should have known."

"You'll learn," she assured him.

"With you as my teacher, I'm sure I will learn far more than I bargained."

"Already having second thoughts?"

"Never," he proclaimed.

Gathering Maggie in his arms, Captain Garrett pulled her against his heart and kissed her with such passion and promise she knew they were destined for more joy than her heart could hold. Making the stiff-necked captain of the *Guillemot* her Christmas project had been divine inspiration.

She could hardly wait to begin the adventure.

Apache Snow

by
Doreen Owens Malek

Oklahoma Territory
December 1875

Rachel Worthington looked out the side window of the coach as its wheels hit a rut and the vehicle jolted forward, almost pitching her out of her seat. She grabbed her spoon bonnet and resettled her reticule in her lap, thinking that she should not have worn her new outfit for the last leg of the trip home from St. Louis. She had wanted to look nice in case Jesse saw her when she arrived. But the train ride from St. Louis to Oklahoma City had been a summer holiday by comparison with the subsequent dangerous stagecoach journey across Indian country that had brought her to Fort Broward. As the huge wooden gate in the wall surrounding the fort opened to admit the stage, the other two passengers with her smiled at Rachel and each other. They had made it.

One man was going south to Texas and the other was going farther west to Denver. Only Rachel was remaining at the fort for Christmas.

She peered out the isinglass window at the combination post office and stage depot as the coach lurched to a stop. She saw her friend Mary Turner waving to her excitedly. The stage driver jumped down from his seat above the horses and came around to stand on the running board and open the passenger doors.

"Rachel!" Mary called, jumping up and down as Rachel alighted from the coach. "Welcome home!"

Rachel rushed to embrace her friend as the driver tossed assorted luggage down from the top of the coach. Her trunk landed with a thud behind her as Mary smothered her in a hug, then held her off to look at her.

"Oh, you look just fine! Gotten even prettier, if that's possible. And your traveling costume is so becoming. You have to tell me all about St. Louis, I can't wait to hear, it's been so dull here without you I thought I was just going to die!"

Mary's father was a colonel in the cavalry and she had been living at Fort Broward for over four years.

"Come inside before we both catch our death of cold," Mary added.

The two women went through the station door as Rachel straightened the bow at the neck of her cloak and tucked a few loose strands of hair back into her chignon. She glanced around the warm station covertly, all the while smiling back at Mary. Except for the postmaster in his eye shade and gartered sleeves composing a telegram, the place was empty, the dusty floor-boards bare and dully reflecting the glow of the potbellied stove standing in the middle of the room

"Is Jesse here?" she finally said in an undertone to Mary, the need to know overcoming the conventions of small talk.

Mary glanced meaningfully over her shoulder at Charlie Sedge, who looked up at the women and smiled.

"Hello, Rachel," the postmaster said. "Your father will be so glad to see you. He said to leave your trunk here and he'll be in to fetch it when he gets back from Haven Springs."

"Thanks, Charlie. Merry Christmas."

"Jesse hasn't been seen here since October," Mary whispered, taking Rachel's arm and steering her away from Charlie, who thought it was part of his job to disseminate gossip.

Rachel turned pale. "Jesse hasn't been around for over two months?" she said.

Mary shook her head.

"Well, where is he?"

"Nobody knows."

"I'm leaving, Miss Worthington," the stagecoach driver said, opening the station door and sticking his head in through it. "The horses are in the stable and your trunk's out back with the deliveries."

Rachel managed to nod and smile. "Thank you, Mr. Hastings. You're a very efficient driver."

"Well, no Injuns this time out, that always makes for a safe trip. Arapahos are quiet, even the Blackfeet haven't been stirring up trouble. Must be the weather, there's a big snow coming. They always know before we do. Well, good afternoon ladies, I'm off to wet my whistle at the Copper Pot." He tipped his hat, pulled up the collar of his sheepskin jacket and stomped off the porch in front of the post office. Rachel waited until he had gone a good distance toward the tavern with her two fellow passengers, then tugged Mary back outside with her urgently.

"Has something happened to Jesse?" she hissed.

Mary shrugged.

"He always stops off at the fort when he brings the wagon trains through to Texas. Has he ever been away so long before this fall?"

"Rachel, I don't know, I never paid attention. All I can tell you is that he showed up in October. He asked where you were, I told him you had gone to St. Louis for school in September, and that was the last I saw of him. Do we absolutely have to have this conversation out here? I'm freezing; my feet are like ice. Let's go to your house. Your father said he won't be back until late tonight but Mattie would leave a cold supper for you."

"All right. Let's go."

The two young women hurried down the dirt-packed main street of the fort, heading for the Worthington house on the last corner near the sentry stand, at the opposite end of the thorough-fare from the church. Rachel's father was a circuit-riding doctor who traveled to the U.S. cavalry installations in the surrounding

Indian country and was gone for a day or two, or a week, or a month at a time. He had taken the job when his wife died back East, wanting to give his bereft daughter a change of scene and a new start. Rachel had come out to Oklahoma from their former home in Hartford, Connecticut, during the previous spring, three months after her father's arrival. But she had only been there one short summer before her father decided to send her away to school.

The reason for that decision was Jesse Kincaid.

Rachel and Mary entered the doctor's quarters from the shared boardwalk that fronted all the fort's homes. The walk served as a protection against the rains that flooded the Washita River Valley every spring and turned the streets into mud, against the dust that blew incessantly during the dry summers, and against the ice that formed in sheets during the bitter winters. Dr. Worthington's door was not locked; nobody at the fort had anything worth stealing.

Once inside, Rachel took Mary's cloak and hung it on the clothes tree which stood inside her father's door. Then Rachel untied her green silk bonnet and took off her own brown-and-green tweed traveling cloak. Underneath the cape she wore a dark-brown silk afternoon dress with an apron front and a full bustle, draped up below the waist in the front to show a floral lining of apple green and sable. The underskirt of copper silk was fringed and pleated, and Cluny lace showed at the high neckline and at the ends of the sleeves.

"What a beautiful dress!" Mary said, impressed.

"It should be," Rachel replied. "It cost me every penny of the allowance my father sent me while I was at school. I saved it up and bought this before I left St. Louis." She went over to the cast iron stove and shook the kettle to see if it was filled with water, then bent down to check if the firebox was full. It was. Mattie, the day worker who had taken over Rachel's chores while she was away at school, had proven to be very dependable.

Rachel lit the dry kindling under the small pile of coal with one of the cordite matches her father kept handy for the purpose. "We'll have a pot of tea as soon as this boils."

"Somehow I don't think you're wearing that dress for me," Mary said dryly, sitting at the scrubbed deal table.

Rachel closed her eyes. "I know what happened, Mary. When you told him I had gone to St. Louis he thought that I went voluntarily. He assumed last summer meant nothing to me, maybe even that I thought better of the whole thing and was trying to get away from him. He won't come back here, I just know it." She covered her face with her hands.

Mary got up and touched her shoulder comfortingly. "Rachel, I meant to explain to Jesse that your father packed you off to that school, that you didn't want to go, but my mother saw me talking to him and came running over to drag me away. I didn't get to tell him the whole story, and after that day he didn't come back again. I tried to do as you asked. I'm sorry."

"It's not your fault," Rachel said, sighing. "If anyone is to blame for this, it's my father. He wanted to separate Jesse and me and it looks like he's done it." Her tone was hard.

"Why didn't you leave a letter for Jesse?"

"I promised my father I wouldn't communicate with him. He said he would make trouble for Jesse if I didn't just go off to school without a word."

"What kind of trouble?"

Rachel shrugged wearily. "Who knows? I wasn't going to find out. People around here are only too willing to think the worst of a half-breed."

"People already knew you were spending a lot of time with Jesse while your father was away last summer. It wasn't exactly a secret."

"That was precisely the problem. I was 'making a spectacle of myself,' according to my dad. That's an exact quote." Rachel removed the checkered napkin from a plate on the shelf above

the stove and carried it to the table. It contained strips of beef
jerky, a cornbread biscuit, and two cold slices of ham. Mary sat
again in the rocking chair by the window as Rachel picked up
the biscuit and nibbled at it desultorily.

"Don't look so sad, Ray. Maybe he'll come back here for
Christmas," Mary said.

Rachel shook her head. "I don't know. I don't think the holidays mean much to him, since he has no family. After his father
was killed and his mother died of smallpox, he wound up in an
orphanage run by French nuns. He hardly remembers his parents, much less happy Yuletide gatherings."

"Where was he from?" Mary asked curiously. "You never
told me."

"I don't know that much myself, he never talked about his
past. I got some information from one of the other scouts who
came through here last August. He said that Jesse was born in
the Arizona mountains. His mother was an Athapaskan traded
to his father, an Irish fur trapper, because she had been raped
by another white man and was considered unsuitable for an
Apache husband."

Mary was silent a long moment, then said, "Half-breeds have
a hard life."

"The good people of this fort treated him like he was a dangerous animal who had to be watched, even though he guided
half the wagon trains bringing them here. And now he thinks
I'm one of them. No wonder he's keeping his distance." Rachel
brooded, chewing without enthusiasm as she looked around at
the furnishings her father had brought all the way from Hartford:
her mother's pine hutch, the rocking chair in which Mary sat,
the wicker-patterned dishes and other homely items filling the
single main room. It served as kitchen, living room, and dining
area. The rest of the flat consisted of two bedrooms off a back
hall and a tiny keeping pantry behind the stove.

It wasn't much, but by Fort Broward standards it was luxurious. Most apartments had only one bedroom, and the main room was much smaller. The rent of this place had been thrown in free along with Rachel's father's substantial salary; both were paid by the U.S. Cavalry.

It was difficult to lure qualified medical people away from eastern cities to the Indian frontier, and the offer had to be made as attractive as possible to get Dr. Worthington to come west from Connecticut.

"You were going to tell me about St. Louis," Mary reminded Rachel.

"I didn't see it. I told you that in my letters."

"You were *there,* Rachel Worthington. You must have seen something."

"The school was a very strict ladies' academy, a finishing school where we were supervised at all times, even when we were sleeping. It was on five acres out in the country, a forty-minute coach ride from the city. I only went there twice, on supervised shopping trips. If you're expecting a tale of scarlet sin I fear you are going to be severely disappointed." Rachel dropped the biscuit she'd been gnawing, examined a slice of fatty ham with distaste, then pushed the plate away from her.

"It had to be more exciting than Fort Broward. The only event that livens things up around here is an Indian attack," Mary said, rolling her eyes.

"I would have preferred to be here, believe me. At least I could have talked to you. My classmates at Briarview were all eastern snobs from wealthy families who thought Fort Broward was the back of the beyond. They kept asking me if I knew any red Indians, like I was having Sunday dinner with them."

Mary chuckled. "We all thought *you* were an eastern snob when you first came here. Your father had talked about like you were Queen Victoria."

"I imagine that's who he wants me to be," Rachel said sadly. The kettle began to hiss and she rose to make the tea, shaking the leaves into the strainer, then letting them steep. When it was ready she handed Mary a cup; they both drank it straight, since there was rarely enough milk or sugar available at the fort to waste those precious items flavoring tea.

Early winter darkness was falling; Rachel bent to light the oil lamp on the table. Mary glanced toward the window. "I guess I'd better be going home as soon as I finish this. My mother will want me to help her get dinner."

Rachel nodded.

"I hate to leave you like this," Mary said. "I know you're upset about Jesse."

Rachel shrugged. "I'll be all right. I'll just go to bed early. I'm exhausted from the trip anyway."

"When do you have to be back at the school?"

"February first. I'll be here for over a month."

Mary put her cup on the window ledge and rose to embrace Rachel. "It will be fun having you here. Cheer up, we'll have some good times. And maybe Jesse will come back."

Rachel nodded, managing a smile as Mary picked up her cape and draped it around her shoulders.

"I'll be over to see you in the morning," Mary said, opening the door to the street and shuddering as a gust of wind blew back her clothes. "It's getting really cold," she added. "I'm going to run home. Good night!"

"Good night," Rachel replied, pulling the door closed behind her. Mary lived only a few doors away and Rachel watched her progress through the front window. There was no one else abroad on the dark winter street, but Rachel knew that an occasional renegade Indian, in desperate search of food or supplies, occasionally slipped into the fort and might dispatch anyone he encountered. When Mary was safely inside her house, Rachel went to the stone fireplace which shared a flue with the stove. She lit the fire which had been laid there with the flame from the oil lamp and then dragged the rocking chair over to the hearth to sit in front of the growing blaze. On cold nights the warmth from the stove was not enough to drive off the penetrating chill, and she and her father took turns feeding the fire. She stared into the flames and thought back to the previous summer, when she had met Jesse Kincaid.

The Blackfeet were on the warpath and the Indian raids prevented the wagon trains from running, so Jesse had stayed at the Broward boardinghouse for a couple of months. He took his meals in the cafe there and helped out at the stables, shoeing and exercising the horses until he could begin scouting again. Rachel had heard stories about the half-breed scout but never met him. Then one day when her father was away in Kansas she decided that she should learn to ride a horse. Jesse spotted her fumbling efforts and offered to give her lessons. Half fearful, half intrigued, powerfully attracted to the intense, long-haired loner with the pale-blue eyes, Rachel accepted. By the time her father returned to the fort, she was hopelessly in love with Jesse Kincaid.

Rachel didn't realize she was crying until a tear ran into her mouth. She brushed at her cheeks impatiently, blinking, recalling the strength of Jesse's hands as he lifted her into the saddle, the white flash of his teeth when he smiled, the tender look in his light eyes, so brilliant in his tanned face as he gazed down at her. They didn't know him, any of them, not her father who had called him a "buckskin savage," not the townspeople who whispered about his "squaw" mother and "trashy" father behind his back. Jesse had only kissed her once, that day in the stables when her father had come to fetch her and found her locked in the scout's embrace. But she felt the touch of his lips still, light at first, then pressing hers with a growing demand until her father had grabbed her by the shoulders and pulled her away, shouting with rage. She saw again the stony look on Jesse's face as Dr. Worthington dragged Rachel out of the stables, muttering imprecations under his breath.

It was the last time she saw Jesse. They'd been saying goodbye because the Indian raids had stopped and he was leaving with a wagon train the next day. Dr. Worthington waited until he was gone and then enrolled Rachel at Briarview for the fall term. She had no way of telling Jesse that she would not be there when he returned to see her, as he'd promised. She'd spent the four months in St. Louis living on memories and waiting for the day when she would come back to Fort Broward and see Jesse again.

Now it seemed that wait had been in vain.

Rachel got up from the rocking chair and carried the oil lamp into her bedroom, a plain cell which contained a bed, a dresser, and her grandmother's maple chifforobe. Rachel had made the curtains hanging on the single window facing the street, and she had stitched a quilt in colors to match them. She opened the chifforobe and saw that Mattie had hung one of her old night-gowns on a peg for her. Rachel undressed, going through the motions of removing dress and corset and crinoline, stockings and high-button shoes, draping her things on a chair and then slipping into the muslin nightgown, tying it at the neck. She went back into the other room to fetch two loose bricks kept on the hearth to warm there. She wrapped the bricks in flannel cloths and carried them to her bed, placing them at her feet and then slipping inside the cold sheets, drawing the patchwork quilt up to her neck. She shivered until the heat became trapped under the covers and engulfed her, and then she swam in a dreamy lassitude, remembering her summer romance with Jesse.

What if she never saw him again?

Rachel awoke in the morning to find that her father had returned during the night. She made breakfast for the two of them, since Mattie had been dismissed for the duration of Rachel's visit, and then endured a tense discussion of her grades at Briarview. She had come back to Fort Broward with a handwritten report card signed by Headmistress Madsen. This document indicated that while Rachel Worthington was certainly bright enough, even exceptional in English Usage and Applied Mathematics, she was sorely lacking in something called "Ladies' Deportment" (this meant Rachel had argued with Miss Durand, the Home Skills teacher, about the necessity of memorizing the correct placement of butter knives). Miss Madsen had also added a cautionary word in the space labeled "Other Comments," indicating that Rachel "took direction poorly" and "lacked the impetus for social interaction." This provoked a lecture from Dr. Worthington on Rachel's uncooperative attitude, willful behavior, and determination not to fit in at one of the finest finishing schools in the country.

"I don't understand you, Rachel," Dr. Worthington said, patting the knot of his four-in-hand tie. "You are refusing to take advantage of an opportunity not offered to many young women of your age. I should think you would be grateful and try to absorb some lessons, as well as make some friends." He smoothed the lapels of his black frock coat and then picked up his medical bag.

"I didn't want to go there in the first place," Rachel said quietly. "I didn't feel like socializing."

"You could make the best of the situation nevertheless," he said frostily. "No chance to learn should be wasted."

"I might be interested in learning if they taught anything worthwhile there," Rachel shot back. "I'm sorry to say it, Father, but the most effective way to polish a cut wineglass is not a subject of endless fascination for me. I don't polish too many wineglasses around here."

"You will need to know these things to please your future husband," her father replied. "The efficient running of a well-kept home is important to a successful man."

Rachel said nothing. They'd had this conversation before, and it never went anywhere.

"I'm going back to Haven Springs for the day," Dr. Worthington said. "I should return in time for supper."

Rachel nodded.

"What do you have planned for the day?" Dr. Worthington asked, opening the door.

"Just washing the clothes I brought back from school. And I thought I might go down to Jenkins's and see if they have any of those little Christmas trees people have been putting up in their houses. It might be fun to have one."

"Barbaric German custom," her father said shortly, and left, pulling the door shut after him.

Rachel sighed as she began to clear away the breakfast dishes. She had looked forward to coming home so much, but without Jesse, the prospect of a month in her father's censorious company loomed like a sentence of doom. After Mary's visit, she occupied herself sorting out the trunk her father had retrieved from the depot early that morning. By the time she had brought water from the well, fighting the wind and cold all the way, then heated the water on the stove, then scrubbed her chemises and shirtwaists on the washboard with brown soap, *then* rinsed them and hung them up to dry by the fire, she was ready for a break.

She went into her bedroom and studied herself in the dresser's mirror as she brushed out her long black hair and then pinned it up in a loose knot. She decided that her gingham dress was good enough for a trip to the general store; the pink-and-white checks brought color to her cheeks and sparkle to her almond-shaped brown eyes. She draped her everyday dark-blue cloak about her shoulders, tying its navy grosgrain ribbon at her neck, and fastened a flat gypsy bonnet trimmed with lace around its crown to her hair. Then she went out to the main room to tamp down the fire; she would rebuild it when she returned. She picked up her gloves and reticule as she went out the door.

The cold had kept most people indoors, but those who were abroad hurried along with their heads down, nodding to Rachel briefly as they passed. The sun was bright but offered no warmth as Rachel walked down the main street, which was really the *only* street, since the passages that gave off it leading to side dwellings were merely alleys. She passed the livery stable with Dr. Worthington's office above it, the combination post office and depot, Mrs. Curtin's millinery shop, the U.S. Cavalry installation flying the American flag, the boardinghouse run by Mrs. Hanely, the Copper Pot and the dressmaker's and the carpenter's. Mr. Jenkins's general store was at the end of the street on the right, just before the nondenominational Protestant church. The bell on the door rang cheerfully as she entered, and Mr. Jenkins looked up inquiringly from sorting bags of coffee.

"Well, Rachel Worthington, I heard that you were home. How was St. Louis?"

"Big," Rachel said.

Mr. Jenkins chuckled as several of the matrons shopping in the store glanced over at her curiously.

"How did you like that school?" he asked.

Rachel shrugged. "It was a change, I guess."

"Going back there?"

"In February."

"None too soon," Mrs. Tewksbury whispered waspishly to Mrs. Hutsall, who nodded.

"What's that, Mrs. Tewksbury?" Mr. Jenkins said, looking over at the two middle-aged women, who were lingering near the sacks of dried rice.

"I was just wondering if you had any hard tack," Mrs. Tewksbury said quickly.

"Over by the sourballs and licorice whips, same place it always was and always is," he replied, and the women turned to look at the storage bins, their heads together.

"Now, what can I do for you, Rachel?" Mr. Jenkins said innocently. He winked at Rachel and she smiled.

"Mary Turner told me this morning that your son George

went out into the woods and cut down some little firs for Christmas trees," she said. "I'd like to buy one."

"Sure enough," Mr. Jenkins replied, beaming. "That custom really looks like it's catching on, doesn't it? The Queen of England got the habit from her husband, Prince Albert, and it looks like we have to do everything the Brits do. Well, I'm not complaining, it's good for business. I got a stack of trees out back. What size?"

"Oh, about this high," Rachel said, holding her hand out at her waist.

"Good enough. Just you wait here. I'll be right back with it." Jenkins left the store to go out to his shed. Rachel remained to look around the big room, at the garlands strung from the bare rafters in honor of the season, at the floor-to-ceiling shelves stacked with shirts and hats and gloves and rolls of yard goods, at the bins that lined the floor filled with sacks of beans and tobacco and rice and coffee. The weighing scales stood on the counter next to Mr. Jenkins's cash box. She wandered over to look at several yards of calico marked down for a sale, and when she turned back to the store, Mrs. Tewksbury was standing right behind her.

"Welcome home, Rachel," the older woman said.

"Thank you."

"We were all surprised when you left for school so abruptly," she added.

In a pig's eye, Rachel thought. Mrs. Tewksbury knew every detail of the reason for Rachel's departure; she and her cohort Mrs. Hutsall had cast a disapproving eye on her relationship with Jesse and had not been shy about letting everyone know it. Rachel noticed that this little interchange was acquiring an audience. Mrs. Hutsall was watching from a few yards away and three or four of the other women were looking in Rachel's direction.

"It wasn't abrupt, Mrs. Tewksbury," Rachel said smoothly.

"My father had been planning to send me to school in St. Louis for some time."

This was a bald-faced lie, and they both knew it. Mrs. Tewksbury had the choice of challenging Rachel or letting it pass. Rachel guessed that Mrs. Tewksbury, like most bullies, was at heart a coward, and expected her to let it pass.

She did. She stared hard at Rachel and then opted for a parting shot. "You must be so happy to be back at home with your father," she said sweetly.

"Yes, I have so many fond memories of Fort Broward," Rachel replied, and walked away, leaving the old harpy to make what she could of that.

Mr. Jenkins returned carrying a three-foot balsam sapling, its base still running with sap. As Rachel watched he wrapped its stem in burlap and tied the bundle closed.

"Here you go," he said. "Fresh cut this morning."

"You decorate it?" Rachel asked.

"Yup. My wife did up our first one last year. She draped it with pinecones and strings of berries and popped corn . . ."

"Popped corn?" Rachel said, laughing.

"Yes, yes, you should ask her, she'll tell you all about it. We had a great time. You can make any decorations you like, really. Some people put candles in the branches, but that can be dangerous because the branches can catch fire as the tree dries out. I understand that in the big cities they're making ornaments of crystal and silk and other expensive materials just to hang on the trees."

"All right, Mr. Jenkins, you've convinced me. I'll take it. How much?"

He pondered the question, then smiled. "For you, it's free. Think of it as a welcome-home present." His grin widened. "I never could resist a pretty girl."

Rachel smiled back, holding out her hand. "Oh, you don't

have to carry it back," he said. "I'll have George bring it over to your place later. You might get sap on your clothes."

"Thanks, Mr. Jenkins," Rachel said as the matrons turned away, satisfied that she was leaving.

"Don't pay any mind to those poisonous old biddies," Mr. Jenkins whispered conspiratorially, leaning across the counter. "They're just jealous of a frisky young filly."

Rachel bit her lip and nodded, touched.

She turned and took two steps toward the door, then stopped short as it opened and Jesse Kincaid came into the store.

Rachel felt as if her stomach were plummeting toward her toes. A hush seemed to fall over the store; she could sense that behind her, everyone was transfixed, waiting for the coming scene.

For a moment Jesse didn't see her, and she got a good look at the man she had so longed to see all the while she was gone.

Jesse was dressed in a fringed buckskin jacket and leggings, his light-brown hair shot through with blond highlights from the sun. His tan had faded, but his blue eyes were still arresting as his gaze roamed casually around the shop, then came to rest on Rachel's face.

He didn't move, but she saw the impact of her presence in the way his expression changed. He looked at her a long moment, and then walked past her, going over to the counter and asking Mr. Jenkins for a tin of tobacco.

Rachel watched as Jesse paid for the purchase and walked back out of the store. Her audience forgotten, she dashed out after him and grabbed his arm.

"Jesse!" she said, hanging on to him and preventing him from crossing the street.

He turned to look at her.

"Aren't you even going to say hello to me?"

He shrugged slightly. "Hello."

"Is that all you have to say?"

"What else is there to say?" His beautiful eyes were as cold as a mountain stream high in the Sierra Nevadas.

"We haven't seen each other for four months!"

"So?" He stared down at her, the legacy of his Irish father in his features and coloring, the contribution of his Apache mother in his lean body and lithe carriage.

"So, over the summer I thought that . . ." she stopped, trailing off in confusion.

"You thought what?"

"That we were . . ."

He waited.

"That last day, you kissed me!" she blurted out, unable to stop herself.

"I've kissed lots of girls all over this territory," he said, his face expressionless. "I wouldn't attach too much importance to that if I were you."

Rachel stared up at him, her eyes filling with tears. She gasped and put her hand to her mouth and ran past him blindly, oblivious to the clutch of women standing at the windows of Jenkins's general store, watching the encounter intently.

Jesse looked after her, his face set, and then walked off in the other direction, heading for the Copper Pot.

Rachel did not know how she made it back to her house that day, or through the miserable days that followed. She saw Jesse several times around the fort, and caught him watching her on more than one occasion, but they never spoke again. She went through the motions of decorating the tree she had bought and getting ready for Christmas, but her heart was not in it. As she put the finishing touches on the socks she was knitting for her father and the handkerchiefs she was embroidering for Mary, as she baked trays of cookies and iced ginger cakes, the memory of her encounter with Jesse drove her to tears more than once.

She didn't even get a chance to tell him that her father had forced her into going away to school; Jesse had made it clear that she was nothing special to him, so why would he care? But still she looked for him everywhere she went. She knew he must be staying at the boardinghouse and she had to stop herself from passing by there too often. She had some pride left. Everyone must know by now that he had snubbed her and she'd made a fool of herself chasing after him into the street, but she didn't have to add to her humiliation by lurking in his shadow, hoping for a glance in her direction.

Rachel was making the stuffing for the turkey dinner she had planned for the next day when a knock sounded at her door the afternoon of Christmas Eve.

"Come in," she called.

Her door opened and Mary blew in, dropping her hood and pulling the door closed quickly behind her.

"It smells like snow out there," Mary said, removing her cloak and hanging it up carelessly. "There's a storm coming for sure." She went over to the fire and held her hands out to its warmth.

"Everyone's been saying that since I got back here, but I haven't seen one flake."

"When the sky is blue-white like it's been, you know it's going to storm," Mary said.

"You sound like . . ." Rachel stopped.

"Like who?"

"I was going to say that you sound like Jesse, but I promised myself I wasn't going to talk about him."

"You haven't seen him?"

"Oh, sure, I've seen him. I've seen him from a distance walking into the livery stable, I've seen him through the window of the boardinghouse sitting at a table and eating a plate of ham and eggs, I've seen him coming out of the Copper Pot with two of his trail drivers." She could not disguise the bitter tone of her voice.

"Ray, don't," Mary said softly.

"How could I have been so stupid?" Rachel asked, covering the mixing bowl with a cloth and setting the bowl on a shelf. 'He thought of me as a casual summer toy to play with and forget, a silly teenager with a crush, and there I was, sitting up in St. Louis for four endless months, planning my whole future around him. I feel like the world's biggest idiot."

Mary stood staring somberly at the flames for a long moment and then brightened. "I know what you need. Why don't you come with me to the dance at the church tonight?"

Rachel looked at her in amazement, mouth agape. "Are you kidding, Mary? That's the last thing I need, all those evil women shaking their heads over me and saying, 'There's Dr. Worthington's girl, what a shame. She completely lost her head over that Indian scout and he wants nothing at all to do with her.' I can just picture it. No, thank you."

Mary looked down at her hands. "Of course, if you want everybody to think you're hiding out here, too embarrassed to show your face . . ." She let the sentence dangle tantalizingly.

Rachel gazed at her friend with narrowed eyes. "That won't work, Mary. I'm staying home."

Mary came over to her and seized her hands. "Oh, come on. What are you going to do? Sit here all alone and feel sorry for yourself? Your father's not going to be home until late and you have that beautiful dress that no one has even seen. It's Christmas! Don't you want to have a good time?"

"I won't have a good time," Rachel said darkly.

"How do you know unless you go?"

"What if Jesse is there?" Rachel countered.

"At a church dance? Are you serious?"

Rachel thought it over; she guessed it *was* unlikely.

"Let's get the dress," Mary said, sensing that Rachel was weakening.

"I don't know how I let you talk me into this," Rachel said

as they went into her room and lifted her new silk gown from the chifforobe.

"Look, you can remove this lace at the neck. It's just a fichu that buttons in, so you can lower the neckline for evening wear," Mary said delightedly.

"I know, Mary. I bought the dress."

"Well, come on, change into it. Then we can stop off at my house and have dinner before I get ready."

Rachel hesitated.

"Rachel, don't you want to see the look on Mrs. Tewksbury's face when you come sailing in wearing this ensemble?" Mary asked archly.

Rachel shook her head resignedly and began to unbutton her shirtwaist with nimble fingers.

"That's the spirit," Mary said, assisting in the transformation as Rachel dressed, put up her hair, and added her mother's pearl necklace and earrings to create the final effect.

"You look lovely," Mary said, nodding approvingly.

"One more thing." Rachel opened the top drawer of her dresser and removed from it the reticule she had brought back from St. Louis. From the depths of the drawstring purse she extracted a small crystal vial with a fluted stopper.

"What's that?" Mary asked.

"Je Reviens from the House of Worth, Paris. There's nothing to boost the confidence like a drop of French perfume."

"Did you get that in St Louis?"

Rachel nodded. "One of the other girls in my dormitory always smelled so nice, and I finally asked her what she was wearing. She told me and I looked for it at Famous Barr's. This little bit cost me half what the dress did." She dabbed the scent on the pulse points of her wrists and temples.

Mary whistled appreciatively.

"Well, I guess I'm ready." Rachel replaced the perfume in her drawer and hung the reticule on her wrist. She picked up the

oak which matched the dress and the two of them left her
om.

"I'd better bank the fire and leave a note for my father before
e go," Rachel said.

Mary went to the window and looked out as Rachel rustled
ound behind her.

"What did I tell you?" she said. "It's snowing."

Rachel left the oil lamp burning low and joined Mary at the
indow.

"It's so beautiful, isn't it?" Rachel said softly.

"It's only beautiful in the beginning," said Mary, the veteran
several punishing Oklahoma winters. "When it gets deep and
e supply wagons can't get through so there's nothing in
nkins's store but sacks of dried beans and nothing to eat but
ardtack, your opinion will change. By the spring you'll be hop-
g never to see snow again."

"So for tonight I'll enjoy it," Rachel said, closing her door
hind them and then turning up her face for the touch of the
et flakes against her skin. She closed her eyes and felt the
oth's wings against her eyelashes.

"My mother will be happy I'm bringing you over for dinner,"
ary said. "She keeps asking me to invite you and your father
er to our place for Sunday lunch, but I've been telling her that
's always away working."

"Thanks, Mary. I don't need him holding forth to anybody
se on what a stubborn and ungrateful brat I am. It's bad enough
aving to listen to it myself."

"I think he's talked to my mother about you already," Mary
id, wincing.

"Wonderful. Next he'll be collaring perfect strangers in the
reet to discuss my foibles."

"There are no strangers in Fort Broward, we're all in each
her's pots. But I understand why he needs advice. I think he's
st worried, Ray," Mary said as they passed a house and the

warm glow of a lamp spilled across their path. Darkness wa
already falling and shapes were merging with shadows, but fro
the church at the extreme end of the street they could hear th
dim echo of choral music, and all its windows facing them wer
yellow with candlelight.

"The choir is rehearsing for tomorrow," she added. "Th
dance is scheduled to begin right after practice."

"What do you think my father is worried about?" Rachε
asked her.

"He's worried that you'll take up with Jesse permanently,
Mary replied.

"Not much chance of that happening, is there?" Rachel sai
dismally.

"My father would be the same way, Rachel, except somebod
like Jesse would never be interested in me."

"Why not?"

"Look in the mirror, Rachel," Mary said dryly.

Rachel didn't reply.

"And then look at Jesse," Mary went on evenly. "He's th
man every mother warns her daughter about when she turr
twelve. And your mother is dead, so your father feels like he ha
to do it all by himself."

A soldier passed, his dark-blue uniform almost invisible i
the gathering dusk. He nodded at them and touched his cap.

"There are supposed to be some visiting soldiers from Fo
Bellingham at the dance tonight," Mary added, brightening a
they entered her house. "I could use some new blood. All m
father's men are three minutes away from retirement."

Mrs. Turner had made a festive dinner. She entertained th
girls with stories of her childhood Christmases in Boston whil
Mary's younger brother Tommy bolted his food and then wer
to play by the fire with his wooden soldiers. Colonel Turne
spent the whole meal studying the winter feed plan for the ca
alry's horses, so Rachel and Mary eased the older woman's lon

liness with chitchat and then Rachel helped Mrs. Turner clear away while Mary changed.

By the time the girls were ready to leave, the night was pitch black and the snow was falling fast. The Turners promised to stop by the dance after Tommy was in bed, and Rachel glanced back longingly at the house as they walked away from it.

It had been nice to be part of a whole family again, she thought as they walked through the winter storm to the party.

The church's common room had been turned into a festive place, draped with wreaths and garlands and with one of Mr. Jenkins's larger Christmas trees on display in a corner. The two brick fireplaces at either end of the long room were blazing. There was a large plank table set with punch and cookies, and after they hung up their cloaks Mary and Rachel helped themselves to a drink.

Rachel swallowed once and then looked at Mary with alarm. "What is this stuff?" she asked.

"Mrs. Hutsall's raspberry shandy," Mary replied. Mary's mother had been chairman of the refreshment committee, and Mary knew who had been responsible for what.

"I don't know what's in this, but I doubt if it has much to do with raspberries," Rachel said, putting the punch cup down on the table firmly.

"It's raspberry juice and ginger beer," Mary said.

"Whoever thought that was a good idea?" Rachel asked, almost gagging.

"Mrs. Hutsall, I guess," Mary said, and they both laughed.

Mrs. Sedge, the wife of the postmaster, was playing "Hark! The Herald Angels Sing," on the upright piano, and Rachel could tell from the instruments propped against the wall that the pianist would be joined later by three fiddlers for the dancing. She followed the direction of Mary's glance and saw a gathering of several young cavalry officers in one corner.

"Is that the group from Fort Benninghall?" she asked Mary, who was studying the men with interest.

"Must be, and I declare that several of them look quite promising. Do you think they're going to spend the whole night talking to each other?"

As if in response to what Mary had just said, two of the young men detached themselves from their group and began walking toward them.

"Are they coming to us?" Mary whispered fiercely.

"I think so."

"Well, smile, will you please?"

Rachel smiled obediently.

The taller of the two soldiers stopped in front of Rachel and inclined his head. "Lieutenant Jeffrey Cable at your service, ma'am," he said.

"Hello. I'm Rachel Worthington."

Cable took her proffered hand and kissed it. Mary received a similar greeting from her young soldier and then shot Rachel an encouraging glance over her shoulder as her escort led her away to the buffet table.

"May I get you something to drink?" Cable asked, looking down at her with friendly brown eyes. His dark-blue uniform was spotless, the gold stripe on his trousers matching the gold scarf at his neck. His boots were highly polished and his belt buckle gleamed, as did the cavalry horseshoe on the band of the hat under his arm.

"Is there anything else but that punch?" Rachel asked doubtfully.

"I don't know. Let me take a look." He went off into the crowd and Rachel's foot began to tap as the fiddlers arrived and started to play a reel. Cable returned shortly with two cups full of an amber liquid.

"What is that?" Rachel asked suspiciously, hoping it had not originated with Mrs. Hutsall.

"Apple juice."

"Fine." Rachel took a sip and found that it was, indeed, plain old apple juice. Cable looked around him. "Would you care to dance?" he said.

Rachel glanced behind him and saw that Mrs. Tewksbury, Mrs. Hutsall, and several of their cohorts were standing in a bunch, watching her progress with the snappy young lieutenant. She extended her hand.

"I'd be delighted," she said.

They galloped through several reels, and after a pause for more apple juice, began to waltz when the fiddlers took up a slower pace. During the next twenty minutes, Rachel learned about Lieutenant Cable, his birth and early life, his enlistment in the cavalry, his posting to Fort Benninghall. She responded with some tidbits of her own, enough to be polite, until the musicians took a break and Cable suggested a walk to the conservatory. This was an open space adjoining the common room where the minister's wife had attempted to establish an outpost of warmth and culture in the midst of the hostile plains. The room was filled with books and sheet music, all available for loan on a signature, as well as such plants as could endure the thin light of an Oklahoma winter and still manage to survive.

"How did you know this was here?" Rachel asked, impressed with Cable's familiarity with the floor plan.

"We arrived early. I had plenty of time to look around and get the lay of the land." He moved to her side and stood so close that Rachel inched back nervously, thinking suddenly that it hadn't been too smart to let him get her alone this way.

"What are you doing?" she said.

"What do you think?" he replied, bending over her as her back collided with the wall.

"I think I'd like to go back to the party," Rachel said quickly, trying to sidestep him.

"Come on, don't play coy with me. Why did you come in

here with me if you didn't want this?" He seized her in his arms and crushed her mouth with his.

Rachel pushed him away, her hands flat against his chest, her head twisting from side to side in a futile attempt to escape his embrace. But he was very strong, and she was losing the battle, until suddenly he wasn't there anymore and she was stumbling to regain her balance.

She looked up and saw that Cable was now engaged in a struggle with a far more formidable opponent than herself: Jesse Kincaid. She watched in astonishment as Jesse flung her erstwhile suitor against a book-lined wall. Volumes tumbled to the floor as Cable rebounded and went back for Jesse, throwing punches that missed wildly as Jesse bobbed and weaved expertly, a veteran of many such contests.

"What the hell do you think you're doing?" Cable demanded breathlessly. "Why don't you mind your own business?"

"You keep your hands off her if you want to leave this little soiree with your hide intact," Jesse replied, lifting his arm to ward off a glancing blow and then punching Cable in the stomach with his other hand.

Cable doubled over as Rachel looked on in horror. When he straightened again and lunged forward, Jesse stuck out his foot and tripped him. Cable sprawled inelegantly on the floor.

"Get up, you scumsucking bluebelly," Jesse said, and kicked him. "Pick on somebody your own size, or are you only good at mauling little girls?"

"What's it to you?" Cable gasped, looking up from his prone position, wiping his bleeding lip with the back of his hand. "I was only trying for a little kiss, the same thing you would do if you had the chance."

"That's where you're wrong, Lieutenant," Jesse said, bending over and hauling the other man up from the floor by his shirtfront. "Unlike you fine officers of the cavalry, I don't force my attentions on unwilling women. Now get the hell out of here before I really lose my temper." Jesse shoved Cable toward the door.

Cable looked back at him and his eyes narrowed. "I know who you are. You're that half-breed scout, Kincaid."

"What of it?" Jesse asked flatly, dangerously, not looking at Rachel, who was still standing against the wall, her eyes wide with apprehension.

"Who the hell are you to lecture me, Kincaid? Your mother was some dog-eating Indian."

Jesse exploded toward Cable, but this time Rachel was ready. She flung herself into Jesse's path and hung on him, halting his forward momentum.

"Jesse, don't," she begged him. "Please let him go. I don't want this to turn into a big incident."

Cable, who thought better of his smart remark once he saw Jesse heading for him again, fled through the door of the conservatory and yanked it shut behind him with a bang.

"Are you all right?" Jesse said, holding Rachel off to look at her.

"Of course I'm all right. He barely touched me. How on earth did you know what was happening?"

"I was up in the rafters, watching you. I saw you come in here with that bluecoat," he said, using the Indian term to describe the cavalry lieutenant.

Rachel gazed up at him in astonishment. "You were up in the catwalk?" she said. The common room had been an addition built after the church and it had an unfinished ceiling, with open beams.

He nodded, as if it were the most natural thing in the world to admit.

"Why?"

"I thought you might show up," he said simply.

"Why didn't you just come to the dance?"

"You think all these good people would be happy to see me at their Christmas party?" he asked sarcastically.

"You might be surprised at how generous some of them could be if you gave them a chance," Rachel said softly, reaching up to touch his face.

He looked down at her, swallowed once, then enfolded her in his arms.

Rachel closed her eyes and rested her head against his chest, drinking in the clean buckskin smell of him, so well remembered from the last time they had been together. His arms felt so strong, his tall body so firm and supple, that she hugged him closer, sighing with gratification.

"Rachel . . ." he began, his voice a deep rumble in his chest under her ear.

She raised her head to look into his eyes.

"Yes?" she said.

The door behind them opened to admit a burst of Christmas music, as well as Mary and Mrs. Turner, the latter carrying a stack of books.

Both women halted in their tracks when they saw Rachel in Jesse's arms. At the same instant, Rachel felt his grip relax and he stepped back from her.

"Rachel!" Mrs. Turner said, not even trying to conceal the shock in her voice. "What is going on here?"

The hopelessness of trying to explain the situation washed over Rachel as Jesse moved behind her and then left the room, his moccasined feet soundless against the wooden floor. When the door had closed behind him Mrs. Turner said, "I had borrowed these books and since I was coming here anyway tonight I thought I'd . . ." Her voice trailed off into silence as she saw the expression of utter misery on Rachel's face.

After a moment she began again. "Rachel, I think it's about time we had a little talk."

"Mom," Mary interrupted tersely, "we should stay out of this. It's between Jesse and Rachel."

"Nonsense," Mrs. Turner replied firmly. "Rachel has no mother now and I feel it is my calling to speak in her place."

Mary's expression registered what she thought of this idea. Neither girl moved as Mrs. Turner set the stack of books she was returning on the check-out desk, bending automatically to replace the volumes Cable had knocked onto the floor. Then she turned and faced Rachel, her determination to do her duty stamped on her plain, well-meaning face.

"Rachel, your father has taken me into his confidence on a number of occasions regarding your relationship with this Kincaid boy," Mrs. Turner said.

"He's not a boy," Rachel replied.

"That's precisely the problem, one of them, anyway. He's much too old for you."

"He's twenty-five and I'm eighteen. Colonel Turner is ten years older than you."

Mrs. Turner looked somewhat taken aback by this rejoinder, but recovered quickly and said, "That's not the only objection your father has to him. Why, look at his background, the way he dresses, that hair . . ."

"His mother was an Indian and he dresses like one. What's wrong with that? And I think his hair is beautiful."

"Why doesn't he get it cut, for heaven's sake?" Mrs. Turner said in annoyance.

"I guess he wants to wear it long, the way the Indians do. What does it matter? What people really object to is his Apache mother, and I think that's hypocrisy, anyway. Doesn't Reverend Larsen preach that we are all God's creatures and we should all love one another?"

Mary smiled slightly, wondering how her mother was going to handle that one. Mary knew what it was like to argue with

Rachel, but for Mrs. Turner this was a new, and unsettling, experience.

"Well, of course, but my dear, no one even knows where this man lives! He wanders in and out of the fort at will, appearing and disappearing . . ."

"He has a cabin near Haven Springs," Rachel interjected, as if that answer would pacify Mrs. Turner.

"And how does he live?" Mrs. Turner went on, not even pausing to draw breath. "Guiding wagon trains, when they run, of course, scouting trails for prospectors and miners, shoeing horses if it comes to that . . ."

"Not everyone can be in the cavalry, Mrs. Turner."

"But at least if you found yourself an officer, like that nice young lieutenant you were dancing with tonight, your future would be secure."

Rachel could feel the rage boiling up within her, but by an extreme effort of will she managed to remain in control. "For your information, Mrs. Turner, just minutes before you came in here Jesse rescued me from the unwanted advances of that 'nice young lieutenant.' I'm sorry if I seem disrespectful, but you don't know Jesse, and you shouldn't offer opinions on someone you don't know. I think it's time for me to go home now. Good night, and Merry Christmas."

Mrs. Turner was rendered speechless. Rachel exchanged a quick glance with Mary as she left, then stalked through the party swiftly, ignoring the curious looks cast in her direction as she wove a path through the dancers. Lieutenant Cable, standing with a couple of his friends, avoided her gaze, turning his back on her. She headed straight for the cloak room, drawing the hood of her cape over her head as she passed through the common room and then out the door of the church.

Outside, the snow was falling thickly, and there was a white blanket two inches deep on the ground. The street ahead of her looked long and dark, almost invisible through the curtain of snow, the blackness punctuated only occasionally by the flickering of a light from a window.

"Do you need an escort, Miss Worthington?"

Rachel turned to see Colonel Turner's second in command, Major Benson, standing on the church steps

"Oh, no, thank you, it's just a short walk."

"Your father asked me to look out for you if you came here tonight," Benson said pleasantly, "but I didn't see you earlier at the party."

Rachel wished her father would stop enlisting the aid of everyone at the fort to keep her in line.

"I was in the conservatory with Mrs. Turner," Rachel said, a partial truth which didn't trouble her conscience much.

"Oh, well, good night then, if you're sure you'll be all right," Benson said.

"Good night."

"And Merry Christmas," he added, opening the door to the church.

"Same to you," Rachel called as he went back inside. She stepped down into the snow, which quickly covered the tops of her boots. She had only gone a few steps when a figure blocked her path and she gasped aloud.

"Take it easy, Rachel, it's me," Jesse said, pulling her into an alley between two buildings.

"Jesse, for heaven's sake, have you been waiting for me this whole time?"

He said nothing, and she realized that he had.

"I have to talk to you," he said.

"We can't talk here," Rachel said, glancing back nervously toward the church. "The dance will be breaking up soon, people will be coming and going and someone will spot us. If my father hears that I've been seen with you twice in one night I don't know what . . ."

As if to confirm her fears, the church door opened and three figures emerged. She and Jesse were close enough to hear the people exclaiming over the snowfall.

"Jesse, you have to go," Rachel said urgently, pushing him away from her. "Just tell me the time and place and I'll meet you there, I promise."

He shook his head. "I'll find you," he said, and melted into the darkness of the alley.

Rachel looked after him and then hurried on ahead, anxious to avoid encountering the group which had just left the church. As she got closer to her destination she could see the dim outline of the sentry walking his patrol along the top of the wall of the fort. When she went into her house she found her father's medical bag and coat on a chair, and knew that he was already asleep in his room. He had left the fire going in the fireplace for her.

Rachel shook out her damp bonnet and cloak and spread them before the fire to dry. She paused for a moment to admire the tree she had decorated, and noticed that there was a wrapped box under it. She picked it up and saw that her name was written on it in her father's rapid scrawl. Feeling a little misty, she replaced the box under the tree.

Poor Daddy. He did try. He had come out west to help Rachel, after all, when she couldn't stand to live in their old house anymore, when the memories of her beloved mother were so strong it was impossible to sit in the living room, surrounded by the things her mother had loved, without weeping. Also spurring the move was her father's wish to escape his own feelings of frustration and guilt. He had aided so many sick people in his career, but when his wife was stricken with influenza, he hadn't been able to save her.

Rachel sighed as she banked the fire. She knew that he was genuinely concerned about her, but she suspected that he was also afraid to lose his only child to the handsome half-breed who looked at his daughter with such a hot eye. He would be alone, his wife and his little girl gone in the space of one year, and so his antipathy to Jesse had an element of selfishness in it.

Rachel didn't know what to do. She felt affection and loyalty for her father, but the pull toward Jesse was so strong, the strongest emotion she had ever experienced in her life. How could she ignore it, now that her encounters with him tonight had given her hope? Her mother and father, happy for twenty years, had married against the wishes of her father's parents, who'd thought Rachel's mother not good enough for their physician son. Didn't she have the same right to choose that her father had exercised? Could he have forgotten those days so completely that he didn't see the parallel he now shared with his daughter?

Tired of thinking about it, Rachel carried the oil lamp into her bedroom and discovered that her father had built a fire in the small grate there. She rarely used her fireplace because it had a narrow flue and it was usually too much trouble to get a fire started in it. Surprised and touched, she undressed and slipped into her nightgown, placing her wet boots before her hearth. Dispensing with the hot bricks since her room was already so warm, she slipped under the covers, thinking that she would get up early in the morning and put her father's gifts under the tree before he arose.

The slight sound of wet snowflakes pattering lightly against her window was soothing and the fire crackled companionably, but sleep simply would not come. She tried to put the events of the night out of her mind, but they kept sneaking back into her thoughts. She was finally drifting off to sleep when she heard a sound at the window behind her. Startled out of her doze, she sat up in alarm. Her eyes widened as she saw her window sash go up and a long, leather-clad leg thrust itself over the sill.

"Jesse?" she whispered.

The rest of him came through the window and Rachel stared in amazement as he dropped, cat-footed, to the floor, then whirled to pull the window closed behind him. When he turned back to face her she yanked the bedclothes up to her neck.

"I told you I'd come to you," he said simply, brushing snow off his shoulders.

"How can you be sure that nobody saw you come in here?" Rachel asked in a low tone. Her bedroom window faced directly onto the street, and the sentry on the wall of the fort passed within fifty feet of her house at the farthest point of his patrol.

"I waited until the sentry was at the far end of the compound. It's two o'clock Christmas morning, Rachel. Everybody is in bed."

"Everybody except you," Rachel replied, tossing back her covers when she saw that his hair was wringing wet and his jacket and moccasins soaked through, the leather stained dark. She forgot the thin nightgown she was wearing as she padded toward him barefoot, pushing her straight-backed chair next to the fire.

"Take off those wet things, sit next to the fire and get warm," she said quietly. "How long were you hanging around outside the house?"

"Long enough," he replied, kicking off his shoes and stripping off his jacket. She saw that his shirt was damp in patches also, its collar plastered to his neck.

"That, too," she said.

He shrugged and unbuttoned it, handing it to her as it came off his arms. Rachel looked long and hungrily at his sculpted torso before she turned away, her face flushing.

"I have to go into the keeping room to get you a dry shirt and some towels," she said. "For God's sake just sit there and be quiet. If my father finds you in here he'll skin us both alive."

"I'm not afraid of your father, Rachel," he said quietly.

"Well, since I am, please humor me. Hang up your jacket so it will dry."

"Rachel, will you stop fluttering around and issuing orders? I came here to talk to you."

"We'll talk when I get back. First things first. I'm a doctor's daughter and I can't have you getting pneumonia."

He shook his head as if she were a hopeless case and watched Rachel creep stealthily to her door and open it a crack.

She heard nothing. Emboldened, she stepped into the hall and took a few steps, listening hard. Still nothing. Finally, she went to her father's door and pressed her ear to the oak paneling.

She could hear him snoring lightly inside.

Satisfied, she tiptoed back through the main room and sought out the cedar chest in the alcove behind the kitchen. There were two shirts of her father's in there that needed mending; surely one of them would not be missed. She found it, and grabbed two threadbare towels that had been judged ready for the rag bag. Thus armed, she made her way carefully back to her bedroom, sidestepping a floorboard that she knew creaked loudly and pulling her door closed behind her with a relieved sigh.

Jesse was kneeling before the fire, shaking out his damp hair. She crouched next to him and offered him a towel, then drew her hand back when he reached for it.

"I'll do it," she said softly.

He bent his head obediently and she began to rub his glossy, light-brown hair, abundantly thick and streaked with red and gold highlights. At first her movements were brisk and efficient, but soon she had dropped the towel and was stroking his hair caressingly with her hands. When he felt the change in her touch he looked up, and she could not mask her expression, which showed everything she was feeling.

"I missed you so much," she whispered, her eyes filling, and he swept her into his arms.

"I missed you, too," he said, his mouth against her ear. "I went crazy when I thought you took off for that school in St.

Louis to get away from me. I only came here for Christmas because I hoped you would be here, too."

"My father forced me to go to St. Louis, Jesse. He said he would make trouble for you if I didn't obey him and I was afraid of what he might do. I wanted to tell you that when I saw you the other day in Jenkins's store."

He sighed, pulling her tighter against him. Rachel closed her eyes as she felt the satiny skin of his arms and chest, radiant with inner heat, burning through the cotton tissue of the nightgown she wore. He was naked to the waist, and the thin barrier of her gossamer gown was like nothing at all. It was a potentially explosive combination.

"I know I was mean to you then," he murmured, his breath warm on her neck, "but I wasn't sure what had happened, why you had disappeared. I came back here to find out but when I saw you so suddenly, I kind of . . . lost my nerve."

The thought of Jesse, who feared nothing, losing his nerve at the sight of her gave her a strange feeling. What was it? Excitement? Power?

"Why did you lose your nerve?" she murmured, rubbing her cheek along the smooth expanse of his bare shoulder. His arms tightened reflexively.

"I thought maybe when I kissed you that last day I scared you off."

"I wanted you to kiss me, Jesse, so much. I want you to kiss me now."

She felt his movement and lifted her face up to his. When his lips touched hers she knew that this was what she'd been waiting for during her painful time in Missouri, what she had been waiting for her all of her life.

His mouth was firm and sweet, tasting faintly of tobacco. He was hungry and she was eager; his lips moved to her face, her neck, his tongue invading the collar of her gown as she responded avidly, twining her fingers in his hair and sighing blissfully. She heard his answering sound of satisfaction when she shifted her weight and pressed against him; Rachel's head fell back in abandonment and her hands fluttered down his bare, muscular back as he strained her closer, ever closer. Finally, he swept her up as if she weighed nothing and carried her to the bed.

Rachel lay back and opened her arms; Jesse fell against her, enveloping her with his body. He kissed her again, and she wrapped her legs around his hips, imprisoning him, her ardent innocence inflaming him. He tore his mouth from hers and ducked his head to her breasts, teasing and nipping her through the thin cloth until she was moaning, and, in frustration, he ripped the tie at her neck, shoving the gown off her shoulders and down to her waist. He took one rigid nipple in his mouth and covered the other with a large, sunbrowned hand. Rachel tossed her head on her pillow, biting her lip as his mouth evoked sensations she had never before experienced. When he lifted his head she whimpered and clutched at him, drawing him down to her again forcefully.

"Don't stop," she whispered.

He looked at her, his expression unguarded and vulnerable in the dancing firelight. "I love you, Rachel," he said huskily. "I want to take you right here, right now, with your father sleeping in the next room."

"Then do it," she murmured, twining her arms around his neck. Unable to resist her invitation, he slid his palms along her sides and pushed her gown up to her knees. Rachel dropped her head to his shoulder in submission, moaning, as he ran his hand up her thigh. She turned to accommodate him and then gasped aloud when he touched her intimately.

In the next instant he had thrust her aside and she was alone in the bed. She sat up, her gown disarrayed, her hair over one eye, to see see him sitting in the chair by the fire, his head bent and his arms across his knees.

"Jesse," she said plaintively, and moved to follow him.

He held up his hand. "Stay where you are," he said, in a tone of command that brooked no argument.

She stayed where she was.

After a long minute he looked up at her. She was watching him intently, and he could tell that if he crooked his finger she would come to him, his for the taking again.

But he could not do it.

"Why did you stop?" she whispered.

"You're a nice girl, Rachel, not some mining camp whore to be tumbled in a back room. I didn't mean to get carried away, but you feel so soft and you smell so good, I was . . ." He stopped and ran his hand through his hair, then added, "I want to do this right."

She waited. It was clear he had more to say.

"Would you please cover yourself up?" he said suddenly in an exasperated tone.

She pulled the quilt up to her neck quickly.

He took a deep breath. "I can't let you go, Rachel. Maybe I should, for your own good, I'm aware that I don't have much to offer . . ."

"You have yourself, that's all I want," Rachel began, and he shook his head, silencing her.

"Let me finish," he said. "I've thought about this and I want to get it all out." He paused. "If you go back to school this time I know I'll never see you again."

"Don't say that," Rachel pleaded in an agonized tone, closing her eyes.

"You know it's true, Rachel. Your father will marry you off to some officer or rancher, somebody he thinks is respectable and our chance will be gone forever."

"Our chance?" she echoed.

He stood and began to pace the small room, the firelight casting shadows on the planes of his face.

"I have the promise of a job in Fort Worth, a steady job driving for the Butterfield Overland Mail. I'll take it if you'll come with me. We can get married there, find a place to live. It won't be much at first. I know you're used to better, but I promise I'll always take care of you. I've never really had anything to call my own, but I'd like that to change. I want you, and I want to make a life with you."

He let out his breath in a long exhalation. He had evidently rehearsed this speech many times.

Rachel was silent, tears clogging her throat.

"Well?" he said anxiously. "Will you think about it? I know what you'd be giving up here . . ."

"Oh, Jesse, I'd go anywhere in the world with you, don't you know that?" Rachel whispered, climbing out of the bed and embracing him, her tears spilling over and wetting his skin. His arms came around her convulsively and he held her for a long time, neither one of them saying anything.

Conversation wasn't necessary.

Finally, he pried her arms loose from his neck and held her off to look at her.

"I have to talk to your father," he said, "and ask him for your hand."

Rachel shook her head, her mind already made up on this subject. "Jesse, you must listen to me. He would never understand. If you talk to him you'll only give him a warning of what we want to do and he will try to find a way to stop it."

"You're of age now, Rachel. You told me last summer that your eighteenth birthday was in November. What can he do?"

"I don't know, I don't know, but I'm afraid to take the chance. He's irrational on the subject of my having anything to do with you. Maybe he would try to have you arrested or something."

"Arrested for what? Rachel, you're talking crazy.

"Am I? He's the cavalry doctor and you're the half-breed. The people here at the fort treat you like you're a dangerous character, is it so foolish to think they would take his word over yours? Please trust me on this, Jesse. When it comes to Harold Worthington, I'm an expert. We'll have to elope."

He looked at her hard for a moment, and then nodded. "All right. You know the old man better than I do. I'll load up my buckboard and come back for you tomorrow night at midnight. You be packed and ready, and we'll head for Texas."

She threw her arms around his neck, nuzzling him. "Jesse, I'm so happy. I can't believe that we'll finally be together, I had almost given up hope."

He kissed the top of her head. "Don't you worry. We'll slip away from here and have a life together. You do what you're supposed to do for the holiday tomorrow, then go to your room to sleep as usual, and I'll climb through the window just like I did tonight."

She drew away from him and extended her hand. "Now come back to bed."

"That's not such a good idea, Rachel. I really think I'd better leave."

"You're going to walk back to the boardinghouse now? There must be six inches of snow out there and it's still falling! What if the sentry sees you?"

"He didn't see me on the way in," Jesse replied, stepping into his half-dried, stiffening moccasins.

"Jesse, please stay."

"Rachel, if I get back into that bed with you . . ." He threw up his hands.

"If we're going to be married in a few days anyway, what difference does it make?"

"It makes a difference to me," he said stubbornly.

Rachel, who could only imagine his life before they met, realized that his determination to put his relationship with her into a separate category from his previous experiences was very important to him.

"Then sleep on the floor by the fire," Rachel said, relenting, pleased with the compromise. "I'll give you my quilt."

He hesitated.

"I just want to wake up in the morning with you. It will be the best Christmas present I ever had."

He sighed.

"I promise not to ravish you during the night," she said solemnly.

He grinned, and her heart turned over in her breast. Did this gorgeous creature really plan to take her away with him and make her his wife?

"All right, Rachel, I'm too tired to argue with you anymore." He kicked off his shoes and added two more logs to the fire from the stack in a corner of the room. Then he wedged the top rail of the straight chair under Rachel's doorknob and reached for the quilt she was holding out to him.

"That chair won't keep my father out if he gets suspicious," Rachel said.

"It will give us some advance notice if he tries to get in," Jesse replied.

"I won't be able to sleep," she said archly, watching him spread the quilt on the floor.

"You'd *better* sleep. We have a long journey ahead of us tomorrow night."

"I'd sleep sounder if you were holding me."

"Rachel . . ."

"All right, all right." She punched her feather pillow and settled down as he rolled up in the quilt and lay prone before the fire. She listened and waited until his breathing was deep and even, then joined him on the floor, tying the neck of her gown and curling up next to him with her head on his shoulder.

Then she went to sleep.

* * *

Rachel awoke as the first light was stealing through the curtains on the window of her room. Jesse was still asleep, his arm draped around her loosely, his face eased of care, making him look very young.

Rachel sat up and shook his shoulder. He came awake immediately, his lashes lifting. He looked at her and then bolted to his feet.

"What time is it?" he asked, looking around for his shoes and then slipping into them.

"Just dawn, but you'd better hurry. My father gets up early. Here, put this on." Rachel handed him her father's shirt, which he donned hastily, rolling the sleeves to his elbows when they were too short and stuffing the excess material around his midriff into his pants. He pulled on his jacket, stuck his own rolled-up shirt under his arm, and went to the window to raise the sash.

"Come here," he said.

Rachel ran to him and he embraced her.

"I'll be back for you at midnight. Is that late enough?"

Rachel nodded. "My father always goes to bed by ten."

He kissed her forehead. "Be strong. We'll make it. Don't tell anybody about our plans. I'll see you tonight."

"Tonight," she whispered.

He stuck his head out and looked around the street. There were a few people abroad, but they were a distance away. He glanced at the sentry, whose back was to them, and then vaulted over the sill. He looked back at Rachel, winked, then disappeared around the corner into the alley that ran alongside the house.

Rachel closed the window and then collapsed onto her bed, her heart pounding. She lay there thinking, planning what she would take with her and the letters she would leave for Mary and her father, until she heard him stirring. Then she put on her robe and went out to make breakfast.

Christmas Day was the longest day of Rachel's life. She managed to exchange gifts with her father, sit through the church service and then serve dinner to Dr. Closter and his wife, who were visiting with the soldiers from Fort Bellingham. Dr. Closter was another circuit-riding doctor, and he and Rachel's father told stories of their travels as the women straightened up after dinner. When the Closters left at six Rachel asked her father if she might visit with Mary and give her friend her Christmas present. He nodded, absorbed in a medical journal Dr. Closter had lent him, and Rachel put on her cloak and walked over to the Turner house.

She was sorely tempted to tell Mary about her plans for later that night, but mindful of Jesse's warning, she didn't. She visited with the Turners, and came away with a new shirtwaist Mary had made for her and a packet of lemon verbena sachets from Mrs. Turner, who was kind enough to overlook her disagreement with Rachel at the church party. When Rachel returned to the house, her father was still reading by the fire. She announced that she was going to her room to work on a sampler, and he merely nodded. Once safely inside her room, Rachel began to empty drawers and fold clothes, stowing everything in her mother's old carpetbag. She planned to take only one piece of luggage with her. In the letter she wrote to Mary she told her friend that she could have everything else.

As Rachel put down her pen she heard the clock on the mantel in the living room strike ten. Her father knocked on her door shortly afterward and called out, "Good night, sweetheart. Thanks for a lovely dinner. I'm sure you made a very nice impression on Dr. Closter. And Merry Christmas."

Rachel felt the sting of tears behind her eyes and cleared her throat before answering, "Good night, Daddy. Merry Christmas to you, too."

She listened for his footsteps going down the hall, then blinked the tears away. She couldn't let a momentary feeling of tenderness for her father weaken her resolve. She was not going to the moon, after all. She would see him again.

Rachel was ready long before midnight, fully dressed and

sitting on her bed with her bag on her lap. When she heard the clock strike twelve she got up, left the letters for Mary and her father on her dresser, and went to the window.

Jesse was coming down the street; she could see the team leading his buckboard tied to the hitching post a few doors away. She raised the window as he approached and he took her bag, then lifted her over the sill. The second he closed the window she was in his arms.

"Ready?" he said into her ear.

"Never more ready," she replied.

He took her hand and they were running toward the buggy when the door of the Worthington house opened and the doctor emerged, carrying the shotgun he stored in the keeping room behind the kitchen.

Rachel gasped and flung herself on Jesse, who pushed her aside and then stepped in front of her.

"I heard the sound of horses arriving and looked outside," Rachel's father said. "Kincaid, where do you think you are going with my daughter?"

"I'm leaving the fort tonight and I'm taking Rachel with me," Jesse replied flatly, restraining Rachel when she tried to dash past him.

"The hell you are," Dr. Worthington replied, raising the shotgun. "I sent Rachel to St. Louis to end this nonsense between the two of you. Do you think I will stand by and let you run off with her now?"

"I'm going with him, Daddy. If you stop me now, I'll just find another way, another time," Rachel said.

"Not if this young buck is dead," her father answered, aiming his weapon.

"You can shoot me, but Rachel will hate you for the rest of her life if you do. Is that what you want? Are you going to kill any man who comes courting her?" Jesse said.

"Jesse, let me talk to him," Rachel said in a low tone. "You're only making him angrier."

Jesse looked down at her and then released her slowly. She took a few steps forward. "Daddy, please try to understand. It's time for me to live my own life," she said. "I'm in love with Jesse, we're going to get married. Can't I have the same chance for happiness that you and Mama had?"

"You can't compare the two situations, Rachel. I had an education and a profession. This drifter will never be able to take care of you."

"I have a steady job waiting for me in Texas," Jesse interjected.

Dr. Worthington eyed him narrowly. "Where?"

"Fort Worth."

"Doing what?"

"Driving for the Butterfield Overland Mail."

Dr. Worthington lowered his shotgun slowly and made a helpless gesture. "I've been afraid of this for some time, Rachel. I know how headstrong you are, I'm sure you think you are right, but you're too young to know what you're doing."

"Mama was a year younger than I am when she married you," Rachel replied.

Her father sagged visibly at the mention of his wife. "She wanted so much for you, Rachel," her father said sadly. "And I wanted you to have everything your mother planned for you. She loved you so much."

"I have what *I* want, Daddy. She would have wished for love and happiness to come my way, and it has." Rachel walked over to her father and embraced him, kissing his cheek. He hugged her back.

"I'm going to miss you so much," he said in surrender, his eyes closed, fighting tears. Jesse looked away.

"Fort Worth is not so far, I'll come and visit you. And I'll write to you every week. Charlie Sedge won't be able to keep up with the mail," Rachel replied jokingly.

"And what about tonight?" Dr. Worthington said, looking down at his daughter as he released her.

"We're going to my cabin, then we'll leave for Fort Worth in the morning," Jesse replied.

"You'll marry my daughter?" Dr. Worthington said to him, man to man.

"First chance I get, sir," Jesse replied. "And she'll be safer with me than with any other man in the fort. Ask Colonel Turner or Major Benson if you're concerned about that. I love Rachel. I'll take the best care of her that I know how."

Rachel's father nodded resignedly. "I had a feeling all along that it would turn out this way." He sighed. "I'm sorry I sent you to that school, Rachel. It was not my intention to make you unhappy. I knew it was lonely for you here, with me gone so much of the time. I thought that sending you to St. Louis would give you a chance to be with young women your own age and get an education at the same time."

"And it kept me away from Jesse," Rachel said.

"Yes," he admitted. "I saw what was coming, and it was just too hard to lose your mother and you so close together."

Rachel kissed him again. "That's what I thought, but you're not losing me. I love you and I'll be back to see you. Now will you please go into the house before you freeze to death in your nightshirt?"

Dr. Worthington obeyed as Rachel walked over to Jesse and took his hand. Rachel's father looked at the two of them standing in the snow. "I knew that first day I saw you together that this outcome was fated," he said. "You just looked . . . right."

Jesse squeezed Rachel's hand.

"I'll say good night, Daddy, not goodbye," she said.

Dr. Worthington waved sadly, then smiled. "Good night, and Godspeed." He shut the door.

Rachel leaned against Jesse, clutching his jacket. "I was really afraid he was going to shoot you," she said, shuddering.

Jesse turned her face up to his. "Are you crying?" he asked gently.

"Just a little. I do love him, Jesse."

"I know, but you'll see him again soon, and maybe with his first grandchild." He kissed her lightly. "Come on. I told the sentries I would be coming through with a passenger, and they'll be watching for us."

They climbed into the buggy for the trip to Jesse's cabin, about two miles outside of the fort on the post road. As they went through the gates Jesse saluted the sentries. It began to snow lightly.

Rachel put her head on Jesse's shoulder. "I love the snow, it makes everything look so clean and white," she said softly.

"It's an Apache snow."

"What's that?"

"Silent. You don't know it's out there until you see it."

"Will it stop us from getting to Texas?" Rachel asked.

"Nothing will stop us now," Jesse replied, and Rachel smiled.

The Forgiving Season

by
Dana Ransom

"Well, Merry Christmas, anyway. You sure you don't want to step inside for a minute, sugar . . . for a little cheer? Just to show there are no hard feelings?"

The young bank employee's face fused six shades of crimson. He nearly fell backward down the front steps in his haste to escape the offer of sin that lingered within what was once the finest whorehouse in Memphis. He tried to issue what he hoped would sound like a dignified refusal but it came out as a breathy squeak.

"N-no, thank you, Miss Leslie. I really have to be going back to work . . . right now, but thank you. Maybe—" He let that dangle, a dreamy anticipation as his gaze canted a glimpse over her shoulder toward where a bevy of barely clad beauties was said to lounge in the parlor. Mimi Leslie concluded for him with a knowing smile.

"Maybe another time. Sure thing, honey. Anytime. You get on back to the bank before you catch your death out in this weather. And remember me fondly to Mr. Owen."

The flustered youth sobered at the mention of his boss and tipped his hat with a mutter of, "Yessum," then bolted down the chill December street.

Mimi Leslie pushed the ornate front door closed against the bluster of winter wind and found herself confronted by the other occupants of the house who were still idle in the late-afternoon hour. She had no time to assume a cheery smile that would have reassured no one. The time for pretense had long since past.

"Is that it, then?" one of the women asked, nodding her head toward the document in Mimi's hand.

" 'Fraid so, sweetie. All signed and legal, giving us the heave ho."

A groan of dismay rose from the glum-faced gathering.

"How long do we have, Miss Mimi?"

It was hard to keep the bitterness from her voice. "The bank isn't of a very charitable mind. We have two weeks to shut down and vacate."

"Over the Christmas holiday?" cried one of them in outrage. "That Emmitt Owen has a heart of stone!"

"Now, LaWanda—"

"Don't go taking up his side, Miss Mimi! How could he do this to us? I thought he was your friend."

Suddenly, all Mimi's ire was replaced by a weary inevitability. "It's not his decision, child, and it's not the bank's fault." But the harlots had no patience with Mimi's absolution. They were seeking a villain for their troubles and the bank owner would do nicely.

"Then whose fault is it that we'll be tossed out of the only home we've practically ever known on Christmas Eve?"

Never one to try to wriggle out of blame, Mimi Leslie gave a great sigh and said, "It's mine. It's my fault, girls. I made those poor investments, not the bank. I was the one who cost us our futures by trying to better them, not Mr. Owen."

Not a one of the young women could think to accuse their benefactress of wrongdoing, not she who was well known for her smart decisions in business. If the investment failed, it wasn't because of any negligence on Mimi Leslie's part. But that didn't change the fact that they were soon to be homeless.

"But Miss Mimi, how can the folks of this city turn their backs on you after all you done for them?"

"Now, Zoe, Memphis doesn't owe me a thing."

There was a quick denying chorus, but Mimi waved it down.

"Ladies, we've got a business to open in an hour or so. Go on about yours and give me some time to think this out. You all have my word that none of you will be on the street on Christmas Eve. Now, go on with you." As the group began to disperse, she called, "And no long faces, you hear!"

She didn't let her own reflect her worry until she was safely behind the door to her private parlor. Then her features slumped to the same depths as her spirits. Oh, Lordy Lord, what was she going to do?

It wasn't like she didn't know it was coming. Mimi chided herself for holding to an unreasonable optimism. Must be the season. Miracles and all. No miracles in Memphis for this ol' harlot. Not that she was deserving of one.

After pouring herself a liberal glass of peach brandy, Mimi leaned back upon her favorite chaise to do some hard, fast thinking; the kind she was best known for. Zoe said Memphis owed her. Maybe the little Cajun was right. Maybe she wasn't. Many a broken marriage had been mended in this sumptuous parlor late at night by advice from Miriam Leslie. Many an affluent family and small business had been saved by under-the-table loans from the bawdy house proprietress. But folks tended not to remember such things when they were within the comforting embrace of plenty. No one wanted to look back and admit they owed all to the tender-hearted madame of the local parlor house. And Mimi couldn't blame them. Or, at least, she tried not to. This being the forgiving season and all.

She had no time to wallow in self-blame or add up who was beholden to her past generosities. She had more pressing matters to attend. Like what would happen to her girls once they shut their doors. It didn't have to be her responsibility. She could turn away as unsympathetically as this Tennessee town but that wasn't in her nature. In her eyes, the ladies who lived beneath her roof were family and one didn't abandon family, one provided for them. And that's what she would do.

The six of them had shared the same table, traded gossip,
tended the occasional bruises and unplanned heartaches.
LaWanda had been there the longest, almost seven years, and
sweet-featured Priscilla with her angelic voice for only six
months, but Mimi loved each and all who fell between equally.
And she couldn't bear the thought that any of them would fall
on harder times because of her mistakes in judgment.

No, she couldn't blame Emmitt Owen, Memphis's most re-
spected banker. He'd tried to warn her off investing in the fly-
by-night scheme that offered grand returns at a tremendous risk.
But Mimi was a gambler. She'd survived the war years on shrewd
instinct and common sense, and unlike many of her Confederate
brethren, she'd come out of it a wealthy woman. Some called
her activities treasonous, but she called them just plain smart.
It might not have been the smartest thing to do, but instead of
placing her money in the bank as her old friend suggested, she
was of the mind that good fortune was meant to be shared. And
she'd shared liberally until all she had left was enough to get by
modestly for the next few years. If she hoarded it. But that wasn't
in her nature, either.

Sipping her brandy, Mimi reflected upon her options. They
were grim, indeed. She'd mortgaged the house to throw in with
a slick-talking fellow from Cincinnati who swore his steamboat
design would revolutionize river travel. Maybe it would have if
the sleek sidewheeler hadn't been scuttled on its maiden voyage
by river pirates. Maybe it could have been repaired if its owner
hadn't hopped another reliable boat for New Orleans carrying
all the company's assets in the best northern carpetbagger tradition. There were whispers that maybe he had arranged for his
own boat to be scuttled, but the point was moot to Mimi. Those
maybes didn't go far in returning her investment. In fact, she'd
gone broke trying to make good on the promises that scalawag
had left behind. Emmitt had warned her, and now the only option
left was to appeal to him and his bank for salvation. But she

couldn't bring herself to that level of humility. She wasn't one
to go begging pardon for her mistakes. She took them like a
man and she went on from there. And that's what she'd do this
time, too. Even if it cost her everything. And it looked like it
would.

From below, she heard the joyful tinkling of a Christmas tune
coaxed from the ancient piano. Time to open the doors for business as usual and put on a happy face—for at least a few more
days.

And dressed in her favorite midnight-colored satin, she was
there, as always, to greet her guests as if without a care in the
world, inviting them out of the cold to snuggle up to a warm
drink and a warmer woman, a tireless and gracious hostess until
the early hours of morning. Looking at her, none would guess
she was troubled or that the affluent life she'd made for herself
was about to end. She made no petitions to those who came in
bearing a debt of gratitude to her nor did she make them feel
uncomfortably accountable. She bid each and every one of them
a congenial good morning when they left and wished her best
to their families for a happy holiday. Then, when the last of them
had gone, she closed the doors and assembled her sleepy-eyed
crew in her parlor for some serious discussion.

"I'll be shutting up our doors for good on Christmas Eve,"
Mimi announced, then suppressed the anxious outcries with a
calming gesture. "Mr. Adams has already agreed to handle the
sale of all the furnishings so the bank can take possession the
first of the year. Between now and then, I aim to see each and
every one of you has someplace to go and the means to get by."

There was a murmur of relief. They were all used to depending
upon the big-hearted, shrewd-thinking proprietress, and if she
said things would work out, things would work out.

"But Miss Mimi, what about you?" asked Mabel, her long,
homely face awash with tears. "Everything you have is tied up
in this place. What will you do?"

"Now, sugar, don't you go worrying about me. I'll do just fine. Just fine. We got us a lot of planning to do. Anything you bring in over the next few days, I want you to keep. Consider it your retirement pay from Miss Mimi's Hospitality House." She smiled, and, one by one, her girls smiled back, encouraged by her infectious confidence.

Mimi wished she could be similarly inspired.

"You'll come to live with me, of course."

Cherice Amory had come to make that offer as soon as she heard of her only relative's plight. Bad news always traveled fast, even in a place as bustling in recovering industry as Memphis. She, more than any of the others, owed her aunt a greater sum than she could ever repay. But Mimi gave a whoop of laughter at her niece's solution.

"Oh, Cheri, honey, come live under the same roof with the widow of my former lover? I think not."

"If not for you, Mother Amory wouldn't have a roof over her own head," Cherice protested.

Mimi only smiled at her stubbornness. True, the funds for the revival of the Amory plantation, Stillwater, had come from her own coffer, but it had been an even trade to her thinking; money well spent to assure her beloved niece of a fine home and loving husband. Another of Mimi's risky investments, one that had paid off handsomely with a beautiful new grand-nephew.

"Aunt Mimi, please reconsider. The feud between you and Lilith has come a long way toward mending since Ruben and I married. She's become a wonderful mother-in-law to me and positively dotes on little Johnny. Surely she won't begrudge you a place to stay."

Mimi felt a clog of emotion rise within her chest, the way it did whenever she thought of the chubby little babe who bore the name of the man she'd loved and lost. Every time the infant regarded her through his somber gray eyes, she saw John Amory all over again, and the pain and pleasure was almost too much to bear. Being under the same roof, viewing the familial happiness fate and the Union army had denied her would be a daily heartbreak too strong to endure. Because little Johnny might have been her grandbaby had John come home to see to his promises.

"Now, Cheri, you know the peace between us is kept by a respectful distance. Stillwater is her home and I've no business intruding there."

"But—"

"No, Cherice." At her niece's determined pout, she added, "Have you discussed this with Ruben?"

"Well—no."

"I can imagine what he'd have to say, all very polite and gentlemanly, of course. I'm sure he'd be thrilled at the idea of having me and his mama at points over the supper table every night. The poor man has enough on his mind, what with building up from scratch. I like Ruben too much to wish that upon him. No, Cheri, in the interest of your marital harmony, I must decline. You deserve the happiness you've found with your new family."

"But you're my family, too."

That impassioned cry warmed Mimi's heart, but she wouldn't allow it to sway her. She wouldn't give in before her niece's emotional blackmail, no matter how tempting. Seeing that, Cherice searched desperately for another avenue of rescue.

"If you won't move in, let us loan you enough to set you up in a place of your own. You carried us until we got Stillwater making a profit. It's the least we can do."

Mimi gave her a wry smile. "Now, Cheri, you know I've never allowed myself to be a kept woman and I'm proud of my independence. I've always paved my own way, be it straight and narrow or wide and wicked. It's my road and I choose my own direction. You keep your profits. Your husband has worked hard for them and you've got a little one to think of now."

"Then dissolve the trust fund you set up for Johnny."

"No! Absolutely not! I'd rather work the harbor shacks on my back than steal from that little darlin'."

"Aunt Mimi!"

"Now, honey, I said that for effect not as fact. You look as pale as paper. Have a touch of brandy before you go swooning dead away. I won't have your husband storming in here blaming me for upsetting your delicate constitution." Cherice had to smile at that. They both knew she had the constitution of a Rebel general. Still, Mimi continued her gentle soothing as if the young wife and mother was still the child under her care. "You just relax, sugar. I'm too old to ply a trade. Who'd go paying money for an ol' tart like me?"

Cherice looked her aunt over, seeing a sleek, sophisticated female with good looks aplenty and a firmness of form that had her answering, "Any man with eyes, Aunt Mimi."

Mimi flushed and waved off the remark as empty flattery. "Oh, how you go on. Anyway, I mean to do no such thing. My situation is not that bad, I assure you. I'll do just fine. I wouldn't let the war get the best of me and I'll be dogged if I'll bend under the bank's thumb." Her expression grew sly. "Perhaps I'll take to writing my memoirs. That ought to have the good citizens of Memphis reaching for their pockets right quick."

"Aunt Mimi, no one would believe such maliciousness of you. If you've got a reputation, it's for your fairness."

"Hummph. It was just a thought. I've got entirely too many scruples for my line of employment."

Cherice relaxed a bit seeing that familiar fire flare. She was more than a little worried over Mimi's acceptance of her fate. It wasn't like her to let go of what she had without a splendid fight. Her heart ached for her aunt's predicament but she could see no way to better it; none that the proud Mimi would allow,

that is. If only the woman would tell her how bad her circumstances were. But that Mimi would never do.

"Have you gone to the bank again? Maybe Mr. Owen—"

"Sugar, me and the bank have us an understanding. They take
my money and don't ask how it was made and I don't ask them
any favors."

"But surely seeing as how Mr. Owen and Ruben's daddy were
such close friends—"

"Cherice, let it be." That quiet statement was no less a command. Then Mimi patted her niece's hand and she managed a
smile that could almost pass for genuine cheer. "Perhaps it's just
my time to be moving on. Memphis and I have quite a past
between us. Maybe it's time I left my memories behind."

At Cherice's instant look of alarm, Mimi decided to say no
more. And she was right proud of the way the girl recovered,
quickly taking possession of her fears to present a calm front.
Like a real lady; a true Amory bride.

"You'll come dine with us on Christmas, of course." Cherice
was quite the order giver herself. "Ruben and I will expect you.
Lilith, too."

Mimi answered with an evasive, "I'll have to let you know,
honey. I've got so many things to tend to. But I surely do thank
you for thinking of me."

"You're family, Aunt Mimi, and no one's ever done as much
for the Amory family as you have."

Mimi fought to secure her smile from taking a wry twist. No,
no one had done as much *to* the Amory family as she had. She
walked her niece to the door, well knowing that she already held
passage on a steamship downriver leaving on Christmas Day.
There would be no family gathering over an elegant table for
Mimi Leslie. Not when she'd done her best to divide that family
and ruin all they held to. No, much better that she should be
traveling alone toward an uncertain future than to remain in
Memphis as a burden upon those who cared.

* * *

She was leaving.

Emmitt Owen received the news with a deep, desperate panic
while behind his big desk at the First Federal Reserve Bank of
Memphis. Though he couldn't quite believe it, he couldn't afford
to discount it.

Mimi Leslie had booked a spot on the *Maribelle* bound for
New Orleans on Christmas Day. She was leaving Memphis. She
was leaving him.

For years, he'd tried every way he knew to court the lovely
and compassionate Miss Mimi, but she'd refused to take his suit
seriously, citing the fact that he was a prominent businessman
and she, a lowly brothel owner. As if that mattered to him. He
was well aware that she hadn't directly plied her trade since her
lover, John Amory, was killed in the war. In her own way, she
had been more faithful to his memory than most women were
to their husbands, mourning him to the exclusion of her own
happiness. Emmitt had tried his best to charm her back to life.
She'd let him close enough at one time for him to know he'd
never love another, then she'd pushed him to a cool and coy
arm's length, preferring to pretend that what had shaken him to
the soul stirred her not at all.

He and John Amory had been the best of friends. In their
youth, they'd hunted and fished the sloughs of the Mississippi,
had schemed and dreamed together about how they'd both make
their mark on Memphis and the world. John had gone on to take
himself a young bride and to determinedly carve a plantation
from Tennessee wilderness. Emmitt had followed the safer, more
dependable path in his father's footsteps and had gone into business. When John came into town, it was as if they were boys
again, eager to get into trouble over cards and drink and women.
And Emmitt never envied his friend anything until the day Mimi
Leslie fell in love with him.

Not that he could blame Mimi. John Amory was a strong, vital man with proud, aristocratic looks and a fire of ambition burning bright about him that attracted folks like June bugs to an open flame. In his flamboyant wake, Emmitt was a somber shadow; less handsome, less charismatic, less wealthy, less wild, with eyesight so bad from all the evenings studying over a poor lamp, he couldn't find his way across the street without his spectacles. He'd never done a crazy or impulsive thing until he'd fallen in love with a Memphis brothel girl.

Mimi Leslie had been something to see; all glossy dark hair and sultry eyes with a smile that was sass and sweetness in one. She was working hard the only way she knew how to raise her dead sister's child, Cherice, and looking back, Emmitt could remember when she was an innocent child herself, from a good family of modest means until the harsh whispers of scandal forced her from the road of respectable southern womanhood into the role of harlot. She'd never let circumstance harden or embitter her. In fact, she was one of the most genuinely generous-spirited people Emmitt knew. And unfortunately, she had eyes only for John.

If John had a fault, it was that he espoused the male myth surrounding the plantation class. He truly believed that if he was a success and he minded the rules of gentility, he could get by with whatever he pleased. And it pleased him to have a lovely and refined wife at home to raise his heir and a lively lady in town to serve his passions. He saw both as conveniences for the taking; his wife giving respectability, his mistress, pleasure, and he never considered the consequences, as if he were somehow above them. He never trusted heart and soul to either woman. Those things he sank into his rich riverbed soil. And in his foolishness, he never saw Mimi Leslie as worthy of his respect.

But Emmitt did, right from the start. He saw a woman working a thankless and demeaning job to provide for her young niece. He watched her protect that girl from the advances of the men she herself was paid to welcome and had seen her come close to crumpling when she bartered to send Cherice to safety and a better life in the North when the bitter war years came. Over those harsh times, he saw her use an intelligent mind to survive their country's clash and to profit within a world gone mad. She managed to invest shrewdly in schemes that secretly aided the southern cause and provided her with the money to buy the house in which she'd worked. And while he stayed home from the fighting to salvage his dying father's business, he heard rumors of her suspected traitorous activities by welcoming the conquering North into her house of pleasure. But what most of Memphis didn't know was how much sensitive information her girls gained from their clients while tossing in the sheets; information that saved many rebel lives. Mimi never desired thanks for her dangerous covert work nor did she try to scotch the rumbles of discontent as she seemingly gave comfort to the enemy. That wasn't the kind of woman Mimi Leslie was. She was the woman Emmitt admired for her unflagging courage. She was the woman he loved for her generosity of heart. But his best friend John was able to look right over all her finer qualities. And it seemed damned unfair that he was the brave gray-clad hero Mimi cried for.

It was an arrogant sense of infallibility that carried John Amory off to war in the first rush and probably that same notion of superiority that had him taking a fatal bullet in a front-line charge. It was hard to believe that such a bold, bright spirit was gone in an instant. Emmitt had missed him and Mimi mourned him and it only seemed right that they should take solace from each other.

He hadn't meant for comforting to turn so suddenly to romance. He'd only the purest intentions when he went to call to express his condolences to the woman who had no right to request them. He'd gone to her right after John was laid to rest by his widow, to share with Mimi the serenity found in the graveside service. And soon they were sharing a compassionate embrace that evolved quite unplanned into a passionate union; an intimacy that continued for four glorious days and nights. The best damned days of his whole uneventful and predictable life. It wasn't the loving; though certainly that part of it was spectacular. It was the talking; deep, heartfelt conversations that went on until early-morning light. She spoke of John, of her past, of the desperation that forced her to send Cherice to New York, away from a budding romance with John Amory's son in a trip funded by Lilith Amory's money. She listened while he shared the dreams he and John spun on a sweltering summer's day, dreams that John could no longer see come true. And he found in Mimi Leslie not just the means for physical gratification that his friend had enjoyed so cavalierly, but a soul steeped in goodness and warmth. A soul that had twined about his so perfectly and completely that his spirit was torn asunder when she looked up at him one morning to calmly tell him to go home.

A mistake, she called it. How could anything so marvelous, so perfect, be a mistake? Just a reaction to losing John that couldn't mean anything, she'd said. Hell, it meant everything to him! When he called it love, she laughed gently and somewhat sadly, calling it infatuation. Infatuation didn't bring a man to his knees for the purpose of proposing, he'd told her. She stopped laughing at that and had gone very still. *Get that nonsense right out of your head, Emmitt Owen. Get yourself a good woman, the right kind of woman.* That's what she'd said, refusing to hear his insistence that she was that woman. And then she'd told him she could never love him, not after John, and that had broken his heart.

Even after that crushing announcement, he'd never truly given up hope or pursuit, though both were carried on discreetly. He was a very stubborn and methodical man. By then, Mimi had bought out the former owner of the house where she was working and moved herself out of the role of prostitute to one of

proprietress. He watched her garner a success that paralleled his
own. She was a smart woman; but he'd known that all along.
After much persistence, she allowed him to escort her to several
decorous dinners where nothing was exchanged except discus-
sions on politics and other equally safe topics. He'd thought that
would be enough until the chaste offer of her hand at the evening's end left him burning restlessly for days. He didn't want
her for friendly debates over dinner. He didn't want her for a
night at the cost of a few coins. He wanted her for always, and
it maddened him that she could never take that seriously.

Her profession was just an excuse. His staid and stainless
reputation could balance out any malicious gossip. Marrying
Cherice hadn't sullied Ruben, after all. The war had left them
with a different world, with a different set of standards. All he
had to do was convince Mimi of that.

All he had to do was convince her to marry him.

He couldn't very well do that if she left for New Orleans.
Though he'd hated being the instrument of foreclosure on all
she owned, secretly he'd been filled with anticipation. Surely
now she'd come to him for aid; as her banker, as her friend, as
her former lover. Surely now she'd let him be generous and allow
him to demonstrate how much he cared. But no, not the strong
and independent Miss Mimi. The proud woman chose surrender
over his terms of continuation. As much as he admired her, he
was annoyed by her decision. And he was more than a little
afraid that she meant to carry it out.

Not while he could do anything about it.

"Gather around, girls. I know we're jumping the gun by a day
or two but I want to give you your presents now."

A mood of expectation mingled with the sadness that had
tinged all else since the date of their eviction was made known.
The five parlor girls crowded into Mimi's posh private quarters

like children. And Mimi felt a swell of affection threaten her tenacious control. If she could get through this, she could survive anything. And she was a survivor.

So she poured out glasses of her favorite brandy and they raised a toast to the New Year before she swallowed quickly. The sear of good liquor helped cut through the massing constriction in her throat.

"Well now, darlins, let's see what ol' Saint Nick managed to find for you." She grinned with an enthusiasm she was far from feeling, for this would be their last night together as a family. She reached into the box on her table that usually held expensive cigars for her preferred male guests and pulled out the first envelope. "This here's for Priscilla."

The redhead reached for it with an excited giggle and eagerly broke the seal. Then her features puckered. "What's this, Miss Mimi? A ticket to Denver?"

"Remember that fast-talking fellow you entertained a few months back, the one who paid you to sing all night? Well, it seems he's opened up his own music hall and he's right interested in having you there to bring in the customers with that angel's voice of yours."

Priscilla stared at the voucher for a long moment. They'd all been hearing for so long how much she wanted to make a success of herself with her vocal talent. And this was her ticket. "Oh, Mimi, how can I thank you?"

"By doing what you was born to do best—singing for your supper." Mimi smiled at her and looked away before she was brought to a similar edge of tears. She pulled out another envelope. "This says Soulie."

The delicate Oriental girl took it in anxious hands. The contents included another ticket; this one to California, and a slip of paper listing a date and a dock number. When she looked up in confusion, Mimi was happy to explain.

"You be at that pier on that day and you open your arms wide, sugar. How long have you been saving to bring your mama and sister from China?"

"For over a year but you know I only had enough money for one passage."

"Well, now there's two, already paid for. I couldn't very well turn you out of one family unless I knew you had another to go to."

Soulie was plainly speechless, but the way she crushed the envelope to her breast said plenty.

"Now, here's something for Zoe." She passed over a slim box that when opened, revealed scissors and a silver thimble. "You can use those come morning. Mrs. Jessup has plenty of use for a talent like yours. She told me she had orders to fill for the New Year stacked to the ceiling in her shop, and when I went in to pick up some alterations, I got to bragging about one of my girls with a natural gift for a neat seam. She's more than willing to provide you with a room and all the work you can handle. Providing you want the job."

"Want it?" Zoe surged up to throw her arms about Mimi's shoulders. "After stitching for nine brothers and sisters for all my growing-up years down on the bayou, it'll be something to get paid for it!" Then she quieted and settled back on her heels with a pensive expression. "Mrs. Jessup takes in orders from all the finest ladies in Memphis. Are you sure she wants to have me work for her . . . considering?"

"Now, you go getting those kind of thoughts right out of your head," Mimi charged with an intimidating fury. "You were offered this job because of what you can do not because of what you were. If those fine ladies don't want you touching their pretty silks and satins, let them run their own seams!"

Zoe's eyes were downcast and full of uncomfortable disbelief. It was an unspoken shame they all shared; that they weren't good enough to mix with the city's gentry because of the trade they'd plied. Mimi patted her shoulder reassuringly and backed down her temper. Her words came out smooth as that fancy silk.

"Now, honey, Mrs. Jessup is looking for a clever hand with a needle. She knows who you are and where you been living and it doesn't matter to her. You can't let it matter to you. Do you want this job or not?"

Zoe's head came up. Her dark gaze was glittering but her chin was squared with determination. "Yes, I do."

"Fine then. The ladies of Memphis will look better for that decision." Then Mimi turned her attention to Mabel, whose homely face was filled with cautious anticipation.

"Whatcha got in there for me, Miss Mimi?" Her voice was wavering slightly. Mabel had always been Mimi's secret favorite. She'd come from a dreadful family, filled with abuse from both parents. After their thankful deaths while she was still at a young age, she'd known nothing but cruelty from the hands of caregivers at a string of orphanages until she was finally forced out to survive on the streets. Because of her less than perfect features, she'd found the streets a harsh place to be and had taken to her position at Mimi's as if it was a shelter from the evils of life. She was clearly apprehensive at the thought of returning to them.

"It's not a what but a where. It's a place that won't pay well, that'll work you long, hard hours and come near to breaking your heart, but I always said, you got the biggest heart of anyone I know. You recall an Amos Mitchell?"

"From the St. Ambrose Home for Foundling Children?"

"That's the one. Well, it seems one of his co-workers was visiting here one night and got a taste of your cooking. Mr. Mitchell would be mighty grateful if you was to come to St. Ambrose. They got lots of little mouths to feed and lots of little souls that need all the love they can get. He was hoping you could be there to make up Christmas dinner and help pass out the gifts donated by the charities here in town."

They all knew those charities narrowed down to one. Since Mabel had come to live with them, Mimi had taken a special interest in St. Ambrose, which was the only institution to try to help the poor frightened child Mabel had been. And Mimi never forgot or dismissed a debt.

"What can I tell Mr. Mitchell?" Mimi prompted gently.

"You can ask him if he prefers spuds or sweet potatoes."

"Good for you, sugar." Mimi was smiling, sure the children at St. Ambrose would know their best Christmas ever if Mabel had anything to say about it. Mabel had arms made for hugging and a soul big enough to heal the tender hurts of the abandoned during the season of family celebration.

LaWanda leaned back with a negligent grace upon the sofa and pursed her pouty lips. "Well, guess that just leaves me, now don't it? I can't sing, I can't sew, I can't cook and I gots no family. What miracle you gonna pull outta that box for me, Mimi? I can't think of a one. Probably be best if I was to look for work down at the High Roller or the Full House. They's always hiring when it comes to upstairs help."

"What kind of life would that be?" Zoe chided.

"You can't go to work at one of those places," Priscilla agreed in a tone of dismay. "We all know how their girls end up; living in them shacks, living on liquor until disease or despair ends it for 'em. You can't mean to do that, LaWanda."

"Fine for you to say! But I been a whore for half my life. That's all I know how to be." A prickly pride rose up in her defense, a pride that had protected her heart from the callousness of her profession . . . and kept her from admitting just how scared she was when considering the life she'd have without Mimi's pampering care. None of the others who ran women would give two hoots about her as long as she was bringing in money. And when she wasn't pretty enough or healthy enough to earn her way, she'd be discarded like the morning garbage into the indifferent stench of the back alleyways. Still, even knowing that and that all the others knew it, too, she said, "I'll get by. Just see if I don't."

"Why don't you read this first," Mimi suggested, holding out a letter. When LaWanda eyeballed it suspiciously, she added, "It's from Jimmy Bishop."

"The farmer?"

"The one who asks for you every time he comes into town. I took the liberty of sending him a note saying you might be leaving for parts unknown and he was right quick about answering."

LaWanda took the letter and the other girls leaned forward in anticipation while she scanned the contents. Then she looked up in frustration. "Mimi, you know I can't read no more than my name."

"I'll tell you what it says then. It says he's been working his place for a lot of years and it's a fine place on fine soil. It says he'd be right proud if you was to want to come live with him on it."

"As what?"

"Says he remembers the way you talked fondly of the farm you grew up on and that he could use a woman of your character who wouldn't be afraid of hard work, who could take care of a lonely man's heart."

"Sounds like a proposal, LaWanda!"

"Sounds like a good deal to me!"

"Get packing, girl."

Mimi held out the letter to the stunned harlot, nodding her head toward the last line. "He says he'd like to take you for his bride if you'd be willing."

"Mimi, what'll I do?" The big, brassy blonde was reduced to a humbled confusion. "A wife? What do I know about caring for one man?"

"The question is, are you willing to learn?"

"A wife," she murmured again, trying to get used to the idea.

"I'll have to think on it some." But she was touching the single page of childlike block printing with an obvious reverence. Mimi sat back on her chaise, appeased, sure she'd be hearing chapel bells within the next few days.

"What about you, Miss Mimi? What did St. Nick leave you?" Mabel asked, and then all the girls were clamoring to know.

"He gave me the joy of seeing you all happy."

But they wouldn't settle for that. Not after all she'd done for them.

"How you gonna get by, Mimi?" LaWanda demanded. "How much you got left after seeing to us and our troubles? You manage to save anything to live on?"

"Now, LaWanda, you know me better than that. I'm a survivor, honey. I always see to myself. I got plans. I'm heading down to New Orleans on Christmas Day. Got some investments to check on down there that could pan out to plenty. I'll be in tall cotton again in no time, don't you worry."

She'd be worrying enough for all of them.

All day, Mimi listened to the sounds of industry in the rooms around hers. She tried to think of them as positive sounds foretelling of a forward movement toward better things, but her heavy heart reminded her that it was the sound of family getting ready to go separate ways.

She told herself she should be gathering her own things together, but she couldn't seem to shake her immobilizing melancholy. These rooms, this house, these women represented the best part of her life and she wasn't ready to face what it would take to start packing parts of it away. She wasn't usually one for looking back and she wouldn't now. She'd seen that all her girls had something to look forward to. That should be satisfaction enough, yet she was sitting in the thickening shadows, steeping in her own self-pity. It was the season, she told herself. Her first

Christmas alone. She was half tempted in that low moment to cancel her riverboat reservation and take Cherice up on her offer of dinner. But what purpose would that serve? Stillwater would never open its doors for her in welcome, not as long as Lilith Amory was within. Lilith was mistress of the house, while Mimi had been mistress to her husband.

Better she just stick to her plans and let the wide, muddy river carry her away from memories she'd drown in.

"Miss Mimi, you got yourself a gentleman caller."

With a sigh of indifference, she replied, "I'm not in the mood for entertaining company, Pris. Send whoever it is away."

"It's Mr. Owen from the bank."

Mimi was startled by the hot flash of anticipation that spiked through her; an excitement that had more to do with herself than her situation. Emmitt was here. To see her. She swallowed hastily, then said, "Tell Mr. Owen to come up. He knows the way."

She surged off the chaise to pace the room restlessly. Her hands fluttered to the neckline of her dressing gown, then to her hair. She must look a sight. If she kept the lights down, maybe he wouldn't notice that her eyes were circled from lack of sleep and that her faced was lined by pending sorrow. But maybe he'd take those lowered lights as an encouragement of a different kind. Another shiver of expectation shook through her. Defiantly, she reached to turn up the lamp. Let him see her with mussed hair and worry-bruised eyes. He was the only man to have ever seen her looking worse.

At his quiet knock, Mimi was beset by a flutter of nerves. Unwilling for him to see her so discomposed, she turned her back to the door before calling for him to come in. The sound of his heavy tread had her hands trembling as she reached for the brandy decanter.

"I was about to pour myself a drink. Join me?"

"If you're having one."

The sound of his voice poured over her senses as smooth and

warm as the brandy flowing into the two glasses. Lord, she'd missed hearing a man's voice in her parlor. She refused to believe it was just the particular cadence of his speech that she'd longed for. Steadying her hands with conscious effort, she turned toward him. And her reaction to seeing him knocked all her defenses askew.

Emmitt Owen was a big man. Everything about him was huge and solid; his business success, his broad-shouldered build, and his unshakable beliefs. He wasn't handsome, not the way John Amory had been with all his dash and charm, but there was an appealing strength in his less than perfect features. Behind steel-rimmed spectacles, his eyes were blue and bright with a penetrating insight into the human spirit. His ability to read whomever he fixed with that intense gaze was what made him so good at what he did. He could spot weakness and insincerity at a glance and knew where a good investment lay. To offset his shrewd stare was a generous mouth that was quick to smile and soften with compassion. The other reason he'd achieved so much in the banking arena: that contrast of forcefulness and forgiving. And those two characteristics acted upon Mimi's reserve with devastating result. Her conclusion surprised and scared her.

How long had she been in love with him?

He thanked her for the brandy in that low, soothing drawl of his and took a leisurely sip to her hurried gulp. The burn of it gave her back her breath.

"It's been a long time, Emmitt. Did you come to say good-bye?"

"No." Just that without explanation.

"To wish me a Merry Christmas, then? Or to see that we were properly vacating the bank's property?"

"You know me better than that, Mimi."

His soft chide made her blush. And that provoked her. Better to keep it business. She could maintain her distance there. "Do I, Mr. Owen? I'd have thought so until the papers were served."

"I couldn't do anything about it, Mimi. You know that."

There was no use blaming him when she knew that was true. She gave a harried sigh. "I know. I'm sorry.

"I'm sorry, too." No I-told-you-so's, but instead, "Why didn't you come to me?"

"You just got through saying you couldn't do anything."

"Not as a banker, no. But you could have come to me."

His meaning struck her and struck hard. Her smile wavered in a brave attempt at pride. "Now, Emmitt, you know *me* better than that. I'd never take advantage of our friendship."

"Why not?"

"Why not?" For a moment, she floundered helplessly, then came up with a staunch, "Because I don't like to be beholden to anybody."

"I'm not just anybody."

"Maybe that's why." Her fingertip lingered distractedly across one wide shoulder before she could stop herself. And once she'd touched him, however innocently, it was that much harder to pull away and pretend indifference. Because she was remembering all too well what it was like in his embrace. It was as close to heaven as she was likely to get.

"Mimi," he began with a quiet determination. That tone scared her to death. She jumped in to interrupt whatever brought that somber emphasis to his voice.

"Well, now, sugar, if you came out on this cold night just to offer a personal loan, I'm afraid you've made the trip for nothing. I've already got plans, Mr. Owen, and they don't include begging for charity. So if that was all you had in mind, I've got lots of packing to do."

"No, that's not all I had in mind."

She was standing too close to evade him. His move was unexpected but not exactly unwanted. His warm kiss pressed to her temple, then against the firm angle of her jaw. Only after he'd tasted the rapid pulse at her throat and felt her anxious swallowing did he shift to sample from her lips. He found them parted and already moistened by a blot of anticipation. He kept it short and bittersweet, then drew back with obvious difficulty to gauge her response through those unfailingly perceptive blue eyes.

He was letting the choice be hers by that hesitation. Mimi realized she still had the chance to control what would happen between them as she had once before. That decision then was one of the hardest she'd ever had to make. And she couldn't help the one she made this time.

She lifted her hands to his face, cupping his warm, slightly rough cheeks between her palms. And she coaxed him back down to lips that waited with the eagerness of a hunger long denied. She hadn't tasted passion since . . . since she'd asked him to leave all those years ago. And she'd never tasted it anywhere quite so sweetly. Like a fuse touched off, once it burned, the desire was impossible to extinguish until it ran its course, a course that led quite naturally from heated tongue-tangling in the parlor to more intimate exchanges on the other side of the bedroom door.

There, in those shadow-steeped surroundings, they stood toe-to-toe, locked together by deep, mating kisses and slow, reacquainting caresses. And when the lingering inquiries had her rubbing and arching against him like a languid cat, Mimi murmured with a husky intensity, "Emmitt, honey, you're wearing entirely too many clothes. I feel like I'm trying to coerce a loan from my banker."

"Are you?"

Her immediate stiffening was his reply. "No. If that's what you think, you can just go to—"

The hard clamp of his mouth over hers stifled her from speaking the destination she had in mind and got her thinking of another. Paradise. He continued the insistent pressure until her tension eased and her arms curled back around his middle with a forgiving tightness.

"I was hoping that's what you'd say," he whispered in a gentling kiss. His big hands combed her loose hair back away from her upturned face. "Not that you can't have a loan if you want one."

Her eyes flickered open to reflect a growing need and a disinterest in further talk. "No more business tonight, Emmitt." And her hands pushed his finely tailored coat from the wide rack of his shoulders.

"I agree," he murmured. "It's time things got personal between us."

And he was starting down his shirt buttons as she was busy with his trouser flap. Then he drew a shaky breath as her hand closed over him. Her long strokes admired the proportioned way he was sized; all of him was as impressive as his stature. His fingers flew unsteadily over the rest of the upper fastenings and his shirt went sailing over his head. That brought her attention up a notch to the heavy furring of his chest. Her fingers played through that springy mat for a moment until her breathing began to labor. With an earthy laugh, she let her hands reluctantly drop away.

"Oh, sugar, I'd almost forgotten what an incredible man you are."

But that wasn't really true. She'd been trying hard to forget.

His forefinger crooked beneath her chin, lifting her for a soulful kiss that lasted until he had her dressing gown in a glimmering pool around her ankles. He didn't bother with a lustful look but instead, carried her straight to bed. He didn't need to look. The memory of her pearlescent skin was braised upon his mind, just as the feel of her all soft and yielding beneath him was engraved upon his soul. How he'd wanted her . . . wanted this, but she wasn't about to let him savor it too long. Her knees pushed up on either side of his sturdy thighs and her back arched, initiating a contact that scorched clean through him. And as if that didn't make her purpose clear enough, her hands cupped the hard curve of his buttocks, urging him to seek out that which she was eager to give.

"We've got all night," he said, struggling for control. And failing miserably.

"Maybe you do, but I don't." She was too aroused to put it in fancy terms. The truth would do. "I want you now."

So he complied with a smooth, deep plunge that had her eyelids opening wide, then sinking down in a sensual half-mast as his name purred up from her throat. And once she closed about him in that hot grip of pleasure, there were no more thoughts of a slow, easy restraint. They moved together with a sleek, primitive abandon, both well versed on the reward that awaited.

The culmination came so hard and fast, Mimi gave herself over with a keening cry even as she felt his concluding tremors. Then there was a long, lush silence with only the rasp of breathing to disturb it. The delicate chain of his kisses from ear to collarbone woke her from her sated doze. Her hands came up to rub along the firm contour of his shoulders, plying muscle and absorbing damp heat.

"I didn't mean to rush you, darlin'," she cooed contentedly. "It's been so long, I guess I just got greedy. I hope you got your money's worth."

He paused in his suckling at her throat. "How much were you planning to charge?"

"How much do you think I was worth?" She made her question coquettish, hoping he couldn't read the insecurity beneath it. She'd wanted so much to please him. Odd sentiments coming from one in her profession.

Then he lifted up on his elbows to say with a heart-shaking sincerity, "All I own and all I can borrow."

His reply unsettled her because it sounded as if he meant it. It was what she wanted to hear yet feared to believe. So she made the situation into a teasing game to reduce the intensity. "Good thing for you that you're the only man I've ever given it to for free."

But he wasn't willing to let the mood relax, prompting her with a quiet, "Really?"

"Yes" was all she'd say. She didn't want to tell him that even John Amory had always left coin for her favor. He'd told her that to lay with her without paying would be cheating on his wife. Apparently, he'd felt there was an acceptable difference between a whore and a lover and she never told him how much that differentiation hurt her. She didn't want to confide that to Emmitt who'd always made her feel as if their unions were ones of shared bliss rather than bartered pleasure. And that brought up a longtime source of curiosity.

"Emmitt, why is it you have never married?"

His hands began to plump her breasts with a gentle kneading, his touch so tender and insightful, she felt that stir of passion all over again. Feeling it now, looking at him now, reminded her of how it had been for them in the days after John's funeral. How guilty and confused she'd been giving herself over so easily to his loving. His first kiss had shaken her from her grief, and after their first union, she'd known as if lightning-struck, how shallow her love for John had been. John had never cleansed her soul from the stigma of sin or treated her with a cherishing tenderness. Waking to find Emmitt stretched out asleep beside her had given her a glimpse into what a normal existence would be; one in which a man and woman loved one another exclusively enough to share more than the night heat. That look into what her life might have been with just one man who would be there every morning had purely terrified her. Because she wasn't the kind of woman who deserved devotion from a man like Emmitt Owen. Not then.

Not now.

Tactfully, she wriggled away from his spirit-quickening caresses, pushing his hands aside with a feigned playfulness. "Are you trying to avoid the question, sugar?"

He shifted to one side but stayed propped up to look down upon her. Sometime during their passionate thrashings, he'd taken off his glasses, and without them, his eye color softened, betraying a surprising vulnerability. His smile tore her heart in two. "It's your fault. You made me forget what the question was. You're just too darned distracting. A man's mind goes to mush when he's near you."

She swallowed hard and struggled to retain her resolve. Though she wanted nothing more than to succumb once again to the temptation of his touch, she knew she couldn't afford to. They'd both read too much into it. Once could be excused as a reckless passion but not twice. Her expression was flirtatious by design. "I asked why you never married? Remember?"

"Oh. When I was younger, I was too busy building up a strong business foundation. No woman in her right thinking could have been expected to put up with my selfish hours."

Was he funning her or did he really believe that? That's exactly what women were expected to do, and do it without complaint. His näiveté amused and touched her deeply. A man considerate of what a woman was feeling . . . what a rarity that was. It made him all the more precious in her eyes. She began to absently twine her fingers through the nap of his chest hairs, unable and unwilling to stop touching him. He, also, was just too damned distracting. "So what's your excuse now that you're so successful?"

"I'm waiting for you."

Mimi was startled into a nervous laugh. "Now, what would you want with an old harlot like me?"

"Don't," he said sternly. "Don't laugh at me."

The anxious chuckles dried up into an uncomfortable tightness. "Then don't make fun of me."

"I've never done that, Mimi. Never." And the intensity of his words terrified her. Because she feared he meant them. Again, she tried to defuse the moment by refusing to act upon his emotions. She touched his jaw with gentle fingertips.

"I know that, Emmitt. You've been a wonderful friend to me. I wish I'd listened to you better."

"I wish you'd listen to me now. I love you, Mimi."

She just stared at him in stark dismay while her heart began a wild rhythm. Those few words were enough to upend her world, but there was more he would say.

"I've loved you almost from the start, but I couldn't compete with John when he was alive and it seems I can't compete with his ghost now that he's gone. I've tried to win your affection every way I knew how."

Panic settled inside her, stirring her to take the defensive in an effort to stave off the pain. "Did you think I'd love you if you forced me out of business? Did you think I'd turn to you if you gave me no other choice except to starve? Is that what you thought?"

"Mimi—"

But her ire was gathering the momentum needed to conquer her fright and her inappropriate longing for what could never be. "Did you think to bankrupt me into your bed? I won't be bought, Emmitt. Your money can't buy away the shame of what I am."

"What you are is the most generous, loving woman I've ever known."

"I'm a whore!"

"That's what you *did,* not who you are. Mimi, I don't care about that—"

"No? Well, I care. And so will everyone else. We've had this conversation before, Emmitt. Nothing has changed." She was sitting up, reaching for her robe when he caught her up in his arms and struggled to hold her close. With the heat and strength of him wrapped around her, she almost relented. She could almost believe it possible that a man like this could take her from what she was. But that was a familiar harlot's dream; always holding out for that hero who could erase the stain of truth. It was just a fantasy. She'd been in the business long enough to know that. There was no reason for her to think otherwise and risk the pain of disillusionment that would follow when reality overcame this moment of tender folly. When he would regret the unwise sentiments.

His words brushed softly along her cheek, a whisper-sweet argument. "Lots of things have changed. Mimi, this town isn't going to judge you for your past mistakes."

How wrong he was! The truth gave her the strength to resist him.

"Don't tell me about this town! Don't try to get me to believe it will be forgiving. I know different. This town listened to the cries of a fifteen-year-old girl who was carried off at a barbecue and forced to submit against her will, and then it turned a deaf ear to her call for justice. You know why? Because the man came from a better family than she did. Because he said the girl enticed him and they believed him because of all the land and slaves his daddy owned. He didn't care that he ruined that girl's future with his careless lust, and the town didn't care that she didn't do anything wrong. They made her family hide in shame. Their disdain drove her parents to push her out of their home to save the reputations of their two younger daughters. Don't tell me about forgetting the past. If I'd have been smart, I'd have let that boy have his way and said nothing. I'd have seen him at parties later on and smiled as if he'd never done a wrong thing. But *that* would have been wrong. This town never forgave me for pointing the finger at one of their finest and they'll never forgive me for what I became because of it."

He said nothing for the longest time, just staring down at her through those penetrating eyes as if he could read the anguish carring her soul. Then he told her with a quiet forcefulness, "Mimi, I'm not like them."

"You're part of this town, Emmitt. You're one of the city's finest. They look up to you. You can't step down to my level of sin and you can't drag me up to where you walk among them."

"Yes. I can. Tonight I'm going to a charity auction. I'll be sitting with the mayor. Come with me."

"What?"

"Come with me."

She was searching wildly for a way to discourage him from his madness, all the while loving him so much it hurt to draw a decent breath. "And have half the men there murmuring and remembering how I was in my younger days beneath the sheets?"

"I won't let it bother me."

"Well, it will bother *me!* I'm not ashamed of the choices I had to make. And I'll be damned if I'll let a passel of snotty aristocrats who'd gladly accept my charity but give none in return look down their thin noses at me." She jerked free of him and tugged on her dressing gown, too angry and distressed to care if tears streaked her flushed features.

"Mimi, I want you. I love you. What do I have to do to make you care?"

"You'll have to pay me for the privilege, just like everyone else. I don't want your charity. I've heard too many pretty promises."

His expression took on the hard edge of determination she was sure he wore when arguing his right to foreclose in the bank's best interest. "Will buying back your business for you convince you that I love you enough to look beyond what it is you do?"

"I won't be owned, Emmitt Owen. I won't be controlled. Not by you, not by any man."

They regarded each other for a tension-charged moment, both

too stubborn and prideful to give away when they knew the
were right in what they were doing. Then Emmitt's gaze softene
as he reached for her. She realized the danger in remaining i
such close proximity and she shoved his hand away.

"I think it's time you were going to your fancy party. I've g
clients to see."

And with that coldly spoken falsehood, she stalked out of th
bedroom to give him time to dress and herself the chance to pu
together her resources. But she was nowhere near composu
when he stormed out a moment later in hastily donned attire 1
confront her in an impressive rage.

"You want to be a whore, be a whore. You want me to tre
you like a whore, I will." And with that, he stuffed a handful
greenbacks down the overlap of her gown. "There. And believ
me, you were worth that and more." That was a backhande
compliment if she ever heard one. He hesitated, giving her
chance to respond but there was no slackening to her will. Seeir
that they'd reached an impasse, there was little more Emmi
could do except relent. "Good night, Miss Mimi. I won't kee
you from your other customers."

Her heart was pounding crazily against the padding of co
siderable cash money. Reaching into her gown, she drew o
what had to be at least several hundred dollars. A terrible trem
bling got a hold of her and then she was racing after him, shou
ing down at him as he stomped down the stairs.

"Take your money, Emmitt Owen! It's no good here."

And as he paused to look up at her, she flung the greenbacl
at him so that they rained down upon him where he stood. H
made no move to catch them. His eyes were on Mimi. His e>
pression was hard and unreadable.

"I'm not the first man to make a fool of himself over yo
Mimi, but I had hoped to be the last. Guess I was wrong. I car
make a future with you if you won't let go of the past."

Then he turned to continue the rest of the way down and w

out the front door without ever looking back again to where she'd collapsed upon the top step to weep woefully into her hands.

Eventually, Mimi was aware of her audience. Several of the girls were staring up at her in an uncomfortable sympathy. LaWanda was gathering up the money, and when it was all neatly stacked in her hand, the blonde came up to sit on the step beside her to offer the silent support of her shoulder and the understanding curl of her embrace.

Within the next three days, the working women of Miss Mimi's Hospitality House left for new employment, one by one. The last to go was LaWanda, who departed with uncharacteristic tears in the early afternoon on Christmas Eve. Then Mimi was alone in the big house. Silence settled in around her like a deepening northern snowfall. blanketing her emotions with an ever-increasing chill. As she moved from room to empty room, she was sure she would never be warm again.

Then came a knock on the front door.

"Sorry, we're closed for business," Mimi was saying by rote as she swung the heavy door inward. Then she saw who stood there and words and coherent thought vanished.

Lilith Amory was on her front steps.

"May I come in?"

At one time, Mimi might have enjoyed a rollicking laugh at the thought of the pristine Mrs. Amory requesting entrance into a house of ill repute, but on this night, she just stepped aside to let her pass. The other woman eased into the foyer and stole a covert look at her surroundings. A nun couldn't have acted more ill ease in Satan's parlor. That thought woke Mimi from her stupor.

"Mrs. Amory, won't you make yourself comfortable." A polite but impossible suggestion. "May I take your coat?"

"No, thank you." Her arms clutched at the fine material as i[f] she feared it would be somehow damaged by the contact. I[t] wasn't a conscious act, so Mimi tried not to take offense. "[I] don't mean to stay long. I'm sure you're very busy and I hav[e] a family to get home to."

That factual reminder wounded more deeply than the earlie[r] unintentioned snub. Mimi found her teeth gritted as she fough[t] the desire to toss the pompous Mrs. Amory out on her well-bre[d] rump. Instead, she murmured smoothly, "Then why don't yo[u] sit down and get right to the point of this . . . most unexpecte[d] call."

Lilith followed her gesture into the parlor proper and stoo[d] there for a moment staring with a gentle woman's unabashe[d] curiosity.

"I'd thought there'd be gilt cupids," she muttered to herself.

"I beg your pardon?"

"Nothing." But Lilith continued to gawk in obvious surprise[.] This was not at all what she'd imagined when she thought o[f] Mimi Leslie's bawdy house. She'd pictured garish crimson wal[l] hangings and yards of tassels, tasteless paintings, and vulga[r] statuary. Instead, she found the room decorated with a sumptu[-] ous elegance, all in shades of muted pink and silvery grays tha[t] was inviting to the refined eye and soothing to the senses. It wa[s] every bit as fashionable as her own parlor. A place one coul[d] relax in comfort. And somehow, that made it all the worse. A[ll] the more dangerous. It was easier to think of her husband's mis[-] tress as a bit of cheap flash instead of a serious rival.

"Can I offer you some sherry or maybe, under the circum[-] stances, something a little more bracing?"

"A shot of something bracing, I think."

Mimi smiled and poured as Lilith perched awkwardly on th[e] edge of a tufted sofa. She had to be wondering if her husban[d] had ever sprawled there in the arms of another woman listenin[g] to the piano play while drinking from the same decanter. Mim[i]

ould have told her no. She could have relieved much of the
woman's misery by telling her that John had always been the
oul of tasteful discretion, but she didn't attempt to set the other's
mind at ease. Mimi had suffered enough in her own imaginings;
ohn at the dinner table with his wife and son in dutiful attendance, saying grace with heads bowed and hearts humbled as
they murmured proper thanks for their prosperity. Those pictures
of domestic tranquility had been a terrible pain to bear on the
nights when she was entertaining a revolving cadre of the uncaring. Let Mrs. Amory be tormented by her visions just as she
was tortured by hers.

"Here you go."

The two woman took down the fiery liquor like seasoned
dockhands, anxious to get over the discomfort of the situation.

"So, Mrs. Amory, what brings you here?"

Instead of answering, Lilith regarded her for a long, scruti-
nizing second before speaking. "I wanted to hate you, Miss
Leslie. I wanted to believe you were the worst kind of woman
so I could feel better about myself, but seeing Cherice and the
way she's been reared, I know better."

Mimi could think of nothing to say, so she waited for the
woman to go on.

"Ironic, isn't it, how much we've shared over the years: the
same man, the same grief, Cherice, and now little Johnny. We've
too much in common to be enemies."

"If you've come to invite me to move in—"

"Lands, no!"

That honest response won a respectful smile from Mimi, and
once she got over her embarrassment, Lilith was smiling, too.

"I think we both realize how . . . awkward that would be, Miss
Leslie."

"Then why have you come? To wish me well or just to get a
look at the infamous Miss Mimi's before the doors are closed
for good?"

Lilith's color heightened, but she said truthfully, "Yes, wanted to see for myself, but I came to talk to you because o something Cherice said to me. She told me you denied yoursel any happiness because you felt guilty about John."

Mimi's jaw dropped. She wanted to issue an objection but the protesting words wouldn't come. So she shut her mouth an listened to what the other woman would say.

"Cherice said you felt responsible for my failed marriage and that's why you were leaving Memphis instead of seeking hel from your family."

How could Cherice have spoken of such personal things t this woman, of all people! However, she was too astonished t be angry with her indiscreet niece. And suddenly all too vulner able. "That's not it at all," she whispered at last, but Lilith pai no attention to her weak argument.

"What went wrong with my marriage had nothing to do wit you, Mimi. I wanted to think so for my vanity's sake, but wit age comes a certain wisdom, whether you wish it or not. I'v watched Cherice and my son together. If I'd had half their spiri and unselfish love, I'd have marched here with a scatter gun t take my husband home where he belonged. You couldn't hav made him come here against his will but perhaps I could hav put a stop to it by making him prefer to stay at home. But I wa raised to believe a woman had no right to demand a man b faithful, only that he provide for her and her children. And that he did most generously. I was too busy tending his home an his social status to take care of the needs of the man. I wa willing to let you do that for me. We married so young, you see and I was so unschooled in things of a personal nature." He blush increased, but she continued determinedly. It was impor tant that she get it all out now, both for Mimi and for herself.

"I didn't realize how much I loved John until he went off t war. I let him go without ever telling him that. I saw my chanc to make amends when Ruben was planning to ask Cherice fo

er hand. I saw you in her. I thought if he married her, he'd be
neating himself out of what I'd just discovered—how good life
ould be with the right person at your side. I didn't believe then
aat Cherice could be that woman. I know now that I was
rong."

She paused and took a deep breath, risking a cautious look
t the impassive face of the woman opposite her. Lilith couldn't
ll how Mimi was taking things, so she plunged on while her
ourage held.

"The war took John away from me and Ruben, not you. Had
e come home, it would have been to Stillwater and his family
nere. Cherice told me you believed he was coming here to you,
aat he was going to leave me, but that's not true. He wrote me
ght up until the end, telling me of his plans after the fighting.
hey were plans filled with hope for his plantation and for
uben. He never would have left Stillwater, and I, by virtue of
is name, was Stillwater. He never would have sullied Ruben's
ture with scandal. That was the kind of man he was."

"I know all about that kind of man, Mrs. Amory."

Those words were said in a small, taut voice but without any
etraying emotion. Lilith couldn't tell if she was angry or hurt
y the information she was hearing. She only knew how she
erself would feel if told all her treasured dreams were found
be a lie. And for all his infidelity, her husband had never lied
her.

"I'm not telling you this to cause you any pain. Lord knows,
e've both suffered enough of that over the last few years. I just
vanted to let you know so you wouldn't go on mourning him
nd the future you might have had together. It would have come
nothing, Miss Leslie. Cherice has brought new life into my
orld and a new chance to discover what love is. I aim to spoil
ly grandchild something fierce, as I will any more who follow.
would hate to think you would deny yourself the same pleasure
ecause of something we should have put to rest between us

long ago. Cherice is fond of quoting something you told her. I
believe it goes, 'You're not where you've been but where you're
going.' I think that means it's time we let memories go and moved
on with our lives. If yours take you from Memphis, I want you
to know I really do wish you well, and that I'll see to Cherice
and the baby for you. And if you stay and there's anything I can
do, I would be honored if you'd call on me."

With that, she stood, and Mimi rose as well. The two regarded
each other for a long moment, then Mimi said, "You are a gracious woman, Mrs. Amory. Not many would be willing to hum-
ble themselves before someone like me. Not after all the pain I
caused you."

"It's Lilith. And much of the pain was brought on by my own
pride. A sin of the South, I believe."

"There are worse sins," Mimi reflected. Then she offered her
hand and the other woman took it. "I'm glad we had this talk . . .
Lilith."

They smiled cautiously, testing the new ground laid between
them that was not quite friendship but was no longer a bitter
battlefield.

"Well, I must be going. It's Johnny's first Christmas, you
know."

"I know," Mimi echoed softly, and Lilith's gaze filled with a
surprising empathy as she remembered that this woman was
denied the small daily joys she doted upon. And the last of the
jealous spite she held for Mimi Leslie died in that pensive moment.

"The invitation to dinner tomorrow stands. We'd be happy if
you'd join us. Our Maddy always makes enough to feed a hungry
regiment." Then, more persuasively, she added, "Christmas is a
time for family to be together."

Mimi saw her to the door and out into the frigid evening where
her buggy waited, its team blowing frosty plumes into the gathering shadows. Despite the chill, she remained, hugging her arms

while standing upon those front steps until the conveyance was out of sight. Then she returned inside where there was warmth but no longer welcome. She climbed the stairs as if all her nerve endings were still numbed by the cold, but the thaw she hoped to avoid began as she resumed her packing. And with it, came incredible pain.

John Amory had never meant any of his promises. Deep in her heart, she'd always known that, but there was a part of her, a part raised under a shadow of shame, that made her believe she was responsible for his death. When the news had come that he'd been killed, her conscience cried out that he'd died to punish her for the sin of adultery, to prevent her from finding happiness with him as a result of wrongdoing. The guilt of that had weighed upon her shoulders for years, and it was nothing short of amazing that John Amory's widow was the one to lift it from her.

He hadn't planned to come back to her. In his death, he'd managed to manipulate her emotions just as he'd done in life. He'd blinded her with his surface charm into thinking what she felt for him was love, and the blame she harbored over his tragic end had convinced her to wear her martyred devotion to his memory like sackcloth and ashes. She had never loved him. She had never understood love until Emmitt Owen.

I'm not just anybody.

I'm not like them.

No, Emmitt wasn't like the others. He wasn't like John who would never have seen her as anything but a whore handing out pleasure for profit. John would never—ever—have left his lovely home and respectable wife to make an honest woman out of her. Lilith had been right about that, but she'd been kind enough not to point out the true reason. It was because he never viewed Mimi as an honest woman. She'd been a convenience afforded by his life of planter privilege, nothing more. And for five years, he'd dragged her heart down into the grave alongside him and she'd allowed it to remain buried with him because she'd been taught that she deserved no better than the misery her lifestyle led to.

Hadn't he stolen enough of her life from her? Him and that fellow who'd taken her virtue so long ago? The shame was theirs, not hers. It always had been.

Wasn't it time to resurrect the redeemable spirit of Miriam Leslie?

Wasn't it time she stopped apologizing and started in living again?

And part of living was loving. And the man she loved was Emmitt. Had she taken the time to look beyond the guilt and confusion, she would have known it always had been.

She was standing over her partially packed trunk, staring down blindly through her tears at the rich satins and sleek silks she'd worn in the reception foyer of this house for the last five years. But the clothes and the surroundings that claimed her as a fallen woman could be changed. They could be put aside and forgotten. If she had the strength to walk away. If she could wash away the stain of shame upon her soul that reduced her pride the way no outward stigma could.

It was time she stopped punishing herself for her family's shallow vanity and John Amory's deceit. It was time she held her head up high to proclaim herself as good as any who walked the streets of Memphis. If only she could take that first terrifying step.

A staccato of sound announced another visitor. Wondering if Lilith had forgotten something, Mimi wiped away her tears with an impatient hand and hurried down the steps to throw open the door. And she froze.

For there beneath the light filtering snow fall was Emmitt Owen come to call.

Only the absence of a smile upon his face held her back from filling his arms with a gladsome cry. His look was not inviting, nor was his tone. It was painfully neutral. A remote banker's voice.

"Good evening, Mimi. I know it's late and I'm sorry to disturb you, but I've a gift for you."

"A gift?" She drew a shaky breath, at first uncertain then touched by a surge of joy. "Oh, Emmitt, you shouldn't have done—"

"I didn't," he corrected crisply, and her expectations plummeted only to be teased up again by his next curious words. "It's a gift from the city of Memphis to wish you a Merry Christmas."

She took the folded paper from his hand and stared incomprehensibly upon the words as snowflakes made damp blotches upon the parchment. "I don't understand," she said at last.

It was the deed to her house. Paid in full.

Then she was afraid she understood all too well. "Emmitt, you didn't—"

But he cut off her angry accusation. "No, I didn't. All day anonymous donations have appeared on my desk at the bank, funds marked for the payment of your loan. There was more than enough to see your debt erased by closing time. I took the liberty of opening an account for the rest. I'll hold it there until you decide—until you decide where I should forward it. If you still mean to go, that is.

And then all the hurtful indifference melted from his eyes the way the white powder disappeared upon the warmth of his exposed skin.

"You'll let me know, Mimi, won't you, one way or another?"

When she didn't answer—couldn't—answer, he sighed and began to turn away. That's when her shock gave way to opportunity.

"Emmitt?"

He looked back at her.

"Won't you—would you come in for a moment? Join me in a toast to the holiday?"

He studied her face as if he was afraid he was interpreting her invitation incorrectly. Then an almost imperceptible nod.

Mimi held the door open and she was quick to relieve him of his damp outer coat. She sucked in a deep breath, tasting the crispness of the weather and the heat of man in that lingering inhalation. And nothing had ever seemed more invigorating. He walked into the parlor with a heartrending familiarity and neither said anything until both had a sip of brandy. Then he spoke first.

"I guess the folks here in Memphis are a lot more forgiving than you gave them credit for."

Mimi regarded the deed still clutched in one hand. "But why? I don't understand why they would have done such a thing." For her. For a harlot of no importance.

"Because you've touched a lot of lives here, Mimi. You've done a lot of good and people remember that when they've got the chance. I think they're trying to thank you for being there when they needed you by being there when you needed them."

"Who—?"

"Does it matter?"

She smiled slightly. "No. Not really."

Emmitt was watching her, puzzled by her subdued reaction. This wasn't what he'd hoped for when he'd brought her the un-expected peace offering from the city of Memphis. Finally, he asked, "Will you reopen your doors?" *Will you stay now?* was his unspoken question.

Mimi thought a moment, and a poignant expression crossed her face. She looked about the parlor room, seeing the ghosts of the past: a young Cherice in white playing the piano, a love-struck Ruben Amory at his father's side unable to take his eyes from her. John, with his dazzling smile like a beacon to a girl's heart, curling his arm about her waist to tug her toward the stairs in lustful urgency. Emmitt at cards here in the parlor, watching through somber eyes as they ascended the steps. Had he loved her even then?

"No," she murmured quietly. "I won't reopen. I can't. The girls have all gone on to better things. I think it's time I did, too."

He stared hard into his glass. Tension leaped along his jaw until the words worked their way out. "Then I guess you really are saying goodbye."

"Goodbye? Yes, I am. Goodbye to all that is past and hello to what's to come."

"There's no reason for you to go. I mean, this place is paid for now. You have a home here. You could turn this place into a—"

Her smile grew wry at his desperate mental groping. "Into what? A boardinghouse for respectable young church-going girls? No, Emmitt, it's time I moved out from under the memories in these rooms. Besides, I'm all packed."

"Then come live with me."

His offer was so unexpected, she just stared. Then she found her voice. It was painfully frail as she echoed LaWanda's earlier insecurity. "As what?"

"Whatever you want to be."

Her heart was pounding up in her throat, a hurried pulse of anticipation. But still, she protested. She felt she had to. "I need a fresh start, Emmitt."

"You don't need to go all the way to New Orleans to have that." Her eyes widened in surprise that he'd known her plans. And her intent. "That'd be running away, Mimi. That's not like you. You want to start over, start here. The best way to effect change is to force it head-on. If you can't see the change in folks with your own eyes, you won't believe it was possible. Mimi, you need to see it happen. You're the one who needs to make it happen."

He was right. She knew it. But what he was suggesting called for more courage than she could muster. She'd faced down Union soldiers and drunken customers but the thought of battling scornful opinion on the boardwalks and in the marketplace day to day made her turn away from him to utter a soft, cowardly admission.

"I'm scared, Emmitt."

"I'll be right here to help you be strong."

And his arms banded about her in a tight wrap of security. His big frame became an unyielding wall of support at her back, one she could lean upon, one that would provide ample shelter. Unconsciously, she was clutching at his sturdy forearms, testing their strength, knowing it wouldn't fail her. She trembled as his kiss whispered along her temple. She realized it was time for a little more truth on her end. It was important for him to understand before things went any further.

"I've always made such big talk about not apologizing for who I am, but that kind of talk's easy when you've got a sullied reputation to hide behind. I've been using this place to keep the world out, to shield me from its opinions. There won't be anything to hide behind once I step outside."

"Walk at my side, Mimi, and walk proud. You've got more starch than most petticoats. I won't let anyone hurt you with loose talk."

"But you can't stop what they're thinking."

"I don't care *what* they're thinking. Why should you? This whole country's starting over fresh. Why should we be less forgiving toward one another when we've got wounds so much greater to forget?"

She was rubbing his sleeves, delighting in the hard feel of his flesh, in the powerful cadence of his voice. "You make it sound easy."

"We both know that's not going to be true."

His fingertips rose to stroke down her cheek, then curved around her jaw to angle her head up and about. She met the warm pressure of his mouth with all the welcome he could want. It was a taste of paradise neither cared to surrender.

"Marry me, Mimi. Let's show them all we don't care what they think. I'll protect you from their gossip."

Her chuckle was a low and throaty surprise. It was the most enticing sound he'd ever heard. "Oh, sugar, gossip can't hurt my reputation. It's yours I'm worried about."

"Mine?" He clearly didn't understand. Or didn't want to understand. Mimi swallowed hard, figuring she owed it to him to put it blunt and plain so he'd know exactly what he was getting into.

"Emmitt, you can only be hurt by your association with me. I don't want to be responsible for pulling your name into scandal."

"I'll survive it. Ask Ruben if he values a sterling name over the love of his wife."

"But it's not the same thing. Cherice was never—she never—Oh, tarnation! Emmitt, everyone in Memphis knows what I am. There's no hiding it, no explaining it away, no pretending it's something less offensive. I've been a whore and I ran a whorehouse. Think what that will do to your standing in town. I'm afraid for you, Emmitt."

He gave a scoffing laugh. "I'm not. Not now. I've been afraid for five long years wondering if I'd ever hold you in my arms again. I know what you've done and I know why. I don't care if the entire army of the Potomoc was lined up outside your bedroom door. As long as I'm last in line. I'd rather be last than first." He adored her uplifted features with his gliding touch, gently brushing away the steady advance of tears she was unaware of shedding. "Is that why you sent me away after John died? Because you thought you'd ruin me?"

"You were just starting out, Emmitt. It was such a fragile time for you. I didn't want you to risk everything for me. I didn't want to risk you hating me for it later."

"Then you must have cared for me." There was a hushed hope in those words that touched her heart to hear.

"I've always cared for you." But instead of expounding upon that long-sought sentiment, she cautioned, "What'll they say when staid and respectable Emmitt Owen, owner of the bank, takes a harlot into his house?"

"They'll probably cluck in disapproval and secretly think, 'Why, I never thought that stuffy ol' Emmitt Owen had it in him!' The men will envy me my nights and just maybe some of the women will envy you your bank account. I'm not such a bad catch, you know."

Her fingers threaded back through his hair to lace behind his head. "I know," she told him as she drew him down to her parted lips. Her response encouraged him to grow bolder in his proposal.

"Say you'll marry me, Mimi. Tell me there's a chance someday you'll grow to love me."

"Honey, I couldn't grow to love you any more than I do right now."

His bright eyes penetrated straight to her soul in his search for the truth of that statement. Then he bent down to kiss her, a hard, claiming kiss, a branding kiss of passion and possession. He gave way with reluctance when she pushed her palms against his chest.

"I've got a present for you, too, Emmitt. You wait right here while I get it." She wriggled free of his embrace and was out of the room in a swirl of silk, returning a moment later with something in her hand. He took what she offered to him and studied it in bewilderment. It was a one-way ticket to New Orleans.

"Merry Christmas, Emmitt. I won't be needing that anymore."

Smiling, he tore it in half and let the pieces fall.

"Be my wife."

"Make the arrangements. I'm all packed."

His grin broke wide, strong and satisfied. "Right after Christmas. We'll start the New Year together. How'd that be?"

"That'd be fine, Mr. Owen. But as long as you're here tonight . . ." She reached out to possess herself of his big hand, giving it a slight tug. "We've got all night to discuss wedding plans and a half dozen rooms upstairs that could use one more good memory before I close them up for good. And we've been invited to Christmas dinner at my niece's house. We might as well start by telling them the news first. If you're willing."

He drew her up close against him. "Willing and able. Lead the way, Miss Mimi. The spirit of giving is upon me."

She turned down the lamp so their shadows no longer mixed with the memories within the parlor room. And hand in hand, they climbed the stairs together as Miss Mimi's Hospitality House closed for business and Miriam Leslie's heart opened to embrace a flood of long overdue personal happiness.

The Spirit of Christmas

by
Bobbi Smith

Prologue

St. Louis, 1878

It was Christmas Eve. Stephanie Charless sat alone in the parlor of her family home on Lucas Place, staring out the window at the deserted, night-shrouded street beyond. Freezing rain borne by the icy wind splattered against the panes, blurring the view. The dark-haired, green-eyed beauty didn't notice, though, for her tears had already blinded her. It seemed to Stephanie that she hadn't stopped crying since she'd gotten the news three days earlier that her beloved parents and only sister, ten-year-old Jenny, had been killed in a tragic accident. The funeral had been the afternoon before, and now, for the first time in her life, she was alone.

Pain stabbed at Stephanie as she glanced across the room at the Christmas tree they'd decorated as a family the day before the accident. It had been a warm, loving, festive time, stringing popcorn and putting the candles and ornaments on the tree. The memory of Jenny's happy, delighted laughter echoed hauntingly in her mind. Sweet, angelic Jenny had loved everything about Christmas—the jingle bells, the caroling, the pure joy of the season. Every year from Thanksgiving on, her sister had eagerly counted the days until Christmas Eve, carefully marking them off on a calendar in her room. Stephanie knew that this year's calendar would forever remain marked only until December 21.

For Stephanie, the spirit of Christmas had died along with he family.

As she stared at the gaily wrapped presents piled under th tree, Stephanie's soul ached with the knowledge that her littl sister would never unwrap them. A sob tore through her as sh realized with desolate, desperate clarity that she would neve see her parents or her sister again.

"Stephanie?"

At the sound of her maiden aunt's voice, she turned her tearfu gaze to the woman who'd come to live with her now that he parents were gone. "Yes, Aunt Rose?"

"Is there anything I can do for you, sweetheart? Anything a all?" The gray-haired, elderly woman moved into the room. Sh loved Stephanie like her own and had been giving her som private time, but the sound of her crying had torn at her heart

Stephanie managed a teary, brittle smile. "I only want Mam and Papa and Jenny back. Can you get them for me?"

"I wish with all my heart I could." Thoughts of her belove sister, brother-in-law, and niece besieged her, and she fough futilely against the tears that threatened.

Stephanie stood and went to her aunt, hugging her as the shared their loss.

"What are we going to do without them?" her aunt asked.

"I don't know, Aunt Rose. I wish I did."

After a long moment, they moved apart.

"I know this isn't a good time to tell you this, but I was puttin some of my clothes in the closet in the bedroom I'm using, an I found something I think you need to see."

Stephanie followed Rose upstairs, and when they entered th room she saw another pile of presents on the bed.

"Your mother evidently had these hidden away. They're he Santa gifts for Jenny."

Stephanie moved forward and touched each lovingly wrappe present. Her mother had always had extra presents for Jenny o

hristmas morning because her little sister had clung fiercely
her belief in Santa.

Stephanie's thoughts drifted for a moment to the Christmas
ve two years before. As they'd been leaving Midnight Mass,
nny had seen a poor man begging outside of church. She'd
oken away from her father and hurried to the man to give him
e last few pennies she had in her pocket. Her parents had been
touched by her display that they, too, had helped the man.
nny had known the true meaning of the season even as an
ght-year-old.

"They're mostly toys," Rose was saying. "I helped your
other wrap them. Do you want to keep them or should I return
em?"

"No! We won't return them," Stephanie replied quickly as a
immer of inspiration sparked in her numb heart. "What time
it?"

"A little after eight. Why?"

"I have an idea, and there's still time."

"Time for what?" She had no idea what Stephanie was
inking.

"I need to send a message to Father Finn. I need him right
vay."

"But why?"

"You'll see." She'd known the priest since she was a child.
e'd been a close friend to her parents, and he'd told her at the
neral if she ever needed him all she had to do was call. Tonight,
e needed him.

Stephanie and Rose went back downstairs and called one of
e servants to take the message to the priest.

Father Robert Finn read Stephanie's note as soon as it came,
d he immediately left the warmth of the rectory and started
1 his way to see her. He kept his overcoat wrapped tightly

around him in defense against the miserable weather as he hur
ried through the streets to the Charless household. A worried
frown creased his brow as he thought about the sense of urgency
in her missive, and he was concerned that something was terribly
wrong. He'd promised Stephanie that he would be there for her
if she needed him, and, being a man of his word, he would.

He turned the corner onto Lucas Place and hunched his broad
shoulders against a blast of wintry wind that battered him. The
promise of warmth at the Charless home just down the block
made him quicken his pace. He reached the door and knocked,
and he was glad when Sam the butler quickly opened it to admit
him.

"Father, come in where it's warm. It's terrible out there." The
old servant smiled in welcome as he recognized the tall, dark
haired priest.

"Thanks, Sam. I got a note from Stephanie saying that she
needed to see me right away. Is she all right?" he asked as he
shed his coat and handed it to him.

He nodded in response as he took the damp garment. "She
and Miss Rose are waiting for you in the parlor, Father."

Father Finn started toward the parlor just as Stephanie
emerged from the room.

"You came! I hoped you would!" At the sight of him before
her, she smiled. He'd been a close friend to her family for a long
time, and his gentle, deep, abiding faith had helped her through
the trauma of the last few days. She'd been praying that he would
come right away, and she was thrilled that her prayers had been
answered.

"What is it? Is something wrong?" His dark-eyed gaze mir
rored the confusion and concern as he crossed the foyer to go
to her. He'd thought she might be depressed and lonely and miss
ing her family at this most holy time; yet, instead, she seemed
almost happy.

"No, nothing's wrong. In fact, I think something's very right. Come and sit down. I have something I want your opinion on."

She drew him into the parlor where he greeted Rose and then sat down with them. They had a hot cup of tea as she began to explain.

Father Finn listened as the young woman told him her inspired plan.

"Will you do it? Will you help me tonight?" she pleaded. "We can go right after Midnight Mass."

"Are you sure about this, Stephanie? These were your parents' last gifts to you and your sister. Are you certain you want to give them away?" He knew she'd been devastated by her loss and that it would take time for her to recover. He didn't want her to do anything tonight that she might regret later.

For the first time in days, she was filled with a sense of peace. She was determined to turn her own pain into an act of goodness. She met his caring regard without hesitation. "Yes, Father, I'm sure. I'm doing this for my parents, but mostly I'm doing it for Jenny. She would have wanted me to."

Father Finn touched her hand in a gesture of understanding and support. "I'll be back as soon as I can."

"I'll have everything loaded in the carriage, ready to go. You know the families who are in most need?"

"Yes."

"Perhaps this Christmas will be the one that makes a difference in their lives."

They met at two A.M., the priest and the mysterious veiled woman in mourning clothes. Together, they made silent rounds through the city's streets, delivering the presents to doorsteps of families in need.

No one saw them.

On Christmas morning, children believed.

One

A St. Louis Post-Dispatch *Editorial*
November 23, 1882

The Spirit of Christmas? Don't Believe it!
Zachary Madison

The Spirit of Christmas is at it again. In case you've missed past coverage, each holiday season from Thanksgiving to Christmas for the last four years a mysterious person identified only as the Spirit of Christmas has been doling out presents and money to the less fortunate of our city. There are those who would have us believe that this Spirit is acting out of kindness and concern, but this reporter disagrees. Nothing is ever done in this life without some promise of a return. Whoever this Spirit is, rest assured they're receiving some kind of payoff for their efforts. And for all the Spirit's supposed generosity, what real good does it do? For one day out of the year, the poor child has a toy and the parents have a dollar in their pockets. Are those paltry gifts going to change their lives? Is that surprise on the doorstep going to lift the family out of poverty? Hardly.

The actions of the Spirit are cruel. It's far better never to know better things exist than to have a glimpse of the joy that could be theirs only to have it snatched away with the brutal dawning of a cold new day. The Spirit of Christmas? To quote Dickens: Bah! Humbug!

* * *

Dark-haired, dark-eyed Zach Madison put the finishing touches on his editorial and then handed it to John Molloy, one of the other reporters at the paper. "Here, see what you think," he said as he leaned back in his desk chair in the newspaper office.

John read it quickly, then looked up at him, his expression a bit puzzled. "You're being a little hard on our 'Spirit', Zach. From the sound of this, you could rival Scrooge in the beginning of *A Christmas Carol* for being the most hard-hearted, cynical man alive. You don't really feel this way, do you?"

"Would it matter if I did?"

"But 'Bah! Humbug'? Come on. This Spirit of Christmas we've got running around the city every year is a good thing. Why try to ruin it?"

"I'm not trying ruin anything. I'm just trying to show it for what it is."

"But do you really believe this? Do you really think that everyone has an ulterior motive for what they do? And that people never do good things just for the joy of it?"

"We're reporters, John. We're supposed to tell the truth. That's all I'm doing."

"The truth as you see it," he countered.

Zach shrugged. "This is an editorial."

"You honestly don't believe in Christmas, do you? Or Santa?" John studied Zach as he spoke. He'd worked with him for two years, and yet even after all that time, he still didn't know him well. Zach was an excellent reporter, one of the best on the paper, but he was a private man, a lone wolf, and he liked it that way.

"Sure, I believe in Christmas and Santa, and the tooth fairy, too." Zach dismissed his question.

"I just don't understand why you have to be so negative about something that does good?"

"What good is it doing? Like I said in the editorial, why taunt the poor kids with something they can never have? Why build up their hopes? They know the world's a miserable place, why let them hope for something better?"

"Because things *can* get better."

"Maybe you're the Spirit, John. You sound just like a do-gooder."

"I'm not the Spirit, but I wish I had the money to do what the Spirit is doing."

"You're too soft-hearted," Zach counseled.

"And you're too hard. I can't believe if you feel this way that you're going to cover the Annual Charity Awards on the fifteenth." The Awards Banquet was an annual event, hosted by the mayor, in which civic honors were bestowed upon all those who gave selflessly of their time in service to others during the course of the year.

"Rest assured, I'll cover it to the best of my ability."

"That's what I'm afraid of," John remarked.

"What's wrong with the truth, John? One of these days you're going to find out that, no matter how much you wish it were different, the world and most of the people in it are just not nice."

John refused to be converted to his harsh outlook. "I disagree with you. Life is what we make of it. You look at everything too dispassionately. Sometimes it seems as if you judge things without any emotion at all. Don't you ever feel the joy that comes just from doing good for others?"

"Sure I do."

"Oh, really? When?"

"Right now," Zach said with a grin. "I'm a real nice guy. Why, I just agreed to cover the Presentation Ball for Andrews Saturday night."

"The Presentation Ball?" John stared at him in complete surprise. This ball was one of the biggest of the season, and every-

one who was anyone showed up. It was commonly know
around the office that Zach had little taste for such social event
"How'd he talk you into it? Blackmail?" He was chuckling a
he asked the question.

"He caught me in a weak moment." Zach grimaced inward
at the thought of spending an entire evening in the company o
the elite. The liquor was free, though, and there was one othe
bright spot . . .

"I wish Andrews had asked me."

"I owed him, and he collected—in spades."

"Hey, Zach, it's a tough, ugly job covering the social scen
but someone's got to do it. You want me to take it for you?
could force myself to go, knowing I was doing you a favor," h
volunteered, excited by the prospect of hobnobbing with the ri
and famous.

"No, that's okay. I don't like owing anybody anything."

"Well, enjoy yourself, but if you change your mind . . ." Joh
handed the editorial back as he started from the room.

"Goodbye, John."

When the other reporter had gone, Zach reread his wor
As he did, John's question about whether or not he believe
in the goodness of people kept intruding in his thoughts. H
paused and, after a period of reflection, decided that he trul
didn't believe men harbored any innate kindness in their heart
He'd seen too much ugliness in his twenty-eight years of livin
to be convinced that people really did want to do the rig
thing.

Zach had learned early in life that it was every man for hin
self. At age four, he'd been abandoned by his mother at an o
phanage in Chicago. He'd never seen her again after that col
November night when she'd left him at the door of the foundlir
home and had started to walk away. Frightened, he'd run aft
her, but she'd spanked him and forced him to stay there. She

isappeared into the darkness and had never looked back, not ven when he cried out to her over and over again.

Zach remembered vividly those first weeks in the home when, errified and lonely, he'd cried every night at bedtime for his mother, wanting her desperately. The other, older boys had taken o interest in him. They'd been annoyed by his whining and had eaten and intimidated him into silence. That was his first lesson t the home; nobody really cares and only the strong survive.

The people who'd run the orphanage had tried in their own ay to help, but times had been hard and he'd been just one of many. From that Thanksgiving on, he'd learned that the holidays ere not for the likes of him. He'd prayed silently at night that is mother would come back for him on Christmas. When he'd wakened at dawn that day and found that his prayers had gone nanswered, he still hadn't given up. With all the hope of an nnocent, he'd been sure that she'd return for him. All Christmas ay he'd kept vigil at the orphanage's front window, watching s people passed by carrying gaily wrapped packages and laugh- ng cheerfully in the spirit of the season. He'd stoically endured e taunts and jeering laughter of the other boys as he'd contin- ed to watch, but the long hours passed and she'd never come. When at nightfall he'd been herded off to dinner and then to bed, e pain of the realization that he was all alone had been almost o much for him to bear. From that night on, the night that his ope had died, he'd begun to harden his heart. He'd been alone en, and he still was today.

By his twelfth birthday, he was big enough and strong enough o make his own decisions. He'd run away and had never gone ack. Now, here he was. Through sheer grit and hard work, he'd nade something out of himself. He'd done it on his own, without ny help from anybody. That's the way life was. You were on our own.

* * *

Father Finn worked side by side with Stephanie, wrapping th
gifts and adorning each one with a bright holiday bow. When a
last the final bow had been tied, he looked up and smiled at he

"You've outdone yourself this year." He gazed around th
room full of presents, amazed and proud of all that she'd accom
plished. What had begun as a simple giving from the heart th
first Christmas, had now turned into an annual endeavor, and
was one of which he was particularly fond. Anytime he coul
help to bring the joy of Christmas to others, Father Finn wa
happy.

Stephanie looked up at the priest who'd been her secret partne
since the very first and returned his smile. "I would never hav
guessed it would have turned into anything of this magnitud
That first year, I just wanted to help a few children have th
happy Christmas that Jenny had missed, and now . . ." She ges
tured to gifts waiting to be distributed by the Spirit. "It's gettin
to be a challenge trying to buy all these without anyone figurin
out what we're doing."

"It's a good thing you've got your aunt Rose and Sam t
help."

"They're wonderful."

"Yes, they are, but none of this would have happened withou
you. You're a legend in your own time."

"I don't want to be that. I'm not doing this for glory. I'r
doing it for Jenny. You know how much Christmas meant t
her. I just want to carry on with her spirit of goodness an
generosity."

"I know, and you are."

"But am I doing enough?" she worried.

He met her gaze and saw reflected there the truth of her co
cern for the less fortunate. When he spoke it was from his hear
"The poor will always be with us. There's never an end to th
need. All we can do is our best, and you've done that."

Stephanie glanced around again and saw the fruits of her tit

ing stacked up and ready to be distributed. It was amazing the amount of gifts she had this year. She'd set aside a portion of the profits from her family's business and, with Aunt Rose and Sam helping her with the shopping, they'd purchased as many things as they could. There had been a time when she'd considered revealing the truth and asking for donations, but she'd decided to keep the secret of the Spirit. Only Aunt Rose, Sam, and Father Finn knew she was the one responsible, and she enjoyed the anonymity of it.

"It's been five years now. . . ." she said softly, recalling as she always did at this time of the year the happiness of her childhood and the tragedy that had ended it. "It's hard to believe that I've accumulated so much that we have to start giving things out right after Thanksgiving again."

"Your parents and sister would be proud of you."

"I hope so." Her eyes shone with tears at his praise. His support meant a lot to her.

"Do you have the bells and your notes ready?" the priest asked.

"I'm all set." Though that first year, Stephanie had only given out the presents, she'd been so touched by the plight of the people she'd visited in secret that night, she'd been inspired to continue the following year. That second Christmas she'd begun to leave a string of jingle bells like the ones Jenny had loved so much with each gift, along with a note wishing the recipient a wonderful season and asking them to pass along their good fortune when they were able. She'd signed the note "The Spirit of Christmas," and the newspapers had been calling her that ever since.

"What time do you want to leave tonight?"

"After eleven, I think. It should be quiet enough on the streets then."

"I'll be here," Father Finn promised, knowing he was going to enjoy the evening as much as she would.

"See you then."

Two

"I don't believe this," Stephanie blurted out as she stared down at the copy of the *Post-Dispatch* she held.

"Believe what, dear?" Aunt Rose asked solicitously, looking up from her needlepoint.

"There's an editorial in the *Post* by that . . . that Zachary Madison! It's incredible!" Her anger was obvious.

"We've met him, haven't we? As I recall, I thought he was rather nice. What's he written that's upset you so?" She lay her stitchery aside and gave her niece her full attention.

"Yes, we've met him, several times, and I thought he was nice, too. But listen to this . . ." Stephanie began to read the offending article to her. " *'The actions of the Spirit are cruel. It's far better never to know better things exist, than to have a glimpse of the joy that could be theirs only to have it snatched away with the brutal dawning of a new day. The Spirit of Christmas? To quote Dickens: Bah! Humbug!'* " She paused to draw a breath. "Do you believe it? He's infuriating! How can he possibly believe that the Spirit does these things for payment?!" Righteously outraged, she tossed the paper aside as if it were some vile thing.

"I don't feel angry at him, I feel sorry for him," Rose said quietly. She could hear in Zach's condemnation of the Spirit the sound of someone who'd never known true love and affection.

"Sorry for him?" Stephanie glared at her aunt. "Maybe he just doesn't understand true goodness in anyone."

"There are people out there who never had a family like yours. Think what your life would have been like if your parents had died when you were very young and you'd been left poor with no relations to care for you. I doubt you'd be the same young woman you are now."

Stephanie refused to budge on her condemnation of the reporter. "That may very well be, but he's supposed to report the truth."

"No, dear, that's an editorial. That's his opinion."

"Well, he doesn't know what he's talking about. He sounds like a mean, spiteful man. I've got a notion to write him back and straighten him out about a few things."

"Why don't you? Write to him as the Spirit and try to convince him he's wrong. It might prove entertaining to see what kind of response you get."

"Indeed, it might," she replied thoughtfully as she recalled the first time she'd met the good-looking Zach Madison. It had been in the spring at the grand opening of the newly rebuilt Olympic Theater. He'd been covering the event for the newspaper. They'd run into each other several times since then, and she'd always found him interesting and entertaining. Before today, she'd thought him quite intelligent, but now, she had her doubts. "Excuse me, Aunt Rose, I believe you're right. I do have some correspondence to catch up on."

"Don't get so wrapped up in your letter-writing that you forget about the ball tonight," Rose called after her as she started from the room.

"It's a good thing you said something," Stephanie replied as she stopped in the doorway. "I'd almost forgotten about the Presentation Ball. Michael said he'd be here around eight."

"I'm sure he'll be on time. He's quite fond of you, you know, and I'm certain *he* hasn't forgotten about your engagement this evening."

She smiled gently at her aunt. "I know you like Michael, Aunt Rose, but he isn't the man for me. We're just good friends."

"I happen to think he'd be the perfect husband for you. He's handsome and wealthy and—"

"And I'm sure he'd be thrilled to hear you say all that," she interrupted her match-making relative, "but I'm not romantically interested in him. I like him, but I don't love him."

"Love sometimes takes time."

"That may be true. I may not know what real love is yet, but I do know enough to realize it's not what I feel for Michael."

"Pity."

Stephanie's smile turned a trifle wicked as she imagined her aunt on the arm of the handsome, blond, blue-eyed young man. "Perhaps I should ask him if he'd be interested in an older woman."

"Oh, you!" Rose blushed in girlish pleasure at her teasing. "If I were forty years younger, I just might take you up on that."

They shared a moment of laughter, and then Stephanie headed upstairs to write her letter to Zach Madison. "Don't worry, I'll be ready for Michael when he gets here."

Retreating to her bedroom, Stephanie sat down at her desk and took out pen and paper. She waited a few minutes, taking the time to bring her anger under control. She wanted to be certain that what she was going to put on paper would sound intelligent and not shrill. Finally, she began to write:

An Open Letter to Mr. Zachary Madison

Sir,

In your editorial of the twenty-third entitled The Spirit of Christmas? Don't Believe it!, *you contend that the works of the person known as Spirit of Christmas in our community are being done strictly for a calculated reason and not for the love of the season and God's people. You also state that the Spirit's good deeds are cruel in that they nurture hope where there should be none.*

Sir, I maintain that you do not know the true meaning of Christmas. Christmas is hope. Christmas is unconditional love. Christmas is the joy of giving from one's heart with no promise or thought of repayment. Perhaps you need to experience these gifts of the Spirit so that in the future you'll be able to recognize them for what they are—presents freely given in loving appreciation of the season.

If the gifts I bring lighten one heart, brighten one day or bring faith to one lost soul, then all will have been worth it. I claim no reward other than the knowledge that somewhere on Christmas morning, a child is smiling.

I remain,
The Spirit of Christmas

When she'd finished the letter, Stephanie read it again. Pleased with the results, she copied it in a plain yet neat script on unmarked white stationery before sealing it in an envelope to be mailed the next day. She didn't know if her letter would make it into print in the paper, but at least she had the pleasure of knowing that Zach Madison was going to hear about it one way or another.

"Are you having a good time?" Michael Hunt asked as he stood at Stephanie's side, watching the couples swirling about the dance floor.

They'd been dancing almost nonstop since they'd arrived, and they'd finally decided to sit this one out.

"Oh, yes. I always have a good time with you," she told him. The evening was proving to be very enjoyable. The ballroom in the Merchant's Exchange Building had been gaily decorated for the holiday season, and everyone in attendance seemed to be in the spirit of things.

"I enjoy being with you, too," he said earnestly.

Stephanie recognized the tone in his voice, and she regretted that she didn't harbor deeper feelings for him. Michael was one of the nicest men she knew. His Nordic good looks coupled with his extensive fortune made him one of the most eligible bachelors in town. She knew there were a number of young women in the room who would have traded places with her in a second.

"You look lovely tonight," he complimented, his gaze warm upon her. The emerald silk-and-velvet gown she wore emphasized the green of her eyes. The bodice was modest yet enticingly cut, the waist was fitted and showed off her slender figure. The skirt flared out over a soft bustle and fell gracefully in a train behind her. She'd arranged her hair up in a sophisticated style, and at her throat, she wore a pearl-and-emerald choker. Stephanie was everything he wanted in a woman. She was beautiful, she came from a good family, and she had a fortune in her own right. Theirs would be the perfect match.

"Thank you." She felt the heat of his regard and turned her full attention back to the dancers, falling silent as she sipped from her drink.

It was then as Stephanie was casually watching the crowd that she caught sight of a tall, dark-haired man across the room. Her gaze seemed magnetically drawn to him, and it irked her when he turned in her direction and she discovered it was none other than the infamous Zach Madison, author of the editorial that had prompted her to write that very day.

"I see Zach Madison is here," she remarked more to herself than to Michael.

"The reporter?" he asked, following the direction of her gaze. "He must be here covering the ball for the paper. I seriously doubt that he got an invitation."

There were occasions, like right now, when Michael's arrogance irritated Stephanie. Not wanting to argue with him and cause a scene, she chose to let his rather callous remark pass. "Did you happen to read his editorial in the paper today?"

"No, I didn't have time."

"He seems to think that our town's Spirit of Christmas is not altruistic at all, but someone who does the gift-giving strictly for some greedy reason."

Michael couldn't have cared less. "You know how the *Post* is. They're always trying to stir things up, looking for a secret, hidden meaning to everything."

"That's true enough, but I think Zach's wrong. The Spirit of Christmas is a fine thing. The poor need all the help they can get."

"You're a very caring person, Stephanie. Not everyone feels as you do, though."

"Obviously. I certainly don't see the upstanding Zach Madison at any of the charity functions I attend. He was very callous in the article and sounded a lot like Scrooge."

Michael wondered why she was letting something so ridiculous annoy her. "Why worry about it? It doesn't really concern you. I know how good you are with the children at the orphans' home. You give of yourself freely. A man like Madison wouldn't understand that."

"What do you mean, 'a man like Madison'?" She was curious to find out what Michael knew that she didn't.

"He came up from the streets."

Stephanie's gaze remained on the reporter as she listened to Michael. She thought he made Zach's less than privileged background sound like some kind of criminal offense. "Why would that make him less understanding of others' needs? It seems to me that those who know what it's like to do without would be more apt to help those who are less fortunate."

"Who knows? He probably just wrote the editorial from that

angle to get everyone talking. I wouldn't let it bother you. What does it really matter?"

His dismissive, patronizing tone annoyed Stephanie. She knew he had no idea she was the Spirit, but the fact that he hadn't bothered to defend the Spirit grated on her and left her wondering just how sensitive *he* was. When David Walton, a handsome young man she'd known for years, approached her and asked her for the next dance, she was almost relieved to get away.

Zach had had his reason for wanting to cover the ball for the paper, and that reason—Stephanie Charless—was circling the ballroom floor right now in the arms of one of the wealthy young scions of St. Louis society. He kept his efforts subtle, yet he managed to keep an eye on her. They'd met the previous spring, and he'd spoken with her several times at various functions since. Though he'd told himself that he was way out of his class, it hadn't seemed to matter. She'd been in his thoughts ever since.

Zach read of her activities through the society section of the paper and knew all about her association with the rich heir, Michael Hunt. It seemed they attended nearly every ball together, and he was surprised they hadn't become engaged by now. Secretly, he cheered the thought that she remained uncommitted, yet another small, nagging part of him, the part that had dealt with the harshness of the streets and the orphanage, cautioned him not to reach too high above his station. Zach prided himself on always being a risktaker, though, when he believed the prize was worth it, and as his gaze followed Stephanie's progress around the dance floor, he knew she was worth it. With his goal set, he crossed the dance floor, shouldering his way through the smiling couples to tap the unsuspecting David Walton on the shoulder.

Walton, a bespectacled, well-mannered young man, turned quickly, surprised by the intrusion.

"May I cut in?" Zach requested.

"Stephanie?" David deferred to his partner.

Stephanie, too, was surprised by Zach's action, and she could only nod in assent. David reluctantly handed her over.

Stephanie moved into his arms, and when Zach's hand settled warmly at her waist, a shiver frissoned up her spine. He whisked her out onto the dance floor, spinning her through the other dancers with grace and skill. She was quickly impressed by his waltzing ability.

"Good evening, Mr. Madison," she said as she gazed up at him, trying not to think about how right the touch of his hand felt at her waist or of how handsome he was.

"The last time we met, Stephanie, you were calling me Zach," he said with an engaging smile. She felt as wonderful in his arms as he'd thought she would.

"I suppose it was just the surprise of seeing you here tonight. I thought you didn't care for the social scene."

"I have to admit this isn't my idea of a good time, but sometimes we do things for our friends that are above and beyond the call of duty."

"How noble of you. It must have been a terrible sacrifice for you, giving up your evening to join us tonight. Perhaps you're filled with a little of the *Christmas spirit?"*

She said the last with emphasis, and his smile widened perceptively.

"Ah, so that's why you're being so formal tonight. You read my editorial today."

"I'm tempted to call you Mr. Humbug instead of Mr. Madison," she countered.

"Zach is much better."

"All right, Zach," she conceded, remembering her mother's admonition that you could catch more flies with honey than vinegar. "But I don't understand why you were so hard on the Spirit of Christmas."

The music ended just as she was speaking, and Zach wasn't the least bit ready to relinquish her company just yet.

"Why don't we go out in the entryway where we can talk for a few minutes?" he suggested, leading her from the ballroom into a deserted area.

"You know, Zach. I usually enjoy reading the editorials. Unlike some, I like to be challenged to think in different ways and consider things from different perspectives, but this time I firmly believe you're wrong. *You're* the one who needs to look at things differently. I'm sure the poor children and the children in the orphanage appreciate the presents they get."

"I think I know more about what goes on in orphanages than you do," he answered, a hard note sounding in his voice.

"And why is that?"

"Because I was raised in one."

His terse answer surprised her, and she glanced up at him. In that fleeting moment, she caught a glimpse of a shadow of pain mirrored in his dark eyes. It was so quickly masked that she almost wondered if she'd imagined it.

"How much can you know about what those kids need?" he continued. "Do you know what it's like to be homeless or without a family? You were born with the proverbial silver spoon in your mouth. You haven't got any idea what it's like to live any other way."

"I may have been blessed with a loving family, but that doesn't mean I'm a stranger to pain and sorrow. I know things can be bad for people, but I am also a firm believer in the power of the human soul to overcome adversity. People have the ability to rise above their circumstances. All they need is encouragement and the opportunity. I go to St. Christopher's once a month to work with the children, and I've seen what some of these kids can do once they're given a little love."

"How generous of you to give one day a month to the children. What about the other twenty-nine or thirty days that they have to make it on their own?" he challenged.

For the second time that day, she felt anger toward this man. "I really don't see where you have any right to criticize me. I haven't seen you volunteering your time to help anyone. You certainly haven't made your presence known at any of the functions I attend or at any of the organizations I work for."

"Like I wrote in the editorial, I think a lot of those charities are a waste of time. I don't think they're helping anybody."

"And I think you've been working on hard, ugly cases too long. You're a hard man, Zach Madison. You seem to have lost the ability to see good in people."

"Oh, I don't know about that," he countered as he deliberately looked up at the ceiling above her. They were standing in an alcove out of view of the crowd in the ballroom.

There, suspended from the ceiling by a string, was a ball of mistletoe.

"You look awfully good to me," he murmured as his head dipped toward hers and he claimed the prize of a kiss.

Stephanie had followed his gaze to the mistletoe and had been about to protest, when his sensuous assault caught her off-guard. She gave a little gasp of surprise as his lips found hers.

Zach was never a man to do anything half measure. He had the opportunity and the will, and he was determined to press his advantage. He had allowed himself to imagine what it would be like to kiss her before, but the reality far surpassed his pleasant, sensuous musings. The feel of her in his arms and the sweet taste of her was heaven for him. For that moment, the rest of the world faded away, and it was just the two of them, sharing that intimacy for the first time. His mouth moved over hers, possessively, hungrily. It took an effort on his part to end the embrace.

When Zach drew away, Stephanie stared up at him in confusion. Her emotions were a mixture of amazement at the sensations that had swept through her and irritation at his boldness. She'd been kissed before and she'd found Michael's kisses rather nice, but this . . . this had been totally different. She'd forgotten everything while she'd been in Zach's arms, and that was very uncharacteristic for her. She liked being in control, and for that fleeting instant, she had been lost.

"We were talking about helping people," Stephanie said quickly to hide the dilemma of her conflicting emotions.

"Ah, yes, your monthly visit to the orphanage."

She refused to accept to his scathing attitude. She was going to prove to him that she was making a difference. She couldn't reveal herself as the Spirit, but she certainly could show him how much joy she got out of being with the children at the home. "Why don't you go with me to St. Christopher's on Monday? Maybe if you see what really goes on there, you'll change your mind."

Not about to miss an opportunity to be with her again, he gave her an easy grin. "Never let it be said that I'm not open-minded and willing to be proven wrong."

"Stephanie?"

The sound of Michael calling her name as he looked for her in the crowd interrupted their privacy.

"What time?" Zach quickly asked.

"Meet me there at three in the afternoon."

"I'll be there."

Three

Zach was smiling as he read the Spirit's letter. The reporter in him was feeling a bit smug as he considered the fact that he was the first and only media person to make contact with the Spirit. Confident of his own ability, he turned his well-honed investigative skills to the physical aspects of the letter, trying to figure out where it had been posted and who had written it. The script was ordinary, showing no particular peculiarities that would help to identify the author. Frustrated in his first attempt to discover the Spirit's identity, but not about to give up, he hurried off to talk to his boss.

"Walter, I know how much you want to sell papers, and I've got an idea for the scoop of the year. If you give me the go-ahead, I can double our circulation in the next week."

Walter Curtis, a portly, balding man, looked up from the articles he was editing to pin his best reporter with a piercing gaze. "Let's hear it." He set his work aside to concentrate on what Zach was going to pitch.

"I have here the letter of the century," he announced, handing over the Spirit's correspondence.

The editor scanned it quickly, his eyes widening as he realized who'd written it. "This is great stuff! I knew that editorial of yours was going to ruffle some feathers, but I didn't know we'd get to the Spirit himself. What do you want to do?"

"I want to get an exclusive interview with the Spirit."

"That's a great idea, but how?"

"I want to approach the Spirit with the idea that I'm giving him the opportunity to tell the world the truth about himself."

There was an eager, hungry glow in Zach's eyes that Walter had seen before when he was on an important story. Usually, he appreciated Zach's zealousness where his job was concerned, but this time he had a few doubts. The Spirit wasn't a criminal or crooked politician who had to be exposed or brought to justice. The Spirit did good works and brought joy to people. Walter paused thoughtfully.

Zach was a hard, driven man. Walter knew that. It was a rare occasion when he saw evidence of any softer emotion in him. Though they were not close friends, he knew more about Zach than anyone in the office, and he knew he was basically a good man who'd lived a rough life. It was that very hardness that made him a damned good reporter—when the story called for it. The Spirit, however, wasn't a hard-edged story.

"Well?" Zach asked, puzzled by his boss's hesitation. "Do run with it?"

Walter frowned slightly at Zach's eagerness to go after a story that he thought he could use as an exposé, for he had experienced the power of the Spirit. Walter had visited the homes of those who'd been graced by the Spirit, and he'd seen what goodwill and joy the anonymous benefactor had brought. "Follow it up, but keep me informed. I want this handled right."

"Don't worry. We'll sell papers. Think of the headlines we'll have once I find out the Spirit's identity."

"There's no need to reveal his identity—if you find it out, that is."

"But that's the whole point of doing this!" he protested.

"You sound like a crusader going after corrupt officials."

"Are you saying you won't back me up if I discover who this man is?"

"I'm saying that there's no need for you to reveal the identity of the Spirit. If you can get an interview with our city's generous

enefactor, all the better for publicity. Our readership might very
vell triple instead of double when we run the story. But as far
s giving away his identity, well, I may just have to draw the
ne there."

Zach didn't like being leashed this way, but he agreed just so
e could get started. "All right. I'll take this as far as I can."

As Walter watched Zach leave his office, he wondered about
ne outcome of what he'd just put in motion. Zach was like a
ulldog when it came to getting to the bottom of a story. Once
e started, there would be no stopping him—unless the Spirit
utsmarted him.

A smile lit the editor's face as he considered the chance that
is ambitious reporter might just have met his match in this
uest. The Spirit had been around for quite a while and no one
ad caught him yet.

Thinking of Zach and his determined pursuit, Walter silently
oped the Spirit turned the tables on him. It would be a good
ning if, through his goodness and joy, the Spirit overcame Zach's
oubts and hardness. If the Spirit could somehow show Zach
ne true meaning of Christmas, it might be just what the younger
nan needed to soften his hardened heart. All things were pos-
ible at Christmastime, and Walter wouldn't underestimate the
ower of the Spirit of Christmas.

Zach returned to his desk and sat pondering the best way to
onvince the Spirit to agree to an interview. Finally, he decided
n open challenge was the best way.

An Open Letter to the Spirit of Christmas

*You stated in your response to my editorial that I didn't
know the true meaning of Christmas, but you're wrong. I
know what Christmas is all about. It's about peace on Earth*

*and goodwill toward men. It's about caring for one another
and giving our best to each other—not just on December
25th, but the other 364 days of the year, as well.*

*It's a good thing that you do in giving your presents, but
why not come out in the open with it? Let the people see
who you are. Why do you go about your works in secret?
Why are you afraid of being discovered?*

*Let me interview you and give you the acclaim you de-
serve. Your Christmas Spirit is a light to the world. Why
hide it under the cover of darkness? Give me the opportunity to tell the world about you and shine your light across
the land.*

                                        Zachary Madison

"We'll run it tomorrow," Walter promised when he approve
the letter an hour later.

"Good. This could prove interesting."

"I'm looking forward to seeing what kind of response yo
get—if any."

Zach had been so caught up in writing the letter that when h
finally looked at the time, he was shocked to find it was afte
three.

"I'm on my way to St. Christopher's Orphanage right now.
thought a connecting story about the good works the voluntee
do all year would work well, especially with the Charity Banqu
coming up."

"Good, good," he said, relieved that Zach was taking a mo
positive angle. "We've had enough letters complaining abo
the editorial. The Spirit wasn't the only one who wrote, yo
know." He held up a sheaf of letters from the readers. "An articl
on St. Christopher's will quiet them down."

"I'll try to find something good to say about the place."

"I hear it's well run."

"As far as orphanages go," Zach countered. "No matter how well it's run, it's still an orphanage. I'll see you tomorrow."

Stephanie told herself she wasn't disappointed, but no matter how much she tried to deny it, she had been looking forward to seeing Zach again. Ever since he'd stolen the kiss under the mistletoe, he'd been in her thoughts. She'd managed to make it through the rest of the night with Michael, but every chance she'd gotten she'd watched for Zach among the crowd, keeping track of his movements around the room. When at last the evening had come to an end and Michael had escorted her home, she'd accepted his good-night kiss with almost regret. Her traitorous heart was wanting the man kissing her to be Zach, not Michael. Michael's kisses were sweet and nice, warm and comforting, but Zach's had made her forget everything—the ball, the danger of discovery, *everything*. She wondered if it had been a fluke, a moment of madness, or if her reaction to him had been real.

"Miss Stephanie?"

The sound of towheaded Billy Roberts's call interrupted her romantic musings and forced her back to the present . . . to the myriad of children who were clamoring for her attention.

"What were ya thinkin' about, Miss Stephanie?" Billy asked, having seen the faraway look in her eyes and knowing it meant she was daydreaming about something important. *He* daydreamed all the time. "Were you wonderin' what Santa's bringin' ya for Christmas?"

"That's exactly what I was thinking about, Billy. How did you know?"

" 'Cause it's almost Christmas," the ten-year-old replied sagely.

"Have you children made your lists yet?" Stephanie asked as she sat down on a stool in the midst of the youngsters.

"Yes, ma'am!" the mix of boys and girls ages three to eleven replied as they quickly gathered around her, each jockeying for the seat on the floor closest to her, for they loved her and wanted to be as near to her as they could.

"All right, then, I want each one of you to tell me what you want the most for Christmas this year," she encouraged.

As the little ones told her of their dreams, she listened intently and kept careful track. She was so engrossed in their fantasies that for the moment, she forgot all about Zach not showing up and thought only of the children.

When Zach finally arrived at St. Christopher's, he was nearly an hour late. As he started up the walk to the three-story, seemingly dark and imposing building, he found his steps measured. A part of him was telling him to run away, to escape while he still had time. He knew it was foolish to feel that way after all this time. He was a man now, an adult, but there was no denying the feelings of desolation and abandonment that still lurked in the deepest recesses of his heart and soul. With an effort, Zach put aside his childish fears. His emotional armor back in place, he was ready to go in. He moved on up the walk and knocked on the door. The sound echoed hollowly, and again a sinking feeling came over him.

When the door swung open, though, and the friendly, welcoming, smiling face of an aged nun greeted him, he was startled. He was used to sad faces and sorrowful looks at orphanages. This woman looked to be happy and joyful, as if she were actually glad to be there and certainly glad to see him.

"Welcome to St. Christopher's. I'm Sister Mary Louise. Can I help you?" she asked as she held the door wide in invitation for him to come in out of the cold.

"Yes, I'm Zach Madison, and I was supposed to meet Miss Charless here this afternoon. Is she still here?"

"Oh, yes, Miss Stephanie always stays until suppertime. Come, let me have your coat and then I'll take you to her."

Zach obediently did as he'd been told, handing over his coat and then following the diminutive nun down a long, wide, spacious hallway toward a large room at the back of the building.

Zach had expected the home to be dark and depressing. He'd expected to feel trapped and uncomfortable. He was surprised on all accounts. The orphanage was a light-hearted, seemingly happy place. He could heard the sounds of children's laughter coming from the room where they were heading, and he tried to remember if he had ever heard such spontaneous laughter in all the years he'd been in the home in Chicago.

"Shall I let her know you're here?" Sister Mary Louise offered as they reached the doorway.

Zach glanced in and saw Stephanie, surrounded by a sea of smiling, happy children, and he knew he couldn't interrupt the moment. "No, Sister, thank you. I'll just stay here and watch."

"If you need anything, let me know."

"Thanks."

Zach remained where he was, quietly watching the scene before him. Stephanie was mesmerizing as she entertained the youngsters. They were respectful of her, yet full of the joy and excitement that went with childhood.

Zach felt a pang of envy, for he had never known a moment like that in his whole life. His days at the orphanage had been overshadowed with a sense of fear and constant uncertainty. He'd never known how the bigger, older boys were going to treat him on any given day. There had been no sharing and little caring at the home. As he was recalling those cold, desperate days of his childhood, a squabble broke out between two boys who were about nine years old.

Zach watched in almost suspended horror as one of the bigger boys got up and went after the two of smaller ones. Memories of how the bullies at the home had beaten him assailed Zach, and he almost started into the room to protect the two, when he was stopped by the big boy's actions.

Billy was used to Ronny and Fred always fighting. As designated peacemaker among the children, he quickly grabbed Ronny by the collar and dragged him off of Fred.

"Quit it, you two. We're sick of your fighting all the time. You don't want to mess up Miss Stephanie's visit," he scolded.

Ronny was red-faced and still trying to swing at Fred who was just getting back to his feet. "But he hit me first!"

"Only after you said I wasn't gettin' nothin' this year for Christmas!" Fred shouted back.

"You're both dumb," Billy told them so loudly everyone around was giggling at them. "Fighting don't do no good. It just makes you look stupid. Now be quiet, or I'll get Sister and you can help her fix dinner." Billy let go of Ronny.

Though he shot him a sullen look, Ronny had sense enough to move to another part of the room and sit down. No one wanted to cook. That was girls' work. Fred settled in next to Billy, and Stephanie smiled at the older boy.

"Thank you, Billy. We were having so much fun, I hate for anyone to start fighting."

"They won't do it again, ma'am. Will you, Ronny? Fred?"

They both answered in unison, "No, ma'am."

"That's wonderful. Christmas is a time of peace and goodwill, not fighting and arguing," she instructed. "Now, where were we?"

At that particular moment, she happened to glance toward the door and saw Zach. As their gazes met across the room, a soft smile curved her lips. He was there . . . He'd come . . . Stephanie couldn't believe how rapidly her heart started beating at the sight of him. She tried to cover her flustered moment by drawing the children in on it.

"Hello. Zach." Her voice was soft and throaty.

"Hello, Stephanie," he returned, unable to look away from her.

"Children, I have a surprise for you today. We have a visitor." She gestured toward Zach. "This is Mr. Madison. He works for the *Post-Dispatch* newspaper. He's a reporter. Can you welcome him to St. Christopher's?"

"Hello, Mr. Madison," they chorused, and one little girl named Annie, who was only four, got up and ran over to him.

"C'mon and sit with us. We're telling Miss Stephanie what we want for Christmas." She took his hand and drew him forward.

Zach clasped her hand in his. He was amazed at how tiny she was. When Annie tugged him down beside her, he sat on the floor without thought. He found himself grinning as he joined the circle of adoring children at her feet. It was obvious they loved her dearly, and as he gazed at her he realized that loving her wouldn't be a very difficult thing to do.

"What do you want for Christmas, Mr. Madison?" Annie asked, turning innocent blue eyes on him.

"I . . . uh . . . I hadn't really thought about it."

"You haven't?" She was shocked.

"Don't you get lotsa presents?" another child asked. "You're a grown-up."

"No, actually, I don't get any presents at all."

"You don't?" The children were all horrified. "That's terrible. Everyone should get a present at Christmas."

"Why don't you?" another pressed.

He shrugged. "It never seemed important."

"Well, tell Miss Stephanie what you want. Maybe she can help you get it this year."

"Yes, Zach, what would you like for Christmas?' Stephanie asked, her eyes twinkling.

Your love forged unbidden into his thoughts, and Zach was stunned by the revelation. He didn't know if his surprise showed

on his face as he struggled to think of a more appropriate answer.
Ever the reporter, he came back with, "How about peace on
Earth?"

The children groaned. "That's boring. Don't you want a pony
or some paints or a jump rope or—"

"His is a very admirable request," Stephanie interrupted. "I
just wish there was some way we could all pitch in and get it
for Mr. Madison."

"Can you buy it, Miss Stephanie?" Annie asked sweetly.

"No, I'm afraid you can't. Peace comes to each one of us
individually. We can share our peace, but we truly can't create
it for someone else. They must find their own."

"We could help him find his," another young boy offered.

"We'll see. Now, who hasn't told me what they wanted yet?"
She changed the topic.

Zach sat next to Annie as Stephanie worked her magic with
the children. It was nearly an hour later when the children were
called to dinner and they were finally alone.

"Do you have time to go to dinner with me?" Zach asked.

"I'd love to have dinner with you."

Zach took her to a restaurant in one of the better hotels in
town. They ate a delicious dinner and were relaxing over hot
cups of coffee when Stephanie brought up the orphanage.

"You're very good with the children, you know. You should
go there more often. They liked you, they really did."

"I was impressed by the way you handled them, too." He
wondered if this was just some playful pastime for her. He
wondered, too, if she realized the effect she was having on the
children.

"I wasn't 'handling' them," she said quietly. "They're my
friends. I like them, and I hope they like me."

"They more than like you," he said. He wanted to tell her that
he "more than liked her," too, but he didn't. "But can they count
on you?"

"For anything," she said with a fierceness that surprised him.

"That's good. Too often, people come into their lives and then leave again. It's good that you're there for them. They need that stability, that trust."

"You're very insightful. I'm surprised, as much as you understand human nature, that your column about the Spirit of Christmas was so negative."

"Well, if nothing else, my negative column—as you call it—certainly stirred up the readers. I even heard from the Spirit of Christmas himself today."

"You did?" She managed to act shocked. She found it amusing that he assumed the Spirit was a man.

"The Spirit wrote that I didn't know the meaning of Christmas. We'll be running his letter in the paper tomorrow along with my response."

"And how did you answer him?"

"I challenged him to let me interview him. My boss was supportive, and it'll certainly help to sell newspapers if I can get the interview."

"That's a wonderful idea. Will you reveal his identity if he agrees to talk to you?"

"Of course. If the Spirit is doing all of this for goodwill, why not reveal who he is? If people could, they'd help him, and he could do even more good works, if indeed that's what he really wants to do."

"I see your reasoning, but I have a feeling after all these years that the Spirit just wants to quietly do what he does best—give away gifts."

"We'll see. I'll let you know what kind of response I get to my letter."

"I'll be interested in knowing. The Spirit has always meant a lot to me. It's nice to know people are out there doing nice things."

Zach hired a carriage to take them back to her house, and as the conveyance drew a stop before her home, he couldn't resist kissing her again.

"Stephanie . . ." He said her name softly as, with infinite care, he framed her face with his hands and claimed her mouth with his.

In the privacy of the carriage, they clung together, tasting of the promise of their passion and catching a glimpse of what could be theirs. It was heaven.

As they moved apart, Stephanie eyes were shining with an inner light, and she lifted one hand to gently touch his cheek. "You're a very special man, Zach Madison."

Her words penetrated to his heart. He gazed at her, thinking she was beauty and innocence and kindness—all the good things of the world—all the things that were missing in his life. No one had ever told him he was special before. A crack formed in the protective armor around his soul. He leaned forward and pressed a sweet-soft kiss to her lips.

A feeling, deep, warm, and abiding, filled Stephanie, and when they moved apart, she gazed at him in wonder. He was so handsome, and for all that before she'd thought him a hard, un-feeling man, she now sensed the gentleness in him.

"I'd better go in," she said softly.

"I know." He opened the door to the carriage and climbed out, then helped her down. He took her arm and escorted her to the door.

"Good night," she whispered as she started inside.

"Good night." He started to turn away, but in a moment he would later consider to be one of total insanity, he turned back. "Stephanie?"

"Yes, Zach?" She glanced at him expectantly.

"I'll be covering the Charity Awards for the paper. Would you like to go with me?"

Stephanie was thrilled that he'd asked. After being with him, she knew she could never spend another evening with Michael.

Zach was the only man she wanted to be with. She sensed there was so much more to him. She was challenged by the inner man, and she wanted to get to know him.

"I'd love to go with you, Zach."

Zach didn't realize he'd been holding his breath until she answered. The realization that her response meant that much to him annoyed him slightly, but her answer eliminated any objections he might have had. "Wonderful." He found he was grinning like a schoolboy, and he suddenly didn't care. "I'll pick you up at six-thirty on the fifteenth."

"I'll be looking forward to it."

"Go on in so I'll know you're safe."

"Good night, Zach." She was smiling as she disappeared into the house.

As Zach returned to the waiting carriage, he was still grinning, his steps were light, and he felt very good inside.

Four

The St. Louis Post-Dispatch
December 8, 1882

A Message to Zach Madison

Sir,

    I found your request for an interview intriguing, but I must decline your generous offer. While your prose was perfect, I felt no warmth in your response. Your heart isn't open to the joy and love of the season, so I can see no reason for us to speak. It is my prayer that something or someone touches you this Christmas and helps you understand and believe in the Spirit. Then, perhaps once you do believe, we can meet and talk.

I remain,
The Spirit of Christmas

"Well, Zach, it seems our Spirit isn't being very cooperative. What are you going to do now?" Walter asked as he stood before his favorite reporter's desk, trying not to grin as he confronted him with the news of the Spirit's response.

"It's not over yet. You've seen how our circulation is up just from the letters going back and forth. I'm going to issue another challenge. Who knows? Maybe I can strike a nerve and draw him out."

"Why do you want to 'strike a nerve'?"

Zach looked up at his boss. "I don't like being told no."

"Ah, young man, you've still got a lot of living to do. Most of life is being told no."

"Not this time. Somehow, some way, I'm going to find out who the Spirit is."

"Good luck, Zach. Oh, by the way, the response to your articles on volunteers has been very good. Keep up the good work." Walter returned to his own office.

Zach grunted. Those articles were nice to do, but he liked stories with real meat to them. He wanted to solve the unsolvable, to discover the unknown. He wanted to unmask the Spirit and he intended to do it.

Picking up his pen, Zach began writing his challenge. It ran the following day.

To The Spirit of Christmas

You said in your last letter to me that you hoped someone or something would touch me this Christmas and show me the true meaning of the season. Why don't you come out of your hiding place and be the one to make a believer out of me? Meet with me and show me why Christmas is the day of love and joy. I challenge you to prove my editorial wrong.

You're one of the most influential of all the charitable groups in town. I'm sure most of St. Louis is eager to hear from you. Let me do the interview. You have my word that I'll be fair and unbiased in my reporting. The coverage I could give you would increase public awareness of your efforts even more and bring additional attention to the goodness that you do. I look forward to hearing from you.

Zach Madison

The Spirit responded to his request a few days later.

Mr. Madison,

While I appreciate your interest in my contributions to the city, I have no interest in garnering any extra publicity for myself or my efforts. I give from my heart and for no other reason.

I understand why you're pursuing this matter now. An interview with me at this time of the year would guarantee your newspaper a very sensational headline. But I have no wish to sensationalize what I do.

It seems, Mr. Madison, that you do not understand this season. I'm sorry that the hardness of your heart keeps you from seeing the goodness in people. If I could give you that gift—the gift of understanding, of peace of the heart, and of love, I would.

I wish you happiness this Christmas. This will be my last correspondence with you.

The Spirit of Christmas

Zach was livid as he read the Spirit's answer to his challenge. "Are you going to print it?" he asked Walter.

"Of course. The public's been following this entire battle of words between the two of you. We can't cut them out now."

Zach ground his teeth in frustration, then made his decision. "I'm going to do it anyway."

"Do what?"

"I'm going ahead with my plan to find out who the Spirit is."

"But how? He refuses to meet you or speak with you. What can you do to draw him out?"

"I'm not going to draw him out. I'm going to go after him. I'll find out where he went last year and stake out the the same areas this year. He's bound to show up one night, and when he does, I'll be there waiting. I'll get my interview."

Walter chuckled. "You're determined, but I'm beginning to think you may have met your match this time."

"We'll see."

Zach spent the next three nights haunting the streets of St. Louis's poorer sections in hopes of catching the Spirit in action. Instead of the Spirit, he roamed silently and alone in the cold, dark alleyways that ran behind the shanties. He hadn't meant to spy on anyone, but there had been several homes where he'd been able to look inside, and he'd caught glimpses of hungry families, whose clothes were little better than rags, huddled together for warmth. Stray, hungry dogs and some horrible rodents of the night that bore not mentioning were his companions as he continued to search, but try as he might, he could not find the Spirit.

Zach was frustrated when he returned to his room in the boardinghouse late that night, and he grew determined to keep up his effort to find the Spirit. As he settled into bed, thoughts about what he'd seen kept playing through his mind. It touched him to realize that maybe there *were* things in life worse than living as he had in the home. There had always been three meals a day in the orphanage, and with the coming of the cold weather every year, each child had been given a warm coat. He was surprised by the thought and remained awake long after he'd settled in.

The night of the Annual Charity Awards arrived. Had Zach been going with anyone other than Stephanie, he probably would have only stayed long enough to get the information he needed to do an adequate article about it and then would have left to return to the streets and his feverish pursuit of the elusive Christmas Spirit. It seemed that each morning when he'd returned to work at the paper, he'd discover that the Spirit had indeed been out making his round and that he'd missed him by only a few blocks or a few hours. It was driving him crazy, but there was something, or rather someone, more pressing in his thoughts . . .

Stephanie. It was thoughts of her and the wonder of her kiss that had kept him warm on those cold, lonely nights he'd hunted in vain for the Spirit, and for just tonight, he was determined to put aside his driving need to find the Spirit just for this evening and enjoy himself.

Zach had to admit that he was eager to see her again. He'd never felt this kind of warmth for anyone before, and he was looking forward to being with her. She was one of those people who was to receive an award tonight, and he was honored to be her escort. He wore his best suit and even left early to make sure he wouldn't be late.

"Good evening," he greeted her warmly as she came down the stairs to meet him after Sam had let him in. He watched her descend, his eyes alight at the sight of her. She looked elegant and incredibly lovely in her high-necked, long-sleeved demure gown of midnight blue velvet, and had they been alone, Zach would have kissed her. With Sam standing nearby and Aunt Rose hovering in the other room, he could only dream.

"Good evening," she returned, her gaze just as warm and hungry upon him. She thought him the handsomest man she'd ever seen. She realized as she smiled at him that she'd missed him in the days they'd been apart. She'd missed his intelligent conversation, his keen wit, his dark expressive eyes, but most of all . . . she'd missed his kiss and his touch. She'd never felt this way about a man before, and it was positively exhilarating for her.

Stephanie held out her hand to him as she reached the bottom of the steps, and Zach took it in his, then linked her arms through his.

"I missed you," he admitted freely, savoring having her by his side again.

"I missed you, too," she told him, looking up at him from beneath lowered lashes, and confirming in that moment in her mind that he was indeed the most handsome man alive. She thought his features classic, his strong, broad shoulders just the right width, his height a perfect match for hers.

Zach was about to tell her how lovely she looked when Rose came out of the parlor. She was dressed fashionably for the evening and was carrying her purse.

"Mr. Madison, it's so good to see you again. Are we ready to go, dear?" Rose asked Stephanie.

Zach glanced from Rose to Stephanie. "Go?"

"Zach, you know my aunt Rose. She's invited to the banquet, too. I hope you don't mind if she accompanies us." Stephanie knew she should have mentioned it when she'd accepted his invitation, but she'd been so caught up in the joy of being with him that Aunt Rose had completely slipped her mind.

"Not at all," Zach answered quickly. Though he would have loved to have spent the evening with just Stephanie, he knew this was a good opportunity to get to know more about her and her family. "What man in his right mind would turn down the chance to accompany two of the most beautiful women in St. Louis to the banquet tonight?"

Rose was delighted by his flirting. "Why thank you, sir."

"My pleasure." He gave her a courtly half-bow as he continued his play. "Shall we go?"

"Of course."

After the ladies had donned their coats, they left for the banquet in Zach's hired carriage. The grand hall was crowded with the best of the best in St. Louis society. The dinner was excellent as was to be expected in such company.

Zach sat between Stephanie and Rose, entertaining them with tales of his work. Though Rose had been very taken with Michael, Zach intrigued her. As the evening progressed, she found herself laughing at his comments and enjoying his company immensely.

Stephanie was pleased that Zach was being so kind to her aunt. And by the end of the meal, Rose was having serious doubts about her judgment that Michael would be the perfect husband for Stephanie. Furthermore, she was certain that, had she been forty years younger, she would have been after Zach for herself!

The awards ceremony began after dessert, and lasted hours. When he'd first taken the assignment, Zach had anticipated that he would be bored the entire evening. Instead, he found that the time was flying while he was with Rose and Stephanie. When the mayor took the podium to announce the next award presentation, they fell silent to pay attention.

"Our next winner, for all her youth, has been a mainstay in our community for several years now. Stephanie Charless is an extraordinary young woman. She's lived through the devastating loss of all her immediate family, and yet this experience has not hardened her to the sorrows of the world, but made her more sensitive to them. The needs of others are paramount to her. She gives freely of herself and is always there to help. Just ask the children at St. Christopher's if you have any doubts. I am proud to present this next award to Miss Stephanie Charless. Stephanie? Please come up and accept your award with our most heartfelt congratulations."

Stephanie looked over at Zach as she started to rise. For just a fleeting moment, she saw a flicker of emotion in his regard that touched her heart. It was a look of pride in her accomplishments and something more . . . something she was almost afraid to put a name to. As quickly as it had been mirrored there, it was gone, and she hurried to the front of the banquet hall to accept her award.

Tears filled Stephanie's eyes as she stood before the room crowded with her friends and acquaintances. "Thank you," she said in a husky, emotional voice as she held the award before her. "You'll never know how much this means to me. It's a wonderful thing in itself to do good works for others, but it's even more wonderful when you know it's appreciated. My prayer for the coming year is that life will get better for everyone and tha someday very soon, there will be no poverty, no sickness, and no despair in our community. I wish each and every one of you a blessed holiday season and a New Year filled with joy, hope, and, most of all, love."

"Isn't she wonderful?" Rose asked as Stephanie was making her acceptance speech.

"Most assuredly," he agreed, his gaze riveted on her.

Applause echoed through the room as she returned to their table.

Zach stood up as she neared, and Rose got up to hug her. When Stephanie looked to Zach, their eyes met and held. He saw in the depths of her gaze all the gentleness and love that filled her and guided her through life. He'd never known anyone like her before.

"Congratulations," he said as he held her chair for her.

"Thank you." Her answer was softly spoken as she sat back down next to him. She did not object when he reached over and took her hand in his, but reveled in the warmth of his touch.

They sat quietly as the ceremony continued.

"We have one last award tonight, but I fear it might go unclaimed by the winner. Our council voted unanimously to give an award to the Spirit of Christmas for the unfailing joy and happiness he brings to so many every year." The mayor held up the Spirit's award for all to see. "I have a feeling that even if he were here, he wouldn't come forward to accept it."

There was an expectant pause as everyone waited for the Spirit to reveal himself. But no one stood to take the honor.

"As we suspected, the award remains unclaimed, yet the sentiment behind it is just as heartfelt. The Spirit of Christmas—whoever you are, and I hope you're here among us tonight—thank you from the City of St. Louis."

The crowd thundered its approval with applause.

At the mention of the Spirit, Zach started scowling for the

first time that night. Stephanie glanced over at him and couldn
help but notice.

"You shouldn't look so angry."

"I'm not angry, just annoyed."

"Why now, after all this time and all these awards?"

"I know you do your work at the orphanage because you trul
care about the children. I've seen it. I believed it. I'm just n
so sure about these other 'winners' who are here tonight, but
least they don't hide what they're doing and why they're doin
it. The Spirit, however . . ."

"The Spirit is different, Zach."

"The Spirit's a coward."

"No he's not. It says in the Bible, one should do good work
quietly."

"And you actually believe that's his reason for being so s
cretive?" he scoffed.

She managed a little shrug. "I'd like to think so."

"Well, I don't."

"Zach." She touched his arm. "Have all your Christmas
been that bad? Have you been hurt so much that you can't ju
accept the Spirit's actions for what they are?"

Her words were like arrows to his heart. "My life is just fin
thanks. I'm happy. But I am determined to find out who th
Spirit is."

"What are you going to do?"

"I've been patrolling the streets at night, trying to catch hi
in the act, and I'm going keep it up until I do. One way or t
other I'm going to get my interview."

"Where have you been looking?" she asked innocently.

He told her the areas he'd already checked and explained ho
frustrated he was by his inability to track the Spirit down.

"I'm going to keep rechecking the places he went last ye
and hope I get lucky."

Sadness filled her as she studied him. "If that's what you really want, Zach, I wish you well."

The banquet over, they made the trip home in the carriage. With Aunt Rose along as chaperone, there was no opportunity to be alone with Stephanie, though Zach wanted to kiss her badly.

"Thank you for escorting us," Rose told him as he walked them to the door.

"Yes, thank you, Zach. It was a lovely night."

"It was my pleasure."

Once Stephanie and Aunt Rose were safe inside and Zach had gone, Rose turned to Stephanie, her expression worried.

"He's a very determined young man."

"A very sad one, too."

"He sounds like he fully intends to pursue the Spirit no matter what."

"I know," she worried.

"Zach's a very sharp reporter, you know. What are you going to do?"

"The only thing I can do. I'm going to be extra careful. I'll talk to Father Finn tomorrow and tell him what's happening. He'll know what to do. Good night, Aunt Rose."

"Good night, dear."

The next night, Zach again searched the streets hoping to catch the Spirit in action, and again his search proved futile. He'd been surprised, pleasantly so, when Stephanie had stopped by the newspaper that morning to see him and to invite him to spend Christmas Eve with her at the orphanage and then go back to her home for dinner with her aunt. He'd accepted gladly, and he regretted that the holiday was still so far away.

As he thought about spending Christmas Eve with Stephanie and Rose, it occurred to him that he should bring them presents.

Christmas shopping was a new experience for him, but he a
tacked it as he did everything, straight on. The clerks in th
stores were friendly and smiling, and he found himself smilin
in return. The other shoppers were bustling about, smiling, too
and chatting as they carried their packages and he found himse
speaking to complete strangers. He saw little children who wei
wide-eyed with wonder over the coming of the holiday, and the
happiness was infectious. By the time he finished purchasing
silk scarf for Aunt Rose, he was humming Christmas carols.

Zach left the shop with Rose's scarf already gift-wrapped ar
started hunting for the perfect present for Stephanie. He wai
dered down Fourth Street, looking in the shop windows ar
finally stopped before a jeweler's display. There in the windo
resting on a bed of midnight-blue velvet, the same color as th
dress she'd worn to the banquet, was the most beautiful diamor
ring he'd ever seen. He stood there in the cold for what seeme
like eternity, staring down at the precious gem and thinkir
about a life with Stephanie. He hadn't even told her he love
her yet—he hadn't even been sure until that moment, but as I
fantasized about spending the rest of his life with her, he kne
that was what he wanted most in the world. Zach could think
no better time than Christmas Eve to propose. He finally we
into the shop. When he came back out a half an hour later, I
was carrying another gift-wrapped box.

It was late the night of the twenty-second when Father Fir
met Stephanie at their prearranged time. After loading the pre
ents into the carriage, they set off on their rounds with Sa
driving.

"You've almost finished another year of giving, Stephanie
Father Finn remarked as they rode through the deserted stree

"It seems hard to believe that the past four weeks have go

by so quickly," she sighed. "I couldn't have done it without you. Your help means a lot."

"I appreciate your praise, but it's not true. You enjoy this so much that I'm certain you'd find a way to bring these presents to the people no matter what."

She smiled at him. "It's a good feeling to know that my efforts are for a worthy cause." She paused thoughtfully for a moment. "You don't think Zach Madison is right, do you? You don't think I should come forward and let everyone know who I am?"

Father Finn had sensed all along that the reporter's columns and letters had been troubling her. "I don't think you should come forward, but his opinion matters to you, doesn't it?"

"Yes, it does. I'm afraid I've fallen in love with him."

"But that's wonderful," he replied, pleased with her good news. "Does he feel the same way?"

"I don't know yet. He's a good man, Father, but I don't think he's known much love in his life."

"From the edge in his letters, I have to agree with you. But you have so much love to give, Stephanie. Zach would be a very lucky man to have you."

"Thank you."

"There's no need to thank me for speaking the truth."

"The trouble is, when I finally tell him the truth, he might be very angry with me. You see, he's confided in me about his search for the Spirit and talked about his determination to reveal the Spirit's identity."

"Or he might be very impressed. You may be underestimating him. You said yourself that you won him over at St. Christopher. You may just be what the man needs to soften his heart and help him understand."

"I'd like to think you're right." She turned to stare out the carriage window as Sam slowed their pace near their first stop. "Zach's out on the streets again tonight trying to find us. He's very good at what he does."

"So are you. Don't worry. We'll be fine. Everything's going to work out perfectly."

They shared a knowing look as the carriage came to a halt. He opened the door for her and they climbed out, their arms loaded with the presents for the family that lived in this run-down little house.

Three hours later, tired but happy, they were on their way to their last stop. They'd gone there the year before, for the mother had been desperately ill and the father had been working long hours to support her and their five children. Father Finn had told Stephanie how the mother had passed away in the spring and how the children were facing their first Christmas without her. The children were young, all of them under twelve.

Stephanie knew the sadness of the holidays without a mother, and she identified personally with their pain and loss. Though she couldn't bring their mother back, she could at least bring them some presents this Christmas and let them know that somebody cared for them.

They stopped a block away from the house, and, after pausing to draw her veil down in disguise, she descended from the carriage. With Father Finn's help, they gathered up the last of the packages and made their way quietly down the street to the front door. After stacking the presents on the stoop, Stephanie lay the strip of bells and her note on the top so they would be seen right away. She and Father Finn shared a secret smile and then slipped away, sight unseen.

As they neared the carriage, though, a voice rang out in the silence of the predawn hour.

"Wait . . . hold it right there . . . I want to talk to you!"

Stephanie knew the voice as well as her own, and she took refuge behind the priest as Zach emerged from a darkened alley just beyond their parked and waiting carriage. Sam had pulled his coat collar up so his face couldn't be seen, and he huddled down, trying not to let Zach get a look at him. Father Finn took

:o her defense, too, positioning himself between them as they
<ept walking toward the carriage.

Zach had been exhausted, cold, and sleepy until he'd heard
:he carriage coming up the street. He'd sat and watched outside
:hree different houses tonight, and he'd been about to give up
:he hope that he would ever get his story when the sound of the
1orses stopping nearby had roused him from his irritated mus-
ngs. He'd crept to the street to watch, and it had been then that
1e'd seen a priest descend from the carriage followed by a
woman dressed in mourning clothes. He'd continued to watch,
and when they'd both gathered up gift-wrapped packages, he'd
<nown he had the Spirit. He'd kept watch over them as they'd
juietly delivered the presents to one of the houses farther down
:he street.

Now, as he confronted the pair, Zach realized that he'd seen
:he priest around somewhere before and that there was some-
:hing strangely familiar about the woman . . . something about
:he way she moved . . . something elusive that he *almost* recog-
1ized but not quite . . . Before he could reach them, though, the
woman climbed hastily into the carriage and shut the door, pull-
ng down the shade so he couldn't see her.

"What can I do for you?" Father Finn asked when they came
:ace-to-face.

"I'm Zach Madison from the *Post-Dispatch,* and I've been
:rying to find our elusive Spirit of Christmas. Are you the Spirit,
:ather?"

Father Finn smiled at the man whose determination had
›rought him this close to discovering the secret. "I would like
:o think that I have the Spirit of Christmas in my heart. What
ibout you, Mr. Madison?"

"I'm not here to talk about me, Father, and I didn't ask you
f you *had* the Spirit. I asked if you *were* the Spirit."

"Does it matter? What matters is the spirit of the season,
wouldn't you agree?"

Zach took an aggressive step toward him, wanting to somehow get another look at the woman in the carriage. Something about her was nagging at him. Zach started to reach around the priest to the door, but the priest moved to block him again and grabbed his arm.

"I'm not a believer in violence, but there are occasions when it might be necessary to make a point." He stood his ground, refusing to allow him access. "Surely you wouldn't want to force me to do something that is so foreign to my nature, would you, Mr. Madison?"

Zach ground his teeth in frustration at being thwarted. He was so close. The answer he'd been seeking was arm's length away, and yet . . .

"Good night, Mr. Madison. Have a blessed Christmas."

Father Finn stood before Zach, a symbol of God's authority on Earth, and Zach's only choices were to respect his wish and stay away or physically challenge him and open the door to the carriage. Something inside Zach told him to choose the first option.

When Zach made no further threatening moves, Father Finn nodded toward him and then opened the carriage door and climbed in, shutting it quickly behind himself.

Zach watched in frustration as the vehicle moved off. He followed it as far as he could on foot, but it disappeared in the distant darkness.

His frustration knew no bounds, and he did not sleep at all that night. He returned to his room and lay wide-awake, staring at the ceiling, trying to put together the pieces of the puzzle he'd just been handed. When the realization came to him, he was amazed that he hadn't realized it sooner. He told himself he was seven kinds of a fool to have been so close to it all along and not to have seen it before. He'd been arrogant to assume the spirit was a man, yet everyone had. No one had ever even considered that the Spirit might be a woman.

Zach showed up at the office early the next morning and began checking back through issues of the paper for articles about Stephanie. It took him a while, but he finally found what he was looking for—the notice of the terrible deaths of her parents and sister. It was as he'd suspected. They had died just before Christmas in the very year the Spirit had begun to distribute presents.

Zach was lost in thought as he realized what he'd just discovered. He still wasn't absolutely sure, but if it was Stephanie, her family's deaths explained the reason that the woman he'd seen last night had been wearing mourning clothes. Not only did the black gown and veil provide a disguise, but they also acted as a tribute to what she'd lost. Zach knew he would have his answer that very night. Instead of watching the streets at random in hopes of catching a glimpse of the Spirit again, tonight he would watch Stephanie. He would wait outside of her house all night if he had to, and if and when she left, he would follow her.

Five

The following night was cold and clear. A silver moon hung low in the sky and a myriad of twinkling stars adorned the heavens.

It was just after eleven as Zach stood in a secluded, shadowed corner just down the street from Stephanie's house. With his coat collar turned up against the chill and his hands thrust deep in his coat pockets, he maintained his vigil, watching and waiting. Several times he saw Stephanie move past the window. She looked quite warm and happy and very beautiful. He longed to be inside with her, and more than once, he asked himself why he was standing out there all alone in the freezing cold.

Hours passed, and still there was no unusual activity at the Charless household. Eventually, the lights downstairs were extinguished and lights upstairs were lighted. Still, he waited.

Zach considered leaving, but something held him there. He knew it was still early by the Spirit's standard, so he huddled down against the cold and girded himself for a longer wait.

He allowed his mind to drift, and he thought of Stephanie's engagement ring safely locked away in his room. By this time tomorrow, he hoped she would be his fiancée. All his Christmases until now had been spent alone or a lot like tonight, standing on the outside looking in. If he married Stephanie and were blessed with children, he would make sure his children's Christmases were joyous and filled with wonderful, loving memories.

Zach was tired, but he clung to thoughts of making Stephanie his bride and they kept him warm.

Zach debated with himself about what to do if his hunch about Stephanie being the Spirit proved true. If she was, he knew he should be angry with her, for it meant that she'd been playing with him almost from the first. Yet, even as he considered being angry with her, he knew he wouldn't be. He remembered the tone of her last letter to him, and her wish that she could give him those special gifts of the Spirit for the holiday. Heartfelt emotions stirred in his chest as he thought of the gifts she'd wanted to give him, the gifts of understanding, peace of the heart, and love. It was painful for him to concede that she'd already given him those priceless presents just by being who she was.

Lost deep in thought, Zach almost missed the arrival of the priest shortly before one A.M.. Zach watched as the priest went around to the back of the house. Reining in his own desire to charge over and confront them both, he forced himself to stay where he was and watch. He was rewarded when just a few minutes later the carriage came slowly out of the drive.

Zach had tied his horse nearby, and as soon as the carriage moved off down the street, he got his mount and he followed the vehicle at a measured distance as it crossed town. The carriage stayed to the back streets and avoided any and all of the major thoroughfares. Their trip this night took them to the north side of town. Zach watched covertly from a block away as the priest and the mourning woman delivered the gifts to the door of a run-down shanty, then slipped away to deliver more gifts to a house just three blocks over.

Zach was feeling quite triumphant about himself and his investigative abilities. He was ready to confront them right then and there, but as he was watching them deliver packages to another house, he saw a light go on inside just as they were putting the jingle bells on the presents on the stoop.

"Who's out there?" came the muffled call of a woman's voice from inside.

Stephanie and Father Finn were shocked at being discovered. They fled as silently as they could down the street. They had just managed to get out of sight around the corner when the door flew open.

"Dear Lord!" came the woman's cry as she found the unexpected pile of gifts on her doorstep. "But who . . . Why?" She stuck her head out to take a better look, but there was no one around. All was quiet.

Bending down, she picked up the strand of jingle bells, and at their sweet sound, she knew. "The Spirit . . ." she said as her children, freshly roused from sleep, came running to join her at the door.

"What is it, Mama?"

"Children, the Spirit of Christmas has come to us tonight . . ."

"Did he bring presents, Mama?"

"Yes, sweetheart, he did."

"Oh, boy!" Their excitement was obvious in their voices.

As Zach stayed in the darkness watching unobserved, he guessed that the children were about four and six years old. He kept watch as the woman glanced around outside once more and then picked up the packages and took them in. As she ushered the children back inside, she looked outside one last time and said in a soft, thankful voice, "God bless you, Spirit of Christmas."

She closed the door, but even that solid barrier could not block the sounds of their joy and laughter.

Zach stood there, his throat tight, his heart actually hurting in his chest. He didn't understand why his eyes were burning. He heard Stephanie's carriage drive away, but he didn't go after it. Instead, he stayed where he was, sharing vicariously in the destitute family's happiness as they opened the presents from the Spirit.

When at last Zach turned away from the family in the shanty, he mounted his horse and headed back. His decision had already been made, and it had been made in his heart. He would not stop the Spirit from doing her good works. There was no secret payback for giving gifts to a family living just above the level of starvation and hopelessness. It was as if his eyes had been opened for the first time, for he understood now that there was no secret meaning to her goodness. There was only a deep, abiding wish to make people happy and to give to others the same joy that she'd had while her family had been alive. The Spirit wanted families to love and celebrate the holiday together. The Spirit wanted to share the peace and joy that comes only from the heart. At last, Zach understood.

He did not go after the carriage.

Stephanie and Father Finn stopped at several more houses in the same neighborhood and then began working their way back toward Lucas Place.

"Tired?" Stephanie asked Father Finn as he climbed into the carriage with her after their last stop.

"Yes, but it's a good tired. I'll be over right after Midnight Mass, and then we can visit the orphanage just as we'd planned."

"I managed to get each child one thing that they said they wanted."

"They're blessed to have you."

"I'm blessed to have them."

Stephanie dropped him at the rectory and then told Sam to take her home. Sam let her out near the door then pulled the carriage on into the stable. She had just started up the steps when he spoke, startling her.

"Good evening, Madam Spirit, or should I say good morning?" he asked quietly.

"Zach . . ." Stephanie gasped his name as she quickly turned to face him.

"Hello, Stephanie."

"You know . . ." She was hesitant, not certain whether he was friend or foe. "How did you find out?"

"When I saw you last night . . . Well, I'd know you anywhere, wearing anything," he answered.

"I was afraid this was going to happen . . ." Suddenly she saw her time as the Spirit ending, and her heart grew heavy. She knew what Zach was after. He wanted the big news story, the headlines. It was well known that the *Post-Dispatch* sensationalized everything, and the revelation of her identity would no doubt be big news for several days. Their circulation would probably double from twenty to forty thousand and then it would be over. They would have had their big story just in time for the holiday, and then when all was said and done, there would be no more Spirit of Christmas and no more surprises for the children. There would be only open charity, the kind that destroys souls and damages the heart.

"Why were you afraid?" he asked.

"Because I know why you were doing all this."

He moved closer, taking her hand in his. "There's no need to be afraid." His voice was gentle and filled with deep emotion. "The secret of the Spirit will remain with me."

"It will? You won't give it away?"

"No, Stephanie. I understand now. I've seen the good you do and the joy you bring." He was about to kiss her to seal his promise to her when Sam's call interrupted them.

"Miss Stephanie? You all right?" Sam heard them talking and came from the stable to check on her and make sure she was all right.

"Yes, Sam. I'm fine. It's just Mr. Madison."

"He ain't going to tell, is he, Miss Stephanie?" The old man came to her side to defend her. His rheumy-eyed gaze was sharp and condemning as it rested on Zach.

"Zach?" She looked to him, wanting him to answer Sam.

"No, Sam, I'm not going to tell. Stephanie's secret is too important to reveal."

"That's good. Very good. Well, good night," he mumbled as he went off to his rooms above the stable, leaving them alone once more.

"Will you come in, Zach?"

"For a minute. Just to make sure you're safe."

She led him into the darkened house. Once they were inside the door, Zach could no longer refrain from taking her in his arms. He'd been longing to hold her and kiss her all night, and at the feel of her in his embrace, he crushed her to his chest, savoring her nearness. She was special, so very special, and he wanted to keep her with him always, to make her his own.

"Stephanie . . ." he said her name in a love-husky whisper. When she looked up at him, he finally spoke the words that had been in his heart and mind for days. "I love you."

"Oh, Zach!" she whispered, lifting her lips to his.

They kissed, sweetly at first, then more deeply.

"I love you, too, Zach," she returned when they finally broke apart. "I was so afraid that I'd never be able to reach you . . . to help you understand . . ."

"You were right to refuse me the interview. I didn't understand then," he admitted.

"But you do now?"

He nodded, thinking of the family he'd watched that night. His expression was one of fierce devotion as he drew her close again and kissed her once more. His mouth slanted across hers in a possessive exchange that lighted a fire of desire that would never be fully sated between them.

"It took me awhile to realize how much you mean to me, but now that I know, I never want to let you go." He looked down at her and asked the loving question. "Stephanie, will you marry me?"

A soft smile curved her lips as she gazed up at the man of her dreams. She wanted to spend the rest of her life giving him all the love he'd been missing. "Yes, Zach, I'll marry you. I can think of no Christmas gift I'd rather have than your love."

He stared at her in disbelief as the realization that she'd said yes pounded through him. He'd expected her to refuse him, to tell him that she wanted nothing to do with a man like him—a man whose heart was hard and uncaring. She certainly could have had her pick of any of the men in the city, yet she'd just accepted his proposal. He gave a delighted laugh of surprise. "You said yes."

"Of course I did. I love you, Zach," she repeated, her eyes glowing with the deep emotion she felt for him. She went to him and rested her hands on his chest as she lifted her gaze to his. "I want to spend the rest of my life loving you."

Zach covered her hands with his. "You were right about a lot of things in your letters to me, Stephanie. I'm a hard man. I haven't known much gentleness in my life."

"I know, and I plan to make up for that." She rose up and kissed him. "Starting right now."

He pulled her close, holding her to his heart. "Marry me tonight . . . right now. We can elope."

"No . . ."

Her refusal startled him, and at his puzzled look, she hurried to explain.

"I want to be married in church."

"Wouldn't that take weeks?"

"We'll go see Father Finn first thing in the morning. If anyone can help us, he can."

"Stephanie? What's going on down here?" Aunt Rose called

out as she came down the staircase carrying a lamp to light her way.

"I'm here with Zach, Aunt Rose. He's just proposed and I've accepted."

"Zach did? This is wonderful!" Rose exclaimed excitedly as she toddled into the kitchen to find them standing there, still wrapped in each other's arms.

"We're going to be married right away if we can get Father Finn to perform the ceremony."

"What about the banns?"

"We'll have to ask him. Will you go with us in the morning? Will you be our witness?" Stephanie asked.

"I wouldn't miss it for the world!" She was beaming at the thought of the happiness they could give each other.

Zach touched Stephanie's cheek as he drew away from her. "I'd better go now. What time do you want to go see Father Finn?"

"At ten?"

"I'll be here."

"I'll be waiting."

Rose politely made herself scarce so the two young lovers could say a proper good night, and they quickly took advantage of her discretion. When Zach had gone, Stephanie went up to bed feeling happier than she ever had in her whole life. Zach loved her and she loved him. It would be the perfect Christmas.

Zach returned to his room, but he was too excited to sleep. Suddenly, everything seemed so very clear to him, and so very wonderful. He went to stare out the window for a while at the beautiful night sky, and after a moment of being lost deep in thought, he knew what he had to do. Sitting down at his desk, he took out pen and paper, He was smiling as he began to write:

To The Spirit of Christmas

It is Christmas Eve as I write this open letter to you. While it is still difficult for me to believe, I wanted you to know that your prayers for me have been answered. I have been touched by the love and joy of the season, and I now understand all that you are trying to accomplish.

There are some matters that are better left to the heart and not to the avid intrusion of a newspaper reporter in search of a story. The Spirit's identity is one of them. Who the Spirit is, isn't important. What the Spirit does, is what matters. Thank you, Spirit of Christmas, for showing us the true light of the world—generous, unselfish love, and thank you for bringing that light into my life.

Zachary Madison

Zach reread it once more to be sure it was right and then sealed it in an envelope. He would drop it off with Walter at the office first thing in the morning just to make sure it ran in the next edition. It would be his Christmas present to Stephanie. Feeling more content than he had in years, he lay down on his bed and waited eagerly for the new day to dawn. He was smiling.

Father Finn stared at Zach as he sat across from him at his desk in his office in the rectory. Stephanie and Rose were sitting beside him. "So you're saying that you were there last night, and you saw everything?"

"Yes. After seeing you and the mysterious veiled woman the night before, I started putting two and two together. I did some research, and when I realized it just might be Stephanie, I waited outside her house last night. I saw you leave together and followed you on your rounds."

The priest looked over at Stephanie, expecting her to be upset,

ut she looked serene and perfectly happy. He frowned, confused. When they'd come there so early in the day to speak to
him, he'd feared trouble. But neither of them seem distressed.
"I see. So, Mr. Madison . . ."

"Zach, please, Father."

"All right, Zach, what are you going to do with this newfound
information?" He waited, expecting the worst.

"Nothing." He smiled at him. "I understand now just what
Stephanie's doing and why. There's no reason to tell anyone
about it. The gifts of the Spirit should continue to be given every
year—anonymously."

Father Finn felt as if a great weight had been lifted from his
shoulders. "Thank you."

"Now, there was another reason why we've come to see you
so early today, and why Aunt Rose is with us," Stephanie spoke
up.

"Yes?"

"We want you to marry us."

"That's wonderful." The priest smiled. He remembered
Stephanie's words from several days before when she'd told him
that she was in love with Zach, and he was happy for her. If ever
anyone deserved happiness and love in her life, it was Stephanie.

"There's just one thing, Father . . ."

"We'd like you to marry us today, if you can," Stephanie
added. "I know there might be a problem with the banns, but
just this one time, do you think . . . ?"

He was quiet for a moment then stood up. "Let me call Mrs.
Sutton in here."

"Mrs. Sutton?" Stephanie, Zach, and Rose exchanged puzzled glances.

"Well, we'll need two witnesses," he explained.

Their joy was obvious. "Thank you, Father."

They were married a short time later in church with Rose and
Mrs. Sutton looking on approvingly. As they promised to love,

honor, cherish, and obey, a feeling of peace and contentmen
filled them. When Zach took the diamond ring out of his pocke
and slipped it on Stephanie's finger, she gasped at the beauty o
it. Their gazes met and locked and they knew in that momen
that they were meant to be together, and that their marriag
would be a one made in heaven.

"I now pronounce you man and wife," Father Finn intoned
knowing he'd bent the rules, but knowing he'd done so for a
good cause.

Zach was filled with a depth of emotion unlike anything he'
ever experienced in his life as he took his wife in his arms and
kissed her. The moment was so romantic that Aunt Rose and
Mrs. Sutton both sighed as they smiled at the happy, embracing
couple.

When the kiss ended, Zach did not release Stephanie but kep
a warm, possessive arm around her as he thanked the priest.

"This will be one Christmas I'll never forget," Stephanie tol
Father Finn as she looked up at her husband adoringly. "You'v
given me the perfect gift, Father."

"What about you, Zach?" Father asked him.

"This is my best Christmas ever." He gazed down at Stephani
with love in his eyes. She was his soulmate, his life. He was n
longer alone.

Stephanie left Zach's side to go to her friend and kiss hin
sweetly on the cheek.

Father Finn grinned in delight. "Merry Christmas, Stephani
and Zach. You, too, Rose."

"Will you still go with me tonight?" Stephanie asked him.

"Do you still want to?"

"Of course. It's Christmas Eve. The Spirit can't disappoin
the children. They'll be expecting me."

"Then I'll be there. What about you, Zach? Will you help us
We can use all the willing hands we can get."

"I wouldn't miss it for the world."

Zach, Stephanie, and Rose passed the afternoon at the orphanage celebrating at a Christmas party for the children. They returned to the house to spend Christmas Eve together, and Rose announced that after she attended Midnight Mass with them, she was going home with her best friend Matilda to spend the night with her. Zach and Stephanie were touched by her thoughtfulness in giving them a night alone together. They shared a wonderful dinner, and after they'd eaten, Zach gave Aunt Rose the scarf he'd picked out for her. She loved it and thanked him profusely. She gave him a set of cufflinks, and he was touched by her thoughtfulness. He hadn't expected her to have a present for him.

"Thank you, Rose. They're beautiful."

The little old lady gave him a hug and a Christmas kiss.

They attended the Midnight Mass, and it was a deeply emotional time for Zach. He'd never worshipped with family before. It was a feeling he hoped he'd never lose.

Father Finn met them at the house afterward, and the three of them made the Spirit's last trip of the year. This time the trip was to St. Christopher's. It was the first time ever that Stephanie did not wear her mourning clothes on their excursion. Her Christmas would no longer be a time of sadness for her. She had Zach now.

Zach helped deliver the presents that Stephanie had so personally selected and wrapped for the children. The orphanage was dark as they crept in through the door the sisters had left open for them, and Zach knew a moment of dread as he entered the silent building. Earlier in the day when they'd visited, there had been laughing and caroling and joy. Now, at night, it reminded him once again of the home he'd lived in, and he had to fight down his fear as he kept his eyes on Stephanie and followed her. She was the light in his life now. As long as he was with her, he would never be lonely again.

Stephanie led the way to the main dining room where the tree was set up. They stacked the multitude of packages beneath it, taking care to be as quiet as they could. It wouldn't do to have the children awaken and find them there. When they were finished, they stood back to survey their handiwork. The tree and the presents looked beautiful, and the protective armor that had shielded Zach's heart for so long was finally shattered. He could give to these children what he'd needed all those years ago. He tightened his arm around his wife and gave her a kiss before starting from the building.

Sam drove them back to the rectory to drop off Father Finn. As he prepared to climb out, Stephanie stopped him.

"Father?"

"Yes, Stephanie?"

"Merry Christmas," she said as she pressed her gift to him into his hand. It was an envelope with enough money to help him finance his favorite charities for the next year and support the small school he ran just west of St. Louis.

"Thank you." His words were heartfelt. "Bless you both."

As the carriage started up again, Zach drew Stephanie across his lap and, cradling her to him, he kissed her.

"I love you, Mrs. Madison."

"I like the sound of that," she said as she clung to him, enjoying the intimacy of finally being alone with her husband.

When they reached the house, they bid Sam good night and went inside.

Stephanie led him upstairs to the master bedroom suite. Aunt Rose had insisted that they use that room for their own from now on. Stephanie was thrilled to find that Rose had taken care of everything and had had the room readied for them.

They gazed at each other in the privacy of the bedroom, and they both knew they could deny themselves no longer. They wanted each other desperately, and they came together, celebrating each touch and kiss.

Zach was exquisitely gentle with her, leading her slowly

through her initiation to love. She was the most precious thing in his life, and he would always treat her that way.

As their kisses grew hungrier, he grew bolder with his caresses. When at last the barriers of their clothing had been stripped away and they lay together for the first time, he marveled at her beauty. Had he dreamed the perfect woman, she could not have been more beautiful than Stephanie was to him that night.

"I love you," he whispered as he held her close.

The feel of her silken flesh pressed fully against him stirred his passion to a raging fire, but he held himself back, not wanting to frighten her with the power of his need. He kept himself under tight control. With the most infinite of care, he gentled her to his touch, easing her slowly closer to the full knowledge of a man's possession.

Stephanie had never realized that loving Zach would be so exciting. She'd known his kisses were heady and wonderful, but his touch had created fires within her that were building to a fever pitch. She clung to her love, eagerly giving herself over to his sensual expertise. As she'd grown more bold, she began to caress him with the same intimacy he was touching her. His reaction was instant and passionate, and for the first time in her life, she'd discovered the true power of being a woman.

When Zach could wait no longer, he moved over her and claimed her for his own, filling the silken heat of her with the strength of his love.

Stephanie gasped at the sensation, so foreign yet somehow so very right. She instinctively matched his loving rhythm and they celebrated the love that was a gift to them both. As one, they sought the heights of ecstasy. When the rapture of their need burst around them, they clung together, giving each other love's most perfect gift.

Zach had never known life could be so sweet. In the aftermath of their loving, he cradled her to him. No longer was his heart shielded from life's most powerful emotions. He loved and was loved. Stephanie was his world, and he would protect her with his life.

Zach held her close to his heart through the long, dark hours of the night. This night, there was no cold loneliness for him. This night, there was only love and the promise of a beautiful future together.

On Christmas morning, the hope that had died within Zach all those years before was reborn.

On Christmas morning, Zach believed.